ARIS & PHILLIPS HISPANIC CLASSICS

MIGUEL DE UNAMUNO

Aunt Tula

La tía Tula

A Novel

Translated with an Introduction by

Julia Biggane

Aris & Phillips
is an imprint of
Oxbow Books, Oxford, UK

© J. Biggane, 2013

ISBN   hardback: 978-0-85668-323-9
ISBN   paper: 978-0-85668-322-2

A CIP record for this book is available from the British Library.

This book is available direct from

Oxbow Books, Oxford, UK
Phone: 01865-241249; Fax: 01865-794449

and

The David Brown Book Company
PO Box 511, Oakville, CT 06779, USA
Phone: 860-945-9329; Fax: 860-945-9468

or from our website

www.oxbowbooks.com

Cover image: Spanish Woman in a Red Shawl *by Robert Henri (1907),*
creative commons licence

Printed and bound by CPI Group (UK) Ltd, Croydon, CR0 4YY

CONTENTS

ACKNOWLEDGMENTS

I am deeply grateful to John Macklin for his generous encouragement and advice; I am also grateful to Francisca Sánchez Ortiz for her advice on 1920s sociolect and literary style. I am indebted, too, to my inspiring students on the 2011–2012 Advanced Translation Skills course at the University of Aberdeen.

INTRODUCTION

As a novelist, dramatist, essayist, poet and public intellectual, Miguel de Unamuno (1864–1936) was a towering figure in twentieth-century Spanish cultural and political life. Widely recognised and translated during his lifetime, his work has retained academic currency: scholarly studies continue to appear each year, and his fiction is still commonly taught in universities across Europe and the Americas. He was a strikingly energetic and prolific writer too, producing five novels, seven novellas, eleven plays, scores of short stories, dozens of essays – major and minor – many hundreds of poems, an extensive body of travel writing and several memoirs. He also wrote a vast quantity of articles on diverse subjects for a wide range of newspapers and journals in Spain, wider Europe and Latin America.

Unamuno's literary fame rests principally on his novels, novellas and later drama. Unsurprisingly, the thematic and stylistic emphases of his prose fiction changed significantly over the course of an almost forty-year writing career: the metafictionality, parody, anti-realism, subversion of the authoritative third-person narrator and incorporation of disparate subject matter in earlier novels such as *Amor y pedagogía* (Love and Pedagogy) (1902) and *Niebla* (*Mist*) (1914) gave way in later years to more sober character studies such as *Abel Sánchez* (1917), *La tía Tula* (*Aunt Tula*) (1921) and *San Manuel Bueno, mártir* (*St Manuel Bueno, Martyr*) (1930). Nevertheless, there are important continuities across his fiction: his characters are often lonely, alienated or conflicted figures, assailed by profound doubts about the nature and purpose of their existence; they all hunger after some form of immortality or afterlife; they are all also anxious to leave a lasting stamp on their immediate social environment, or on generations to come – sexuality, reproduction and parenthood are major concerns. While struggling to make their mark on those around them, his characters perceive themselves as vulnerable to destruction or annihilating absorption by a threatening 'other' – be that the author-figure himself in *Niebla*, an envied rival in *Abel Sánchez*, or

even a much-loved figure in *San Manuel Bueno, mártir* and *La tía Tula*. Across most of his fiction, temporal settings and locations are sketchy or only broadly defined, so giving the impression that the novelist is concerned more with universal human experience than specific circumstance or period.

Certainly the travails of Unamuno's protagonists are consonant with his reflections on the human condition as laid out in his most famous essay, *Tragic Sense of Life*.[1] This 1912 work, which sets out Unamuno's philosophy of existence, is central to his thought, and, as several scholars have argued, some of its arguments are embodied in *Aunt Tula*, so a brief outline may be helpful here. Unamuno's is a decidedly unsystematic philosophy, drawing eclectically and idiosyncratically on disparate sources, but his starting point is the early-Enlightenment Dutch philosopher Baruch Spinoza's premise that what essentially defines the living being is its effort to survive indefinitely. For Unamuno, in humans, this entails a yearning for personal immortality, which is one of the conditions giving rise to religious faith. But if a longing for eternal life is an essential part of the human condition, so is reason, because without it, mankind cannot perceive, reflect or communicate. Yet a reason depending upon sceptical enquiry is not, in Unamuno's representation, compatible with religious faith. Human subjects are, then, for Unamuno, fundamentally riven by the competing but interdependent claims of reason and faith: a hunger for immortality is not rational, and cannot be assuaged or extinguished by arguments from reason, but nor can it be understood or expressed without the reflective, communicative capacities lent by reason; reason may operate on the basis of sceptical enquiry, yet its scepticism can never be absolute (otherwise, Unamuno argues, the thinking subject would have to doubt his or her own existence), so it can only sustain itself by leaning upon faith, even if only upon faith in reason. That humans must live with this constant, irreconcilable conflict is, for Unamuno, what makes them tragic.

Of course the relation between reason and faith is a hoary question in theology and philosophy: what is distinctive about Unamuno's representation of the problem is the deeply combative yet intimate dynamism of faith and reason's interdependence. And though in

---

[1]   *Tragic Sense of Life*, trans. J. E. Crawford Fitch (New York: Dover, 1954) [*Del sentimiento trágico de la vida en los hombres y en los pueblos*].

Unamuno's eyes tragic, the uncertainty about life after death arising from this conflictive relationship should form the basis not of despairing inertia, but, on the contrary, a vigorous personal ethics. Unamuno summarises this ethics by quoting a dictum from the French essayist Senancour's early nineteenth-century novel *Obermann*: 'Man may very well be perishable. But let us resist such a possibility, and, if nothingness is what really awaits us, let us make it an injustice'.[2] For Unamuno, in order that death be an injustice, the individual must pursue a vocation in life (whether a calling, or an imposed or accidental path) with such commitment and passion that he becomes irreplaceable.[3] In terms of interpersonal relations and collective co-existence, the essay advocates an ethics of 'mutual imposition': Unamuno adapts the Christian biblical command to 'love thy neighbour', and argues that 'it is by imposing my ideas upon my neighbour that I become the recipient of his ideas. My endeavour to impose myself upon another – to be and live in him, and by him, to make him mine (which is the same as making myself his) – is what gives religious meaning to human collectivity, to human solidarity.'[4] Once again the basis of human existence is represented by Unamuno as intimate combat and struggle – both with oneself and with others.

It should be clear that Unamuno's preoccupation with religious uncertainty, with reproduction (and the questions about gender and sexuality it throws up), as well as the presence of a potentially threatening but necessary and intimate 'other', cannot be read solely in terms of a timeless philosophy of existence. The struggles undergone by his tragic philosophical subject, or his fictional protagonists, are not easily abstracted from the dramatic material shifts in gender roles and relations taking place across European and American societies in the early years of the twentieth century, nor from contemporaneous debates about secularism and the entrenchment both of explicitly atheist political philosophies or movements and reactionary religious politics in the Spain of the time. And the potentially usurping or dominating 'other'

---

2   'L'homme est périssable. Il se peut; mais périssons en résistant, et si la néant nous est reservé, ne faisons pas que ce soit une justice.' Etienne Pivert de Senancour, *Obermann*, (Paris: Ledoux, 1833), Lettre XC.
3   See note 27 for remarks about the gender of this subject.
4   Unamuno, *Tragic Sense of Life*, 278.

may be read as a figure obliquely representative of any number of emerging threats to the established socio-economic, cultural or political order in Spain during the early part of the twentieth century. Even though an explicit, detailed social context may be absent, it is impossible, then, to remove Unamuno's tragically uncertain philosophical subject, or his lonely, ambivalent characters, from the prevailing social, scientific/ technological and philosophical dislocations of late modernity. Most of his fiction – not solely the avant-garde *Mist* and *Love and Pedagogy* – deserves a prominent place in the Spanish modernist archive, and his thought, for all its eclecticism and idiosyncrasy, is also of its moment, sharing preoccupations with philosophers such as William James, Henri Bergson, Edmund Husserl and Martin Heidegger.

Unamuno's significance is certainly not limited to his fictional output or his philosophy of existence: he was amongst Spain's first modern intellectuals, and took his role as a public commentator very seriously. In addition to his responsibilities as professor and rector at Salamanca – Spain's oldest university – he was a prolific newspaper essayist, and occupied a prominent position in the early twentieth-century political sphere. His own allegiances shifted over the course of his life: an early sympathy for Basque autonomous rights (Unamuno had been born and raised in Bilbao) was supplanted by membership of the socialist party for a period in the 1890s; thereafter his politics were that of a broadly liberal republicanism containing both progressive and conservative elements. He was a mordant critic of King Alfonso XIII, and of Primo de Rivera's proto-fascist military dictatorship during the 1920s. Unamuno's opposition to the dictatorship, which had the backing of Alfonso, earned him internal exile to the Canary Islands in 1924. He escaped to France, and was pardoned by the regime, but, on principle, remained in exile until the dictatorship collapsed in 1930. Alfonso left the throne after Republican victory in the major cities in the first municipal elections since the dictatorship. During the early period of the subsequently-declared Second Republic, Unamuno briefly became a member of the Spanish parliament during the Republican-Socialist coalition government. But he soon became disenchanted with the Republic, and later, his hostility to the broad-left Popular Front coalition led him initially to support the military coup mounted against it in July 1936, a coup which triggered the Civil War. Unamuno soon recanted, condemning the ideological poverty and the savagery of the Nationalist

rebels. He died, unreconciled to either the Republican or Nationalist side, at the very end of the same year.

Unamuno's social and political writings tackled some of the deepest fault lines of Spanish society in the period leading up to the Civil War: he wrote on Spanish nationhood and nationalism, was critical of the powers of the Catholic Church and the military, and was excoriating about the imperial ambitions and political meddling of Alfonso XIII. He wrote controversially on the politics of language – particularly the status of Castilian Spanish in relation to Spain's other languages. Although at times his analyses were less than coherent, or were characterised by polemical provocation rather than nuanced enquiry, all his political writing stemmed from a deep, sustained and intimately-felt engagement with some of the most sensitive issues in national life. This engagement was not limited to his non-literary output: a substantial portion of his poetry is politically inspired, and his prose fiction is far from being apolitical, though much scholarship tends to ignore or underplay its socio-political dimensions. Many of Unamuno's novels need to be seen, at least in part, as 'political fictions', and, as this introduction will argue, *Aunt Tula* is no exception.

Aunt Tula may not have the prominence of Unamuno's most famous texts, *Mist* and *San Manuel Bueno, mártir*, but is nevertheless an important novel for what it might tell us about Unamuno's views on gender, religion and civil society – all crucial issues in early twentieth-century Spain. It appears to have had a long, if not continuous, gestation: as early as 1902, Unamuno had written to a friend

> Right now I am working on a new novel called *The Aunt*. It's the story of a young woman who turns down various suitors, remaining unmarried to look after her nieces and nephews, the children of her dead sister. She lives with her brother-in-law, whom she rejects as a prospective husband, as she does not want conjugal duties to *sully* the chaste air breathed within the home by her *sons and daughters*. Given that her maternal instinct had already been fulfilled, why would she feel obliged to lose her virginity? She's a virgin mother. I know of at least one case.[5]

---

[5]   Emphasis in original. Cited in Geoffrey Ribbans, 'El autógrafo de parte de *La tía Tula* y su significado para la evolución de la novela', in *Volumen-homenaje a Miguel de Unamuno*, ed. D. Gómez Molleda (Salamanca: Universidad de Salamanca/Casa Museo Unamuno, 1986), 475–494 (477)

Needless to say, the published novel that appeared almost twenty years later as *Aunt Tula* is far more elaborate than this bare-bones summary suggests. In particular, the motives for Tula's virginal 'maternity', and her relationship with her brother-in-law, Ramiro, become much more ambiguous. Tula's chastity may partly be determined by her frustrated love for Ramiro (realising that her sister is also enamoured of him, Tula sacrifices her own feelings and urges the two to marry). When her sister dies, Tula is reluctant to consider a marriage proposal from Ramiro, in part because she does not want to be a substitute for her sister. She dismisses marriage to him completely after he seduces and impregnates the family maid. Tula's desire for motherhood by proxy is also given a strikingly ruthless quality in the published text: it is at Tula's insistence that Rosa has three children in quick succession, despite Rosa's increasing physical fragility. Rosa dies in childbirth, as does the sickly family maid during her second labour, having been obliged to marry Ramiro by Tula. Even while they are still alive, Tula largely usurps the care of the children from the two mothers.

Although she may consider herself a virgin mother, the 1921 Tula is certainly not a meek, long-suffering Marian figure. She is outspoken about the submissive, instrumental role expected of married women, and unafraid of challenging those males who urge such a role on her, including members of the clergy and the family doctor. In contrast to the uncomplicated embrace of virgin motherhood implied in the 1902 précis, it is also suggested in the novel that Tula's avoidance of marriage is at least partly driven by a pathological fear of the bodily, and the sexual. Moreover, Tula seems increasingly to come to regret her choices, warning her 'children' at the end of the novel to avoid her own mistakes. The novel is prefaced by a substantial prologue that ranges much further than the subject of virgin motherhood, exploring the historical and social significance of sorority, aunthood, domesticity and what Unamuno calls 'civilization' – the formation of a strong and healthy civil society.

Amongst other things, then, Unamuno fleshes out an intricate psychological portrait from the original anecdote.[6] Tula (or Gertrudis,

---

[6]   For a particularly interesting psychoanalytic reading of the novel, see Alison Sinclair, *Uncovering the Mind: Unamuno, the Unknown and the Vicissitudes of Self* (Manchester: Manchester University Press, 2001), Chapter 8 'Envy: reconstruction and destruction of maternity in *La tía Tula*', 140–152; for an alternative Lacanian

as she is more formally known) is anxious to protect her own autonomy while limiting that of others (though she is self-aware enough to come to realise that); she is deeply compassionate and gentle with the children she cares for, while capable of displaying a remarkable harshness and lack of empathy with the adults around her. Deeply religious, she finds herself at odds with the spiritual advice she receives from the church; desperately lonely at times, the only intimacy she actively seeks is maternal contact with her charges. In love with Ramiro, she resists being subsumed within the institution of marriage, which in her eyes would risk turning her into merely a respectable release mechanism for his sexual or amorous longing; moreover, its legal identity would turn her from her charges' *de facto* 'mother' into their *de jure* 'stepmother', a relation from which she has vowed to protect them.

Most critical studies of *Aunt Tula* agree that Tula is ambivalently presented, though they categorise and interpret this ambivalence in several very different ways. She has been seen, for example, as an androgynous figure,[7] a feminist or proto-feminist[8] and as a Jekyll and Hyde-like monster hiding a selfish, destructive possessiveness behind a facade of self-abnegation.[9] The complexity of her character has been seen both as a function of the text's realism[10] and as the result of apparently inadvertent

reading, see Gonzalo Navajas, 'The Self and the Symbolic in Unamuno's *La tía Tula*', *Revista de Estudios Hispánicos*, 19 (1985) 117–37.

[7]   See, for example, Juan Rof Carballo, 'El erotismo en Unamuno', *Revista de Occidente*, 7 (1964), 71–96, Gonzalo Navajas, 'The Self and the Symbolic in Unamuno's *La tía Tula*', Paciencia Ontañón de Lope, 'En torno a *La tía Tula*', in *Actas del Octavo Congreso de la AIH*, ed. D. Kossoff, J. Amor y Vázquez, R. H. Kossoff / G. W. Ribbans (Madrid: Ediciones Istmo, 1986), 383–89, and Harriet Turner, 'Distorsiones teresianas de *La tía Tula*', in *Los hallazgos de la lectura: Estudios dedicados a Miguel Enguidanos*, ed. J. Crispin, E. Pupo-Walker, L. Lorenzo Rivero (Madrid: José Porrúa Turanzas, 1989), 131–51.

[8]   See Laura Hynes, '*La tía Tula*: Forerunner of Radical Feminism', *Hispanófila*, 117 (1996), 45–54, Carlos Feal, 'Nada menos que toda una mujer: *La tía Tula* de Unamuno', in *Estelas, laberintos, nuevas sendas: Unamuno, Valle Inclán, García Lorca, la Guerra Civil*, ed. A. Loureiro *et al.* (Barcelona: Anthropos, 1988), 65–79, and John P. Gabrièle, 'From Sex to Gender: Towards Feminocentric Narrative in Unamuno's *La tía Tula*, or "Cómo se hace una novela feminista"', *Hispanic Journal*, 20 (1999), 105–117.

[9]   See Ricardo Gullón, *Autobiografías de Unamuno* (Madrid: 1964), 194–217.

[10] Antonio Sánchez Barbudo, 'Introducción', *La tía Tula*, (Madrid: Taurus, 1981), 7–40.

8 *Introduction*

contradiction and disparity in the narrative;[11] the prologue's relation to the novel has also been seen as a source of the text's overall ambivalence.[12] Mary Lee Bretz is right to point out that neither protagonist nor novel is altogether coherent.[13] But if the text's ambivalences are not entirely resolvable, they can at least be better understood if placed in context – both in relation to Unamuno's fictional work before 1921, and to the evolution of his female characters in particular – and also in relation to the wider social conditions of early twentieth-century Spain. Without historicising, it is certainly not possible satisfactorily to address the question of the text's representation of gender roles and relations – a question to which almost all critical studies since the late 1980s have turned their attention. Yet a historicising approach is one that no study has undertaken so far in any detail. Some earlier studies even counsel against such an approach: Geoffrey Ribbans, for example, argues that *Aunt Tula* is concerned with 'abstractions and personified ideas, not social interaction', and so should not be judged in relation with conventional notions of realism, verisimilitude or social representativeness; Julián Marías notes the lack of any precise temporal or locational indicators in the text, and refers to it as a 'timeless' novel (and therefore, by implication, one that would be inappropriate to read in terms of a specific historical moment).[14] Perhaps

---

[11] Frances Wyers, *Miguel de Unamuno: the Contrary Self* (London: Tamesis, 1976), Part 2, Chapter I 'Masters and Slaves', 78–81.

[12] See, for example, Gullón, *Autobiografías de Unamuno*, 194–217, and David Turner, *Unamuno's Webs of Fatality* (London: Tamesis, 1974), Chapter VI 'The Religion of Domesticity in *La tía Tula*', 92–106.

[13] Mary Lee Bretz, 'The Role of Negativity in Unamuno's *La tía Tula*', *Revista Canadiense de Estudios Hispánicos*, XVIII (1) (1993), 17–29, (28).

[14] Geoffrey Ribbans, 'A New Look at *La tía Tula*', *Revista Canadiense de Estudios Hispánicos*, XI (2) (1987), 403–419 (p. 410); Julián Marías, *Miguel de Unamuno*, trans. F. M. López-Morillas (Cambridge, Mass.: Harvard University Press, 1966) [1943], Chapter V 'Unamuno's Narratives', esp. 104–113, 105; 'Prólogo de Julián Marías,' *La tía Tula*, (Madrid: Salvat/Alianza, 1970), 11–15, 11). Of the scholars who do consider the novel in relation to the time in which it was written, Mary Lee Bretz historicises the text primarily in aesthetic terms, insisting that the text's tensions and negations suggest that it should be read as an unequivocally modernist text ('The Role of Negativity in Unamuno's *La tía Tula*'). Roberta Johnson notes that much of what Tula, 'says about her own situation echoes what Spanish feminists [...] were saying about women's general social situation – their subordination to a patriarchal legal system, their lack of options outside marriage' (*Gender and Nation*, 167–68), but does not examine the particular nature of the contemporaneous feminist

taking their cue from Unamuno himself, who suggests in the prologue to *Aunt Tula* that it may be seen in some ways as a companion piece to his 1917 novel *Abel Sánchez*, which bore the subtitle 'a story of passion', some critics have seen the text as focused on singular emotion, and therefore one not easily susceptible to historicisation. But that the text itself does not provide concrete detail about its location or moment does not make it a category error to place it in historical context; nor are abstractions or passions without historicity. This Introduction will attempt to historicise the text, and will argue for a new reading of the novel, proposing that *Aunt Tula* may be seen in part as a symbolic resolution of what, for Unamuno, were two pressing socio-political problems for Spain in the 1920s: the place of women and the place of the Church.

It should not come as a surprise that the representation of female characters in Unamuno's work changed as the social horizons of women in Spain shifted over the course of the late nineteenth- and early twentieth century. Although feminist ideas had been circulating in Spain, albeit on a local or relatively small scale, since before the mid-nineteenth century,[15] and although a proposal for limited women's franchise had first been submitted to the Spanish parliament in 1877, it was not until the late 1880s/early 1890s – precisely the period in which Unamuno began his writing career – that feminism began to occupy a more prominent place in public debate. However, there were still no national organized movements at this time: feminist ideas and arguments continued to be disseminated largely by small groups, or a few notable figures such the social campaigner and essayist Concepción Arenal and the writer Emilia Pardo Bazán. It was not until the beginning of the twentieth century that the issue of women's civil rights and suffrage became a more substantive issue in Spanish political life: the campaigns of the British suffragettes received widespread international press attention; the extension of the franchise to women was debated in the Spanish parliament – though again without success – in 1907 and 1908, and new pro-suffrage commentators and journals began to emerge.

movements emerging in Spain at the end of the second decade of the twentieth century.

[15] See Concha Fagoaga, *La voz y el voto de las mujeres: el sufragismo en España* (Barcelona: Icaria, 1985), esp. Chapter 1, 'Los canales del mensaje sufragista', 29–81.

Nevertheless, organized feminism was still not able to gain a foothold at this time, so it is not remarkable that before 1914, the figure of the feminist or modern emancipated woman is absent from Unamuno's fiction and dramatic work. In his earliest, turn-of-the century novels – *Paz en la guerra* (1897) and *Amor y pedagogía* (1902) – the female characters are demure, domestic, deeply Catholic, traditional figures.[16] The most striking feature of these women – who are all represented in positive terms – is how deeply and all-encompassingly maternal they are: they mother not just their children, but also act as redemptive and healing motherly figures to their husbands or fiancés as well.[17] And all these female characters remain firmly within the home. For all the modernist reflexivity and playfulness of a text such as *Amor y pedagogía*, Unamuno's representation of gender roles and relations cleaves closely to a traditional separate-spheres model.

As elsewhere across Europe, it was the far-reaching consequences of the First World War that accelerated changes to the gradually and unevenly shifting situation of women within society, even in a non-belligerent country like Spain. The increase in war-related industrial production for export, and the rise in prices of basic commodities and consumer goods brought more Spanish women into the workforce, both in traditional and new roles.[18] The second decade of the twentieth century also saw the official opening-up of higher education to women.[19] The question of women's legal status and civil, educational and professional capacities or rights became ever more prominent, and the first national

---

[16]   *Paz en la guerra* has been translated into English as *Peace in War* by A. Lacy and M. Nosick (Princeton University Press, 1983). *Amor y pedagogía* (Love and Pedagogy) has not yet been translated into English.

[17]   Of course the figure of the *femme fatale* or the mercenary woman also appears. But the *femme fatale*, even if broadly modern, is not here an emancipated woman.

[18]   For incisive studies in English of how economic and social change in the early twentieth century affected women, see Catherine Davies, *Spanish Women's Writing 1849–1996* (London: Athlone Press, 1998), Chapter 5 'Skirts on the Horizon: Women and Political Reform 1912–1940', esp. 99–103, and Adrian Shubert, *A Social History of Modern Spain* (London and New York: Routledge, 1990), Chapter 1 'A Century of Dynamism', especially the section 'Men, Women and Children', 23–43.

[19]   The numbers were initially tiny, but nevertheless, admission was an important step forward. For an interesting study of this widening access, see Mercedes Montero, 'First steps towards equality: Spanish women in higher education (1910–1936)', *International Journal of Iberian Studies*, 24 (1) (2011), 17–33.

feminist and mass women's associations began to appear at this time. There were two main strands to this mobilisation. Secular bourgeois feminism was represented most notably by the Asociación Nacional de Mujeres Españolas (ANME, or the National Women's Association, loosely affiliated to the Conservative Party), which was founded in 1918. ANME's campaigning had different emphases from its Anglo-American feminist analogues: achieving suffrage was given less importance than greater access to the public sphere, legal reform or protection of professional, educational and labour rights. Approximately a year later, the first mass national Catholic women's association, Acción Católica de la Mujer (ACM, or Women's Catholic Action) was founded. This was, like ANME, a socially conservative movement which also campaigned for greater access to the public sphere, and professional and legal reform of women's rights. It deployed the concept of the *madre social* ('social mother') to argue that the feminine traits of maternal self-sacrifice were necessary and beneficial not just within the domestic sphere, but could be exercised outside the home for the good of the nation as a whole.[20]

When the figure of the non-traditional woman who left the home – or who was otherwise diverted from a conventional maternal or religious path – began to be registered in Unamuno's fictional work in the second decade of the twentieth century, the representation was not flattering. The 'new woman' Eugenia in his 1914 novel *Mist* who insists on her independence and works to support herself financially is a coldly selfish, manipulative and deceitful figure. And as the number of women entering the workforce or higher education grew during this decade, so the female figures in Unamuno's fiction who ventured into civil society, or who made use of civil law and contract, became more monstrous. Their maternal vocation was as strong as the early, traditional figures, and it is indeed precisely the fierce protectiveness of or loyalty to their offspring that is shown to be incompatible with other roles within society: the characters' maternal drive consumes and indeed annihilates any sense

---

[20] Catherine Davies writes incisively about ANME in *Spanish Women's Writing 1849–1996*, 101–2; there are no studies in English on ACM, but Inmaculada Blasco Herranz's 'Ciudadanía y militancia católica femenina en la España de los años veinte' (*Ayer*, 57 (1) (2005), 223–246) is a superb introduction to the movement, and provides much valuable context about women and Catholicism in the 1920s.

of civic or wider ethical responsibility they might have.[21] For example, the widow Raquel in *Dos madres* (Two Mothers) (1920) is shockingly ruthless in pursuit of her maternal ambitions. Unable biologically to have children, she uses her financial and contractual expertise to arrange what is, in effect, surrogate motherhood, destroying the life of the innocent, young woman she uses for her scheme, and driving the father of her acquired baby to his death. The figure of Carolina in *El marqués de Lumbría* (The Marquis of Lumbría) (1920) is similarly cruel: she is dismissive of tradition and propriety, and is utterly unconcerned about betraying and destroying her wider family in order to secure advantage for her son, born out of wedlock. It is significant that both figures, a widow and (initially) a single woman respectively, are not subject to the Civil Code, a body of law which, amongst other things, severely restricted married women's activity outside the domestic sphere: the two women, are in this sense 'outlaws', uncontainable and free to manipulate civil society and its rules in the service of their blind, anti-social maternal devotion to their offspring, unburdened by broader moral considerations. In these two tales, written precisely at the point that organised feminism was emerging in Spain, female participation in civil society is portrayed as pernicious because women seem unable to detach their maternal drive from a wider, disinterested good. Conversely, the protagonist of Unamuno's 1921 play *Raquel, encadenada* (Raquel, Enchained), who renounces a prestigious professional career as a musician to adopt a small child, is presented in positive and highly sympathetic terms.[22]

Unamuno's representation of female characters in the period up to the early 1920s may have had its basis in traditional social Catholic teachings on men and women's roles – Unamuno was brought up in a strictly religious household – and may also have been shaped by elements of the social philosophy of Hegel, a thinker who had exercised

---

[21]   The only apparent exception is *Niebla*'s Eugenia, whose lack of maternal feeling may be a function of her youth.
[22]   See Miguel de Unamuno, *Teatro completo*, ed. M. García Blanco (Madrid: Aguilar, 1959), 776–838.

great influence on the younger Unamuno.[23] An important defender of the separate-spheres thesis, Hegel argued that women's natural attachment and loyalty to family made her unsuitable for participation in civil society, let alone in the life of the state.[24] Certainly the equation in Unamuno's work between the positive representation of domestic mothers and the negative representation of women – particularly mothers – who enter civil society is consonant with this division. And in 1920, a year before *Aunt Tula* was published, Unamuno had made the rather Hegelian assertion that '[w]omen lack a sense of the civic and substitute the domestic for it: for women, the family *is* the fatherland'.[25]

Where, then, should we place Tula? She is a character who appears at around the same time as the quotation above; she is contemporaneous also with the protagonists of *Dos madres* and the *El marqués de Lumbría*, and, like Raquel in *Dos madres*, hungrily takes on a proxy motherhood role, even while the biological mother of her charges is still alive and healthy. But Tula complicates the binary division between Unamuno's domesticated females and the deviant characters who enter the civil

---

23 To be sure, much of the mature Unamuno's tragic philosophy was fundamentally incompatible with that of Hegel's idealism, and he was already gently parodying Hegel's systematicity by 1895, in the essays that would subsequently be published as *En torno al casticismo* (On Authentic Spanishness) (1902). Nevertheless, Unamuno retained respect for Hegel's work, and traces of, or references to Hegelian thought are to be found throughout his later writing. Aspects of Unamuno's representation of women's roles, seem to be particularly sensitive to Hegel's thoughts on the matter, even when Unamuno's own position does not cleave entirely to Hegel's: see, for example, endnote xi in Chapter VI of the translation.

24 Hegel famously argued that 'man has his actual substantive life in the state, in learning, and so forth, as well as in labour and struggle with the external world and with himself'. Because of her natural passivity and subjectivity, '[w]oman, on the other hand, has her substantive destiny in the family, and to be imbued with family piety is her ethical frame of mind.' Commenting on Sophocles' *Antigone* (whom Unamuno also invokes in *Aunt Tula*'s prologue), Hegel notes that 'family piety [is] principally the law of woman and [...] law of a substantiality at once subjective and on the plane of feeling, the law of the inward life [...] a law opposed to public law, to the law of the land. (*Hegel's Philosophy of Right*, trans. T. M. Knox [Oxford: Clarendon, 1952], §166, 114–115).

25 'La mala educación', *El mercantil valenciano*, 16.11.1920, reproduced in G. D. Robertson, *Miguel de Unamuno's Political Writings*, 3 vols. (Lewiston, N.Y: Edwin Mellen, 1996), I, 381–385 (382). Whether this condition was, in Unamuno's opinion, innate to women or was historically contingent was a question he did not address explicitly here or elsewhere in his work.

sphere. She exhibits qualities both of the staple domestic angel figure of Unamuno's earlier work, and of the more emancipated characters of his post-1914 fiction: she can be ruthless, cruel and inhuman in pursuit of her maternal urges and in order to protect her own autonomy; she can also be tender and nurturing; she has a keen intellect and quick wit; she can be emotionally manipulative; she can, too, be a vulnerable figure of great pathos. She is not simply a Hegelian domestic mother, but is also far from being a new or emancipated woman.

There is, of course, one simple possible explanation for this hybridity: the relatively long gestation of Tula's character across time perhaps accounts for her possessing qualities both of the traditional and more modern female figure. Tula may in part be a portmanteau figure because she was originally conceived at one social juncture in terms of women's history in Spain, and completed only at another, transformed juncture. In other words, her ambivalent character is not necessarily a product of inconsistency or carelessness on Unamuno's part, as Frances Wyers has suggested, or deliberate irresolution as Geoffrey Ribbans has proposed; more simply, her hybridity may be a function of the long history of her composition as a character.[26]

But the long gestation does not completely account for Tula's complexity or hybridity: she is more than a combination of traits exhibited by previous Unamunian female figures. In separate important new readings of the novel in the 1980s, Carlos Longhurst and Geoffrey Ribbans persuasively argued that Tula can be seen as personifying the argument that Unamuno laid out in *Tragic Sense of Life*, whereby, in the absence of the guarantee of an afterlife, each individual should strive to become irreplaceable, and should instead pursue a vocation with such conviction and will that a lasting mark be left on others.[27] For Longhurst

---

[26]   Wyers, *Miguel de Unamuno: the Contrary Self*, 80–81; Ribbans, 'A New Look at *La tía Tula*', 417.

[27]   Carlos Longhurst, 'Para una interpretación de *La tía Tula*', *Actas del Congreso Internacional: Cincuentenario de Unamuno* ed. D. Gómez Molleda (Salamanca: Universidad de Salamanca, 1989), 143–51; Ribbans, 'A New Look at *La tía Tula*'. It may be worth noting that the examples Unamuno uses of vocations being exercised in society are all professions or trades that were exclusively masculine at time. It is not easy to say whether Unamuno was simply illustrating his point by drawing on existing practice or convention, or whether he felt that such an existential enterprise was limited to men. There remains, then, a potential difficulty about the translatability

and Ribbans, it is in this way that Tula's choices might be understood: in order to be an ideal, pure mother, Tula must avoid other roles or activities (including conjugal duties and the business of procreation and labour). Hence also, perhaps, the importance the text places on the legacy of Tula's work – in the last words of the novel, Tula's youngest niece, who has assumed her late aunt's mantle, looks to Tula to guide her and her siblings' future. Carlos Longhurst's reading places particular emphasis on the religious dimensions that, for Unamuno, a task such as Tula's entailed: for Unamuno, a religious vocation was not to be understood as being confined to an ecclesiastical or cloistered role. Fulfilling one's own particular role in secular society – as a cobbler, say – with the utmost ethical commitment and will to be unsubstitutable, and to leave a lasting trace on others, could be just as much a religious vocation as being a priest: both vocations derived from humanity's inherent 'religious sense' – both the hunger for immortality and the desire for a binding connection with others. For Longhurst, Tula clearly exemplifies the pursuit of a religious vocation through the uncompromising embrace of a lay role – here the care and nurture of children.[28] Furthermore, as Roberta Johnson later astutely pointed out, Tula 'exhibits the same existential anxieties as her male counterparts'.[29] The crucial – and hitherto unnoticed – point to be taken from both readings is that Tula is the first of Unamuno's female figures to possess such qualities and such anxieties. This is a potentially important development: Unamuno is now prepared to admit an intellectual and existential complexity previously denied to his female characters, and in this sense *Aunt Tula* may represent a change in Unamuno's views perhaps arising from wider shifting perceptions of women's capacities.

There is, though, a clear difference between seeing Tula as the first female character to be an analogue of Unamuno's existentially anxious male characters – or as equivalent to the heroic figure of *Tragic Sense of Life*, fighting against annihilation by the exercise of a vocation – , and seeing her as a feminist, or proto-feminist figure. Critical studies that

---

the figure appearing in *Tragic Sense of Life* to the female sex, despite the importance and attractiveness of Longhurst's and Ribbans' readings.
[28] Longhurst, 'Para una interpretación de *La tía Tula*', 147.
[29] Johnson, *Gender and Nation*, 166. Perhaps this is one reason that so many critical readings see Tula as an androgynous character.

read *Aunt Tula* as a feminist text base their arguments partly on what they see as consonances between Tula's attitudes and later feminist positions. Laura Hynes goes furthest in this regard, arguing that Tula is a precursor of radical feminism as represented by figures such as Andrea Dworkin and Shulamith Firestone, but John P. Gabrièle and Carlos Feal also see her as a vanguard figure.[30] Although Mary Lee Bretz does not label *Aunt Tula* a feminist text, she stresses its 'negation of existing gender socialization and relations' through which it 'provide[s] a glimpse of a different and future world'. She also argues that the novel 'foreshadows the thinking of Simone de Beauvoir and other feminist texts'.[31] Precisely because such studies see Tula as an anticipatory figure, out of joint with the times, they do not contextualise the novel in any detail, either in terms of early twentieth-century social conditions, or Unamuno's wider work. Roberta Johnson's study, which argues against reading *Aunt Tula* as a feminist text, similarly chooses not to historicise the novel in any detail, though she does in passing argue that 'most of what Tula says about her own situation echoes what Spanish feminists [...] were saying about women's general social situation'.[32]

There are problems both with readings that seek to remove *Aunt Tula* from the historical conditions of its production, and with a reading that too casually aligns the protagonist with contemporaneous Spanish feminism. While it would certainly be simplistic and literal-minded to map Tula's feminist credentials primarily in terms of how closely she might be compatible with the actually-existing feminism of the time of the novel's publication, neither should contemporaneous configurations of feminism be ignored. It is surely significant that Tula is unassimilable to either of the two main strands of feminism emerging in Spain at the end of the twentieth century's second decade. Despite Tula's deeply-held religious beliefs, she could not be easily accommodated within the Catholic feminist organization ACM. ACM operated within the institutional and doctrinal strictures of the Catholic church – there was no questioning of Catholic orthodoxy. Tula, on the other hand, has various brushes with the Church and its teachings, most acutely with

---

[30] Hynes, '*La tía Tula*: Forerunner of Radical Feminism'; Gabrièle, 'From Sex to Gender', 116; Feal, 'Nada menos que una mujer', 77
[31] Bretz, 'The Role of Negativity', 19; 22.
[32] Johnson, *Gender and Nation*, 167–68.

Father Alvarez over the role and autonomy of women, but even, albeit much less abrasively, with her uncle Primitivo, who suggests gently that some of her questions and thoughts might be heretical. Furthermore, ACM's project was to address social problems by expanding women's sphere of operation beyond the domestic; Tula works in exactly the opposite direction, addressing the one potential social problem she encounters – Manuela's precarious professional and social position as a single mother-to-be without any family or social network (she is an orphan) by absorbing her *into* the home.

If Tula's attitudes are incompatible with the precepts of ACM, they are no less assimilable to those of the bourgeois lay organization ANME. ANME was above all a legalist movement, pursuing (selective) formal equality as the key to emancipation for women. Tula shows no interest in legal reform: her attitude to the existing law is individualistic and self-servingly partial. She is uncompromising about deploying its protection for others, insisting that Manuela be married to Ramiro, against her and Ramiro's will. In relation to her own position, though, Tula seeks to evade or disobey the law. One of the reasons she will not marry Ramiro is that she does not want merely to be a 'stepmother' to his children: nor does she want her deep bond with the children to be circumscribed by legal limits. And she is prepared to flout the law in pursuit of her own ends, threatening to take Ramiro's children away because she fears they may be corrupted by his extra-marital relationship with the maid Manuela.[33] Of course the law was grossly prejudicial to women at this time; nevertheless, Tula's response to this inequality is individual self-exemption. She exhibits no interest in collective reform – indeed her radical solitude is insisted upon throughout the text. Tula's singularity, both in relation to contemporaneous feminist movements and in terms of her more general individualism, problematizes attempts to view her as even a proto-feminist figure.

All the studies that read Aunt Tula as a feminist text rest their case partly on Tula's criticisms of the subordinate position that patriarchal institutions and practices, for example the Church, and marriage, assign women, and on her rejection of what Bretz refers to as the 'tyranny of

---

[33] Tula is quite explicit about this flouting, vowing in Chapter XIII to take the children 'whatever the law may say' ('diga lo que dijere la ley').

biology'.[34] To be sure, Tula is quick to resist the attempt to instrumentalise her by various male figures in authority, challenging her confessor Father Alvarez's interpretation of the Catechism's teachings on marriage, which, she feels, reduce married women to the role of sanctified remedy for men's appetites and vessel for procreation; she resists just as strongly the attitude of her family doctor, Don Juan, which is no less instrumental in terms of marriage, if this time grounded in rationalist argument. And she offers occasional trenchant criticism of some aspects of female subordination in Catholic doctrine and its institutions. But we should be wary of conflating these criticisms too readily with a feminist position, and not just because of her lack of interest in protecting the liberty and autonomy of other women, or in reforming the structures she criticises. It is important to keep in mind that Tula's rejection of 'biology' is driven primarily not by any anticipatory feminist de-essentialising impulse, but by a desire to rise above the limitations of the flesh in order to reach a more spiritual plane – in other words, her desire is framed in *religious* terms. It might be argued that such framing does not exclude a feminist potential, and may simply be a function of the limits of Tula's education or self-understanding. But the issue is further clouded by the text's suggesting that Tula's privileging of the spiritual is impelled in part by a deeply personal fear of the bodily and the sexual. The whole question, then, of the corporeal is over-determined and ambiguously presented: it is difficult to assimilate straightforwardly to a feminist reading.

And of course one of the criteria by which we might try to evaluate the text's position on feminism – the representation of Tula's aptitude for, and participation in civil society – must remain hypothetical, as Tula remains in the home. As the analysis above indicates, Tula's attitude to the law suggests a certain inaptitude for civil society. And she certainly seems profoundly unsuited to the hierarchies and discipline necessary for associational life or structures outside the home. When asked by Ramiro in Chapter VIII why she has not pursued a religious vocation by becoming a nun, she answers 'I don't like being on the receiving end of orders'. When Ramiro replies that she would surely quickly be given the role of mother superior, she is equally recalcitrant, replying that 'I like *giving* orders even less'. It may be significant that Tula is undoubtedly

---

34   Bretz, 'The Role of Negativity', 23. For Tula's criticisms, see, in particular, her comments towards the end of Chapter XVII.

represented as a more sympathetic – and morally superior – character than the two Unamunian contemporaneous female protagonists who do venture into civil society, Raquel in *Dos madres* and Carolina in *El marqués de Lumbría*. Unlike these characters, whose maternal urges have such destructively anti-social and immoral consequences, Tula is chaste, and she is religious, and there are suggestions that it is perhaps these two qualities that endow her with some ethical potential beyond the limits of maternal love within the household as imagined by the Hegelian model of gender. This potential seems to lie in the sublimated, spiritual nature of her maternal vocation, which transcends the exclusive, possessive and morally blind attachment of biological or fleshly bonds to become something more inclusive. There may, then, be the germ of a civic subject in this chaste, religious character.

Nevertheless, although Tula pursues her calling with the will to be irreplaceable that Unamuno had laid out as a prerequisite for ethical civil-society participation, there are enough counter-indications to suggest that Unamuno retains a wariness about the desirability of women – even chaste, single women – leaving the domestic sphere to enter the public arena. And it is certainly difficult to read the novel's prologue as being sympathetic to feminism's aspirations for greater participation in the civil sphere. Amongst the last parts of the text to be written, and dated 1920, the prologue was composed at a time when Spanish feminism had just begun to organise on a national scale, and women were gaining ever greater entry into the labour market and higher education. Unamuno's invocation of St Teresa of Avila, Abishag the Shunammite and Antigone – all of whom the prologue represents positively – as forebears or relations of Tula does not suggest sympathy with such aspirations for autonomy or freedom to act in civic life. The commonalities between the figures are obvious: like Gertrudis, the three other characters lived out their lives as virgins; like her, they were deeply religious women. St Teresa and Abishag are also associated with sublimated maternity: St Teresa was the spiritual Holy Mother (Santa Madre) of the discalced Carmelites; Unamuno presents Abishag as *sacrificing* her maternity for king and state in tenderly caring for the elderly David in her youth. But it is above all the qualities of sisterliness and aunthood that Unamuno emphasises in relation to St Teresa and Antigone, and it is these qualities that most link them to Gertrudis. Unamuno opens the prologue with a

long quotation from St Teresa's *Life* in which she describes one of her childhood sibling relations; it is followed by an extract from a letter she writes in her capacity as aunt to Lorenzo de Cépeda which is full of tender concern for the wellbeing of her nephew. And, as Unamuno stresses, Antigone's sororal ties are particularly dense: sister to Polynices and Eteocles, she is also sister to her own father, Oedipus; this in turn means that she is also an aunt to her brothers.

What Unamuno's representation of the three figures emphasises above all is familial loyalty, and the equivalence of sisterly, auntly and maternal love: their selfless love for sibling and niece/nephew provides all the qualities that motherhood can (as Tula's own life also seems to attest). They are all also, in various ways, heavily domesticated figures: Abishag's contribution to the life of the state is made indirectly, and from a position ensconced deep within the household, supporting King David's reign by providing him with chaste private comfort. St Teresa is also, in part, domesticated in Unamuno's representation, from the opening quotation describing her efforts to build a dwelling for herself, to the subsequent extract focusing on her family life. There is no reference to her public existence or her complex relations with Church and state.[35] And Antigone, of course, challenges Creon's state law in the name of the Penates – the household deities: for Unamuno, Antigone represents domestic religion in conflict with the (tyrannical) politics of the *civis*. In asking towards the end of the prologue 'Can civility and civilization exist without the foundation stones of domesticity and domestication?', Unamuno suggests that although women are crucial to the life of the *civis* as the bedrock of its existence, they must, by the same token, not undermine its foundations by entering *into* the life of the state.[36] Essentially, this is a restatement of Hegel's position.

Another notable feature of all three figures invoked in the prologue is their solitude, a trait also emphasised in the characterisation of Tula. Abishag appears without kin in the Bible, having no family or

---

[35] It is instructive to compare Unamuno's representation with Gillian Ahlgren's illuminating study, *Teresa of Avila and the Politics of Sanctity* (Ithaca/London: Cornell University Press, 1996), which emphasises Teresa's considerable intellectual and political abilities.

[36] '¿Caben civilidad y civilización donde no tienen como cimientos domesticidad y domesticación?'

companion apart from King David[37]; Antigone fights a lone battle for justice: her sister Ismene is too scared to support her, while her betrothed, Haemon, is unaware of her plight. Unamuno's description of St Teresa as a quixotic figure (without, we might note, a Sancho – or Sancha – Panza) also emphasises her solitary singularity. At a time when women were beginning to campaign and act collectively in pursuit of greater rights and freedoms, this emphasis on the aloneness of the figures that Unamuno writes of so admiringly may be read as a gesture further distancing women from the civic. A similar boundary-setting might also be read into the prologue's insistent valorisation of the chaste sister and aunt figure: at a time when increasing numbers of women were seeking wider horizons than the family home in the public sphere, education or the workplace, and at a time when the number of single women was growing,[38] the prologue's eagerness to categorise unmarried women in terms primarily of their sororal ties seems again part of a desire to keep them firmly yoked to the familial, domestic sphere.

In the light of the above analyses, it is surely difficult to read Tula as even a proto-feminist figure. And it is equally hard to see the gender politics of the novel as anything other than conservative: in response to wider social changes taking place outside the home at the time, rather than opening up the civil sphere to its female characters, *Aunt Tula* expands and diversifies domestic spatiality, whose organization provides what appears to be a substitutory, or compensatory mimicry of work outside the home, at times even reproducing the logic of economic modernisation and industrial rationalisation. It is in this light that we might read the splitting of maternal duties within the text between the material procreation of children (Rosa, Manuela) and the spiritual and emotional nurturer and educator (Tula). For Bretz, Tula's adoption of the latter role is part of her negation of 'the tyranny of biology', but it is possible to read it also not as a rejection of female labour (in all senses), but as a *division* of labour, and a remodelling of maternity and its tasks as a quasi-industrial process. Chapter V notes that a married couple 'at full productive capacity' needs to be left in peace; Chapter XIV refers to the delicate 'production plant' of Manuela's body, unable easily to withstand

---

[37] 1 Kings 1–2.

[38] María Rosa Capel, (co-ord.), *Mujer y sociedad en España (1700–1975)* 2nd edn (Madrid: Dirección General de Juventud y Promoción Socio-Cultural, 1986), 31.

the demands of pregnancy.[39] If this domestic sphere is indeed a mirror of civil-society labour, it is one that softens the rough edges of work outside the home. There is no competition or exploitation in the splitting of maternal duties between Rosa, Manuela and Gertrudis: the biological mothers are grateful for the help, and Gertrudis is omnicompetent and alacritous in her efforts. This model of complementarity contrasts notably with the competition, exploitation and aggression represented in *Dos madres* and the *El marqués de Lumbría*, where female protagonists do enter civil society, and perhaps bring its values back into the home. There is a further palliative engagement with mass industrial society in Chapter XVIII, where, in the absence of a wet nurse for Manuela's second baby, Tula is forced to bottle-feed her. The text notes that the feeding bottle – an "industrially-produced device" – becomes for Tula "the symbol and instrument of a religious rite".[40]

This expansion of the domestic sphere may plausibly be read as part of a reactionary 'solution' to the rise of feminism and female civil-society participation. But it may be serving other, wider, socio-political ends too, particularly if considered in the light of the striking religious agency with which Tula is endowed. In Unamuno's early novels, female characters act largely as simple, intuitive repositories of traditional religious values;[41] after 1914, the – sympathetically represented – female characters in Unamuno's fictional texts often take on roles more traditionally associated with institutionalised male vocations.[42] It is not an exaggeration to say that, at times, Tula takes on a priestly function:

---

[39] '...un matrimonio, y más un matrimonio joven como vosotros y en plena producción, necesita estar solo' (Chapter V); 'La preñez de Manuela fue [...] molestísima. La fragilísima fábrica de cuerpo la soportaba muy mal' (Chapter XIV).

[40] 'El biberón, ese artefacto industrial, llegó a ser para Gertrudis el símbolo y el instrumento de un rito religioso'.

[41] For example, Josefa Ignacio in *Peace in War*, or Marina del Valle in *Amor y pedagogía*, who, in a rare act of independence from her husband, has her son, Apolodoro christened – against the wishes of his rationalistic father – because 'así se ha hecho siempre' ['that has always been the done thing'] (*Amor y pedagogía* (Madrid: Espasa Calpe, 1959 [1902], 44). Here her religious traditionalism outweighs her conjugal obedience.

[42] Joaquina in *Abel Sánchez* (1917) acts as a confessor-figure to her father; Angela Carballino also acts as a confessor-figure to San Manuel Bueno, and becomes his unofficial deaconess in the later novella *San Manuel Bueno, mártir* (1931). Once again, Eugenia in *Niebla* is an exception here.

she is accused of acting like an inquisitorial confessor by Rosa in Chapter II; it is she who, in Chapter XIII, again like a confessor-figure, demands penitence from Ramiro for his sinful relation with Manuela; she aspires to become Ramirín's spiritual director, thus usurping the parish priest, as noted in Chapter XIX. At the same time, Tula rejects the existing social institutions and teachings of religion, as her comments on convent life, and her angry dismissal of Padre Alvarez's advice attest. This transfer of sacerdotal agency may be another dimension of the text's drive to provide a compensatory substitute for women's continued lack of civil agency and the very narrow channels of social participation open to them. But it may also be more than that: it might provide an imaginary solution to another social problem that was exercising Unamuno in the first two decades of the twentieth century: the power of the church in Spanish civil and political life. As *Tragic Sense of Life* had laid out, part of Unamuno's ethical vision for a life lived in the face of uncertainty about the existence of an afterlife entailed an expansion of religiosity – specifically a widening out of the concept of a religious vocation. By fulfilling his labour with the utmost commitment and conscientiousness, the cobbler, say, could achieve transcendent and lasting 'life' in the minds and memories of those he served. This revised understanding of religious work and its proper ambit would involve what Unamuno referred to as a 'disecclesialisation' (*'deseclesiastización'*) of Christianity: rather than being confined to a narrowly-defined role within church structures, religious vocations could be realised in secular/civil life.[43] But there was another welcome aspect to such disecclesialisation for Unamuno: it also entailed the weakening of the social and political power of the Catholic Church in Spain. Press articles Unamuno wrote around the time of *Aunt Tula*'s publication attest to his enduring hostility to the Church's influence on political life.[44]

---

[43] The word '*civil*' in Spanish can mean 'lay' as well as 'civil'.

[44] In 1922, for example, he deprecated the Church hierarchy's approving use of the word *cruzada* (crusade) to describe the ongoing Spanish colonial military campaign in Morocco. Claiming that Christ's reaction to the Church's intrusion into colonialist politics would be to reproduce the words he said on the cross in the Gospel of St. Luke – 'Father, forgive them, for they know not what they do', Unamuno adds 'No, they know not what they do. And if they are bishops [...] even less so. Especially when they are mixed up in nationalist or social campaigns'. 'El proceso de Cristo' ['The Procession of Christ'], (*España*, no. 315, 8.IX.1922), reproduced in Unamuno,

And significantly, there is at times in these writings a conflation of the problem of institutional religion with that of gender, as Unamuno links the improper presence of the Church in socio-political life with that of women in the public sphere. One of the reasons that Unamuno deemed women unsuitable for participation in the life of the state was their sympathy for Catholic institutions that he felt were inimical to a progressive national polity. Writing of the political conflicts between a conservative monarchy and liberal aspiration in nineteenth-century Spain in 1918, Unamuno writes scornfully '[t]he struggle for a modern, secular, democratic, European Spain began in 1833 upon the death of the abject Fernando VII, and in the eighty-five years that have passed since then, this poor nation has been ruled for some fifty years – almost sixty per cent of the time – by women. And a female regime, especially in Spain – tends to be a Jesuitical regime'.[45] Previously, he had described the Church as 'zealous of its own authority', but 'anarchist in relation to the state and its own prerogatives';[46] when discussing the question of women and civilisation in *Aunt Tula*'s prologue, he invokes Creon's accusation that Antigone's burial of Polynices is an act of anarchy, the worst of all evils. Although Unamuno is clearly sympathetic to the family loyalty that Antigone demonstrates, and asks whether it is anarchy, or civilisation that is actually the worse evil, there is no questioning of her identification with anarchic hostility to state law.[47] For Unamuno, then, there seems to have been a parallelism between the threat posed to the healthy, well-functioning state by both Church *and* women. Here it becomes possible to see how *Aunt Tula* could in part represent an ingenious solution to Unamuno's problems: in laying out an expanded role for the (intelligent, questioning) chaste woman to be part of disecclesialisation by taking up in the domestic sphere some of the hitherto institutionalised clerical male

---

Crónica política española, 299–302 (302). See also 'La nueva inquisición' (1919) in the same volume, 756–777.

[45] 'El habsburgianismo jesuítico español' ['Spanish Jesuitical Hapsburgism'], *Crónica política española*, 175–179 (178).

[46] 'La conciencia liberal y española de Bilbao', a speech made at the Sociedad 'El Sitio' in Bilbao, 5 September 1908, reproduced in *Obras completas*, ed. M. Garcia Blanco, XVI vols (Madrid: Afrodisio Aguado, 1959), vol. VII, 756–777 (766).

[47] Once again, Unamuno's position is close to Hegel's, who also expresses sympathy for Antigone, but also uses her as an illustration of the unsuitability of women for participation in the life of the state. See *Hegel's Philosophy of Right*, 114–5.

tasks, secular civil life is insulated from both women and Church, while agency and prestige is added to women's domestic role as a substitute for greater civil rights.

This resolutional dimension of the text may give the impression that, *pace* Bretz's reading, *Aunt Tula* has a degree of coherence, for all its other ambivalences. But it retains a contradictory valence to the last, not least because of the two figures that Unamuno makes fullest use of in the prologue to exemplify the religious domestic: Antigone and St Teresa of Avila. Despite Unamuno's manifest desire to keep them within the realm of the domestic, they in some ways evade the confines of his representation, even if only temporarily. Antigone may well incarnate religious domesticity versus purely civic virtues, as Ribbans argues, or 'domestication' versus 'civilisation' in Unamuno's terms.[48] But Antigone has to enter the civil sphere, and indeed become an interlocutor with the state, in order to assert the values of the household deities. And she wanders across the desert with Oedipus to Colona, a journey alluded to in the prologue as an example of sororal and daughterly fidelity, but also an indication that Antigone cannot be regarded simply as an immured domestic figure. Similarly, St Teresa would not have been able to assume her own domestic religiosity as spiritual mother of her order, or as defender of (potentially subversive) private interior prayer if she had not moved extensively outside the walls of her religious house, influencing figures within wider society and the court. Furthermore, by representing St Teresa as a Quixotic figure in the prologue, Unamuno (apparently unwittingly) underlines her role as woman errant, wandering the territories of Spain in search of her ideal. *Aunt Tula* may, then, represent, in part, an attempted curtailing of the civic agency of women, and an extolling of the contained domestic sister; yet, like the crumbling walls of the young Teresa's hermitages invoked in the opening paragraphs of *Aunt Tula*'s prologue, it is not able fully to contain its mobile female subjects.

As for the women in Spain in the first two decades of the twentieth century, although they made significant inroads into civil society, they would have to wait until after the arrival of the Second Republic in 1931 to see a fuller realization of their civil and political rights, though these were shortly afterwards reversed by the Francoist state. For all its

---

[48] Ribbans, 'A New Look at *La tía Tula*', 415.

defence of domesticity, in representing an intellectually strong, complex and ambivalent female protagonist – Unamuno's first – *Aunt Tula* does, perhaps, in some ways despite itself, allow the reader an oblique glimpse of the profound changes taking place in regard to the conceptualisation of women's capacities in Spain in the years before the Republic. Most importantly, as this Introduction has tried to argue, *Aunt Tula* cannot simply be reduced to a '*historia de pasión*', abstractable from the social conditions of its time; nor can its engagement with the question of what might constitute a good civil society/civic life be reduced to the question of female participation within it; the role of religion and Church are also part of the text's problematic. *Aunt Tula*'s dimension as a 'political fiction' is not one that should be ignored.

Style and translation

The Spanish text of *Aunt Tula* is uncomplex from a lexical and syntactical perspective: Unamuno tends not to use obscure, archaic or neologistic vocabulary, and although some of his sentences can seem lengthy to a reader more familiar with English-language convention, they are not especially long by Peninsular Spanish standards, and only rarely are they structurally convoluted.[49] There is relatively little use of metaphor, wordplay or punning, all of which can present significant difficulties to the translator. Furthermore, there is no regional, dialectal or sociolectal variation marked in characters' speech, which is for the most part characterised by colloquial, middle-class usage pertaining broadly to the provinces of Castile. Nevertheless, the text contains sufficient linguistic challenges and idiosyncrasies to prevent the task of translating it from becoming a tediously easy or mechanical exercise.

Frances Wyers has accurately and incisively characterised the style and structure of Unamuno's novels in the following terms: 'rapid development of plot, reduction of description to a bare minimum, [and] highly charged dialogue that propels events in a swift staccato'.[50] Certainly the most structurally distinctive feature of the novel is the amount of dialogue it contains – some chapters are composed largely,

---

[49]   The only systematic exception is the slightly archaic suffixing of object pronouns to finite verb forms (*e.g.* 'formáronse', 'arrebolóse' *etc.*), not uncommon in 1920s Peninsular educated writing.

[50]   Wyers, *The Contrary Self...*, 80–81.

and in a few cases almost entirely of direct speech between characters.[51] Rarely is this speech accompanied by the usual reporting or attributional clauses, so that, at times, the representation of speech is more akin to that of the script of a theatrical work (see, in particular, the novel's final chapter). The privileging of dialogue over narratorial description may be one factor in the novel's ambivalence: there is relatively little explicit synthetic or over-arching judgement passed by the narrator on Tula and her actions, and readers are only given limited access to her private thoughts; even the third-person description contains a significant quantity of free indirect discourse. This lack of overt narratorial direction may be designed to encourage a more active, questioning attitude on the part of the reader.[52] But the quantity of dialogue, may also be plausibly seen, at least in part, as a function of the speed with which Unamuno was writing, given the volume of his output – literary and non-literary – and his professional duties as a university teacher. Dialogue can be quicker to write than finely-crafted, carefully-articulated, nuanced description.

The frequent use of very short paragraphs contributes to what Wyers calls the 'staccato' rhythm of Unamuno's prose, but may again, perhaps, be partly a result of swift writing. It is not that Unamuno was uninterested in style: he wrote a substantial number of articles on the matter,[53] and as a poet who published many hundreds of sonnets, he was hardly insensitive to the discipline of precise literary composition. But in much of his narrative fiction, it is broad ideas, rather than detail or style that matters to him.[54] It is in this light also that we should read the not infrequent use of '*Y*' ['And'] to begin paragraphs, and even chapters. This tic has been suppressed in the translation merely to avoid

---

51 Abundant dialogue is one of the defining characteristics of Unamuno's longer narrative fiction: see endnote IV in this translation.

52 The reader, that is, who is not simply an uncritical consumer of fiction – the 'lector de novelas' ['(mere) novel reader'] that Unamuno condescendingly exempts from having to read the prologue – see endnote I in the translation.

53 Some of these are collected under the title 'A propósito del estilo (1892–1922)' ('On the question of Style') in volume XI of the Afrodisio Aguado *Obras completas*, XVI vols, ed. M. García Blanco (Madrid, 1959). Unamuno also wrote a series of articles on style in 1924 while exiled from Spain, later collected as *Alrededor del estilo* [On Style]. Interested readers should consult Laureano Robles' edition of the collection (Salamanca: Universidad de Salamanca, 1998).

54 It is in this light that we should perhaps read the confusion over the gender and names of children in Tula's charge: see endnote XII in the translation.

unnecessary repetition and clumsiness. Other stylistic idiosyncrasies are not easily rendered in English without considerable inelegance. There is remarkably frequent use of the deictic '*aquel/aquella*' throughout the text. Spanish has two diectics for the English 'that' (person or object): '*aquel/aquella*' indicates an object or person further away in space or time than the other deictic '*ese/esa*'. '*Aquel/aquella*' might be rendered in English as 'that (person or object) over there/over yonder', and, in certain contexts, has the connotation of 'far away'. Accounting for such a tic is not easy. It perhaps implies some narratorial distance from the events recounted; it might be tempting to think also that this strikingly repetitive use of deictics is part of the sensitivity to spatiality in the text: the novel opens with the evocation of the spaces that St Teresa yearns and struggles to inhabit, and this Introduction has argued that the novel is deeply concerned with the limits and possibilities of domestic space versus the civic sphere. In the translation, the use of '*aquél/aquella*' is almost always rendered less precisely. 'That' house (let alone 'that house yonder') reads oddly/unidiomatically in English. So the deictics '*ese/aquel*' are not marked, but the reader should be aware of this idiosyncrasy. Other translation difficulties pertaining to specific words or phrases appearing in the text are identified in the English version and are discussed in the appropriate endnotes.

Editions of La tía Tula

La tía Tula was first published in 1921 by Editorial Renacimiento in Madrid. Subsequent editions were published posthumously by Espasa Calpe in Buenos Aires (1940) and Austral in Madrid (1964). An edition with an introduction by one of the earliest scholars of Unamuno, the philosopher Julián Marías, was published by Salvat Editores (Madrid) in 1969; an edition with an introduction written by another distinguished early Unamuno scholar, Antonio Sánchez Barbudo, was published by Taurus (Madrid) in 1981. The Planeta publishing house in Barcelona published a critical edition with notes by José Luis Gómez and an introduction by José Jiménez Lozano in 1986. Carlos Longhurst produced an extremely thorough and rigorous critical edition for Cátedra (Madrid) in 1988: it is the best edition available. An edition produced by Manuel Cifo González

was published in Madrid by Alhambra Longman in 1991.

The novel is also published in vol. IX of the Afrodisio Aguado *Obras completas* edited by Manuel García Blanco (1959–1964), and in vol. 2 of the later Escelicer *Obras completas* (1966–1971). It is published in Vol 1 of the Biblioteca Castro *Obras completas* edited by Ricardo Senabre (Madrid: Turner, 1994).

The Spanish text reproduced here is based as closely as possible on the first edition published by Renacimiento. Two corrections to the text are explained in footnotes in Chapter XVII and Chapter XXII of the Spanish text. Elsewhere, corrections of occasional minor inconsistencies of spelling, accentuation and punctuation are not marked. The now-archaic accentuation of third-person singular preterite forms of ver (*vió*) ser/ir (*fué*) and dar (*dió*) has been retained, as has the convention whereby capitalized letters are unaccented.

BIBLIOGRAPHICAL NOTE

Many of the critical studies written on *Aunt Tula* are written in Spanish. Readers of a bilingual edition of the novel may be diffident about approaching such work, so I have limited the bibliography in Spanish to the most important studies. Given the ambivalence of the text, and the widely divergent critical readings it has produced, I have tried to include as wide a range of studies as possible. Some are more carefully grounded and historicised than others, as this Introduction has indicated.

Critical studies in Spanish

Feal, C. 1988. Nada menos que toda una mujer: *La tía Tula* de Unamuno. In *Estelas, laberintos, nuevas sendas: Unamuno, Valle Inclán, García Lorca, la Guerra Civil*, ed. A. Loureiro *et al*. Barcelona: Anthropos, 65–79.

Gullón, R. 1964. *Autobiografías de Unamuno*. Madrid, 194–217.

Longhurst, C. 1989. Para una interpretación de *La tía Tula*. In *Actas del Congreso Internacional: Cincuentenario de Unamuno*, ed. D. Gómez Molleda. Salamanca: Universidad de Salamanca, 143–51.

Regalado García, A. 1968. *El siervo y el señor: la dialéctica agónica de Miguel de Unamuno*. Madrid: Gredos, ch. 6, 'Las ficciones novelescas desrealizadas', 130–158 (esp. 145–148).

Ribbans, G. 1968. El autógrafo de parte de La tía Tula y su significado para la evolución de la novela. In *Volumen-Homenaje a Miguel de Unamuno*, ed. D. Gómez Molleda. Salamanca: Casa-Museo Unamuno, 475–493.

Sánchez Barbudo, A. 1981. Introducción. *La tía Tula*. Madrid: Taurus, 7–40.

Turner, H. S. 1989. Distorsiones teresianas de *La tía Tula*. In *Los hallazgos de la lectura: estudios dedicados a Miguel Enguidanos*, ed. J. Crispin *et al.* Madrid: José Porrúa Turanza, 131–151.

Critical Studies in English

Bretz, M. L. 1993. The Role of Negativity in Unamuno's *La tía Tula*, *Revista Canadiense de Estudios Hispánicos* XVIII (1), 17–29.

Gabrièle, J. P. 1999. From Sex to Gender: Towards Feminocentric Narrative in Unamuno's *La tía Tula* or 'Cómo se hace una novela femenista', *Hispanic Journal* 20, 105–117.

Hynes, L. 1996. *La tía Tula*: Forerunner of Radical Feminism, *Hispanófila* 117, 45–54.

Johnson, R. 2003. *Gender and Nation in the Spanish Modernist Novel*. Nashville: Vanderbilt UP, ch. 4 'Baroja's, Unamuno's and Azorín's Failed Feminists', 145–184, (esp. 166–170).

Julián Marías, J. 1966. [1943] *Miguel de Unamuno*, trans. F. M. López-Morillas. Cambridge, Mass.: Harvard University Press, ch. V, 'Unamuno's Narratives', esp. 104–113.

Navajas, G. 1985. The Self and the Symbolic in Unamuno's *La tía Tula*, *Revista de Estudios Hispánicos* 19, 117–37.

Olson, P. 2003. *The Great Chiasmus: Word and Flesh in the Novels of Unamuno*, West Lafayette, Ind.: Purdue University Press, ch. 3, VI. '*La tía Tula*: Consanguinity and the Cult of Family', 136–153.

Ribbans, G. 1987. A New Look at *La tía Tula*, *Revista Canadiense de Estudios Hispánicos* XI (2), 403–419.

Sinclair, A. 2001. *Uncovering the Mind: Unamuno, the Unknown and the Vicissitudes of Self*. Manchester: Manchester University Press, ch. 8, 'Envy: reconstruction and destruction of maternity in *La tía Tula*', 140–152.

Turner, D. 1974. *Unamuno's Webs of Fatality*. London: Tamesis, ch. VI, 'The Religion of Domesticity in *La tía Tula*', 92–106.

Wyers, F. 1976. *Miguel de Unamuno: the Contrary Self*. London: Tamesis, part 2, ch. I, 'Masters and Slaves', esp. 78–81.

History/context

Baker, E. 2000. *Fin de siècle* culture. In *Spanish History since 1808*, ed. J. Alvarez and A. Shubert. London: Arnold, 155–177.

Davies, C. 1998. *Spanish Women's Writing 1849–1996*. London: Athlone Press, ch. 5, 'Skirts on the Horizon: Women and Political Reform 1912–1940', esp. 99–103.

Johnson, R. 2003. *Gender and Nation in the Spanish Modernist Novel*. Nashville: Vanderbilt UP, esp. Introduction, and ch. 1, 'Women and the Soul of Spain'.

Shubert, A. 1990. *A Social History of Modern Spain*. London and New York: Routledge, ch. 1, 'A Century of Dynamism', esp. the section 'Men, Women and Children', 23–43.

LA TÍA TULA

AUNT TULA

PRÓLOGO

(Que puede saltar el lector de novelas)

TENÍA uno (hermano) casi de mi edad, que era el que yo más quería, aunque a todos tenía gran amor y ellos a mí; juntábamonos entrambos a leer vidas de santos... Espantábanos mucho el decir en lo que leíamos que pena y gloria eran para siempre. Acaecíanos estar muchos ratos tratando desto, y gustábamos de decir muchas veces para siempre, siempre, siempre. En pronunciar esto mucho rato era el Señor servido, me quedase en esta niñez imprimido el camino de la verdad. De que vi que era imposible ir adonde me matasen por Dios, ordenábamos ser ermitaños, y en una huerta que había en casa procurábamos, como podíamos, hacer ermitas poniendo unas piedrecillas, que luego se nos caían, y ansí no hallábamos remedio en nada para nuestro deseo; que ahora me pone devoción ver cómo me daba Dios tan presto lo que yo perdí por mi culpa.

«Acuérdome que cuando murió mi madre quedé yo de edad de doce años, poco menos; como yo comencé a entender lo que había perdido, afligida fuíme a una imagen de Nuestra Señora y supliquéla fuese mi madre con muchas lágrimas. Paréceme que aunque se hizo con simpleza, que me ha valido, pues conocidamente he hallado a esta Virgen Soberana en cuanto me he encomendado a ella y, en fin, me ha tornado a sí.»

(Del capítulo I de la Vida de la santa Madre Teresa de Jesús, que escribió ella misma por mandado de su confesor.)

«Sea (Dios) alabado por siempre, que tanta merced ha hecho a vuestra merced, pues le ha dado mujer, con quien pueda tener mucho descanso. Sea mucho de enhorabuena, que harto consuelo es para mí pensar que le tiene. A la señora doña María beso siempre las manos muchas veces; aquí tiene una capellana y muchas. Harto

PROLOGUE

(Which may be skipped by readers only interested in the story or the action)[1]

'One of my brothers was very close to me in age, and he was the one I was fondest of, although I loved all my siblings very much, and they me. My brother and I used to read the lives of the saints together... It would terrify us to read that both sorrow and heavenly glory were for all eternity. We spent a great deal of time discussing this, and we liked to repeat over and over 'for all eternity, forever and ever'. The Lord's purposes were served in my frequent uttering of this phrase, as I was thus inculcated with the way of truth from an early age. When I learned, to my dismay, that it was not going to be possible for me to go to a place where I would be martyred for my belief in God, my brother and I decreed that we would become hermits, and we tried as best we could to build hermitages out of piled-up stones in a garden within the grounds of the house. These hermitages would all fall down, and so our desire came to naught, but my devotion is heightened even further when I see how God soon afterwards gave me what I had lost through my own fault when younger.'

'I remember that when my mother died, I was a little under twelve years old. When I began to understand what I had lost, I resorted in my grief to an image of Our Lady. Bathed in tears, I begged *her* to be my mother. Although a simple-mindedly naive act, I believe it served me well, because I have always found Our Sovereign Lady when I have commended myself to her, and she has brought me to her.'
(From Chapter 1 of the *Life of St Teresa of Avila*, written by her at the command of her confessor)[2]

'May God be praised for all eternity for the goodness he has showed you sir: he has given you a wife, in whom you will find much respite and comfort. I send you my most heartfelt congratulations: it is a great consolation to me to know that you have taken a wife. I will always kiss the hand of Señora Doña María many times over. Here she will find a chaplain in myself and many others. We very much

quisiéramos poderla gozar; mas si había de ser con los trabajos que por acá hay, más quiero que tenga allá sosiego, que verla acá padecer.»

(De una carta que desde Ávila, a 15 de diciembre de 1581, dirigió la santa Madre y Tía, Teresa de Jesús, a su sobrino don Lorenzo de Cepeda, que estaba en Indias, en el Perú, donde se casó con doña María de Hinojosa, que es la señora doña María de que se habla en ella.)

En el capítulo II de la misma susomentada *Vida*, se dice de la santa Madre Teresa de Jesús que era moza «aficionada a leer libros de caballerías» – los suyos lo son, a lo divino– y en uno de los sonetos, de nuestro Rosario de ellos, la hemos llamado:

Quijotesa
a lo divino, que dejó asentada
nuestra España inmortal, cuya es la empresa:
«sólo existe lo eterno; ¡Dios o nada!»

Lo que acaso alguien crea que diferencia a santa Teresa de Don Quijote, es que este, el Caballero –y tío, tío de su inmortal sobrina–, se puso en ridículo y fue el ludibrio y juguete de padres y madres, de zánganos y de reinas; pero ¿es que santa Teresa escapó al ridículo? ¿Es que no se burlaron de ella? ¿Es que no se estima hoy por muchos quijotesco, o sea ridículo, su instituto, y aventurera, de caballería andante, su obra y su vida?

No crea el lector, por lo que precede, que el relato que se sigue y va a leer es, en modo alguno, un comentario a la vida de la santa española. ¡No, nada de esto! Ni pensábamos en Teresa de Jesús al emprenderlo y desarrollarlo; ni en Don Quijote. Ha sido después de haberlo terminado, cuando aun para nuestro ánimo, que lo concibió, resultó una novedad este parangón, cuando hemos descubierto las raíces de este relato novelesco. Nos fué oculto su más hondo sentido al emprenderlo. No hemos visto sino después, al hacer sobre él examen de conciencia de autor, sus raíces teresianas y quijotescas. Que son una misma raíz.

¿Es acaso este un libro de caballerías? Como el lector quiera tomarlo... Tal vez a alguno pueda parecerle una novela hagiográfica, de vida de santos. Es, de todos modos, una novela, podemos asegurarlo.

hope to enjoy her company, but if your labours in the New World prevent that, I would rather that you both have peace there rather than have her suffering here.'
(From a letter, written in Avila on 15 December in 1581, by the Holy Mother – and Aunt – Teresa to her nephew don Lorenzo de Cepeda, who was in the Indies (in Peru), where he had married doña María de Hinojosa, the 'doña María' referred to in the letter).

In chapter II of the above-mentioned *Life*, St Teresa of Avila notes that as a child, she was an enthusiastic reader of 'romances of chivalry', and her own published works are books of chivalry too – divine chivalry. In one of my own sonnets, collected in the volume *Rosario*, I called her:

A lady Quixote,
A divine Quixotess who established
Our immortal Spain, and whose enterprise can be encapsulated thus:
It is only the eternal that exists: it is either God or nothing!

Some might think that what differentiates St Teresa from Don Quixote is that the latter, the Knight, – and uncle to his immortal niece – made himself ridiculous, becoming an object of scorn and butt of endless jokes for mothers and fathers, drones and queen bees.[3] But did St Teresa escape ridicule? Was she not laughed at? Don't many people think her founding of the Discalced Carmelites, her adventures of errant chivalry and her life and works quixotic or ridiculous?

The reader should not take these opening remarks to indicate that the tale that follows is in any way a commentary on the life of Teresa, the Spanish Saint. Nothing could be further from the truth! I was not thinking of St Teresa when I began it or while I was writing it; nor was I thinking of Don Quixote. It was only after finishing it that I discovered the roots of this novelistic tale, and the comparison came as a surprise even to the mind that had conceived the work. In other words, its deepest meaning was hidden to me when I began it. It has only been after the act, after the author examined his conscience that he saw the Teresian and Quixotic origins of the tale. Which are one and the same origin.

Is this a tale of chivalry? That depends on how each reader takes it. It may be that to some it will seem like a hagiography, the life of a saint. What I can assure you is that it is a novel.

No se nos ocurrió a nosotros, sino que fue cosa de un amigo, francés por más señas, el notar que la inspiración –¡perdón!– de nuestra nivola *Niebla* era de la misma raíz que la de *La vida es sueño*, de Calderón. Mas en este otro caso ha sido cosa nuestra el descubrir, después de concluida esta novela que tienes a la vista, lector, sus raíces quijotescas y teresianas. Lo que no quiere decir, ¡claro está!, que lo que aquí se cuenta no haya podido pasar fuera de España.

Antes de terminar este prólogo queremos hacer otra observación, que le podrá parecer a alguien quizá sutileza de lingüista y filólogo, y no lo es sino de psicología. Aunque ¿es la psicología algo más que lingüística y filología?

La observación es que así como tenemos la palabra *paternal* y *paternidad* que derivan de *pater, padre,* y *maternal* y *maternidad,* de *mater, madre,* y no es lo mismo, ni mucho menos, lo *paternal* y lo *maternal,* ni la *paternidad* y la *maternidad,* es extraño que junto a *fraternal* y *fraternidad,* de *frater, hermano,* no tengamos *sororal* y *sororidad,* de *soror, hermana.* En latín hay *sororius,* a, um, lo de la hermana, y el verbo *sororiare,* crecer por igual y juntamente.

Se nos dirá que la *sororidad* equivaldría a la *fraternidad,* mas no lo creemos así. Como si en latín tuviese la hija un apelativo de raíz distinta que el de hijo, valdría la pena de distinguir entre las dos filialidades.

Sororidad fue la de la admirable Antígona, esta santa del paganismo helénico, la hija de Edipo, que sufrió martirio por amor a su hermano Polinices, y por confesar su fe de que las leyes eternas de la conciencia, las que rigen en el eterno mundo de los muertos, en el mundo de la inmortalidad, no son las que forjan los déspotas y tiranos de la tierra, como era Creonte.

Cuando en la tragedia sofocleana Creonte le acusa a su sobrina Antígona de haber faltado a la ley, al mandato regio, rindiendo servicio fúnebre a su hermano, el fratricida, hay entre aquéllos este duelo de palabras:

«A. –No es nada feo honrar a los de la misma entraña…

»Cr. –¿No era de tu sangre también el que murió contra él?

It had not occurred to me, but was pointed out by a friend (a French friend to be precise) that the inspiration (apologies for the immodesty) for my *nivola*[4] *Niebla* had the same origin as Calderón's *La vida es sueño* [Life is a Dream]. But in this other more recent case, it was I who discovered, after having finished it, the Teresian and Quixotic roots of the novel that you, the reader, hold in your hands. Which is not, of course, to say that what is recounted here could not have happened outside Spain.

Before ending this prologue, I want to make a further observation that to some might seem a mere linguistic or philological subtlety, but it is actually a psychological one. Although is psychology anything more than linguistics and philology? The observation is this: given that we have the words *paternal* and *paternity*, deriving from the Latin *pater* (father) and *maternal* and *maternity* from *mater* (mother) – not that the paternal and the maternal, or paternity and maternity, are anything like each other – it is strange that, alongside *fraternal* and *fraternity*, from *frater* (brother), we do not have *sororal* and *sorority* from *soror* (sister).[5] In Latin there is *sororius, a, um*, (meaning 'pertaining to a sister'), and *sororiare* ('to grow in an equal or similar way').

No doubt I will be told that *sorority* is equivalent to *fraternity*, but I don't believe that to be the case. If in Latin, 'daughter' had an appellative with a different root from 'son', it would be worth the while to distinguish between the two filialities.

Sorority was what was demonstrated by the admirable Antigone, that saint of Hellenic paganism. Daughter of Oedipus, she suffered martyrdom for her love for her brother Polynices, and because she confessed her faith in the eternal laws of conscience, the laws that rule the eternal world of the dead, the immortal world, and not the laws forged by despots and tyrants of the earth such as Creon.

In the tragedy by Sophocles, when Creon accuses his niece Antigone of having broken the law – and his sovereign command – by burying her brother, the fratricide, with proper funeral rites, the following verbal duel between the two characters takes place:

A.   There is nothing shameful in honouring those of one's own flesh and blood.

Cr. Wasn't the one who was killed in opposing Polynices also your flesh and blood?

»A.　–De la misma, por madre y padre...
»Cr.　–¿Y cómo rindes a este un honor impío?
»A.　–No diría eso el muerto...
»Cr.　–Pero es que le honras igual que al impío...
»A.　–No murió su siervo, sino su hermano…
»Cr.　–Asolando esta tierra, y el otro defendiéndola...
»A.　–El otro mundo, sin embargo, gusta de igualdad ante la ley…
»Cr.　–¿Cómo ha de ser igual para el vil que para el noble?
»A.　–Quién sabe si estas máximas son santas allí abajo...»

(*Antígona*, versos 511–521.)

¿Es que acaso lo que a Antígona le permitió descubrir esa ley eterna, apareciendo a los ojos de los ciudadanos de Tebas y de Creonte, su tío, como una anarquista, no fue el que era, por terrible decreto del Hado, hermana carnal de su propio padre, Edipo? Con el que había ejercido oficio de *sororidad* también.

El acto *sororio* de Antígona dando tierra al cadáver insepulto de su hermano y librándolo así del furor regio de su tío Creonte, parecióle a este un acto de anarquista. «¡No hay mal mayor que el de la anarquía!» – declaraba el tirano – .

(*Antígona*, verso 672.) ¿Anarquía? ¿Civilización?

Antígona, la anarquista según su tío, el tirano Creonte, modelo de virilidad, pero no de humanidad; Antígona, hermana de su padre Edipo y, por lo tanto, tía de su hermano Polinices, representa acaso la domesticidad religiosa, la religión doméstica, la del hogar, frente a la civilidad política y tiránica, a la tiranía civil, y acaso también la domesticación frente a la civilización. ¿Aunque es posible civilizarse sin haberse domesticado antes? ¿Caben civilidad y civilización donde no tienen como cimientos domesticidad y domesticación?

Hablamos de *patrias* y sobre ellas de *fraternidad* universal, pero no es una sutileza lingüística el sostener que no pueden prosperar sino sobre *matrias* y *sororidad*. Y habrá barbarie de guerras devastadoras, y

A.   Yes, by the same mother and father...
Cr.   So why do you impiously honour Polynices?
A.   The dead man would not see it thus.
Cr.   But you are honouring the pious and the impious equally.
A.   It was not his slave that died, but his brother.
Cr.   Yes, but while he was destroying this land; the other was
      trying to defend it.
A.   Nevertheless, equality before the law reigns in the other
      world...
Cr.   How can there be equality between the noble and the
      villainous?
A.   Who knows whether such maxims hold in the nether world?

(Antigone, ll. 511–521).

Might it be that what allowed Antigone to discover this eternal law, thus rendering her an anarchist in the eyes of the citizens of Thebes and her uncle Creon, was the fact that, by Fate's terrible decree, she was sister to her own father, Oedipus, for whom she had also performed sororal duties?

It was Antigone's sororal action, covering the exposed body of her brother with earth according to the established funeral rites, that unleashed the fury of her uncle, King Creon, who saw it as an act of anarchy. 'There is no worse evil than anarchy', the tyrant declared (*Antigone*, l. 672). Anarchy? Civilization?

Antigone, an anarchist according to her uncle, the tyrant Creon – who was the very model of virility, though not of humanity; Antigone, sister to her father Oedipus, and therefore aunt to her brother Polynices, is perhaps the representative of religious domesticity, domestic religion, that of the home, set against political and tyrannical civil life, civil tyranny. Perhaps she also represents domestication in opposition to civilisation.[6] That said, is it possible to be civilised if one has not been domesticated beforehand? Can civility and civilization exist without the foundation stones of domesticity and domestication?

We speak of *fatherlands*, and over and above them, of universal *fraternity*, but it is not merely a linguistic nicety to argue that such values cannot thrive except by resting on mother countries and sorority. And the barbarism of devastating wars and other ravages will continue as long as

otros estragos, mientras sean los zánganos, que revolotean en torno de la reina para fecundar y devorar la miel que no hicieron, los que rijan las colmenas.

¿Guerras? El primer acto guerrero fue, según lo que llamamos Historia Sagrada, la de la Biblia, el asesinato de Abel por su hermano Caín. Fué una muerte fraternal, entre hermanos; el primer acto de fraternidad. Y dice el *Génesis* que fué Caín, el fratricida, el que primero edificó una ciudad, a la que llamó del nombre de su hijo – habido en una hermana – Henoc. (Gén., IV, 17). Y en aquella ciudad, polis, debió empezar la vida civil, política, la civilidad y la civilización. Obra, como se ve, del fratricida. Y cuando, siglos más tarde, nuestro Lucano, español, llamó a las guerras entre César y Pompeyo *plusquam civilia*, más que civiles –lo dice en el primer verso de su Pharsalia – quiere decir *fraternales*. Las guerras más que civiles son las *fraternales*.

Aristóteles le llamó al hombre *zoon politicon*, esto es, animal civil o ciudadano – no político, que esto es no traducir – animal que tiende a vivir en ciudades, en mazorcas de casas estadizas, arraigadas en tierra por cimientos, y ese es el hombre y, sobre todo, el varón. Animal civil, urbano, fraternal y... fratricida.–Pero ese animal civil, ¿no ha de depurarse por acción doméstica? Y el hogar, el verdadero hogar, ¿no ha de encontrarse lo mismo en la tienda del pastor errante que se planta al azar de los caminos? Y Antígona acompañó a su padre, ciego y errante, por los senderos del desierto, hasta que desapareció en Colono. ¡Pobre civilidad, fraternal, cainita, si no hubiera la domesticidad sororia!...

Va, pues, el fundamento de la civilidad, la domesticidad, de mano en mano de hermanas, de tías. O de esposas de espíritu, castísimas, como aquella Abisag, la sunamita de que se nos habla en el capítulo I del libro I de los Reyes, aquella doncella que le llevaron al viejo rey David, ya cercano a su muerte, para que le mantuviese en la puesta de su vida, abrigándole y calentándole en la cama mientras dormía. Y Abisag le sacrificó su maternidad, permaneció virgen por él – pues David no la conoció – y fue causa de que más luego Salomón, el hijo del pecado de David con la adúltera Betsabé, hiciese matar a Adonías, su hermanastro, hijo de David y de Hagit, porque pretendió para mujer a Abisag, la última reina con David, pensando así heredar a éste su reino.

it is the drones – who flit around the queen bee in order to fertilise her and to devour the honey that they did not make – who rule over the beehive.

Speaking of wars, the first act of war, according to what we call scripture, or the sacred history recounted in the bible, was the murder of Abel by his brother Cain. It was a fraternal death, an act carried out between brothers, the first act of fraternity. And Genesis says that it was Cain, the fratricide, who was the first to build a city, which he named Enoch, after his son – born of Cain's sister. (Gen IV, 17). And in that city, that *polis*, the political life of the *civis*, civil society and civilization had to begin. As is clear to see, it was the work of a fratricide. And when centuries later, our own Lucan, a Spaniard, called the civil wars between Caesar and Pompey *plusquam civilia* (more than civil) – this is what he says in the opening words of his *Pharsalia* – he meant that they were *fraternal*. Wars that go beyond the civil are fraternal.

Aristotle called man *politikon zōon*, that is, a civic animal or citizen – not a political one (that would be a mistranslation), an animal that tends to live in cities, in stacks of immovable houses, rooted to the ground by their foundations. And the *politikon zōon* is man, and, above all, the male. A civic, urban, fraternal…fratricidal animal. But isn't this civic animal purified through the action of the domestic? And can't home – true home – also be found in the tent belonging to the nomadic shepherd whose home is wherever his tent is pitched during his marathon journeys? Antigone, too, accompanied her father as he blindly wandered through the paths of the desert until he disappeared at Colona. How impoverished fraternal, Cainite civility would be if there were no sisterly domesticity!

Domesticity, the foundation of civility, is intimately connected with sisters and with aunts. Or with spiritual, absolutely chaste wives, such as Abishag the Shunammite, mentioned in the first chapter of the first book of Kings. The maiden Abishag was taken to the elderly King David, by then near death, so that he might be tended to in the twilight of his life: she would warm his bed as he slept. And Abishag sacrificed her maternity for him – she remained a virgin for his sake, David never knowing her as his wife. And this was why Solomon, fruit of the sinful union between David and the adulteress Bathsheba, had Adonias (his stepbrother, son of David and Hagith) killed, because he wanted Abishag, David's last queen, for his wife, intending thus to inherit the kingdom.

Pero a esta Abisag y a su suerte y a su sentido pensamos dedicar todo un libro que no será precisamente una novela. Ni una *nivola*.

Y ahora el lector que ha leído este prólogo – que no es necesario para inteligencia en lo que sigue – puede pasar a hacer conocimiento con la tía Tula, que si supo de santa Teresa y de Don Quijote, acaso no supo ni de Antígona la griega ni de Abisag la israelita.

En mi novela *Abel Sánchez* intenté escarbar en ciertos sótanos y escondrijos del corazón, en ciertas catacumbas del alma, adonde no gustan descender los más de los mortales. Creen que en esas catacumbas hay muertos, a los que lo mejor es no visitar, y esos muertos, sin embargo, nos gobiernan. Es la herencia de Caín. Y aquí, en esta novela, he intentado escarbar en otros sótanos y escondrijos. Y como no ha faltado quien me haya dicho que aquello era inhumano, no faltará quien me lo diga, aunque en otro sentido, de esto. Aquello pareció a alguien inhumano por viril, por fraternal; esto lo parecerá acaso por femenil, por sororio. Sin que quepa negar que el varón hereda feminidad de su madre y la mujer virilidad de su padre. ¿O es que el zángano no tiene algo de abeja y la abeja de zángano? O hay, si se quiere, *abejos* y *zánganas*.

Y nada más, que no debo hacer una novela sobre otra novela.

En Salamanca, ciudad, en el día de los Desposorios de Nuestra Señora del año de gracia milésimo novecentésimo y vigésimo.

I am planning to write an entire book about Abishag, her fate and her significance. It will not quite be a novel.[7] Nor a *nivola*.

But now the reader who has read this prologue – not necessary for an understanding of what follows – can get to know Aunt Tula, who, if she knew of St Teresa and Don Quixote, perhaps did not know of Antigone, or Abishag the Shunammite.

In my novel *Abel Sánchez*, I tried to delve into certain nooks and crannies of the heart, certain catacombs of the soul, spaces into which other mortals do not like to descend.[8] Such mortals believe that there are dead people in the catacombs whom it is best not to visit, but that notwithstanding this, these dead people rule over us. It is the legacy of Cain. And here in this novel, I have tried to delve into other nooks and crannies. Because there was no shortage of people who told me that *Abel Sánchez* was inhuman, there'll doubtless be no shortage who say the same of this novel, even if they deem it inhuman in a different sense. Some considered *Abel Sánchez* inhuman precisely because of its depiction of virility and fraternity, and perhaps this novel will strike some as similarly inhuman, but this time for its portrayal of femininity and sorority. Which is not to deny that the male inherits femininity from his mother, or that the female inherits virility from her father. Does the drone not also possess qualities of the bee, and vice versa?[9]

But enough; I should not be writing a novel here about another novel.

> *The city of Salamanca, the day of Our Lady's betrothal, in the nineteen hundredth and twentieth year of grace.*

I

Era a Rosa y no a su hermana Gertrudis, que siempre salía de casa con ella, a quien ceñían aquellas ansiosas miradas que les enderezaba Ramiro. O por lo menos, así lo creían ambos, Ramiro y Rosa, al atraerse el uno al otro.

Formaban las dos hermanas, siempre juntas, aunque no por eso unidas siempre, una pareja al parecer indisoluble, y como un solo valor. Era la hermosura espléndida y algún tanto provocativa de Rosa, flor de carne que se abría a flor del cielo a toda luz y todo viento, la que llevaba de primera vez las miradas a la pareja; pero eran luego los ojos tenaces de Gertrudis los que sujetaban a los ojos que se habían fijado en ellos y los que a la par les ponían raya. Hubo quien al verlas pasar preparó algún chicoleo un poco más subido de tono; mas tuvo que contenerse al tropezar con el reproche de aquellos ojos de Gertrudis, que hablaban mudamente de seriedad. «Con esta pareja no se juega», parecía decir con sus miradas silenciosas.

Y bien miradas y de cerca aún despertaba más Gertrudis el ansia de goce. Mientras su hermana Rosa abría espléndidamente a todo viento y toda luz la flor de su encarnadura, ella era como un cofre cerrado y sellado en que se adivina un tesoro de ternuras y delicias secretas.

Pero Ramiro, que llevaba el alma toda a flor de los ojos, no creyó ver más que a Rosa, y a Rosa se dirigió desde luego.

–¿Sabes que me ha escrito? – le dijo ésta a su hermana.

–Sí, vi la carta.

–¿Cómo? ¿que la viste? ¿es que me espías?

–¿Podía dejar de haberla visto? No, yo no espío nunca, ya lo sabes, y has dicho eso no más que por decirlo...

–Tienes razón, Tula; perdónamelo.

–Sí, una vez más, porque tú eres así. Yo no espío, pero tampoco oculto nunca nada. Vi la carta.

–Ya lo sé; ya lo sé...

–He visto la carta y la esperaba.

–Y bien, ¿qué te parece de Ramiro?

I

It was to Rosa, and not to her sister Gertrudis – always at Rosa's side when she left the house – that Ramiro's anxious gaze would cling. Or at least that is what the two of them, Rosa and Ramiro, thought when they first became attracted to each other.

The two sisters, who were always together though they did not always see completely eye to eye, seemed to make up an indissoluble couple, as if they together constituted one single value. It was the lavish and rather provocative beauty of Rosa, a living, breathing flower whose bloom was open to the heavens come rain or shine, which first drew others' gazes to the pair. But it was Tula who would then firmly meet those gazes and keep them at bay. Watching the sisters go by, some men would dream up a childish or risqué comment, but they would then be forced to contain it when they met the reproach of Gertrudis's gaze, which expressed a mute but eloquent gravitas. 'This couple is not to be trifled with', her silent glances seemed to say.

And when scrutinized closely, it was actually Gertrudis more than Rosa who awakened others' desire to possess her. While her sister Rosa's magnificent beauty was as open as a flower that blooms in all seasons, Gertrudis was like a sealed treasure chest which, one sensed, contained a trove of tender, delectable secrets.

But Ramiro, whose heart was driven by his eyes and what was on the surface, thought he only had eyes for Rosa, and so of course directed himself to her.

'Guess what? He's written to me…', said Rosa to her sister.

'Yes, I saw the letter.'

'What? You saw the letter? Have you been spying on me?'

'How could I not have seen it? And no, I never spy on people, as you well know. You're just saying that for the sake of it.'

'You're right Tula. Forgive me.'

'All right, I will – yet again – because I know what you're like. I don't spy on people, but I never hide anything either. I saw the letter.'

'I know, I know…'

'I saw the letter and I'd been expecting it.'

'So … what do you think of Ramiro?'

–No le conozco.

–Pero no hace falta conocer a un hombre para decir lo que le parece a una de él.

–A mí, sí.

–Pero lo que se ve, lo que está a la vista...

–Ni de eso puedo juzgar sin conocerle.

–¿Es que no tienes ojos en la cara?

–Acaso no los tenga así…; ya sabes que soy corta de vista.

–¡Pretextos! Pues mira, chica, es un guapo mozo.

–Así parece.

–Y simpático.

–Con que te lo sea a ti, basta.

–Pero ¿es que crees que le he dicho ya que sí?

–Sé que se lo dirás al cabo, y basta.

–No importa; hay que hacerle esperar y hasta rabiar un poco...

–¿Para qué?

–Hay que hacerse valer.

–Así no te haces valer, Rosa; y ese coqueteo es cosa muy fea.

–De modo que tú...

–A mí no se me ha dirigido.

–¿Y si se hubiera dirigido a ti?

–No sirve preguntar cosas sin sustancia.

–Pero tú, si a ti se te dirige, ¿qué le habrías contestado?

–Yo no he dicho que me parece un guapo mozo y que es simpático, y por eso me habría puesto a estudiarle...

–Y entretanto si iba a otra...

–Es lo más probable.

–Pues así, hija, ya puedes prepararte...

–Sí, a ser tía.

–¿Cómo tía?

–Tía de tus hijos, Rosa.

–¡Eh, qué cosas tienes! – y se quebró la voz.

–Vamos, Rosita, no te pongas así, y perdóname – le dijo dándole un beso.

'I don't know him.'

'One doesn't have to know a man to say what one thinks of him.'

'*I* do.'

'But what do you think of what you've been able to *see* of him then?'

'I can't even judge him on that basis without knowing him.'

'Don't you have eyes in your head?'

'Maybe not for things like that ... you know I'm short-sighted.'

'Excuses, excuses! Well, I'll tell you: he's a fine figure of a man.'

'So he seems.'

'And he's nice with it.'

'If he is to you, that's all that matters.'

'But surely you don't think I've already said yes to him?'

'I know what you'll say in the end, and that's enough for me.'

'That's by the by; he has to be made to wait, and even be tormented a little.'

'What for?'

'One has to make oneself appreciated.'

'You won't gain appreciation of your worth like that Rosa, and such coquettishness is deeply unpleasant.'

'So *you* wouldn't...'

'He's not trying to court me.'

'And if he were?'

'There's no point asking hypothetical questions.'

'But just put yourself in my place: if he'd approached you, how would you have responded?'

'Well, I've said nothing about his being a fine figure of a man, or nice with it, so I would start by examining him very carefully...'

'And meanwhile, he would have approached another woman...'

'Yes, most likely...'

'Well, if *that's* how you're going to proceed, you can start preparing...'

'To be an aunt, yes, I know.'

'What do you mean 'to be an aunt'?'

'An aunt to your children, Rosa.'

'The things you say...', and there was a catch in Rosa's voice.

'Now, now, Rosa, don't get upset... I'm sorry', said Gertrudis, giving a sister a kiss.

–Pero si vuelves...

–¡No, no volveré!

–Y bien, ¿qué le digo?

–¡Dile que sí!

–Pero pensará que soy demasiado fácil...

–¡Entonces dile que no!

–Pero es que...

–Sí, que te parece un guapo mozo y simpático. Dile, pues, que sí y no andes con más coqueterías, que eso es feo. Dile que sí. Después de todo, no es fácil que se te presente mejor partido. Ramiro está muy bien, es hijo solo...

–Yo no he hablado de eso.

–Pero yo hablo de ello, Rosa, y es igual.

–¿Y no dirán, Tula, que tengo ganas de novio?

–Y dirán bien.

–¿Otra vez, Tula?

–Y ciento. Tienes ganas de novio y es natural que las tengas. ¿Para qué si no te hizo Dios tan guapa?

–¡Guasitas no!

–Ya sabes que yo no me guaseo. Parézcanos bien o mal, nuestra carrera es el matrimonio o el convento; tú no tienes vocación de monja; Dios te hizo para el mundo y el hogar...vamos, para madre de familia... No vas a quedarte a vestir imágenes. Dile, pues, que sí.

–¿Y tú?

–¿Cómo yo?

–Que tú, luego...

–A mí déjame.

Al día siguiente de estas palabras estaban ya en lo que se llaman relaciones amorosas Rosa y Ramiro.

Lo que empezó a cuajar la soledad de Gertrudis.

Vivían las dos hermanas, huérfanas de padre y madre desde muy niñas, con un tío materno, sacerdote, que no las mantenía, pues ellas disfrutaban de un pequeño patrimonio que les permitía sostenerse en la holgura de la modestia, pero les daba buenos consejos a la hora de comer, en la mesa, dejándolas, por lo demás, a la guía de su buen natural. Los

'But if you change your mind…'

'I won't!'

'Well then, what shall I say to him?'

'Say yes'

'But he will think I am giving in too easily…'

'Well, say no then…'

'But the thing is…'

'Yes, I know, you think he's handsome and nice. So say yes to him then, and let's have no more of this coquettishness, which is really not very nice at all. Say yes. After all, it'd be hard to find a better match. Ramiro is desirable: he's an only child.'

'I didn't mention that.'

'But *I'm* mentioning it Rosa, and it's fine.'

'But won't people say, Tula, that I'm just desperate to land a fiancé?'

'Well they'd be right.'

'We're back to this?'

'I'll keep saying it: it's natural that you want to find a husband. Why else would God have made you so pretty?'

'Don't joke about things like that.'

'You know I never make jokes. Whether we women like it or not, our career is either marriage or the convent. You have no vocation to be a nun; God made you to live in the world and in the home, in other words, to be a wife and mother … you're not made to be left on the shelf, like one of those pious ladies who volunteer to help in the parish church, dressing the statues of the saints. So say yes to him.'

'What about you?'

'What do you *mean*, 'what about you'?'

'What will *you* do…?'

'Don't worry about me.'

The very next day after this exchange, Rosa and Ramiro began courting, as the expression goes.

And Gertrudis's loneliness began to take on an almost concrete form.

The two sisters, who had been orphaned at a young age, lived with an uncle, their mother's brother. He was a priest, and did not need to support the two sisters financially, as a small inheritance allowed the pair to live in modest comfort. What he did give them was good advice when they were at table together; otherwise he allowed them to be guided by their

buenos consejos eran consejos de libros, los mismos que le servían a don Primitivo para formar sus escasos sermones.

«Además – se decía a sí mismo con muy buen acierto don Primitivo –, ¿para qué me voy a meter en sus inclinaciones y sentimientos íntimos? Lo mejor es no hablarlas mucho de eso, que se les abre demasiado los ojos. Aunque... ¿abrirles? ¡Bah!, bien abiertos los tienen, sobre todo las mujeres. Nosotros los hombres no sabemos una palabra de esas cosas. Y los curas, menos. Todo lo que nos dicen los libros son pataratas. ¡Y luego, me mete un miedo esa Tulilla...! Delante de ella no me atrevo..., no me atrevo... ¡Tiene unas preguntas la mocita! Y cuando me mira tan seria, tan seria..., con esos ojazos tristes – los de mi hermana, los de mi madre. ¡Dios las tenga en su santa gloria! – ¡Esos ojazos de luto que se le meten a uno en el corazón...! Muy serios, sí, pero riéndose con el rabillo. Parecen decirme: «¡No diga usted más bobadas, tío!» ¡El demonio de la chiquilla! ¡Todavía me acuerdo el día en que se empeñó en ir, con su hermana, a oírme aquel sermoncete; el rato que pasé, Jesús Santo! ¡Todo se me volvía apartar mis ojos de ella por no cortarme; pero nada, ella tirando de los míos! Lo mismo, lo mismito me pasaba con su santa madre, mi hermana, y con mi santa madre, Dios las tenga en su gloria. Jamás pude predicar a mis anchas delante de ellas, y por eso les tenía dicho que no fuesen a oírme. Madre iba, pero iba a hurtadillas, sin decírmelo, y se ponía detrás de la columna, donde yo no le viera, y luego no me decía nada de mi sermón. Y lo mismo hacía mi hermana. Pero yo sé lo que ésta pensaba, aunque tan cristiana, lo sé. «¡Bobadas de hombres!» Y lo mismo piensa esta mocita, estoy de ello seguro. No, no, ¿delante de ella predicar? ¿Yo? ¿Darle consejos? Una vez se le escapó lo de *¡bobadas de hombres!*, y no dirigiéndose a mí, no; pero yo le entiendo...»

El pobre señor tenía un profundísimo respeto, mezclado de admiración, por su sobrina Gertrudis. Tenía el sentimiento de que la sabiduría iba en su linaje por vía femenina, que su madre había sido la providencia inteligente de la casa en que se crió, que su hermana lo había sido en la suya, tan breve. Y en cuanto a su otra sobrina, a Rosa, le bastaba para

own natural good sense. His good advice was culled from books – the same books that don Primitivo used to prepare his rare sermons.

'In any case,' don Primitivo would say to himself, not unwisely, 'why would I interfere in their inclinations and intimate feelings? The best thing is to keep as quiet as possible about such matters and not open their eyes too much … although what am I saying? All eyes are wide open these days, women's most of all. We men know nothing about any of this. And priests even less. Everything the books say is nonsense. And that little Tula scares me silly! Standing before her, I daren't … I daren't even… That young girl certainly knows how to ask difficult questions. And when she looks at me so very seriously, with her big sad eyes – her mother's eyes, my sister's eyes, God rest their souls! Those mournful eyes which tug at one's heartstrings… They *are* very serious, but there does also seem to be a smile at the corner of her eyes, as if she is saying to me "You've said enough silly things for now uncle". The little devil! I still remember the day that she insisted on going to listen to one of my sermons, along with her sister. Goodness me, the time I had of it! It was so hard to tear my eyes away from her so as not to falter in what I was saying. It was no good – her eyes were fixed so firmly on mine. And the same thing – the *very* same thing – happened with her saintly mother, my sister, and with my own saintly mother, God rest both their souls. I could never be at ease reading the sermon when they were there. That was why I told them – more than once – not to come to hear me. But mother used to sneak in without saying anything, and would sit behind a column where I couldn't see her. She would never say anything about it afterwards. And my sister would do the same thing. But I know what my sister thought, I just know, even though she was so Christian. She was thinking, "Typical men's nonsense!" And I'm convinced that this young girl thinks the same. Preach when she's there watching me? Give her advice? Me? No chance! Once, the phrase "typical men's nonsense!" did actually slip from her lips! Not when she was referring to me, granted, but I know what she meant…'

The poor gentleman felt a deep respect, mingled with admiration, for his niece Gertrudis. He had the feeling that wisdom was passed down the distaff side in his family, and that his mother had been the source of all intelligence in the house where he was raised. His sister had gone on to fulfil the same role in her own household, albeit all too briefly. And as for

protección y guía con su hermana. «Pero qué hermosa la ha hecho Dios, Dios sea alabado – se decía –; esta chica o hace un gran matrimonio, con quien ella quiera, o no tienen los mozos de hoy ojos en la cara.»

Y un día fue Gertrudis la que, después que Rosa se levantó de la mesa fingiendo sentirse algo indispuesta, al quedarse a solas con su tío, le dijo:

–Tengo que decirle a usted, tío, una cosa muy grave.

–Muy grave..., muy grave... – y el pobre señor se azaró, creyendo observar que los rabillos de los ojazos tan serios de su sobrina reían maliciosamente.

–Sí, muy grave.

–Bueno, pues desembucha, hija, que aquí estamos los dos para tomar un consejo.

–El caso es que Rosa tiene ya novio.

–¿Y no es más que eso?

–Pero novio formal, ¿eh?, tío.

–Vamos, sí, para que yo los case.

–¡Naturalmente!

–Y a ti, ¿qué te parece de él?

–Aún no ha preguntado usted quién es...

–¿Y qué más da, si yo apenas conozco a nadie? A ti, ¿qué te parece de él?, contesta.

–Pues tampoco yo le conozco.

–Pero ¿no sabes quién es, tú?

–Sí, sé cómo se llama y de qué familia es y...

–¡Basta! ¿Qué te parece?

–Que es un buen partido para Rosa y que se querrán.

–Pero ¿es que no se quieren ya?

–Pero ¿cree usted, tío, que pueden empezar queriéndose?

–Pues así dicen, chiquilla, y hasta que eso viene como un rayo...

–Son decires, tío.

–Así será; basta que tú lo digas.

–Ramiro..., Ramiro Cuadrado...

–Pero ¿es el hijo de doña Venancia, la viuda? ¡Acabáramos! No hay más que hablar.

his other niece, Rosa, her sister Gertrudis gave her all the guidance and protection she needed. 'And God has made Rosa so beautiful – may He be praised', don Primitivo used to say to himself. 'If she does not make a good marriage, able to choose whomever she wants, then the young men of today don't have eyes in their heads.'

And so one day, after Rosa had risen from the table on the pretext of feeling a little indisposed, it was Gertrudis, now left alone with her uncle, who said,

'I have something very serious to tell you uncle.'

'Very serious…?' The poor gentleman reddened. He thought he saw a mischievous humorousness in the corner of his niece's grave eyes.

'Yes, very serious.'

'Well then, out with it! The two of us are here to talk things over.'

'Well … Rosa has a suitor.'

'Is that *all*?'

'But it's a serious suitor uncle…'

'Well then, I can be the one to marry them!'

'Naturally!'

'And what do you think of him?'

'You haven't asked who he is yet.'

'What does that matter? I hardly know anyone… What do you think of him? Please tell me…'

'I don't know him either.'

'Are you telling me you don't know who he is?'

'I know his name, and the family he comes from, and…'

'Well that's enough! What do you think of him?'

'I think he's a good match for Rosa, and that they will come to love each other.'

'Don't they love each other already?'

'Do you really think they can love each other from the start?'

'That's what they say, my child. I've heard that love can even come like a bolt from the blue.'

'They're just sayings, uncle'

'I'm sure you're right; you know better than me.'

'It's Ramiro…, Ramiro Cuadrado…'

'You mean Doña Venancia's son? Doña Venancia the widow? Say no more … it's all settled.'

–A Ramiro, tío, se le ha metido Rosa por los ojos y cree estar enamorado de ella...

–Y lo estará, Tulilla, lo estará...

–Eso digo yo, tío, que lo estará. Porque como es hombre de vergüenza y de palabra, acabará por cobrar cariño a aquella con la que se ha comprometido ya. No le creo hombre de volver atrás.

–¿Y ella?

–¿Quién? ¿Mi hermana? A ella le pasará lo mismo.

–Sabes más que san Agustín, hija.

–Esto no se aprende, tío.

–¡Pues que se casen, los bendigo y sanseacabó!

–¡O sanseempezó! Pero hay que casarlos y pronto. Antes que él se vuelva...

–Pero ¿temes tú que él pueda volverse ...?

–Yo siempre temo de los hombres, tío.

–¿Y de las mujeres no?

–Esos temores deben quedar para los hombres. Pero sin ánimo de ofender al sexo... fuerte, ¿no se dice así?, le digo que la constancia, que la fortaleza está más bien de parte nuestra...

–Si todas fueran como tú, chiquilla, lo creería así, pero...

–¿Pero qué?

–¡Que tú eres excepcional, Tulilla!

–Le he oído a usted más de una vez, tío, que las excepciones confirman la regla.

–Vamos, que me aturdes... Pues bien, los casaremos, no sea que se vuelva él... o ella...

Por los ojos de Gertrudis pasó como la sombra de una nube de borrasca, y si se hubiera podido oír el silencio habríase oído que en las bóvedas de los sótanos de su alma resonaba como un eco repetido y que va perdiéndose a lo lejos aquello de «o ella...».

'Ramiro only has eyes for Rosa, and he thinks he's in love with her.'

'And he'll come to be, little Tula, he'll come to be…'

'I think so too uncle. He's a man of his word, an honourable man, and will eventually feel love for the woman he has just proposed to. I don't think he's a man who would renege on a promise.'

'And her?'

'Who? My sister? I think the same thing will happen to her.'

'You're more knowledgeable than St Augustine, child.'

'These things aren't learned uncle.'

'Well, let them be married. I'll give them my blessing and that'll be an end to it!'

'Or a beginning! But they must be married quickly. Before he goes back on…'

'But do you think he's capable of changing his mind?'

'I have my fears about men, uncle.'

'And not about women?'

'These kinds of fears are more relevant to men. Without wanting to offend the … what's the phrase?… stronger sex, I think that constancy and fortitude are more attributes of the fairer sex than of men…'

'If all women were like you, my child, I'd believe it, but…'

'But what?'

'You're exceptional Tula!'

'Uncle, I've heard you say more than once that the exception proves the rule.'

'Now you are addling my brains … all right then, let's get them safely married, so that he … or she … can't go back on any word.'

At that, it was as if the shadow of a storm cloud had passed across Gertrudis's eyes, and if it were possible to hear the silence, one would have heard, in the vaults of the cellars of her soul, the echo of the words 'or she' ringing out before they slowly faded away.

II

Pero ¿qué le pasaba a Ramiro, en relaciones ya, y en relaciones formales, con Rosa, y poco menos que entrando en la casa? ¿Qué dilaciones y qué frialdades eran aquéllas?

–Mira, Tula, yo no le entiendo; cada vez le entiendo menos. Parece que está siempre distraído y como si estuviese pensando en otra cosa – o en otra persona, ¡quién sabe! – o temiendo que alguien nos vaya a sorprender de pronto. Y cuando le tiro algún avance y le hablo, así como quien no quiere la cosa, del fin que deben tener nuestras relaciones, hace como que no oye y como si estuviera atendiendo a otra...

–Es porque le hablas como quien no quiere la cosa. Háblale como quien la quiere.

–¡Eso es, y que piense que tengo prisa por casarme!

–¡Pues que lo piense! ¿No es acaso así?

–Pero ¿crees tú, Tula, que yo estoy rabiando por casarme?

–¿Le quieres?

–Eso nada tiene que ver...

–¿Le quieres, di?

–Pues mira...

–¡Pues mira, no! ¿Le quieres? ¡Sí o no!

Rosa bajó la frente con los ojos, arrebolóse toda y llorándole la voz tartamudeó:

–Tienes unas cosas, Tula; ¡pareces un confesor!

Gertrudis tomó la mano de su hermana, con otra le hizo levantar la frente, le clavó los ojos en los ojos y le dijo:

–Vivimos solas, hermana...

–¿Y el tío?

–Vivimos solas, te he dicho. Las mujeres vivimos siempre solas. El pobre tío es un santo, pero un santo de libro, y aunque cura, al fin y al cabo hombre.

–Pero confiesa...

–Acaso por eso sabe menos. Además, se le olvida. Y así debe ser.

II

What, though, was the matter with Ramiro, who was now spoken for, his relations with Rosa formalized to such a degree that his foot was virtually in the marital door? Why was there such a delay? Was he getting cold feet?

'Oh Tula, I understand him less with every passing day. He seems constantly distracted, as if his mind were on something – or *someone* – else. Who knows? It's as if he's frightened that we're about to be suddenly surprised by someone else. And when I throw in a comment about the future and speak casually of the inevitable end of our relationship, he pretends not to hear. His mind is elsewhere, on something or someone else.'

'That's because you're talking to him as if the relationship doesn't mean anything to you. Speak to him as if it actually mattered to you.'

'Oh that's right, so he can think that I'm in a rush to get married! That'll really help!'

'So what if it he does think that? Isn't it the truth, anyway?

'Tula, do *you* really think I'm in a rush to get married?'

'Do you love him?'

'That's beside the point…'

'Do you love him? Tell me.'

'Well…'

'Never mind "well…". Do you love him? Yes or no?'

Rosa lowered her gaze, blushed bright red, and, choking back a sob, stuttered out,

'The things you say Tula! I feel as if I'm in the confessional!'

Gertrudis took Rosa's hand, and with her other hand lifted her sister's chin. Looking deep into Rosa's eyes, she said,

'We live alone sister…'

'What about uncle?'

'I said we live alone. We women always live alone. Poor uncle is a saint, but he's a saint straight from the pages of a book. And although he's a priest, he is, when all is said and done, still a man.'

'But he hears confession…'

'Maybe he knows even less about these things as a result. Anyway, he doesn't remember any of the things he's told. And that's how it should

Vivimos solas, te he dicho. Y ahora lo que debes hacer es confesarte aquí, pero confesarte a ti misma. ¿Le quieres?, repito.

La pobre Rosa se echó a llorar.

—¿Le quieres? – sonó la voz implacable.

Y Rosa llegó a fingirse que aquella pregunta, en una voz pastosa y solemne y que parecía venir de las lontananzas de la vida común de la pureza, era su propia voz, era acaso la de su madre común.

—Sí, creo que le querré... mucho... mucho... – exclamó en voz baja y sollozando.

—¡Sí, le querrás mucho y él te querrá más aún!

—¿Y cómo lo sabes?

—Yo sé que te querrá.

—Entonces, ¿por qué está distraído?, ¿por qué rehuye el que abordemos lo del casorio?

—¡Yo le hablaré de eso, Rosa, déjalo de mi cuenta!

—¿Tú?

—¡Yo, sí! ¿Tiene algo de extraño?

—Pero...

—A mí no puede cohibirme el temor que a ti te cohibe.

—Pero dirá que rabio por casarme.

—¡No, no dirá eso! Dirá, si quiere, que es a mí a quien me conviene que tú te cases para facilitar así el que se me pretenda o para quedarme a mandar aquí sola; y las dos cosas son, como sabes, dos disparates. Dirá lo que quiera, pero yo me las arreglaré.

Rosa cayó en brazos de su hermana, que le dijo al oído:

—Y luego, tienes que quererle mucho, ¿eh?

—¿Y por qué me dices tú eso, Tula?

—Porque es tu deber.

Y al otro día, al ir Ramiro a visitar a su novia, encontróse con la otra, con la hermana. Demudósele el semblante y se le vió vacilar. La seriedad de aquellos serenos ojazos de luto le concentró la sangre toda en el corazón.

—¿Y Rosa? –preguntó sin oírse.

—Rosa ha salido y soy yo quien tengo ahora que hablarte.

be. We live alone, as I said. And now what you must do is confess, here and now, but confess to yourself. I'll ask you again: do you love him?'

Poor Rosa began to cry.

'Do you love him?', the relentless voice asked again.

And Rosa managed to convince herself that the question, voiced in rich, solemn tones, seemed to come from the distant depths of the pure life that the sisters had in common, and that she was being asked in the voice of that same pure life, or perhaps that of their departed mother.

'Yes, I think I'll come to love him a great deal ... very much...', she exclaimed, gently sobbing.

'Yes, you'll love him very much and he'll love you in return even more.'

'How do you know that?'

'I know that he'll love you.'

'But then why is he so distracted? Why does he avoid the topic of marriage?'

'I'll talk to him about it, Rosa, leave it to me!'

'Leave it to *you*?'

'Yes, me. What's so strange about that?'

'But...'

'The fear that's holding you back doesn't hold any terrors for me.'

'He'll say that I'm desperate to get married.'

'He *won't* say that! What he *might* say is that it's me who wants to hurry the marriage along to make it easier for other suitors to then approach me, or because I want to take sole charge of the household. Both those things are absurd, as you know. He can say what he likes: I'll resolve the matter.'

Rosa fell into her sister's arms, and Tula whispered in her ear,

'Now you must love him with all your heart, do you understand?'

'Why are you telling me this Tula?'

'Because it is your duty.'

And the next day when Ramiro went to visit his betrothed, he found himself in the presence of the other sister. Blushing, he hesitated before speaking. The seriousness of Tula's calm and mournful large eyes made his heart pound.

'Where's Rosa?' he asked, without even hearing his own question.

'She has gone out. I'm the one who needs to talk to you right now.'

–¿Tú? – dijo con labios que le temblaban.

–¡Sí, yo!

–¡Grave te pones, chica! – y se esforzó en reírse.

–Nací con esa gravedad encima, dicen. El tío asegura que la heredé de mi madre, su hermana, y de mi abuela, su madre. No lo sé, ni me importa. Lo que sí sé es que me gustan las cosas sencillas y derechas y sin engaño.

–¿Por qué lo dices, Tula?

–¿Y por qué rehúyes hablar de vuestro casamiento a mi hermana? Vamos, dímelo, ¿por qué?

El pobre mozo inclinó la frente arrebolada de vergüenza. Sentíase herido por un golpe inesperado.

–Tú le pediste relaciones con buen fin, como dicen los inocentes.

–¡Tula!

–¡Nada de Tula! Tú te pusiste con ella en relaciones para hacerla tu mujer y madre de tus hijos...

–¡Pero qué de prisa vas...! – y volvió a esforzarse a reirse.

–Es que hay que ir de prisa, porque la vida es corta.

–¡La vida es corta!, ¡y lo dice a los veintidós años!

–Más corta aún. Pues bien, ¿piensas casarte con Rosa, sí o no?

–¡Pues qué duda cabe! – y al decirlo le temblaba el cuerpo todo.

–Pues si piensas casarte con ella, ¿por qué diferirlo así?

–Somos aún jóvenes...

–¡Mejor!

–Tenemos que probarnos...

–¿Qué, qué es eso?, ¿qué es eso de probaros? ¿Crees que la conocerás mejor dentro de un año? Peor, mucho peor...

–Y si luego...

–¡No pensaste en eso al pedirla entrada aquí!

–Pero, Tula...

–¡Nada de Tula! ¿La quieres, sí o no?

–¿Puedes dudarlo, Tula?

–¡Te he dicho que nada de Tula! ¿La quieres?

'You?' he asked, his lip trembling.

'Yes, me.'

'You seem awfully serious…', he said with a forced laugh.

'I'm told that I was born that way. My uncle assures me that it comes down to me from my mother – his sister, and his mother – my grandmother. I don't know about that; nor does it really matter to me. What I *do* know is that I like things to be simple and honest, without deceit.'

'Why do you say that, Tula?'

'Why do *you* avoid the topic of marriage when you talk to my sister? *Why?* Tell me…'

The poor chap, bright red with embarrassment, lowered his gaze. He felt wounded by this unexpected blow.

'You sought relations with her with a certain respectable end in sight, as the gullible might put it.'

'Tula!'

'Don't call me Tula! You courted her in order to make her your wife and the mother of your children…'

'But what's the rush?', Ramiro responded, with another forced laugh.

'The rush is that life is *short*.'

'"Life is short" she says at the grand old age of twenty-two!'

'Shorter still at that age. So, are you planning to marry Rosa or not?'

'Our marriage is not in any doubt!' As Ramiro said this, his whole body was trembling.

'Well, if you're planning to marry her, why are you putting it off like this?'

'We're still young…'

'All the better to marry in that case.'

'We have to try each other out a little.'

'Put each other to the test? Do you think you'll know her any better after a year? You're wrong, you're so wrong…'

'And then there's…'

'You weren't thinking about putting each other to any test when you were looking to become part of this household.'

'But Tula…'.

'Don't call me Tula! Do you love her, yes or no?'

'How can you doubt it Tula?'

'I've told you already – don't call me Tula! Do you love her?'

–¡Claro que la quiero!
–Pues la querrás más todavía. Será una buena mujer para ti. Haréis un buen matrimonio.
–Y con tu consejo...
–Nada de consejo. ¡Yo haré una buena tía, y basta!
Ramiro pareció luchar un breve rato consigo mismo y como si buscase algo, y al cabo, con un gesto de desesperada resolución, exclamó:
–¡Pues bien, Gertrudis, quiero decirte toda la verdad!
–No tienes que decirme más verdad –le atajó severamente–; me has dicho que quieres a Rosa y que estás resuelto a casarte con ella; todo lo demás de la verdad es a ella a quien se la tienes que decir luego que os caséis.
–Pero hay cosas...
–No, no hay cosas que no se deban decir a la mujer...
–¡Pero, Tula!
–Nada de Tula, te he dicho. Si la quieres, a casarte con ella, y si no la quieres, estás de más en esta casa.
Estas palabras le brotaron de los labios fríos y mientras se le paraba el corazón. Siguió a ellas un silencio de hielo, y durante él la sangre, antes represada y ahora suelta, le encendió la cara a la hermana. Y entonces, en el silencio agorero, podía oírsele el galope trepidante del corazón. Al siguiente día se fijaba el de la boda.

'Of course I love her!'

'Well, you'll come to love her even more. She'll be a good wife to you. You'll make a good couple.'

'And with your advice…'

'Forget about advice from *me*! I'll make a good aunt, and that's it.'

Ramiro appeared to struggle with himself briefly, as if he were searching for words. Eventually, wearing an expression that suggested a determination born of desperation, he exclaimed,

'All right then, Gertrudis, I want to tell you the whole truth.'

'I don't need to hear any further truths', she replied severely, cutting him short. 'You have told me that you love Rosa, and that you're set on marrying her; any other truths are for you to tell Rosa after the two of you are married.'

'But there are certain things that one can't…'

'No, there *aren't* certain things that one can't say to one's wife…'

'But Tula…'

'I've already told you not to call me Tula. If you love her, hurry up and marry her; if you don't love her, you've no place in this house.'

These words emerged from Gertrudis's cool lips even as she felt her heart was failing. They were followed by an icy silence. During that time, her blood began to flow again, making Tula, the sister's, face flush bright red. Then, in the ominous silence, the rapid pounding of her heart made itself heard.

The wedding date was fixed the very next day.

III

Don Primitivo autorizó y bendijo la boda de Ramiro con Rosa. Y nadie estuvo en ella más alegre que lo estuvo Gertrudis. A tal punto, que su alegría sorprendió a cuantos la conocían, sin que faltara quien creyese que tenía muy poco de natural.

Fuéronse a su casa los recién casados, y Rosa reclamaba a ella de continuo la presencia de su hermana. Gertrudis le replicaba que a los novios les convenía soledad.

—Pero si es al contrario, hija, si nunca he sentido más tu falta; ahora es cuando comprendo lo que te quería.

Y poníase a abrazarla y besuquearla.

—Sí, sí – le replicaba Gertrudis sonriendo gravemente –; vuestra felicidad necesita de testigos; se os acrecienta la dicha sabiendo que otros se dan cuenta de ella.

Ibase, pues, de cuando en cuando a hacerles compañía; a comer con ellos alguna vez. Su hermana le hacía las más ostentosas demostraciones de cariño, y luego a su marido que, por su parte, aparecía como avergonzado ante su cuñada.

—Mira – llegó a decirle una vez Gertrudis a su hermana ante aquellas señales –, no te pongas así, tan babosa. No parece sino que has inventado lo del matrimonio.

Un día vió un perrito en la casa.

—Y esto ¿qué es?

—Un perro, chica, ¿no lo ves?

—¿Y cómo ha venido?

—Lo encontré ahí, en la calle, abandonado y medio muerto; me dió lástima, le traje, le di de comer, le curé y aquí le tengo –y lo acariciaba en su regazo y le daba besos en el hocico.

—Pues mira, Rosa, me parece que debes regalar el perrito, porque el que le mates me parece una crueldad.

—¿Regalarle? Y ¿por qué? Mira, Tití y al decirlo apechugaba contra su seno al animalito –, le dicen que te eche. ¿Adónde irás tú, pobrecito?

—Vamos, vamos, no seas chiquilla y no lo tomes así. ¿A que tu marido es de mi opinión?

III

It was Don Primitivo that conducted the marriage service of Ramiro and Rosa. During the celebrations, no-one was happier than Gertrudis – so much so that her joy surprised all those who knew her. There were even some who found it slightly unnatural.

The newlyweds settled into their new home-life, and Rosa constantly called for her sister to be there too. Gertrudis would reply that the best thing for newlyweds was to be left alone together.

'Quite the opposite my dear – I have never missed you more than now. Now I understand how much I loved you', and Rosa would embrace her sister, covering her in kisses.

'Yes, that's right,' Gertrudis used to say with a grave smile, 'the happiness of both of you needs witnesses; your joy is heightened by the knowledge that others are aware of it.'

So from time to time, Gertrudis would go and keep them company, occasionally eating with them. Her sister would ostentatiously shower her with affection, and then do the same to her husband, who seemed embarrassed by this behaviour in front of his sister-in-law.

'Look,' Gertrudis once felt compelled to say in the face of yet another display of affection, 'don't be so soppy. Anyone would think that you'd *invented* marriage'.

One day, Gertrudis came across a puppy in the house.

'What's *that*?'

'A dog of course, can't you see?'

'What's it doing here?'

'I found it outside on the street. It had been abandoned and was half dead, and I felt sorry for it, so I brought it back here, gave it something to eat and made it feel better. And here it is', she said, stroking the little dog on her lap and kissing it on the muzzle.

'Well, Rosa, I think you'll have to give it away, because the alternative – killing it – would be cruel.'

'Give him away? Why would I do *that*? Oh, Tití,' she said, clutching the little creature to her breast, 'I'm being told to throw you out of the house. Where will you go, you poor little thing?'

'Oh come, come, Rosa, don't be childish, and don't take it like that. I'm sure your husband agrees with me.'

–¡Claro, en cuanto se lo digas! Como tú eres la sabia...

–Déjate de esas cosas y deja al perro.

–Pero ¿qué? ¿Crees que tendrá Ramiro celos?

–Nunca creí, Rosa, que el matrimonio pudiese entontecer así.

Cuando llegó Ramiro y se enteró de la pequeña disputa por lo del perro, no se atrevió a dar la razón ni a la una ni a la otra, declarando que la cosa no tenía importancia.

–No, nada la tiene y lo tiene todo, según –dijo Gertrudis–. Pero en eso hay algo de chiquillada, y aún más. Serás capaz, Rosa, de haberte traído aquella pepona que guardas desde que nos dieron dos, una a ti y a mí otra, siendo niñas, y serás capaz de haberla puesto ocupando su silla...

–Exacto; allí está, en la sala, con su mejor traje, ocupando toda una silla de respeto. ¿La quieres ver?

–Así es – asintió Ramiro.

–Bueno, ya la quitarás de allí...

–Quia, hija, la guardaré...

–Sí, para juguete de tus hijas...

–¡Qué cosas se te ocurren, Tula...! –y se arreboló.

–No, es a ti a quien se te ocurren cosas como la del perro.

–Y tú – exclamó Rosa, tratando de desasirse de aquella inquisitoria que le molestaba–, ¿no tienes también tu pepona? ¿La has dado, o deshecho acaso?

–No – respondióle resueltamente su hermana –, pero la tengo guardada.

–¡Y tan guardada que no se la he podido descubrir nunca...!

–Es que Gertrudis la guarda para sí sola – dijo Ramiro sin saber lo que decía.

–Dios sabe para qué la guardo. Es un talismán de mi niñez.

El que iba poco, poquísimo, por casa del nuevo matrimonio era el bueno de don Primitivo. «El onceno no estorbar», decía.

Corrían los días, todos iguales, en una y otra casa. Gertrudis se había propuesto visitar lo menos posible a su hermana, pero ésta venía a buscarla en cuanto pasaba un par de días sin que se viesen. «¿Pero qué,

'Well of course he will as soon as *you* say anything to him! As *you're* the sensible one...'

'Stop it, and leave the dog alone.'

'But why? Do you think that Ramiro will be jealous of him?'

'Until now, Rosa, I would never have believed that marriage could make one so stupid...'

When Ramiro came in and found out about the sisters' tiff over the dog, he did not dare take sides, instead dismissing the matter as unimportant.

'It isn't important, and yet it has all the importance in the world, depending on how you see it', said Gertrudis. 'There's something childish about this, and perhaps even something worse. It wouldn't surprise me, Rosa, if you had brought with you that doll you've had since we were each given one as children, and it wouldn't surprise me if you still had her sitting in her own special chair...'

'Of course; she's in the sitting room, dressed in her finest clothes, in the place of honour. Would you like to see her?'

'That's right, so she is', agreed Ramiro.

'Well, you'll have to take her out of there...'

'Never! I'm keeping her...'

'Very well, but as a plaything for your children.'

'The things you think of, Tula...!', Rosa said, flushing deep red.

'Well look at the things *you* think of ... like taking in that dog...'

'What about *your* doll?', Rosa exclaimed, trying to extricate herself from this inquisition, which was upsetting her. 'Didn't you keep yours? Or have you given it away, or perhaps even thrown it away?'

'I still have it,' her sister replied firmly, 'but I've stored it away'.

'That's right. You've stored it so well that I've never been able to discover where...'

'Gertrudis is keeping it for herself', said Ramiro, without realising what he was saying.

'God knows why I am keeping it. It is a mascot from my childhood.'

It was Don Primitivo that visited the newlyweds' home least often: he went only on the rarest of occasions. He used to say, 'The Eleventh Commandment says "Do not get in the way"'.

The days went by, all of them the same, in each of the houses. Gertrudis had made up her mind to visit her sister as little as possible, but Rosa would come looking for her after only a couple of days' absence.

estás mala, chica? ¿O te sigue estorbando el perro? Porque si es así, mira, le echaré. ¿Por qué me dejas así, sola?»

–¿Sola, Rosa? ¿Sola? ¿Y tu marido?

–Pero él se tiene que ir a sus asuntos...

–O los inventa...

–¿Qué, es que crees que me deja aposta? ¿Es que sabes algo? ¡Dilo, Tula, por lo que más quieras, por nuestra madre, dímelo!

–No, es que os aburrís de vuestra felicidad y de vuestra soledad. Ya le echarás el perro o si no te darán antojos, y será peor.

–No digas esas cosas.

–Te darán antojos –replicó con más firmeza.

Y cuando al fin fue un día a decirle que había regalado el perrito, Gertrudis, sonriendo gravemente y acariciándola como a una niña, le preguntó al oído: «Por miedo a los antojos, ¿eh?» Y al oír en respuesta un susurrado «¡sí!» abrazó a su hermana con una efusión de que ésta no la creía capaz.

–Ahora va de veras, Rosa; ahora no os aburriréis de la felicidad ni de la soledad y tendrá varios asuntos tu marido. Esto era lo que os faltaba...

–Y acaso lo que te faltaba... ¿No es así, hermanita?

–¿Y a ti quién te ha dicho eso?

–Mira, aunque soy tan tonta, como he vivido siempre contigo...

–¡Bueno, déjate de bromas!

Y desde entonces empezó Gertrudis a frecuentar más la casa de su hermana.

'What's the matter – aren't you feeling well? Or is it the dog that's still bothering you? Because if it's that, I'll get rid of him. Why are you leaving me on my own?'

'On your *own*? What about your husband?'

'He has to attend to his own matters.'

'Or else he's inventing matters to attend to.'

'What, you think he might be leaving me on my own on purpose? Do you know something that I don't? *Please* say, Tula for the sake of all that you hold most dear ... for mother's sake ... tell me!'

'I think you're both bored with your happiness and with being on your own together. You will have to get rid of that dog, or you'll have cravings during your pregnancy.'

'Don't say that.'

'You'll have cravings and it will make things worse.'[10]

So, when one day Rosa went to tell Tula that she had given the dog away, Gertrudis smiled gravely and, patting her sister as if she were a child, whispered into her ear, 'afraid of the cravings, eh?'. And hearing her sister murmur 'yes' in response, she embraced Rosa more effusively than her sister had thought her capable of.

'Now you'll really see, Rosa ... now neither of you will be bored with your happiness or with being on your own together, and your husband really will have his hands full. This is what you both needed...'

'And perhaps what you needed too, my beloved sister?'

'Who told you *that*?'

'I may not be terribly brainy, but I've lived with you long enough to know you a little...'

'Enough joking...'

From that point on, Gertrudis began to visit her sister at home more often.

IV

En el parto de Rosa, que fue durísimo, nadie estuvo más serena y valerosa que Gertrudis. Creeríase que era una veterana en asistir a trances tales. Llegó a haber peligro de muerte para la madre o la cría que hubiera de salir, y el médico llegó a hablar de sacársela viva o muerta.

–¿Muerta? – exclamó Gertrudis –; ¡eso sí que no!

–¿Pero no ve usted – exclamó el médico – que aunque se muera el crío queda la madre para hacer otros, mientras que si se muere ella no es lo mismo?

Pasó rápidamente por el magín de Gertrudis replicarle que quedaban otras madres, pero se contuvo e insistió:

–Muerta, ¡no!, ¡nunca! Y hay, además, que salvar un alma.

La pobre parturienta ni se enteraba de cosa alguna. Hasta que, rendida al combate, dió a luz un niño.

Recojiólo Gertrudis con avidez, y como si nunca hubiera hecho otra cosa, lo lavó y envolvió en sus pañales.

–Es usted comadrona de nacimiento – le dijo el médico.

Tomó la criaturita y se la llevó a su padre, que en un rincón, aterrado y como contrito de una falta, aguardaba la noticia de la muerte de su mujer.

–¡Aquí tienes tu primer hijo, Ramiro; mírale qué hermoso!

Pero al levantar la vista el padre, libre del peso de su angustia, no vió sino los ojazos de su cuñada, que irradiaban una luz nueva, más negra, pero más brillante que la de antes. Y al ir a besar a aquel rollo de carne que le presentaban como su hijo, rozó su mejilla, encendida, con la de Gertrudis.

–Ahora – le dijo tranquilamente ésta – ve a dar las gracias a tu mujer, a pedirle perdón y a animarla.

–¿A pedirle perdón?

–Sí, a pedirle perdón.

–¿Y por qué?

–Yo me entiendo y ella te entenderá. Y en cuanto a éste –y al decirlo apretábalo contra su seno palpitante– corre ya de mi cuenta, y a poco he de poder o haré de él un hombre.

IV

During Rosa's labour, which was extremely difficult, nobody was calmer or braver than Gertrudis. Anyone would have taken her for a veteran of such processes. Things became so bad that it looked as though a choice might have had to be made between the mother's and the unborn baby's life. The doctor was forced to speak of extracting the baby dead or alive.

'Dead?', cried Gertrudis, 'absolutely not'

'But don't you see?', the doctor exclaimed in response, 'even if the baby dies, the mother can go on to have others. But if she is the one who dies, it's a completely different matter.'

It crossed Gertrudis's mind to reply that there would always be other mothers, but she restrained herself, insisting instead that 'the baby must not die. And, what is more, a soul must be saved.'

Poor Rosa, in the midst of her labour, was completely unaware of what was going on around her until, completely exhausted, she finally managed to give birth.

Gertrudis eagerly snatched up the baby, and, as if she had been doing so all her life, washed and then swaddled it.

'You were born to be a midwife', the doctor told her.

Gertrudis took the baby to its father, who, as though remorseful for some wrongdoing, was fearfully anticipating the news of his wife's death.

'Here is your firstborn son, Ramiro; look how handsome he is!'

But, when freed from the weight of his anxiety, the father looked up, all he could see was his sister-in-law's eyes. A new light was shining from them, blacker but more sparkling than before. And as he leaned toward the little bundle of flesh presented to him as his son, his cheek brushed against Gertrudis's, the contact making him flush bright red.

'Now,' said Gertrudis calmly, 'go and give thanks to your wife, ask for her forgiveness, and cheer her up.'

'Ask her forgiveness?'

'Yes. Ask her forgiveness.'

'What for?'

'I know what I'm talking about, and Rosa will know what you mean. And as far as this little one is concerned,' she said, clutching the baby to her slightly heaving breast, 'he is my responsibility now, and I will make a man of him, or else die trying.'

La casa le daba vueltas en derredor a Ramiro. Y del fondo de su alma salíale una voz diciendo: «¿Cuál es la madre?»

Poco después ponía Gertrudis cuidadosamente el niño al lado de la madre, que parecía dormir extenuada y con la cara blanca como la nieve. Pero Rosa entreabrió los ojos y se encontró con los de su hermana. Al ver a ésta, una corriente de ánimo recorrió el cuerpo todo victorioso de la nueva madre.

–¡Tula! – gimió.

–Aquí estoy, Rosa, aquí estaré. Ahora descansa. Cuando sea, le das de mamar a este crío para que se calle. De todo lo demás no te preocupes.

–Creí morirme, Tula, aun ahora me parece que sueño muerta. Y me daba tanta pena de Ramiro...

–Cállate. El médico ha dicho que no hables mucho. El pobre Ramiro estaba más muerto que tú. ¡Ahora, ánimo, y a otra!

La enferma sonrió tristemente.

–Este se llamará Ramiro, como su padre – decretó luego Gertrudis en pequeño consejo de familia–y la otra, porque la siguiente será niña, Gertrudis como yo.

–¿Pero ya estás pensando en otra – exclamó don Primitivo – y tu pobre hermana de por poco se queda en el trance?

–¿Y qué hacer? – replicó ella –; ¿para qué se han casado si no? ¿No es así, Ramiro? – y le clavó los ojos.

–Ahora lo que importa es que se reponga – dijo el marido sobrecojiéndose bajo aquella mirada.

–¡Bah!, de estas dolencias se repone una mujer pronto.

–Bien dice el médico, sobrina, que parece como si hubieras nacido comadrona.

–Toda mujer nace madre, tío.

Y lo dijo con tan íntima solemnidad casera, que Ramiro se sintió presa de un indefinible desasosiego y de un extraño remordimiento. «¿Querré yo a mi mujer como se merece?», se decía.

–Y ahora, Ramiro –le dijo su cuñada—, ya puedes decir que tienes mujer.

Y a partir de entonces, no faltó Gertrudis un solo día de casa de su

To Ramiro, the room suddenly seemed to be spinning. And from deep inside him, a voice seemed to ask 'Who is the mother here?'

Shortly afterwards, Gertrudis carefully laid the baby down beside his mother. Exhausted, she seemed to be sleeping, her face as white as snow. But then she half-opened her eyes and found herself gazing into those of her sister. A surge of energy seemed to pass through the victorious body of the new mother when she saw her sister.

'Tula,' she groaned.

'I'm here Rosa, I'll be here with you. Get some rest now. When you're ready, you can nurse the baby so that he is soothed. Don't worry about anything else.'

'I thought I was going to die, Tula. Even now I feel as if I'm only dreaming that I'm alive. And I felt so sorry for Ramiro.'

'Shhh now. The doctor says that you mustn't speak too much. Ramiro was nearer death than you were. Now, buck up, and prepare yourself to have another.'

The invalid gave a melancholic smile.

'The baby will be called Ramiro, like his father,' Gertrudis decreed later in a small gathering of the closest family members, 'and the next one – because she'll be a girl – will be called Gertrudis, like me'.

'How can you already be thinking of another when your poor sister has only just come out of labour?' exclaimed Don Primitivo.

'It's only natural,' Gertrudis replied, 'why would they have gone through the effort otherwise? Isn't that right Ramiro?', fixing her gaze on her brother-in-law.

'What's important right now is that Rosa recovers', said her husband, shrinking under Gertrudis's gaze.

'Psh, a woman recovers from such ailments very quickly,'

'My dear niece, the doctor was right when he said that you seem born to have been a midwife.'

'All women are born mothers, uncle.'

And she said it with such intimate, domestic solemnity that Ramiro felt stricken by an indefinable anxiety and a strange remorse. 'Will I be able to love my wife as she deserves to be loved?', he wondered.

'And now Ramiro,' his sister-in-law said to him, 'you can really claim to have a wife.'

And from that day onwards, not a day passed that Gertrudis did not go

hermana. Ella era quien desnudaba y vestía y cuidaba al niño hasta que su madre pudiera hacerlo.

La cual se repuso muy pronto y su hermosura se redondeó más. A la vez extremó sus ternuras para con su marido y aun llegó a culparle de que se le mostraba esquivo.

—Temí por tu vida – le dijo su marido – y estaba aterrado. Aterrado y desesperado y lleno de remordimiento.

—Remordimiento, ¿por qué?

—¡Si llegas a morirte me pego un tiro!

—¡Quia!, ¿a qué? «Cosas de hombres», que diría Tula. Pero eso ya pasó y ya sé lo que es.

—¿Y no has quedado escarmentada, Rosa?

—¿Escarmentada? –y cogiendo a su marido, echándole los brazos al cuello, apechugándole fuertemente a sí, le dijo al oído con un aliento que se lo quemaba: –¡A otra, Ramiro, a otra! ¡Ahora sí que te quiero! ¡Y aunque me mates!

Gertrudis en tanto arrullaba al niño, celosa de que no se percatase – ¡inocente! –de los ardores de sus padres.

Era como una preocupación en la tía de ir sustrayendo al niño, ya desde su más tierna edad de inconsciencia, de conocer, ni en las más leves y remotas señales, el amor de que había brotado. Colgóle al cuello, desde luego, una medalla de la Santísima Virgen, de la Virgen Madre, con su Niño en brazos.

Con frecuencia, cuando veía que su hermana, la madre, se impacientaba en acallar al niño o al envolverlo en sus pañales, le decía:

—Dámelo, Rosa, dámelo, y vete a entretener a tu marido…

—Pero, Tula...

—Sí, tú tienes que atender a los dos y yo sólo a éste.

—Tienes, Tula, una manera de decir las cosas...

—No seas niña, ¡ea!, que eres ya toda una señora mamá. Y da gracias a Dios que podamos así repartirnos el trabajo.

—Tula... Tula...

—Ramiro... Ramiro... Rosa.

La madre se amoscaba, pero iba a su marido.

Y así pasaba el tiempo y llegó otra cría, una niña.

to her sister's house. It was she who dressed, undressed and cared for the baby until his mother was able to take over.

Rosa recovered very quickly, and her beauty became even more radiant. At the same time, she became yet more affectionate towards her husband, to the point where she even accused him of shying away from her.

'I was afraid for your life,' her husband told her, 'I was terrified. Terrified, desperate and filled with remorse.'

'Why remorse?'

'If you had died, I would have killed myself.'

'No! What on earth for?... "Men!", as Tula would say. Anyway, it's all over, and now I know what to expect.'

'Don't you feel wary about going through it all again, Rosa?'

'Wary?' Rosa threw her arms around her husband's neck, and, pulling him close to her, breathed in his ear 'Let's have another, Ramiro! Another! Now I really do love you. Let's have another even if you kill me.'

Gertrudis, meanwhile, was cooing over the baby – innocent little thing! – carefully ensuring that he was not aware of this passionate exchange between his parents.

Despite the baby's tender years and his unawareness, his aunt seemed concerned to make sure that he was not exposed to even the faintest indication of the love that had brought him into the world. Naturally, she hung a medal of the Blessed Virgin Mary around his neck: it was an image of the Virgin Mother, babe in arms.

Often, when Gertrudis saw her sister, the mother, become exasperated when trying to soothe the baby or change its nappy, she would say,

'Give him to me, Rosa, and go and amuse your husband.'

'But Tula...'

'Go on – you have to look after both of them; I only have to occupy myself with this little one...'

'Tula, you have a way of saying things...'

'Don't be childish. Come come now, you're a grown woman and a mother! And give thanks to God that we can share the work out like this.'

'Tula... Tula...'

'Ramiro... Ramiro... Rosa'

The mother would be annoyed, but she would go to her husband.

Time passed, and then another baby arrived, this time a little girl.

V

A poco de nacer la niña encontraron un día muerto al bueno de don Primitivo. Gertrudis le amortajó después de haberle lavado – quería que fuese limpio a la tumba con el mismo esmero con que había envuelto en pañales a sus sobrinos recién nacidos. Y a solas en el cuarto con el cuerpo del buen anciano, le lloró como no se creyera capaz de hacerlo. «Nunca habría creído que le quisiese tanto – se dijo–; era un bendito; de poco llega a hacerme creer que soy un pozo de prudencia; ¡era tan sencillo!»

–Fue nuestro padre – le dijo a su hermana – y jamás le oímos una palabra más alta que otra.

–¡Claro! – exclamó Rosa –; como que siempre nos dejó hacer nuestra santísima voluntad.

–Porque sabía, Rosa, que su sola presencia santificaba nuestra voluntad. Fué nuestro padre; él nos educó. Y para educarnos le bastó la transparencia de su vida, tan sencilla, tan clara...

–Es verdad, sí – dijo Rosa con los ojos henchidos de lágrimas –; como sencillo no he conocido otro.

–Nos habría sido imposible, hermana, habernos criado en un hogar más limpio que éste.

–¿Qué quieres decir con eso, Tula?

–Él nos llenó la vida casi silenciosamente, casi sin decirnos palabra, con el culto de la Santísima Virgen Madre y con el culto también de nuestra madre, su hermana, y de nuestra abuela, su madre. ¿Te acuerdas cuando por las noches nos hacía rezar el rosario, cómo le cambiaba la voz al llegar a aquel padrenuestro y avemaría por el eterno descanso del alma de nuestra madre, y luego aquellos otros por el de su madre, nuestra abuela, a las que no conocimos? En aquel rosario nos daba madre y en aquel rosario te enseñó a serlo.

–¡Y a ti, Tula, a ti! –exclamó entre sollozos Rosa.

–¿A mí?

–¡A ti, sí, a ti! ¿Quién, si no, es la verdadera madre de mis hijos?

–Deja ahora eso. Y ahí le tienes, un santo silencioso. Me han dicho que las pobres beatas lloraban algunas veces al oírle predicar sin percibir

V

One day, not long after the birth of the little girl, kind old Don Primitivo was found dead. It was Gertrudis who wrapped him in his funeral shroud, after having washed him – she wanted him to go to his grave clean – with the same care with which she swaddled her young nephew and niece. And when she was alone with the corpse of the benevolent elderly man, she cried over his death more than she would ever have believed possible. 'I would never have thought that I loved him so much', she said to herself. 'He was saintly. He almost made me believe that I was a fount of wisdom. He was so simple!'

'He was our father,' she said to her sister, 'and he never once raised his voice to us.'

'Well of course not!', exclaimed Rosa, 'He always let us have our own blessed way.'

'That, Rosa, was because his mere presence sanctified our will. He was our father. He was the one who brought us up. And all he needed to do that was the shining example of his own life, which was so simple, so clear...'

'That's true', agreed Rosa, her eyes swollen from crying. 'I have never known anyone so simple.'

'We couldn't have been brought up in a purer household than this.'

'What do you mean, Tula?'

'He filled our life, almost silently, with the veneration of the Blessed Virgin Mary, and with the veneration also of our grandmother, his mother. Do you remember when he used to make us say our rosary at night, and how his voice used to change when he came to the Our Father and the Hail Mary recited for the everlasting peace of our mother, and then the others that he would recite for his mother, the grandmother that you and I never knew? In that rosary he gave us a mother, and in it he taught you to be a mother.

'And he taught you too Tula, you too', Rosa said, sobbing.

'Me?'

'Yes, you! You! Who, if not you, is the true mother of my children?'

'Never mind about that for now. And there he is, a silent saint. I've been told that the poor devout women of the church would sometimes

ni una sola de sus palabras. Y lo comprendo. Su voz sola era un consejo
de serenidad amorosa. ¡Y ahora, Rosa, el rosario!

Arrodilláronse las dos hermanas al pie del lecho mortuorio de su
tío y rezaron el mismo rosario que con él habían rezado durante tantos
años, con dos padrenuestros y avemarías por el eterno descanso de las
almas de su madre y de la del que yacía allí muerto, a que añadieron otro
padrenuestro y otra avemaría por el alma del recién bienaventurado. Y
las lenguas de manso y dulce fuego de los dos cirios que ardían a un lado
y otro del cadáver, haciendo brillar su frente, tan blanca como la cera de
ellos, parecían, vibrando al compás del rezo, acompañar en sus oraciones
a las dos hermanas. Una paz entrañable irradiaba de aquella muerte.
Levantáronse del suelo las dos hermanas, la pareja; besaron, primero
Gertrudis y Rosa después, la frente cérea del anciano y abrazáronse luego
con los ojos ya enjutos.

–Y ahora – le dijo Gertrudis a su hermana al oído – a querer mucho a
tu marido, a hacerle dichoso y... ¡a darnos muchos hijos!

–Y ahora –le respondió Rosa– te vendrás a vivir con nosotros, por
supuesto.

–¡No, eso no! –exclamó súbitamente la otra.

–¿Cómo que no? Y lo dices de un modo...

–Sí, sí, hermana; perdóname la viveza, perdónamela, ¿me la perdonas?
– e hizo mención, ante el cadáver, de volver a arrodillarse.

–Vaya, no te pongas así, Tula, que no es para tanto. Tienes unos
prontos...

–Es verdad, pero me los perdonas, ¿no es verdad, Rosa?, me los
perdonas.

–Eso ni se pregunta. Pero te vendrás con nosotros...

–No insistas, Rosa, no insistas...

–¿Qué? ¿No te vendrás? Dejarás a tus sobrinos, más bien tus hijos
casi...

–Pero si no los he dejado un día...

–¿Te vendrás?

–Lo pensaré, Rosa, lo pensaré...

–Bueno, pues no insisto.

Pero a los pocos días insistió, y Gertrudis se defendía.

cry when hearing him at mass even when they hadn't caught a single word he had said. I can understand that. His very voice was a counsel of loving serenity. Now Rosa, let us say our rosary.'

The two sisters knelt at the foot of their uncle's death-bed and said the same rosary that they had said alongside him for so many years, with two Our Fathers and two Hail Marys, one for the eternal rest of their mother's soul, and one for the man who now lay dead in front of them. They then added a further Our Father and a Hail Mary for the soul of the recently departed. The soft, gentle flames of the two candles burning at either side of the dead body, gave a sheen to his forehead – itself as white as the candle wax – and seemed, as they flickered in time to the sisters' petitions, to accompany Gertrudis and Rosa in their prayers. A profound, familiar peace seemed to radiate from that death. The two sisters got to their feet as one. First Gertrudis, and then Rosa, kissed the waxen brow of the elderly man, and then embraced each other, their eyes now dry.

'Now,' whispered Gertrudis into her sister's ear, 'you must love your husband very much, make him happy ... and give us lots of children!'

'And now,' replied Rosa, 'you will of course come and live with us.'

'No, no I won't', said the other sister quickly.

'What do you mean 'no'? The way you said it...'

'You're right, I'm sorry – forgive the sharpness of my reply. Will you forgive me?' Gertrudis seemed to indicate that she would go down on her knees again in front of the corpse.

'There's no need for that Tula, it's not that serious. You're so impulsive sometimes...'

'You're right, but you do forgive me, don't you Rosa? You do forgive me my impetuousness?'

'You don't even need to ask. But you will come and live with us...'

'Don't go on about it, Rosa.'

'You mean you won't come? But you'd be abandoning your nephew and niece, and they're almost your own children.'

'I've never left them for even a single day...'

'Will you please come and live with us?'

'I'll think about Rosa, I'll think about it.'

'All right, I won't mention it again.'

But in a few days time, Rosa *did* mention it again, and Gertrudis had to defend her decision.

–No, no; no quiero estorbaros...

–¿Estorbarnos? ¿qué dices, Tula?

–Los casados casa quieren.

–¿Y no puede ser la tuya también?

–No, no; aunque tú no lo creas, yo os quitaría libertad. ¿No es así, Ramiro?

–No... no veo... – balbuceó el marido, confuso, como casi siempre le ocurría ante la inesperada interpelación de su cuñada.

–Sí, Rosa; tu marido, aunque no lo dice, comprende que un matrimonio, y más un matrimonio joven como vosotros y en plena producción, necesita estar solo. Yo, la tía, vendré a mis horas a ir enseñando a vuestros hijos todo aquello en que no podáis ocuparos.

Y allá seguía yendo, a las veces desde muy temprano, encontrándose con el niño ya levantado, pero no así sus padres. «Cuando digo que hago yo aquí falta» – se decía.

'No, no, I don't want to get in your way.'

'Get in our way? What do you mean Tula?'

'Married couples need a home to themselves.'

'But can't the home be yours too?'

'No. Although you might not think so, I would limit your freedom. Isn't that right, Ramiro?'

'No, no, I don't see how…' Rosa's husband stuttered, overwhelmed, as usual, when called upon to speak by his sister-in-law.

'See, Rosa? Your husband, although he'd never say so, understands that a married couple – and especially a young couple like you two, at full productive capacity – needs to be alone. I, as aunt, will carry on coming at my usual times, to instruct the children in the things that you cannot take charge of.'

And she kept to her word. Sometimes, when she arrived very early, she would find the little boy already up, even though his parents were still in bed. 'I really am needed here', she said to herself.

VI

Venía ya el tercer hijo al matrimonio. Rosa empezaba a quejarse de su fecundidad. «Vamos a cargarnos de hijos», decía. A lo que su hermana: «¿Pues para qué os habéis casado?» El embarazo fué molestísimo para la madre y tenía que descuidar más que antes a sus otros hijos, que así quedaban al cuidado de su tía, encantada de que se los dejasen. Y hasta consiguió llevárselos más de un día a su casa, a su solitario hogar de soltera, donde vivía con la vieja criada que fué de don Primitivo, y donde los retenía. Y los pequeñuelos se apegaban con ciego cariño a aquella mujer severa y grave.

Ramiro, malhumorado antes en los últimos meses de los embarazos de su mujer, malhumor que desasosegaba a Gertrudis, ahora lo estaba más.

—¡Qué pesado y molesto es esto! – decía.

—¿Para ti? – le preguntaba su cuñada sin levantar los ojos del sobrino o sobrina que de seguro tenía en el regazo.

—Para mí, sí. Vivo en perpetuo sobresalto, temiéndolo todo.

—¡Bah! No será al fin nada. La Naturaleza es sabia.

—Pero tantas veces va el cántaro a la fuente...

—¡Ay, hijo, todo tiene sus riesgos y todo estado sus contrariedades!

Ramiro se sobrecogía al oírse llamar hijo por su cuñada, que rehuía darle su nombre, mientras él, en cambio, se complacía en llamarla por el familiar Tula.

—¡Qué bien has hecho en no casarte, Tula!

—¿De veras? – y levantando los ojos se los clavó en los suyos.

—De veras, sí. Todo son trabajos y aun peligros...

—¿Y sabes tú acaso si no me he de casar todavía?

—Claro. ¡Lo que es por la edad!

—¿Pues por qué ha de quedar?

—Como no te veo con afición a ello...

VI

The couple were expecting a third baby. Rosa began to complain about her fecundity. 'We're going to be overrun with children,' she would say. To which Gertrudis would reply, 'well, why did you get married if not to have children?'

It was an extremely difficult pregnancy for the mother, and she was forced to neglect her children more than she had done previously. They were looked after by Gertrudis, who was thrilled to have them in her care. And on a couple of occasions, she even managed to have them stay in her solitary spinster's home, where she lived with the elderly maid who had served don Primitivo. And the little ones in turn became fiercely attached to this severe and serious woman: they loved her blindly.

Ramiro, who had been bad-tempered in the final months of his wife's previous pregnancies, was even more irascible this time. His attitude made Gertrudis uneasy.

'This is all so tedious and irritating', he would say.

'Tedious and irritating for *you*?', Gertrudis would ask, without lifting her gaze from the nephew or niece that she would almost certainly have sitting in her lap.

'Yes, for me. I'm constantly on edge, afraid of everything.'

'Psh! It will all be fine in the end. Mother nature knows what she is doing.'

'But one can only tempt fate a certain number of times.'

'Oh come, my dear, everything has its risks, and every condition has its setbacks.'

Ramiro was overcome when he heard himself called 'my dear' by his sister-in-law, who usually avoided referring to him by name; he, in contrast, used to like calling her by her pet-name 'Tula'.

'How right you were not to marry, Tula.'

'Really?', and, looking up, she fixed her gaze on his.

'Yes, really. It's all hard work and it even has its dangers at times.'

'And how do you know that I won't still marry?'

'Of course you won't! If you haven't married by now…'

'But things might change – what's to stop me?'

'I don't see you as being very keen on the idea.'

–¿Afición a casarse? ¿Qué es eso?

–Bueno; es que...

–Es que no me ves buscar novio, ¿no es eso?

–No, no es eso.

–Sí, eso es.

–Si tú los aceptaras, de seguro que no te habrían faltado...

–Pero yo no puedo buscarlos. No soy hombre, y la mujer tiene que esperar y ser elegida. Y yo, la verdad, me gusta elegir, pero no ser elegida.

–¿Qué es eso de que estáis hablando? – dijo Rosa acercándose y dejándose caer abatida en un sillón.

–Nada; discreteos de tu marido sobre las ventajas e inconvenientes del matrimonio.

–¡No hables de eso, Ramiro! Vosotros los hombres apenas sabéis de eso. Somos nosotras las que nos casamos, no vosotros.

–¡Pero, mujer!

–Anda, ven, sosténme, que apenas puedo tenerme en pie. Voy a echarme. Adiós, Tula. Ahí te los dejo.

Acercóse a ella su marido; le tomó del brazo con sus dos manos y se incorporó y levantó trabajosamente; luego, tendiéndole un brazo por el hombro, doblando su cabeza hasta casi darle en éste con ella y cogiéndole con la otra mano, con la diestra de su diestra, se fué lentamente así apoyada en él y gimoteando. Gertrudis, teniendo a cada uno de sus sobrinos en sus rodillas, se quedó mirando la marcha trabajosa de su hermana, colgada de su marido como una enredadera de su rodrigón. Llenáronsele los grandes ojazos, aquellos ojos de luto, serenamente graves, gravemente serenos, de lágrimas, y apretando a su seno a los dos pequeños, apretó sus mejillas a cada una de las de ellos. Y el pequeñito, Ramirín, al ver llorar a su tía, la tita Tula, se echó a llorar también.

–Vamos, no llores; vamos a jugar.

De este tercer parto quedó quebrantadísima Rosa.

–Tengo malos presentimientos, Tula.

–No hagas caso de agüeros.

–No es agüero; es que siento que se me va la vida; he quedado sin sangre.

–Ella volverá.

–Por de pronto, ya no puedo criar este niño. Y eso de las amas, Tula, ¡eso me aterra!

'Keen on marrying? What does that mean, anyway?'

'Well, it's...'

'You can't see me looking for a fiancé. Is that it?'

'No, it's not that.'

'Yes it is.'

'You would not have been short of suitors if you'd accepted them...'

'But *I* can't seek *them* out. I'm not a man, and women have to wait to be chosen. Truth to tell, I prefer choosing to being chosen.'

'What are you two talking about?', asked Rosa, who had just come in to the room, flopping exhaustedly into a chair.

'Oh, nothing. *Bon mots* from your husband concerning the good and bad of marriage.'

'You shouldn't be talking about that, Ramiro! You men know hardly anything about it. It's us women who get married, not you men.'

'But my love...'

'Never mind that, come and help me up – I can hardly stand. I'm going to go and have a lie down. Bye Tula! I'm leaving the children with you.'

Her husband went to her side. Rosa took hold of his arm with both hands as she struggled to stand upright. Then, laying her arm on his shoulder, her head bent over so much that it almost bumped against his shoulder, and holding on to him with her other hand, she slowly left the room, leaning on him and whimpering as she went. Gertrudis, who had a child on each knee, watched the laborious departure of her sister, wound around her husband like a climbing plant around its stake.[11] Gertrudis's big, mournful eyes, those serenely grave and gravely serene eyes filled with tears, and, clutching the children to her, she pressed their cheeks to hers. Little Ramiro, seeing his aunt – his beloved aunt Tula cry – also burst into tears.

'Come now, don't cry, we'll play a game.'

Rosa was completely destroyed by this third pregnancy.

'I have a bad feeling about this one Tula.'

'Don't take any notice of supposed omens.'

'It's not an omen; I feel as if my life is slipping away; I've lost so much blood.'

'It will come back.'

'Suddenly I find that I can't feed the baby. And the idea of using a wet nurse terrifies me Tula!'

Y así era, en verdad. En pocos días cambiaron tres. El padre estaba furioso y hablaba de tratarlas a latigazos. Y la madre decaía.

—¡Esto se va! —pronunció un día el médico.

Ramiro vagaba por la casa como atontado, presa de extraños remordimientos y de furias súbitas. Una tarde llegó a decir a su cuñada:

—Pero es que esta Rosa no hace nada por vivir; se le ha metido en la cabeza que tiene que morirse y ¡es claro!, se morirá. ¿Por qué no le animas y le convences a que viva?

—Eso tú, hijo; tú, su marido. Si tú no le infundes apetito de vivir, ¿quién va a infundírselo? Porque sí, no es lo peor lo débil y exangüe que está; lo peor es que no piensa sino en morirse. Ya ves, hasta los chicos la cansan pronto. Y apenas si pregunta por las cosas del ama.

Y era que la pobre Rosa vivía como en sueños, en un constante mareo, viéndolo todo como a través de una niebla.

Una tarde llamó a solas a su hermana y en frases entrecortadas, con un hilito de voz febril, le dijo cogiéndole la mano:

—Mira, Tula, yo me muero y me muero sin remedio. Ahí te dejo mis hijos, los pedazos de mi corazón, y ahí te dejo a Ramiro, que es como otro hijo. Créeme que es otro niño, un niño grande y antojadizo, pero bueno, más bueno que el pan. No me ha dado ni un solo disgusto. Ahí te los dejo, Tula.

—Descuida, Rosa; conozco mis deberes.

—Deberes.... deberes...

—Sí, sé mis amores. A tus hijos no les faltará madre mientras yo viva.

—Gracias, Tula, gracias. Eso quería de ti.

—Pues no lo dudes.

—¡Es decir que mis hijos, los míos, los pedazos de mi corazón, no tendrán madrastra!

—¿Qué quieres decir con eso, Rosa?

—Que como Ramiro volverá a pensar en casarse..., es lo natural..., tan joven... y yo sé que no podrá vivir sin mujer, lo sé .... pues que...

It did indeed prove to be terrifying. They got through three wet nurses in just a couple of days. The baby's father was furious and spoke of taking the horsewhip to them. Meanwhile, the mother's health continued to deteriorate.

'We're losing her', the doctor declared one day.

Ramiro wandered around the house, bewildered, stricken by strange feelings of remorse and sudden rages. One day, he even said to his sister-in-law,

'Rosa's not even making an effort to live. She's got it into her head that she's going to die, and so of course she *will* die! Why don't you try and raise her spirits and convince her that she should live?'

'That's for you, her husband, to do. If *you* can't give her an appetite for life, who can? You're right: her weakness, and the blood she has lost isn't the worst of it. The worst thing is that she thinks of nothing but dying. Even the children tire her in no time. And she hardly asks about the wet nurse.'

In effect, poor Rosa was living as though in some waking dream, in constant confusion, seeing everything as if through a fog.

One afternoon, Rosa, on her own, called Gertrudis to her side. Taking her sister's hand, and in a weak, feverish voice, Rosa said falteringly,

'Look Tula, I'm dying, and there's nothing I can do about it. I'm leaving you my children, whom I love with all my heart, and I'm leaving you Ramiro, and that's one more child. Believe me, he's another child that needs looking after, a big, capricious child, but as good as gold. He's never given me a moment's worry. I leave them all to you Tula.'

'Don't worry, Rosa, I know where my duty lies.'

'Duties .... duties...'

'I know where my heart lies. Your children will have a mother for as long as I live.'

'Thank you Tula, thank you. That's what I wanted from you.'

'Have no fears on that account.'

'What I mean is that my children, my darlings, won't have a stepmother!'

'I don't understand Rosa.'

'Well, Ramiro will think of marrying again ... it's only natural ... he's so young, and I know he won't be able to live without a wife, I know he won't, so...'

–¿Qué quieres decir?

–Que serás tú su mujer, Tula.

–Yo no te he dicho eso, Rosa, y ahora, en este momento, no puedo, ni por piedad, mentir. Yo no te he dicho que me casaré con tu marido si tú le faltas; yo te he dicho que a tus hijos no les faltará madre...

–No, tú me has dicho que no tendrán madrastra.

–¡Pues bien, sí, no tendrán madrastra!

–Y eso no puede ser sino casándote tú con mi Ramiro, y mira, no tengo celos, no. ¡Si ha de ser de otra, que sea tuyo! Que sea tuyo. Acaso...

–¿Y por qué ha de volver a casarse?

–¡Ay, Tula, tú no conoces a los hombres! Tú no conoces a mi marido...

–No, no le conozco.

–¡Pues yo sí!

–Quién sabe...

–La pobre enferma se desvaneció.

Poco después llamaba a su marido. Y al salir este del cuarto iba desencajado y pálido como un cadáver.

La Muerte afilaba su guadaña en la piedra angular del hogar de Rosa y Ramiro, y mientras la vida de la joven madre se iba en rosario de gotas, destilando, había que andar a la busca de una nueva ama de cría para el pequeñito, que iba rindiéndose también de hambre. Y Gertrudis, dejando que su hermana se adormeciese en la cuna de una agonía lenta, no hacía sino agitarse en busca de un seno próvido para su sobrinito. Procuraba irle engañando el hambre, sosteniéndole a biberón.

–¿Y esa ama?

–¡Hasta mañana no podrá venir, señorita!

–Mira, Tula – empezó Ramiro.

–¡Déjame! ¡Déjame! ¡Vete al lado de tu mujer, que se muere de un momento a otro; vete que allí es tu puesto, y déjame con el niño!

–Pero, Tula...

–Déjame, te he dicho. Vete a verla morir; a que entre en la otra vida en tus brazos; ¡vete! ¡Déjame!

Ramiro se fue. Gertrudis tomó a su sobrinillo, que no hacía sino gemir; encerróse con él en un cuarto y sacando uno de sus pechos secos, uno

'What are you trying to say?'

'That you'll be his wife Tula.'

'That is not what I meant, Rosa, and right now I can't lie to you, even out of kindness. I didn't say that I'll marry your husband if you're no longer here; what I said was that they won't want for a mother...'

'No, you said that they wouldn't have a stepmother...'

'All right, then, yes, they won't have a stepmother!'

'Well that can only happen if you marry my Ramiro. Please don't think I'm jealous: if there has to be another woman, let it be you! Let it be you. Perhaps...

'Why must Ramiro remarry?'

'Oh Tula, you don't know anything about men. You don't know my husband...'

'No, I don't know him.'

'Well, *I* do!'

'Who knows...'

The poor invalid lost consciousness.

Shortly afterwards, her husband was called to her side. When he later left the room, he looked unhinged, and was as pale as a corpse.

Death was sharpening its scythe on the cornerstone of Rosa and Ramiro's home, and while the life of the young mother gradually slipped away, sublimating itself into something purer, a new wet nurse had to be found for the youngest child, who was in danger of dying of hunger. Leaving her sister to fall asleep in the cradle of a slow death, Gertrudis occupied herself completely with finding a nurturing breast for her little nephew. Meanwhile, she managed to keep the wolf from the door by feeding him from a bottle.

'What about that wet nurse?'

'She won't be able to come until tomorrow, miss.'

'Look, Tula...', began Ramiro.

'Leave! Leave and go to your wife's side: she's very close to death; go! Your place is with her. Leave the child to me!'

'But Tula...'

'Go, I said. Go and watch over her death; let her enter the next world in your arms. Go! Leave!'

Ramiro left. Gertrudis took her little nephew, who could do nothing but wail, and shut herself in a room with him.[12] She uncovered one of

de sus pechos de doncella, que arrebolado todo él le retemblaba como
con fiebre. Le retemblaba por los latidos del corazón – era el derecho
–, puso el botón de ese pecho en la flor sonrosada pálida de la boca
del pequeñuelo. Y este gemía más estrujando entre sus pálidos labios el
conmovido pezón seco.

–Un milagro, Virgen Santísima – gemía Gertrudis con los ojos velados
por las lágrimas–; un milagro, y nadie lo sabrá, nadie.

Y apretaba como una loca al niño a su seno.

Oyó pasos y luego que intentaban abrir la puerta. Metióse el pecho, lo
cubrió, se enjugó los ojos y salió a abrir. Era Ramiro, que le dijo:

–¡Ya acabó!

–Dios la tenga en su gloria. Y ahora, Ramiro, a cuidar de éstos.

–¿A cuidar? Tú..., tú..., porque sin ti...

–Bueno; ahora a criarlos, te digo.

her dry breasts, one of her maidenly breasts. Completely flushed, it trembled in an almost feverish way, pulsing to her heartbeat – it was the right breast. She put the bud of her breast in the pale rosy-pink flower of the baby's mouth. And the baby wailed even more, latching onto the trembling dry nipple.

'It's a miracle, oh Blessed Virgin Mary', moaned Gertrudis, her eyes blurred by tears; a miracle, and no-one will know about it; no-one.'

And she pressed the baby to her breast like a mad woman.

She heard steps and then someone trying to open the door. She covered her breast, wiped her eyes and went to open the door.

It was Ramiro, who said,

'It's over.'

'God rest her soul. And now, Ramiro, these children need to be looked after.'

'Looked after? You'll...? You'll...?... because without you...'

'As I said, they need to be looked after.'

VII

Ahora, ahora que se había quedado viudo, era cuando Ramiro sentía todo lo que sin él siquiera sospecharlo había querido a Rosa, su mujer. Uno de sus consuelos, el mayor, era recogerse en aquella alcoba en que tanto habían vivido amándose y repasar su vida de matrimonio.

Primero el noviazgo, aquel noviazgo, aunque no muy prolongado, de lento reposo, en que Rosa parecía como que le hurtaba el fondo del alma siempre, y como si por acaso no la tuviese o haciéndole pensar que no la conocería hasta que fuese suya del todo y por entero; aquel noviazgo de recato y de reserva, bajo la mirada de Gertrudis, que era todo alma. Repasaba en su mente Ramiro, lo recordaba bien, cómo la presencia de Gertrudis, la tía Tula de sus hijos, le contenía y desasosegaba, cómo ante ella no se atrevía a soltar ninguna de esas obligadas bromas entre novios, sino a medir sus palabras.

Vino luego la boda y la embriaguez de los primeros meses, de las lunas de miel; Rosa iba abriéndole el espíritu, pero era éste tan sencillo, tan transparente, que cayó en la cuenta Ramiro de que no le había velado ni recatado nada. Porque su mujer vivía con el corazón en la mano y extendía ésta en gesto de oferta y con las entrañas espirituales al aire del mundo, entregada por entero al cuidado del momento, como viven las rosas del campo y las alondras del cielo. Y era a la vez el espíritu de Rosa como un reflejo del de su hermana, como el agua corriente al sol de que aquél era el manantial cerrado.

Llegó, por fin, una mañana en que se le desprendieron a Ramiro las escamas de la vista y, purificada ésta, vió claro con el corazón. Rosa no era una hermosura cual él se había creído y antojado, sino una figura vulgar, pero con todo el más dulce encanto de la vulgaridad recogida y mansa; era como el pan de cada día, como el pan casero y cotidiano, y no un raro manjar de turbadores jugos. Su mirada, que sembraba paz, su

VII

It was only now, now that he had been widowed, that Ramiro realised, without even having suspected it before, just how much he had loved his wife Rosa. One of his consolations – the greatest, in fact – lay in withdrawing to the marital bedroom in which they had spent so much of their lives together, loving each other, so that he could relive their married existence in his own mind.

First, their engagement, that now far-off engagement, which, though not very long, had proceeded at a very leisurely pace. It seemed to him as though Rosa were withholding the most intimate part of her heart from him, in case he did not already have it, or giving him to believe that he would not know her until she was completely and utterly his, body and soul. Their engagement had been characterised by reserve and restraint, everything taking place under the watchful gaze of Gertrudis, who was all soul, and no body. Remembering it all so well, Ramiro went over in his mind how the presence of Gertrudis, his children's Aunt Tula, made him hold back, and made him anxious. It was as if with her there, he could not come out with any of the obligatory teasing or joshing between engaged couples; instead he had to watch his words.

Then came the wedding and the first intoxicating months, the honeymoon period; gradually Rosa opened her heart to him, but it was such a simple, transparent heart that Ramiro came to realise that she had not been veiling or hiding anything from him. His wife wore her heart on her sleeve, offering it up and baring her soul to the world, utterly given over to the cares of the immediate present, just as the roses grow in the field and the larks live in the sky. At the same time, Rosa's spirit was like the mirror image or reflection of her sister's, was all external and open to the skies, just as the running water in the sun is in relation to the hidden, interior spring which feeds it.

Eventually, Ramiro awoke one morning to find that the scales had fallen from his eyes. His gaze thus purified, he saw clearly with his heart. Rosa was not the beauty that he had believed or fancied her to be; she was, instead, an ordinary figure, but one with all the sweetest charm that quiet, gentle ordinariness can offer. She was like his daily bread, like homemade daily bread, not a rare delicacy made up of troublingly

sonrisa, su aire de vida, eran encarnación de un ánimo sedante, sosegado y doméstico. Tenía su pobre mujer algo de planta en la silenciosa mansedumbre, en la callada tarea de beber y atesorar luz con los ojos y derramarla luego convertida en paz; tenía algo de planta en aquella fuerza velada y a la vez poderosa con que de continuo, momento tras momento, chupaba jugos de las entrañas de la vida común ordinaria y en la dulce naturalidad con que abría sus perfumadas corolas.

¡Qué de recuerdos! Aquellos juegos cuando la pobre se le escapaba y la perseguía él por la casa toda fingiendo un triunfo para cobrar como botín besos largos y apretados, boca a boca; aquel cogerle la cara con ambas manos y estarse en silencio mirándole el alma por los ojos y, sobre todo, cuando apoyaba el oído sobre el pecho de ella, ciñéndole con los brazos el talle, y escuchándole la marcha tranquila del corazón le decía: «¡Calla, déjale que hable!»

Y las visitas de Gertrudis, que con su cara grave y sus grandes ojazos de luto a que se asomaba un espíritu embozado, parecía decirles: «Sois unos chiquillos que cuando no os veo estáis jugando a marido y mujer; no es esa la manera de prepararse a criar hijos, pues el matrimonio se instituyó para casar, dar gracia a los casados y que críen hijos para el cielo.»

¡Los hijos! Ellos fueron sus primeras grandes meditaciones. Porque pasó un mes y otro y algunos más, y al no notar señal ni indicio de que hubiese fructificado aquel amor, «¿tendría razón – decíase entonces – Gertrudis? ¿Sería verdad que no estaban sino jugando a marido y mujer y sin querer, con la fuerza toda de la fe en el deber, el fruto de la bendición del amor justo?». Pero lo que más le molestaba entonces, recordábalo bien ahora, era lo que pensarían los demás, pues acaso hubiese quien le creyera a él, por eso de no haber podido hacer hijos, menos hombre que otros. ¿Por qué no había de hacer él, y mejor, lo que cualquier mentecato, enclenque y apocado hace? Heríale en su amor propio; habría querido que su mujer hubiese dado a luz a los nueve meses justos y cabales de haberse ellos casado. Además, eso de tener hijos o no tenerlos debía de depender – decíase entonces – de la mayor o menor fuerza de cariño

exotic flavours. Her pacifying gaze, her smile, her liveliness, were the incarnation of a soothing, serene and domestic disposition. There was something plant-like in his poor wife's silent gentleness, in the way her eyes would quietly drink in and hold the light within them, only then to let it flow out again, now pacified.[13] There was also something plant-like in the hidden yet powerful way that she would constantly, moment-by-moment, drink from the deepest wellsprings of common, ordinary life and in the sweetly natural way the perfumed corolla of her being would open itself to the world.

Such memories! Those games when the poor thing would run away from him and he would chase her around the whole house, feigning triumph in order to be able to claim as his booty long, intimate kisses on the lips; he would hold her face in his hands, look silently into and through her eyes to her soul; most of all, he remembered when he would put his head on her chest, his arms around her waist, and, listening to the tranquil beating of her heart, and he would say to her, 'Stop talking. Let me hear your heart speak'. And then there were the visits from Gertrudis, who, with her serious expression and her big mournful eyes through which a veiled spirit could be glimpsed, seemed to say to them: 'you are just a pair of children who, when I'm not watching over you, are just playing at being husband and wife. That's no way to prepare for having children, because matrimony was instituted so that couples could wed, enjoy grace through the sacrament of marriage, and bring up children to serve God and enter heaven.'[14]

Children! They were amongst the first things that gave him pause for thought. Because as the months went by, there was no immediate sign that their love was going to bear fruit. 'Could it be', Ramiro asked himself, 'that Gertrudis was right? That they were just playing at being husband and wife, without wanting, with all the strength of faith in duty, the fruits of righteous love?' But what had most bothered him at that point, he remembered quite clearly now, was what others might think. He feared that there might be those who thought that because he could not have children, he was less of a man. Why couldn't he do – and do better – what any idiot, weakling or spineless sap could do? It wounded his sense of self-respect; he would have wanted his wife to give birth exactly nine months after they married. Besides, he used to say to himself at that time, having – or not having – children should depend on the strength of the

que los casados se tengan, aunque los hay enamoradísimos uno de otro
y que no dan fruto, y otros, ayuntados por conveniencias de fortuna y
ventura, que se cargan de críos. Pero –y esto sí que lo recordaba bien
ahora– para explicárselo había fraguado su teoría, y era que hay un amor
aparente y consciente, de cabeza, que puede mostrarse muy grande y
ser, sin embargo, infecundo, y otro sustancial y oculto, recatado aun al
propio conocimiento de los mismos que lo alimentan, un amor del alma
y el cuerpo enteros y justos, amor fecundo siempre. ¿No querría él lo
bastante a Rosa o no le querría lo bastante Rosa a él? Y recordaba ahora
cómo había tratado de descifrar el misterio mientras la envolvía en besos,
a solas, en el silencio y oscuro de la noche y susurrándola una y otra vez
al oído, en letanía, un rosario de: «¿Me quieres, me quieres, Rosa?»,
mientras a ella se la escapaban síes desfallecidos. Aquello fue una locura,
una necia locura, de la que se avergonzaba apenas veía entrar a Gertrudis
derramando serena seriedad en torno, y de aquello le curó la sazón del
amor cuando le fue anunciado el hijo. Fue un transporte loco... ¡había
vencido! Y entonces fue cuando vino, con su primer fruto, el verdadero
amor.

El amor, sí. ¿Amor? ¿Amor dicen? ¿Qué saben de él todos esos
escritores amatorios, que no amorosos, que de él hablan y quieren
excitarlo en quien los lee? ¿Qué saben de él los galeotos de las letras?
¿Amor? No amor, sino mejor cariño. Eso de amor – decíase Ramiro
ahora – sabe a libro; sólo en el teatro y en las novelas se oye el *yo te amo;*
en la vida de carne y sangre y hueso el entrañable *¡te quiero!* y el más
entrañable aún callárselo. ¿Amor? No, ni cariño siquiera, sino algo sin
nombre y que no se dice por confundirse ello con la vida misma. Los más
de los cantores amatorios saben de amor lo que de oración los masculla-
jaculatorias, traga-novenas y engulle-rosarios. No, la oración no es tanto
algo que haya de cumplirse a tales o cuales horas, en sitio apartado y
recogido y en postura compuesta, cuanto es un modo de hacerlo todo
votivamente, con toda el alma y viviendo en Dios. Oración ha de ser el
comer, y el beber, y el pasearse, y el jugar, y el leer, y el escribir, y el
conversar, y hasta el dormir, y rezo todo, y nuestra vida un continuo y
mudo «¡hágase tu voluntad!», y un incesante «¡venga a nos el tu reino!»,

love between the married couple, although there were those who were madly in love but whose love did not bear fruit, and there were others, yoked together by fortune or chance, who were overrun with children. He remembered this clearly now. He had come up with a theory to explain it to himself: there was a patent, conscious love, originating in the mind, that could be very strong, and yet be infertile; there was another, hidden, substantial love, inaccessible to the consciousness even of those who fed it, a love originating in the whole, righteous body *and* soul, a love that was always fertile. Didn't he love Rosa sufficiently, or didn't she love him enough? And now he remembered how he had tried to unravel the mystery as he covered her in kisses, alone together in the dark silence of the night, whispering over and over in her ear, 'Do you love me? Do you love me Rosa?' like a litany, or a rosary, while a faint 'yes' would fall from her lips as he did this. It was a form of madness, a folly, and he felt ashamed of it as soon as he saw Gertrudis come in, radiating grave serenity. He was cured by the opportune announcement that they were having a baby. He felt a mad ecstasy overtake him … he had triumphed! And it was then, with its first fruit, that true love arrived.

Love, yes. Love? Love, as they say? What did all those writers know about love – who, not in love themselves, spoke of it and tried to stir loving feelings in those who read their work? What did those literary procurers know? Love? What was important was not love, but rather affection. 'All this about love', Ramiro now said to himself, 'smacks of bookishness: only in novels and in plays does one hear "I am in love with you"; in the flesh-and-blood world, one heard the more homely and affectionate "I love you";[15] and in its homeliest and most affectionate form, the feeling was left altogether unsaid. Love? No, and not even affection, but rather something nameless, something one did not say because it was caught up with life itself. Most of the singers of love songs knew as much about love as the pious or strict rosary-sayers knew about true prayer. Prayer is less something that must be said at such-and-such a time, in a secluded place, with a composed demeanour than something that should be offered up, with all one's heart and by living in God. Prayer had to be the meat and drink, the daily stroll, daily play, one's everyday reading, writing and conversing, and even sleeping; everything should be a prayer in this way, and our lives should be a continuous, silent "Thy will be done", an unceasing "Thy kingdom come", not voiced, nor even thought about,

no ya pronunciados, mas ni aun pensados siquiera, sino vividos. Así oyó la oración una vez Ramiro a un santo varón religioso que pasaba por maestro de ella, y así lo aplicó él al amor luego. Pues el que profesara a su mujer y a ella le apegaba veía bien ahora en que ella se le fue, que se le llegó a fundir con el rutinero andar de la vida diaria, que lo había respirado en las mil naderías y frioleras del vivir doméstico, que le fue como el aire que se respira y al que no se le siente sino en momentos de angustioso ahogo, cuando nos falta. Y ahora ahogábase Ramiro, y la congoja de su viudez reciente le revelaba todo el poderío del amor pasado y vivido.

Al principio de su matrimonio fue, sí, el imperio del deseo; no podía juntar carne con carne sin que la suya se le encendiese y alborotase y empezara a martillarle el corazón, pero era porque la otra no era aún de veras y por entero suya también; pero luego, cuando ponía su mano sobre la carne desnuda de ella, era como si en la propia la hubiese puesto, tan tranquilo se quedaba; mas también si se la hubiesen cortado habríale dolido como si se la cortaran a él. ¿No sintió acaso en sus entrañas los dolores de los partos de su Rosa?

Cuando la vió gozar, sufriendo al darle su primer hijo, es cuando comprendió cómo es el amor más fuerte que la vida y que la muerte, y domina la discordia de estas; cómo el amor hace morirse a la vida y vivir la muerte; cómo él vivía ahora la muerte de su Rosa y se moría en su propia vida. Luego, al ver al niño dormido y sereno, con los labios en flor entreabiertos, vió al amor hecho carne que vive. Y allí, sobre la cuna, contemplando a su fruto, traía a sí a la madre, y mientras el niño sonreía en sueños palpitando sus labios, besaba él a Rosa en la corola de sus labios frescos y en la fuente de paz de sus ojos. Y le decía mostrándole dos dedos de la mano: «¡Otra vez, dos, dos...!» Y ella: «¡No, no, ya no más, uno y no más!» Y se reía. Y él: «¡Dos, dos, me ha entrado el capricho de que tengamos dos mellizos, una parejita, niño y niña!» Y cuando ella volvió a quedarse encinta, a cada paso y tropezón, él: «¡Qué cargado viene eso! ¡Qué granazón! ¡Me voy a salir con la mía; por lo menos dos!» «¡Uno, el último, y basta!», replicaba ella riendo. Y vino el segundo, la niña,

but instead *lived*'. This was what Ramiro had once heard a saintly man of religion, regarded as an authority on prayer, say on the matter, and Ramiro subsequently applied the same description to love. After all, he saw now, the love he had professed for his wife, to whom he had become devoted, had become a very part of her, and their love had fused with the routine course of everyday life: he had breathed it in in the myriad little incidents and trifles of domestic life. To him she was like the air he breathed, and love was something he felt only in moments of breathless distress, when it was missing. And now Ramiro was overcome, and the anguish of his recent widowhood revealed to him all the strength of the past love he had experienced.

At the beginning of his marriage everything had been subject to the laws of desire; he could not touch Rosa without becoming inflamed or without his heart hammering. That was because she was not yet truly and wholly his; later, when he placed his hand on her bare skin, it was as if he had placed it on his own, so calm and unaffected was he; but it was also true that had Rosa's hand been cut off, it would have hurt him as much as if it had been his own. Had he not felt Rosa's labour pains deep inside his own body?

It was only when he saw her take pleasure in the suffering required to give him their first child that he understood that love was stronger than life and death, and that it prevailed over the struggle between the two: he came to understand how love made life die and death live, and how he was now living through the death of Rosa and was dying through his own life. It was later, when he saw the baby calmly sleeping, the little bud of his mouth slightly parted, that he saw love made living flesh. And there, over the cot, contemplating the fruit of his and Rosa's love, he brought the mother closer towards him, and while the baby smiled in his sleep, he kissed Rosa on the corolla of her cool lips, and kissed the peaceful pools of her closed eyes. Counting on his fingers, he said to her 'Yes, two, two', and she replied, 'no, no more. One is enough!' and she laughed. Him again: 'two, two, I want us to have twins, a little pair, a boy and a girl.' And when she became pregnant again, with each stumble or difficulty that Rosa encountered, he would say 'What a load you must be carrying! You are carrying more than one seed! I'm going to get my way – there are two babies there at least!' 'No, there's only one – and it'll be the last!' Rosa would reply, laughing. And the second baby came along, a

Tulita, y luego que salió con vida, cuando descansaba la madre, la besó larga y apretadamente en la boca, como en premio, diciéndose: «¡Bien has trabajado, pobrecilla!»; mientras Rosa, vencedora de la muerte y de la vida, sonreía con los domésticos ojos apacibles.

¡Y murió!; aunque pareciese mentira, se murió. Vino la tarde terrible del combate último. Allí estuvo Gertrudis, mientras el cuidado de la pobrecita niña que desfallecía de hambre se lo permitió, sirviendo medicinas inútiles, componiendo la cama, animando a la enferma, encorazonando a todos. Tendida en el lecho que había sido campo de donde brotaron tres vidas, llegó a faltarle el habla y las fuerzas, y cogida de la mano a la mano de su hombre, del padre de sus hijos, mirábale como el navegante, al ir a perderse en el mar sin orillas, mira al lejano promontorio, lengua de la tierra nativa, que se va desvaneciendo en la lontananza y junto al cielo; en los trances del ahogo miraban sus ojos, desde el borde de la eternidad, a los ojos de su Ramiro. Y parecía aquella mirada una pregunta desesperada y suprema, como si a punto de partirse para nunca más volver a tierra, preguntase por el oculto sentido de la vida. Aquellas miradas de congoja reposada, de acongojado reposo, decían: «Tú, tú que eres mi vida, tú que conmigo has traído al mundo nuevos mortales, tú que me has sacado tres vidas, tú, mi hombre, dime, ¿esto qué es?» Fué una tarde abismática. En momentos de tregua, teniendo Rosa entre sus manos, húmedas y febriles, las manos temblorosas de Ramiro, clavados en los ojos de éste sus ojos henchidos de cansancio de vida, sonreía tristemente, volviéndolos luego al niño, que dormía allí cerca, en su cunita, y decía con los ojos, y alguna vez con un hilito de voz: «¡No despertarle, no! ¡Que duerma, pobrecillo! ¡Que duerma...que duerma hasta hartarse, que duerma!» Llególe por último el supremo trance, el del tránsito, y fue como si en el brocal de las eternas tinieblas, suspendida sobre el abismo, se aferrara a él, a su hombre, que vacilaba sintiéndose arrastrado. Quería abrirse con las uñas la garganta la pobre, mirábale despavorida, pidiéndole con los ojos aire; luego, con ellos le sondó el fondo del alma, y soltando su mano cayó en la cama donde había concebido y parido sus tres hijos. Descansaron los dos; Ramiro, aturdido, con el corazón acorchado, sumergido como en un sueño sin fondo y sin despertar, muerta el alma, mientras dormía el niño.

little girl, Tulita. After she was delivered alive, and as her mother rested, he gave Rosa a big kiss on the lips, as if in reward, as if to say 'You *have* worked hard, you poor little thing'. Rosa looked on, victorious over death and life, smiling with her gentle, homely eyes.

And yet she had died! Although it seemed impossible, she had died. The dreadful evening of the last battle arrived. Gertrudis was there, and, when she was not caring for the poor little starving newborn, she was administering useless medicine, smoothing the bedclothes, encouraging the patient and cheering up all those around her. Rosa lay on the bed that had formed the ground in which three lives had taken seed, her speech and strength beginning to fail her. With the hand of her husband, the father of their children, in hers, she looked at him in the way that a seafarer, about to be lost in the deepest ocean, looks at the far-off headland, that spit of native land that gradually fades from view and merges with the sky; in her last moments of distress, as she approached the edge of eternity, her eyes fastened on Ramiro's. And that final gaze seemed to ask a supremely important question, as if, at the moment she was about to leave the earth for all time, she was asking about the hidden meaning of life. Those glances of reposed anguish, of anguished repose, asked 'You, you who are my life, you who, along with me have brought new mortals into the world, you who have brought three lives out of me, my husband, tell me, what is this all about? It was an evening that plunged them all into the abyss. In moments of respite, Rosa held Ramiro's trembling hands in her own damp, feverish hands; with her swollen eyes, tired of life, firmly fixed on his, Rosa smiled sadly at Ramiro and then turned towards the baby, who was sleeping nearby in his cot. Sometimes with her gaze, sometimes in the faintest of voices, she said, 'Don't wake him! Let the poor mite sleep. Let him sleep away until he's had enough'. The moment finally came when she took her last breaths and departed from the world, and it was as if, on the edge of eternal darkness, hanging over the abyss, she tried to cling to her man. He, in turn, also tottered, feeling himself pulled down too. The poor woman wanted to claw open her own throat, gazing terrified at Ramiro, pleading with her eyes for air; then, her gaze reaching deep into Ramiro's soul, she let go of his hand and fell back onto the bed in which she had conceived and given birth to their three children. The couple rested; a dazed Ramiro, numb to his very heart, felt plunged into something like a bottomless, endless dream. His soul had

Gertrudis fue quien, viniendo con la pequeñita al pecho, cerró luego los ojos a su hermana, la compuso un poco y fuese después a cubrir y arropar mejor al niño dormido, y trasladarle en un beso la tibieza que con otro recogió de la vida que aún tendía sus últimos jirones sobre la frente de la rendida madre.

Pero, ¿murió acaso Rosa? ¿Se murió de veras? ¿Podía haberse muerto viviendo él, Ramiro? No; en sus noches, ahora solitarias, mientras se dormía solo en aquella cama de la muerte y de la vida y del amor, sentía a su lado el ritmo de su respiración, su calor tibio, aunque con una congojosa sensación de vacío. Y tendía la mano, recorriendo con ella la otra mitad de la cama, apretándola algunas veces. Y era lo peor que, cuando recogiéndose se ponía a meditar en ella, no se le ocurrieran sino cosas de libro, cosas de amor de libro y no de cariño de vida, y le escocía que aquel robusto sentimiento, vida de su vida y aire de su espíritu, no se le cuajara más que en abstractas lucubraciones. El dolor se le espiritualizaba, vale decir que se intelectualizaba, y sólo cobraba carne, aunque fuera vaporosa, cuando entraba Gertrudis. Y de todo esto sacábale una de aquellas vocecitas frescas que piaba: «¡Papá!» Ya estaba, pues, allí, ella, la muerta inmortal. Y luego, la misma vocecita: «¡Mamá!» Y la de Gertrudis, gravemente dulce, respondía: «¡Hijo!»

No, Rosa, su Rosa, no se había muerto, no era posible que se le hubiese muerto; la mujer estaba allí, tan viva como antes, y derramando vida en torno; la mujer no podía morir.

died. The baby slept on. It was Gertrudis who, arriving with the little girl clutched to her breast, closed her sister's eyes. She arranged Rosa's body, and then went to wrap up the sleeping baby more snugly. She kissed the baby, and with her kiss, she passed on the warmth that a previous kiss had taken from the last traces of life clinging to the forehead of the exhausted mother.

But had Rosa died? Had she really died? Could she really be dead while he, Ramiro, remained alive? No; during his now solitary nights, while he slept alone in the bed that had now known death, life and love, he felt the rhythm of her breathing by her side, felt her faint warmth, even though it was all accompanied by a distressing feeling of emptiness. And he stretched out his hand, feeling across to the other side of the bed, sometimes pressing it into the mattress. The worst thing about it was that, when he thought about her as he went to bed, the only things that came to mind were notions from books, notions from love stories and not things that came from a living love. And it stung him that his fierce feelings, which were the very life of his life and the oxygen of his spirit, could only take shape as abstract, laboured thoughts. His pain became spiritualised; one might say that it became intellectualised. It only took on flesh, however diaphanously, when Gertrudis arrived. What drew him out of these thoughts was one of those fresh little voices piping up 'Daddy!' Then she was there, the immortal dead woman. Shortly after, the same little voice would pipe up 'Mummy!' And Gertrudis's grave, gentle voice would reply 'My child.'

No, Rosa, his Rosa, had not died. It was not possible that she had died; his wife was there, as alive as she had been before, and was radiating vitality all around her. His wife could not die.

VIII

Gertrudis, que se había instalado en casa de su hermana desde que ésta
dió por última vez a luz y durante su enfermedad última, le dijo un día a
su cuñado:

–Mira, voy a levantar mi casa.

El corazón de Ramiro se puso al galope.

–Sí – añadió ella–, tengo que venir a vivir con vosotros y a cuidar de
los chicos. No se le puede, además, dejar aquí sola a esa buena pécora
del ama.

–Dios te lo pague, Tula.

–Nada de Tula, ya te lo tengo dicho; para ti soy Gertrudis.

–¿Y qué más da?

–Yo lo sé.

–Mira, Gertrudis...

–Bueno, voy a ver qué hace el ama.

A la cual vigilaba sin descanso. No le dejaba dar el pecho al pequeñito
delante del padre de éste, y le regañaba por el poco recato y mucha
desenvoltura con que se desabrochaba el seno.

–Si no hace falta que enseñes eso así; en el niño es en quien hay que
ver si tienes o no leche abundante.

Ramiro sufría y Gertrudis le sentía sufrir.

–¡Pobre Rosa! – decía de continuo.

–Ahora los pobres son los niños y es en ellos en quienes hay que
pensar…

–No basta, no. Apenas descanso. Sobre todo por las noches la soledad
me pesa; las hay que las paso en vela.

–Sal después de cenar, como salías de casado últimamente, y no
vuelvas a casa hasta que sientas sueño. Hay que acostarse con sueño.

–Pero es que siento un vacío...

–¿Vacío teniendo hijos?

–Pero ella es insustituible...

–Así lo creo... Aunque vosotros los hombres...

–No creí que la quería tanto...

–Así nos pasa de continuo. Así me pasó con mi tío y así me ha pasado
con mi hermana, con tu Rosa. Hasta que ha muerto tampoco yo he sabido

VIII

Gertrudis, who had been staying in her sister's home since Rosa's last pregnancy and final illness, said one day to her brother-in-law, 'I am going to move out of my own house.' Ramiro's heart began to thump. 'That's right,' she added, 'I have to come and live here with you and look after the children. That strumpet of a wet nurse can't be left alone here.'

'God bless you, Tula, I am so grateful.'

'I have already told you not to call me Tula. To you, I'm Gertrudis.'

'What does it matter?'

'It matters to me.'

'Look, Gertrudis…'

'I am going to see what that wet nurse is up to'.

Gertrudis watched the wet nurse like a hawk. She would not allow her to breastfeed the baby in front of his father, and she would upbraid the woman for the immodest way she would expose her breast while doing so. 'We don't need you displaying yourself like that: it's the baby who will show us whether you have enough milk for him or not.'

Ramiro felt terrible, and Gertrudis sensed his suffering.

'Poor Rosa', he would say constantly.

'It is the children who deserve compassion, and it is they we should be thinking of…'

'That's not enough. I can't get any rest. It's at night that I feel the greatest weight of the loneliness. There are some nights I can't sleep at all.'

'You should go out after supper, as you used to, not long ago when you were still married, and not come back home until you feel tired. You must go to bed only when you are sleepy.'

'But I feel so empty…'

'Empty? When you have children?'

'But Rosa is irreplaceable.'

'Yes, I agree. Although you men…'

'I never realised how much I loved her…'

'That is what always happens. I felt the same after my uncle died, and now with my sister, your Rosa. Until she died I didn't realise either how

lo que la quería. Lo sé ahora en que cuido a sus hijos, a vuestros hijos. Y es que queremos a los muertos en los vivos...

–¿Y no, acaso, a los vivos en los muertos...?

–No sutilicemos.

Y por las mañanas, luego de haberse levantado Ramiro, iba su cuñada a la alcoba y abría de par en par las hojas del balcón diciéndose: «Para que se vaya el olor a hombre.» Y evitaba luego encontrarse a solas con su cuñado, para lo cual llevaba siempre algún niño delante.

Sentada en la butaca en que solía sentarse la difunta, contemplaba los juegos de los pequeñuelos.

–Es que yo soy chico y tú no eres más que chica – oyó que le decía un día, con su voz de trapo, Ramirín a su hermanita.

–Ramirín, Ramirín – le dijo la tía–, ¿qué es eso? ¿Ya empiezas a ser bruto, a ser hombre?

Un día llegó Ramiro, llamó a su cuñada y le dijo:

–He sorprendido tu secreto, Gertrudis.

–¿Qué secreto?

–Las relaciones que llevabas con Ricardo, mi primo.

–Pues bien, sí es cierto; se empeñó, me hostigó, no me dejaba en paz, y acabó por darme lástima.

–Y tan oculto que lo teníais...

–¿Para qué declararlo?

–Y sé más.

–¿Qué es lo que sabes?

–Que le has despedido.

–También es cierto.

–Me ha enseñado él mismo tu carta.

–¿Cómo? No le creía capaz de eso. Bien he hecho en dejarle: ¡hombre al fin!

Ramiro, en efecto, había visto una carta de su cuñada a Ricardo, que decía así:

«Mi querido Ricardo: No sabes bien qué días tan malos estoy pasando desde que murió la pobre Rosa. Estos últimos han sido terribles y no he cesado de pedir a la Virgen Santísima y a su Hijo que me diesen fuerzas para ver claro en mi porvenir. No sabes bien con cuánta pena te lo digo, pero no pueden continuar nuestras

much I loved her. I know now through my caring for her children, for your children. We love the dead through the living…'

'Or perhaps we love the living through the dead?'

'Let's not split hairs.'

And in the mornings, after Ramiro had got up, his sister-in-law would go to his bedroom and fling open the balcony shutters, saying to herself 'we must get rid of the smell of man here'. She would avoid being alone with her brother-in-law, and so would always have a child with her. Sitting in the armchair that the deceased Rosa had often used, she would watch the little rascals play.

'You see, I'm a *boy*; you're just a girl', she heard little Ramiro, in his child's voice, say to his tiny sister one day.

'Young Ramiro, what is the meaning of this? You're surely not beginning to be brutish? Are you becoming a man?'

One day, Ramiro came home, called for his sister-in-law and said, 'I've discovered your secret Gertrudis.'

'What secret?'

'The relations you had with Ricardo, my cousin.'

'Well, yes, it's true; he was very persistent, he wouldn't take no for an answer nor leave me in peace, and I ended up feeling sorry for him.'

'And you kept it so hidden.'

'But why would I say anything about it?'

'And that's not all I know…'

'Tell me, what else do you know?'

'That you've sent him packing.'

'That's also true.'

'He himself showed me your letter to him!'

'What? I didn't think he was capable of doing something like that. I was obviously right to break things off. Typical man!'

Ramiro had indeed seen a letter from his sister-in-law to his cousin, which read as follows:

"My dear Ricardo,

You cannot imagine how hard things have been since poor Rosa died. These last few days have been terrible, and I have been constantly praying to the Blessed Virgin and to the Holy Child to give me strength so that I can see my future with some clarity. You

relaciones; no puedo casarme. Mi hermana me sigue rogando desde el otro mundo que no abandone a sus hijos y que les haga de madre. Y puesto que tengo estos hijos a que cuidar, no debo ya casarme. Perdóname, Ricardo, perdónamelo, por Dios, y mira bien por qué lo hago. Me cuesta mucha pena porque sé que habría llegado a quererte y, sobre todo, porque sé lo que me quieres y lo que sufrirás con esto. Siento en el alma causarte esta pena, pero tú, que eres bueno, comprenderás mis deberes y los motivos de mi resolución y encontrarás otra mujer que no tenga mis obligaciones sagradas y que te pueda hacer más feliz que yo habría podido hacerte.

Adiós, Ricardo, que seas feliz y hagas felices a otros, y ten por seguro que nunca, nunca te olvidará

Gertrudis.»

–Y ahora – añadió Ramiro–, a pesar de esto Ricardo quiere verte.

–¿Es que yo me oculto acaso?

–No, pero...

–Dile que venga cuando quiera a verme a esta nuestra casa.

–Nuestra casa, Gertrudis, nuestra...

–Nuestra, sí, y de nuestros hijos…

–Si tú quisieras...

–¡No hablemos de eso! – y se levantó.

Al siguiente día se le presentó Ricardo.

–Pero, por Dios, Tula.

–No hablemos más de eso, Ricardo, que es cosa hecha.

–Pero, por Dios –y se le quebró la voz.

–¡Sé hombre, Ricardo; sé fuerte!

–Pero es que ya tienen padre...

–No basta, no tienen madre..., es decir, sí la tienen.

–Puede él volver a casarse.

–¿Volverse a casar él? En ese caso los niños se irán conmigo. Le prometí a su madre, en su lecho de muerte, que no tendrían madrastra.

will never know how sad it makes me to say this, but our relations cannot continue: I will not be able to marry you. My sister continues to ask me from the grave not to abandon her children, and asks me to be a mother to them. And given that I have children to care for, I must not marry. Forgive me Ricardo, please forgive me, for the love of God, and please bear in mind why I am doing this. I feel very sad because I know that I would have come to love you. Above all, it makes me sad because I know how much you love me, and how much this will make you suffer. I am truly sorry to cause you such pain, but, as you are a good man, you will understand my duties, and the reasons behind my decision. You will find another woman who does not have my sacred obligations and who will be able to make you happier than I could have done. Farewell, Ricardo, I hope you are very happy, and that you make others happy. You can be certain that I will never, ever forget you.

Gertrudis."

'And now,' said Ramiro, 'despite this, Ricardo wants to see you.'

'And am I hiding from him?'

'No, but…'

'Tell him that he can come and see me whenever he likes, here in our home.'

'*Our* home, Gertrudis, *our* home?'

'Ours, yes, and our children's home.'

'Well, if you would like it to be like that…'

'I don't want to talk about this!' and she got up and left.

The next day, Ricardo appeared.

'For the love of God, Tula.'

'Let's not discuss this further, Ricardo, it's done now.'

'For the love of God, Tula.'

'Be a man, Ricardo, be strong.'

'But the children already have a father.'

'That's not enough; they don't have a mother…, or rather, they *do*.'

'He can marry again.'

'Remarry? In that case the children will come and live with me. I promised their mother, on her death bed, that they would never have a stepmother.'

–¿Y si llegases a serlo tú, Tula?

–¿Cómo yo? –Sí, tú; casándote con él, con Ramiro.

–¡Eso nunca!

–Pues yo sólo así me lo explico.

–Eso nunca, te he dicho; no me expondría a que unos míos, es decir, de mi vientre, pudiesen mermarme el cariño que a esos tengo. ¿Y más hijos, más? Eso nunca. Bastan estos para bien criarlos.

–Pues a nadie le convencerás, Tula, de que no te has venido a vivir aquí por eso.

–Yo no trato de convencer a nadie de nada. Y en cuanto a ti, basta que yo te lo diga.

Se separaron para siempre.

–¿Y qué? – le preguntó luego Ramiro.

–Que hemos acabado; no podía ser de otro modo.

–Y que has quedado libre...

–Libre estaba, libre estoy, libre pienso morirme.

–Gertrudis...Gertrudis – y su voz temblaba a súplica.

–Le he despedido porque me debo, ya te lo dije, a tus hijos, a los hijos de Rosa...

–Y tuyos...¿no dices así?

–¡Y míos, sí!

–Pero si tú quisieras...

–No insistas; ya te tengo dicho que no debo casarme ni contigo ni con otro menos.

–¿Menos? – y se le abrió el pecho.

–Sí, menos.

–¿Y cómo no fuiste monja?

–No me gusta que me manden.

–Es que en el convento en que entrases serías tú la abadesa, la superiora.

–Menos me gusta mandar. ¡Ramirín!

El niño acudió al reclamo. Y cogiéndole su tía le dijo: «¡Vamos a jugar al escondite, rico!»

–Pero Tula...

'But what if *you* became their stepmother, Tula?'

'What do you mean?'

'Well, if you married Ramiro.'

'I would never do that.'

'Well, that's the only way I can explain it to myself.'

'I've told you: that will never happen. I would never lay myself open to the risk that anything could undermine the love I have for my children, the fruit of my womb. And as for having more children, that will never happen either. I'll have enough to occupy myself bringing up those I already have.'

'Well you won't convince anyone, Tula, that that's the sole reason you have come to live here.'

'I'm not trying to convince anyone of anything. And as far as you are concerned, you should take my word for it.'

And thus they parted forever.

'What happened?' Ramiro asked her afterwards.

'We have broken off relations; it couldn't have been otherwise.'

'And now you are free…'

'I was free before; I'm free now, and I plan to die free.'

'Gertrudis … Gertrudis' – Ramiro's voice trembled in entreaty.'

'I've said goodbye to him because, as I've told you, my duties lie with your children, with Rosa's children.'

'With *your* children, don't you mean?'

'Yes, *my* children too!'

'But if you liked…'

'Don't keep on about it; I've already told you that I cannot marry you, still less anyone else.'

'*Still less…?*', and Ramiro glimpsed some hope.

'That's right, still less anyone else.'

'Why didn't you become a nun?'

'I don't like to be on the receiving end of orders.'

'But in any convent you went into, *you* would be the abbess, the mother superior.'

'I like *giving* orders even less. Ramirín?'

The little boy answered the call. His aunt took his hand and said 'let's go and play hide-and-seek, darling'.

'But Tula…'

–Te he dicho –y para decirle esto se le acercó, teniendo cogido de
la mano al niño, y se lo dijo al oído – que no me llames Tula, y menos
delante de los niños. Ellos sí, pero tú no. Y ten respeto a los pequeños.

—¿En qué les falto al respeto?

–En dejar así al descubierto delante de ellos tus instintos...

–Pero si no comprenden...

–Los niños lo comprenden todo; más que nosotros. Y no olvidan nada.
Y si ahora no lo comprenden, lo comprenderán mañana. Cada cosa de
estas que ve u oye un niño es una semilla en su alma, que luego echa tallo
y da fruto. ¡Y basta!

'I've already told you,' and to say this she stood very close, the little boy's hand still in hers, and said in Ramiro's ear, 'don't call me Tula, and especially not in front of the children. *They* can call me Tula, but you can't. And have some respect for the little ones.'

'In what way am I being disrespectful to them?'

'In letting your instincts out into the open in front of them.'

'But they can't understand...'

'Children understand everything; they understand more than we do. And they forget nothing. And if they don't understand it now, they'll understand it in the future. Every little thing a child sees or hears is a seed planted in his or her soul, which then sprouts and eventually gives fruit. So enough!'

IX

Y empezó una vida de triste desasosiego, de interna lucha en aquel hogar. Ella defendíase con los niños, a los que siempre procuraba tener presentes, y le excitaba a él a que saliese a distraerse. Él, por su parte, extremaba sus caricias a los hijos y no hacía sino hablarles de su madre, de su pobre madre. Cogía a la niña y allí, delante de la tía, se la devoraba a besos.

–No tanto, hombre, no tanto, que así no haces sino molestar a la pobre criatura. Y eso, permíteme que te lo diga, no es natural. Bien está que hagas que me llamen tía y no mamá, pero no tanto; repórtate.

–¿Es que yo no he de tener el consuelo de mis hijos?

–Sí, hijo, sí; pero lo primero es educarlos bien.

–¿Y así?

–Hartándoles de besos y de golosinas se les hace débiles. Y mira que los niños adivinan...

–Y qué culpa tengo yo...

–¿Pero es que puede haber para unos niños, hombre de Dios, un hogar mejor que éste? Tienen hogar, verdadero hogar, con padre y madre, y es un hogar limpio, castísimo, por todos cuyos rincones pueden andar a todas horas, un hogar donde nunca hay que cerrarles puerta alguna, un hogar sin misterios. ¿Quieres más?

Pero él buscaba acercarse a ella, hasta rozarla. Y alguna vez le tuvo que decir en la mesa:

–No me mires así, que los niños ven.

Por las noches solía hacerles rezar por mamá Rosa, por mamita, para que Dios la tuviese en su gloria. Y una noche, después de este rezo y hallándose presente el padre, añadió:

–Ahora, hijos míos, un padrenuestro y avemaría por papá también.

–Pero papá no se ha muerto, mamá Tula.

–No importa, porque se puede morir…

–Eso, también tú.

–Es verdad; otro padrenuestro y avemaría por mí entonces.

Y cuando los niños se hubieron acostado, volviéndose a su cuñado le dijo secamente:

IX

And so began a life of sad anxiety and internal struggle in that household. Gertrudis defended herself from Ramiro's attentions by making sure the children were always around her, and prodded him to go and find some distraction. For his part, Ramiro became even more affectionate and tactile towards the children, speaking to them constantly about their mother, their poor mother. He would grab the little girl, and in front of her aunt, cover her in kisses.

'You're going too far. And you're just bothering the poor mite. And, if I may say so, it's not natural. It's one thing to make them call me "aunt", and not "mother", but this is too much: restrain yourself.'

'Can't I seek consolation in my children?'

'Yes of course, but bringing them up properly comes first.'

'What do you mean by that?'

'Smothering them in kisses and showering them with sweets will enfeeble them. And children are capable of guessing what is going on...'

'And how is that *my* fault?'

'But could there be a better home than this for children? They have a home, a real home, with a mother and a father, and it is a pure, chaste home that they can roam freely in day and night. It's a home where there are no closed doors, a home without mystery. What more could you want?'

But he would try to get close to her, even brushing against her at times. Sometimes she even had to say to him when they were at table, eating together, 'Don't look at me like that: the children can see you.'

At night she would make them pray for mama Rosa, their mummy, God rest her soul. And one night, after this prayer, and in front of Ramiro, she added,

'Now my children, an Our Father and a Hail Mary for papa too.'

'But papa hasn't died, mama Tula.'

'That doesn't matter; he *could* die...'

'You could too...'

'That's true. Another Our Father and a Hail Mary for me then.'

And when the children had gone to bed, she turned to her brother-in-law and said sharply,

–Esto no puede ser así. Si sigues sin reportarte tendré que marcharme de esta casa aunque Rosa no me lo perdone desde el cielo.

–Pero es que...

–Lo dicho; no quiero que ensucies así, ni con miradas, esta casa tan pura y donde mejor pueden criarse las almas de tus hijos. Acuérdate de Rosa.

–¿Pero de qué crees que somos los hombres?

–De carne y muy brutos.

–¿Y tú, no te has mirado nunca?

–¿Qué es eso? – y se le demudó el rostro sereno.

–Que aunque no fueses, como en realidad lo eres, su madre, ¿tienes derecho, Gertrudis, a perseguirme con tu presencia? ¿Es justo que me reproches y estés llenando la casa con tu persona, con el fuego de tus ojos, con el son de tu voz, con el imán de tu cuerpo lleno de alma, pero de un alma llena de cuerpo?

Gertrudis, toda encendida, bajaba la cabeza y se callaba, mientras le tocaba a rebato el corazón.

–¿Quién tiene la culpa de esto?, dime.

–Tienes razón, Ramiro, y si me fuese, los niños piarían por mí, porque me quieren...

–Más que a mí –dijo tristemente el padre.

–Es que yo no les besuqueo como tú ni les sobo, y cuando les beso, ellos sienten que mis besos son más puros, que son para ellos solos...

–Y bien, ¿quién tiene la culpa de esto?, repito.

–Bueno, pues. Espera un año, esperemos un año; déjame un año de plazo para que vea claro en mí, para que veas claro en ti mismo, para que te convenzas...

–Un año...un año...

–¿Te parece mucho?

–¿Y luego, cuando se acabe?

–Entonces... veremos...

–Veremos... veremos...

–Yo no te prometo más.

–Y si en este año...

'This cannot go on. If you cannot control yourself, then I'll have to leave his house even though Rosa, looking down on me from heaven, would never forgive me.'

'But...'

'As I've said, I don't want you sullying – not even with your stares – this house that's so pure and is the best place to bring up your children. Think of Rosa.'

'But what do you think we men are made of?'

'Of flesh. And you're very brutish.'

'And have you ever taken a good look at yourself?'

'I don't know what you are talking about.' But there was a change to her calm expression.

'Even if you were not their mother, though of course you actually are, do you have the right, Gertrudis, to torment me with your presence? Is it fair that you rebuke me while you fill the house with your personality, with the fire in your eyes, with the sound of your voice, with your mesmerising body, a body full of soul, but also a soul full of body.'

Gertrudis, blushing furiously, dropped her gaze and was silent, her heart pounding.

'Whose fault is that? Tell me.'

'You're right Ramiro, and if I went, the children would be clamouring to have me back, because they love me...'

'More than they love me...', said their father sadly.

'I don't smother them in kisses or paw at them all the time. And when I kiss them, they feel that my kisses are purer and that they are all for them, and them alone...'

'So let me ask again, whose fault is that?'

'All right. Wait a year. Let's wait for a year: give me twelve months so I can think clearly for myself, and so that you can think clearly for yourself, so that you can be sure...'

'A year ... a *year*?'

'Does it seem a long time to you?'

'And when it's up?'

'Well, then ... we'll see.'

'We'll see ... *we'll see?*'

'I can't promise any more.'

'And if during that year...'

—¿Qué? Si en este año haces alguna tontería...

—¿A qué llamas hacer una tontería?

—A enamorarte de otra y volverte a casar.

—Eso... ¡nunca!

—Qué pronto lo dijiste...

—Eso... ¡nunca!

—¡Bah!, juramentos de hombres...

—Y si así fuese, ¿quién tendrá la culpa?

—¿Culpa?

—¡Sí, la culpa!

—Eso sólo querría decir...

—¿Qué?

—Que no la quisiste, que no la quieres a tu Rosa como ella te quiso a ti, como ella te habría querido de haber sido ella la viuda...

—No, eso querría decir otra cosa, que no es...

—Bueno, basta. ¡Ramirín!, ¡ven acá, Ramirín! Anda, corre.

Y así se aplacó aquella lucha.

Y ella continuaba su labor de educar a sus sobrinos.

No quiso que a la niña se le ocupase demasiado en aprender costura y cosas así. «¿Labores de su sexo? – decía –, no, nada de labores de su sexo; el oficio de una mujer es hacer hombres y mujeres, y no vestirlos.»

Un día que Ramirín soltó una expresión soez que había aprendido en la calle y su padre iba a reprenderle, interrumpióle Gertrudis, diciéndole bajo. «No, dejarlo; hay que hacer como si no se ha oído; debe de haber un mundo de que ni para condenarlo hay que hablar aquí.»

Una vez que oyó decir de una que se quedaba soltera que quedaba para vestir santos, agregó: «¡o para vestir almas de niños!»

—Tulita es mi novia –dijo una vez Ramirín.

—No digas tonterías; Tulita es tu hermana.

'What, if during that time you do something foolish…?'
'What do you mean by 'something foolish'?'
'Fall in love with someone else and marry her…'
'I'd never do that…'
'How quickly those words come to your lips.'
'I'd never do that…'
'Psh – that's what you men always say.'
'And if I did, whose fault would it be?'
'Fault?'
'Yes! Whose fault would it be?'
'That would only mean…'
'What?'
'That you didn't love her, that you do not love Rosa the way she loved you, the way she would have loved you if she had been the one widowed…'

'No, it wouldn't mean that, it would mean something else … it's not…'

'All right, that's enough. Young Ramiro! Come here! Come along, hurry!'

And that is how that particular battle ended.

And Gertrudis continued the task of bringing up her nephews and nieces.

She did not want her niece to spend too much time learning to sew or undertake similar activities. 'Women's work?', she would say, 'No, no women's work. A woman's job is to make men and women, not dress them.'

One day, little Ramiro let slip a crude phrase he had picked up on the street. His father made to rebuke him, but, interrupting him, Gertrudis said quietly, 'No. Let it pass. We must pretend we haven't heard. We must make a world here in which we never speak of such things even to condemn them.'

Once, she heard someone say of another woman who was unmarried that she would end up an old maid, one of those pious old spinsters who 'helped clothe the saints' statues' in church.[16] Gertrudis added 'or clothed children's souls'.

'Tulita is my sweetheart', little Ramiro said once.
'Don't be silly; Tulita is your sister.'

–¿Y no puede ser novia y hermana?
–No.
–¿Y qué es ser hermana?
–¿Ser hermana? Ser hermana es...
–Vivir en la misma casa – acabó la niña.

Un día llegó la niña llorando y mostrando un dedo en que le había picado una abeja. Lo primero que se le ocurrió a la tía fue ver si con su boca, chupándoselo, podía extraerle el veneno como había leído que se hace con el de ciertas culebras. Luego declararon los niños, y se les unió el padre, que no dejarían viva a ninguna de las abejas que venían al jardín, que las perseguirían a muerte.

–No, eso sí que no –exclamó Gertrudis–; a las abejas no las toca nadie.

–¿Por qué? ¿Por la miel? –preguntó Ramiro.

–No las toca nadie, he dicho.

–Pero si no son madres, Gertrudis.

–Lo sé, lo sé bien. He leído en uno de esos libros tuyos lo que son las abejas, lo he leído. Sé lo que son las abejas estas, las que, pican y hacen la miel; sé lo que es la reina y sé también lo que son los zánganos.

–Los zánganos somos nosotros, los hombres.

–¡Claro está!

–Pues mira, voy a meterme en política; me van a presentar candidato a diputado provincial.

–¿De veras? –preguntó Gertrudis, sin poder disimular su alegría.

–¿Tanto te place?

–Todo lo que te distraiga.

–Faltan once meses, Gertrudis...

–¿Para qué?, ¿para la elección?

–¡Para la elección, sí!

'Can't she be my sweetheart and my sister?'

'No.'

'What does being a sister mean then?'

'Being a sister? It means…'

'Living in the same house,' said the little girl, finishing Gertrudis's sentence.

One day the little girl came in crying, holding out a finger that had been stung by a bee. The first thing that occurred to her aunt was to see if she could suck out the poisonous sting, as she had read one could do with certain snakebites. Then the children, joined by their father, declared that they would not spare the life of a single bee coming into the garden: they would pursue them all to the death.

'No, no!' cried Gertrudis, 'no-one must lay a finger on the bees!'

'Why? Because of the honey?' asked Ramiro.

'I've said no-one must touch the bees.'

'But they are not mothers, Gertrudis.'

'I know, I know that. I've read in one of your books what bees are, I've read all about it. I know about bees, the ones that sting and that make the honey; I know about the queen and I know what drones are.'

'The drones are us, us men.'

'I know!'

'Well then, prepare to be surprised: I'm going into politics! I am going to be put forward for the provincial council.'

'Really?', asked Gertrudis, unable to conceal her happiness.

'Do you really like the idea that much?'

'I like anything that distracts you.'

'There are eleven months left, Gertrudis…!'

'Eleven months till what, the election?'

'Yes, that's right … when the choice has to be made!.'[17]

X

Y era lo cierto que en el alma cerrada de Gertrudis se estaba desencadenando una brava galerna. Su cabeza reñía con su corazón, y ambos, corazón y cabeza, reñían en ella con algo más ahincado, más entrañado, más íntimo, con algo que era como el tuétano de los huesos de su espíritu.

A solas, cuando Ramiro estaba ausente del hogar, cogía al hijo de éste y de Rosa, a Ramirín, al que llamaba su hijo, y se lo apretaba al seno virgen, palpitante de congoja y henchido de zozobra. Y otras veces se quedaba contemplando el retrato de la que fue, de la que era todavía su hermana y como interrogándole si había querido, de veras, que ella, que Gertrudis, le sucediese en Ramiro. «Sí, me dijo que yo habría de llegar a ser la mujer de su hombre, su otra mujer – se decía –, pero no pudo querer eso, no, no pudo quererlo...; yo, en su caso, al menos, no lo habría querido, no podría haberlo querido... ¿De otra? ¡No, de otra no! Ni después de mi muerte... Ni de mi hermana... ¡De otra, no! No se puede ser más que de una... No, no pudo querer eso; no pudo querer que entre él, entre su hombre, entre el padre de sus hijos y yo se interpusiese su sombra... No pudo querer eso. Porque cuando él estuviese a mi lado, arrimado a mí, carne a carne, ¿quién me dice que no estuviese pensando en ella? Yo no sería sino el recuerdo... ¡algo peor que el recuerdo de la otra! No, lo que me pidió es que impida que sus hijos tengan madrastra. ¡Y lo impediré! Y casándome con Ramiro, entregándole mi cuerpo, y no sólo mi alma, no lo impediría... Porque entonces sí que sería madrastra. Y más si llegaba a darme hijos de mi carne y de mi sangre...» Y esto de los hijos de la carne hacía palpitar de sagrado terror el tuétano de los huesos del alma de Gertrudis, que era toda maternidad, pero maternidad de espíritu.

Y encerrábase en su cuarto, en su recatada alcoba, a llorar al pie de una imagen de la Santísima Virgen Madre, a llorar mientras susurraba: «el fruto de tu vientre...».

Una vez que tenía apretado a su seno a Ramirín, éste le dijo:

X

What *was* true was that a strong current had been unleashed in Gertrudis's sealed-off soul. Her head was battling with her heart, and both head and heart were battling inside her with something even more pressing, deeper and more intimate: something like the very marrow of her soul.

When Ramiro was out and she found herself alone, she would pick up Ramiro and Rosa's son, little Ramiro, whom she referred to as her child, and would press him to her virgin breast, burning with anguish, greatly distressed. At other times she would gaze for long periods at the portrait of the woman who had been and still was her sister, as if to ask her whether she had really wanted Gertrudis to take her place with Ramiro. 'Yes, she told me that I was to become wife to her husband, to become his other wife, but she couldn't really have wanted that, surely she couldn't have wanted that… In her situation, that's not what I would have wanted in any case; no, I wouldn't be capable of desiring that … for him to be husband to another woman? Another woman's husband?… Never! Not even after my death, not even if it were my sister … another woman's husband?… No! A man can only belong to one woman … no, she couldn't have wanted that. She couldn't have wanted her shadow to be in the middle between him – the man that belonged to her, the father of their children – and me … she couldn't have wanted that. Because let's suppose that if he were at my side, right next to me, flesh touching flesh, who could say that he wouldn't be thinking of her? I would just be the memory – or something even worse than the memory – of the other woman! No, what she asked of me was that her children should not have a stepmother. And I will not allow that to happen! Marrying Ramiro, giving him my body, and not just my soul, would not prevent that from happening … because then *I* would be the stepmother. And even more so if then he gave me children of my own flesh and blood.' And the thought of flesh-and-blood children made the bones of Gertrudis's soul tremble with sacred terror, because although she was very maternal, it was an entirely spiritual maternity.

And she would lock herself in her room, her modest bedroom, and weep at the foot of the image of the Blessed Virgin Mary, sobbing as she whispered 'the fruit of thy womb'.[18]

One day as she was clutching little Ramiro to her breast, the little boy asked,

–¿Por qué lloras, mamita? –pues habíale enseñado a llamarla así.
–Si no lloro...
–Sí, lloras...
–¿Pero es que me ves llorar...?
–No, pero te siento que lloras... Estás llorando...
–Es que me acuerdo de tu madre...
–¿Pues no dices que lo eres tú...?
–Sí, pero de la otra, de mamá Rosa.
–¡Ah, sí!; la que se murió... la de papá...
–¡Sí la de papá!
–¿Y por qué papá nos dice que no te llamemos mamá, sino tía, tiíta Tula, y tú nos dices que te llamemos mamá y no tía, tiíta Tula...?
–Pero ¿es que papá os dice eso?
–Sí, nos ha dicho que todavía no eras nuestra mamá, que todavía no eres más que nuestra tía...
–¿Todavía?
–Sí, nos ha dicho que todavía no eres nuestra mamá, pero que lo serás... Sí, que vas a ser nuestra mamá cuando pasen unos meses...
«Entonces sería vuestra madrastra», pensó Gertrudis, pero no se atrevió a desnudar este pensamiento pecaminoso ante el niño.
–Bueno, mira, no hagas caso de esas cosas, hijo mío...
Y cuando luego llegó Ramiro, el padre, le llamó aparte y severamente le dijo:
–No andes diciéndole al niño esas cosas. No le digas que yo no soy todavía más que su tía, la tía Tula, y que seré su mamá. Eso es corromperle, eso es abrirle los ojos sobre cosas que no debe ver. Y si lo haces por influir con él sobre mí, si lo haces por moverme...
–Me dijiste que te tomabas un plazo...
–Bueno, si lo haces por eso piensa en el papel que haces hacer a tu hijo, un papel de...
–¡Bueno, calla!
–Las palabras no me asustan, pero lo callaré. Y tú piensa en Rosa, recuerda a Rosa, ¡tu primer... amor!
–¡Tula!
–Basta. Y no busques madrastra para tus hijos, que tienen madre.

'Why are you crying mamita?' ('mamita' was what she had taught him to call her).

'I'm not crying.'

'Yes you are.'

'Do you see any tears?'

'No, but I can feel you crying … you are crying…'

'I'm thinking of your mother…'

'But didn't you say that *you* were our mother?'

'Yes, but I was thinking of your other mother, mama Rosa.'

'Oh yes, the one that died, the one that belonged to papa.'

'That's right, the one that belonged to papa.'

'Why does papa tell us not to call you mama but aunt, auntie Tula, when you tell us to call you mama and not aunt or auntie Tula?'

'Has your papa really told you that?'

'Yes, he told us that you are not our mama yet, that you are still just our aunt…'

'Not *yet* your mother?'

'Yes. He said that you were not yet our mama, but that you will be… Yes, that's right, that you'll be our mama in a few months' time.'

'Then I would be your stepmother', thought Gertrudis, but she did not dare to unveil this sinful thought in front of the child.

'Well now, never mind about that, my child.'

And when Ramiro returned, she took him to one side, and said severely to him,

'Don't go saying things like that to the child. Don't tell him that I am still only his aunt, aunt Tula, but that I'll become his mama. That is to corrupt him, and to open his eyes to things he should not see. And if you are doing it to try and influence me through him, or if you are doing it to move me…'

'You told me that you were going to think about the matter…'

'Well if *that's* why you are doing this, think of the role you are making your son play, the role of…'[19]

'All right, say no more!'

'Words don't frighten me, but I shall keep quiet about it. And you should think about Rosa, and remember her … your first … love!'

'Tula.'

'That's enough. And don't go looking for a stepmother for your children … they already have a mother.'

XI

«Esto necesita campo», se dijo Gertrudis, e indicó a Ramiro la conveniencia de que todos ellos se fuesen a veranear a un pueblecito costero que tuviese montaña, dominando al mar y por éste dominada. Buscó un lugar que no fuese muy de moda, pero donde Ramiro pudiese encontrar compañeros de tresillo, pues tampoco le quería obligado a la continua compañía de los suyos. Era un género de soledad a que Gertrudis temía.

Allí todos los días salían de paseo, por la montaña, dando vista al mar, entre madroñales, ellos dos, Gertrudis y Ramiro, y los tres niños: Ramirín, Rosita y Elvira. Jamás, ni aun allí donde no los conocían –es decir, allí menos –, se hubiese arriesgado Gertrudis a salir de paseo con su cuñado, solos los dos. Al llegar a un punto en que un tronco tendido en tierra, junto al sendero, ofrecía, a modo de banco rústico, asiento, sentábanse en él ellos dos, cara al mar, mientras los niños jugaban allí cerca, lo más cerca posible. Una vez en que Ramiro quiso que se sentaran en el suelo, sobre la yerba montañesa, Gertrudis le contestó: «¡No, en el suelo, no! Yo no me siento en el suelo, sobre la tierra, y menos junto a ti y ante los niños...» « Pero si el suelo está limpio... si hay yerba...» « ¡Te he dicho que no me siento así!» «No, la postura no es cómoda...» «¡Peor que incómoda!»

Desde aquel tronco, mirando al mar, hablaban de mil nonadas, pues en cuanto el hombre deslizaba la conversación a senderos de lo por pacto tácito ya vedado de hablar entre ellos, la tía tenía en la boca un «¡Ramirín!» o «¡Rosita!» o «¡Elvira!». Le hablaba ella del mar y eran sus palabras, que le llegaban a él envueltas en el rumor no lejano de las olas, como la letra vaga de un canto de cuna para el alma. Gertrudis estaba brizando la pasión de Ramiro para adormecérsela. No le miraba casi nunca entonces, miraba al mar; pero en él, en el mar, veía reflejada por misterioso modo la mirada del hombre. El mar purísimo les unía las miradas y las almas.

XI

'We all need a change of air', Gertrudis told herself, and she managed to persuade Ramiro that the whole family would benefit from spending the summer holiday in a little coastal village in the mountains. It was a village that overlooked the sea, and that was in its turn overlooked by its own mountain. She looked for a place that was not too fashionable and so therefore not full of acquaintances, but somewhere that Ramiro would still be able to find agreeable male company to play cards with. After all, she didn't want him to have to deal with the constant enforced presence of his own family. That was a kind of loneliness that made Gertrudis fearful.

Every day, they would go for a walk along the mountainside that overlooked the sea, amongst the strawberry trees. There were the two of them, Gertrudis and Ramiro, and the three children: little Ramiro, Rosita and Elvira. Never, not even in a place where they would pass unrecognised – in fact still less in that case – would Gertrudis have risked going for a walk with just her brother-in-law for company. When they came to a place where a felled tree trunk served as a kind of rustic bench, the two of them would sit down, facing the sea, while the children played nearby – as close as possible. Once, when Ramiro wanted them to sit on the ground, on the mountain grass, Gertrudis answered, 'No, not on the ground! I won't sit on the ground, on the earth, and even less so by your side and in front of the children...' 'But the ground is clean ... it's all grass...' 'I've told you that I won't sit like that. It doesn't feel comfortable... It's worse than uncomfortable...'

Sitting on that tree trunk, looking across at the sea, they would chat about any number of trivial things. As soon as the man steered the conversation along paths that had tacitly been deemed out of bounds, the aunt would always be quick to call out a 'Little Ramiro!' or a 'Rosita' or 'Elvira!' She would speak to him of the sea, and her words, which came to him enveloped in the nearby sound of the waves, wafted over to him like the vague lyrics of a lullaby for the soul. Gertrudis was lulling Ramiro's passion to sleep. She would almost never look at him during these talks; she would look out at the sea. But in some mysterious way, the sea would reflect back the man's gaze. The sea, so clean and pure, joined their gazes and their souls.

Otras veces íbanse al bosque, a un castañar, y allí tenía ella que vigilarle, vigilarse y vigilar a los niños con más cuidado. Y también allí encontró el tronco derribado que le sirviese de asiento.

Quería atemperarle a una vida de familia purísima y campesina, hacer que se acostase cansado de luz y de aire libres, que se durmiese, oyendo fuera al grillo, para dormir sin ensueños, que le despertase el canto del gallo y el trajineo de los campesinos y los marineros.

Por las mañanas bajaban a una pequeña playa, donde se reunía la pequeña colonia veraniega. Los niños, descalzos, entreteníanse, después del baño, en desviar con los pies el curso de un pequeño arroyuelo vagabundo e indeciso que por la arena desaguaba en el mar. Ramiro se unió alguna vez a este juego de los niños.

Pero Gertrudis empezó a temer. Se había equivocado en sus precauciones. Ramiro huía del tresillo con sus compañeros de colonia veraniega y parecía espiar más que nunca la ocasión de hallarse a solas con su cuñada. La casita que habitaban tenía más de tienda de gitanos trashumantes que de otra cosa. El campo, en vez de adormecer no la pasión, el deseo de Ramiro, parecía como si lo excitase más, y ella misma, Gertrudis, empezó a sentirse desasosegada. La vida se les ofrecía más al desnudo en aquellos campos, en el bosque, en los repliegues de la montaña. Y luego había los animales domésticos, los que cría el hombre, con los que era mayor allí la convivencia. Gertrudis sufría al ver la atención con que los pequeños, sus sobrinos, seguían los juegos del averío. No, el campo no rendía una lección de pureza. Lo puro allí era hundir la mirada en el mar. Y aun el mar... La brisa marina les llegaba como un aguijón.

–¡Mira qué hermosura! – exclamó Gertrudis una tarde, al ocaso, en que estaban sentados frente al mar.

Era la luna llena, roja sobre su palidez, que surgía de las olas como una flor gigantesca y solitaria en un yermo palpitante.

–¿Por qué le habrán cantado tanto a la luna los poetas? – dijo Ramiro–; ¿por qué será la luz romántica y de los enamorados?

–No lo sé, pero se me ocurre que es la única tierra, porque es una tierra...

At other times, they would go into the woods, to a chestnut grove, and there she would have to keep a more careful eye on him, on herself and on the children. And there too she found a felled tree trunk that could serve as a seat.

She wanted to reconcile him to a pure, rural way of life, so that he would go to bed tired by the luminosity and the fresh air, and fall asleep to the sound of the crickets outside, and so that he would fall into a dreamless slumber, to be woken only by the cock crowing and the comings and goings of the country folk and the sailors.

In the mornings, they would go to a beach where the holidaymakers congregated. After bathing, the children would amuse themselves by using their bare feet to divert the course of a lazy winding stream that snaked down the beach towards the sea. Sometimes Ramiro joined in the children's game.

But Gertrudis began to be fearful. Her precautions had not been successful. Ramiro spurned the games of cards with his fellow holidaymakers, and seemed increasingly to seek out the opportunity to be alone with his sister-in-law. The little house they were living in was more like a gypsy camp than anything else. And the countryside, rather than quieting Ramiro's passion – or rather his desire, seemed to excite it more. Gertrudis started to feel uneasy. Life seemed to offer itself in a more naked state in those fields, in the woods, in the folds of the mountain. And then there were the animals, those domesticated by man: coexistence with them was more intimate in the countryside. Gertrudis did not like to see how closely the children followed the games of the birds in the aviary. No, the countryside was no classroom of purity. Purity there lay in looking into the depths of the sea. But even the sea … the sea breeze had a sting to it.

'Look, how beautiful!', exclaimed Gertrudis one evening, as the sun set while they sat looking out to sea.

She was referring to the full moon, its pallor tinged with red as it rose from the distant waves like a huge solitary flower growing in the midst of a barren patch of land.

'Why have poets hymned so many verses to the moon?', asked Ramiro. 'And why is moonlight considered romantic, something proper to lovers?'

'I don't know, but it occurs to me that it is the only planet that we can

que vemos sabiendo que nunca llegaremos a ella... es lo inaccesible... El
sol no, el sol nos rechaza; gustamos de bañarnos en su luz, pero sabemos
que es inhabitable, que en él nos quemaríamos, mientras que en la luna
creemos que se podría vivir y en paz y crepúsculo eternos, sin tormentas,
pues no la vemos cambiar, pero sentimos que no se puede llegar a ella...
Es lo intangible...

–Y siempre nos da la misma cara... esa cara tan triste y tan seria... es
decir, siempre ¡no!, porque la va velando poco a poco y la oscurece del
todo y otras veces parece una hoz...

–Sí –y al decirlo parecía como que Gertrudis seguía sus propios
pensamientos sin oír los de su compañero, aunque no era así–; siempre
enseña la misma cara porque es constante, es fiel. No sabemos cómo será
por el otro lado..., cuál será su otra cara...

–Y eso añade a su misterio...

–Puede ser... puede ser... Me explico que alguien anhele llegar a la
luna... ¡lo imposible!... para ver cómo es por el otro lado... para conocer
y explorar su otra cara...

–La oscura...

–¿La oscura? ¡Me parece que no! Ahora que ésta que vemos está
iluminada la otra estará a oscuras, pero o yo sé poco de estas cosas o
cuando esta cara se oscurece del todo, en luna nueva, está en luz por el
otro, es luna llena de la otra parte...

–¿Para quién?

–¿Cómo para quién?

–Sí, que cuando el otro lado alumbra, ¿para quién?

–Para el cielo, y basta. ¿O es que a la luna la hizo Dios no más que para
alumbrarnos de noche a nosotros, los de la tierra? ¿O para que hablemos
estas tonterías?

–Pues bien, mira, Tula...

–¡Rosita!

Y no le dejó comentar la intangibilidad y la plenitud de la luna.

Cuando ella habló de volver ya a la ciudad apresuróse él a aceptarlo.
Aquella temporada en el campo, entre la montaña y el mar, había sido
estéril para sus propósitos. «Me he equivocado – se decía también él – ;

see and yet know that we will never reach ... it represents the inaccessible. It's not like the sun; the sun rebuffs us. We like to bathe in its light, but we know that it is uninhabitable, and that we would burn to death in it, whereas we believe that we could live on the moon, in eternal peace and twilight, with no storms, because we never see it change, but we sense that it's impossible to reach. It represents the intangible...

'And we always see the same side ... like a sad and serious face ... well, actually it's not always the same ... because it becomes eclipsed and then disappears completely, while at other times it looks just like the blade of a scythe.'

'Yes...', and as she spoke, it seemed as though Gertrudis was following the train of her own thoughts without listening to those of her companion – although that was not the case. 'It always shows the same side because it is constant and faithful. We don't know what its other side is like ... what its other side would be.'

'And that adds to its mystery.'

'Perhaps ... perhaps... The way I see it, one might yearn to go to the moon – the impossible – to see what it's like on the other side ... to discover and explore its other side...'

'The dark side...'

'The dark side? I don't think so! Now that the side that we can see is illuminated, the other side will be in darkness, perhaps I don't know enough about these things, but when this side is completely dark, at the new moon, the other side is surely bright: it's a full moon elsewhere.'

'But for whom?'

'What do you mean "for whom"?'

'Well, for whom is the other side shining?'

'For heaven, and that's that. Or did God make the moon just to light the way at night for us on earth? Or perhaps for us to be spouting this nonsense?'

'Well now, Tula...'

'Rosita!'

And Gertrudis allowed no further discussion of the fullness, yet intangibility, of the moon.

When she mentioned the possibility of returning early to the city, he quickly agreed. That period in the countryside, between the mountain and the sea, had been fruitless as far as his purposes were concerned. 'I

aquí está más segura que allí, que en casa; aquí parece embozarse en la montaña, en el bosque, y como si el mar le sirviese de escudo; aquí es tan intangible como la luna, y entre tanto este aire de salina filtrado por entre rayos de sol enciende la sangre... y ella me parece aquí fuera de su ámbito y como si temiese algo; vive alerta y diríase que no duerme...» Y ella a su vez se decía: «No, la pureza no es del campo, la pureza es de celda, de claustro y de ciudad; la pureza se desarrolla entre gentes que se unen en mazorcas de viviendas para mejor aislarse; la ciudad es monasterio, convento de solitarios; aquí la tierra, sobre que casi se acuestan, las une y los animales son otras tantas serpientes del paraíso... ¡A la ciudad, a la ciudad!»

En la ciudad estaba su convento, su hogar, y en él su celda. Y allí adormecería mejor a su cuñado. ¡Oh!, si pudiese decir de él – pensaba – lo que santa Teresa en una carta – Gertrudis leía mucho a santa Teresa – decía de su cuñado don Juan de Ovalle, marido de doña Juana de Ahumada. «Él es de condición en cosas muy aniñado...» ¿Cómo le aniñaría?

was wrong' – he said to himself – 'she is more sure of herself here than back there, at home. Here she seems to cloak herself in the mountain, in the woods, and it's as if the sea acted as a shield to her too. Here she is as intangible as the moon, and meanwhile this sun and sea air inflame one's feelings... She seems out of her element, as if she was fearful of something. She's always on the alert and doesn't seem to sleep...' And she in turn said to herself 'No, the countryside's not pure ... purity is to be found in the cell, the cloister and the city; purity develops amongst people who come together in lines of houses the better to isolate themselves; the city is a monastery, a convent for the solitary; here, the earth, on which people practically have to lie directly, brings them together, and the animals are so many serpents in paradise... To the city! To the city!' The city was her convent, her home, and within it her cell. And there she would better dampen down the desires of her brother-in-law. 'Oh, if only I could say of him', she thought, 'what St Teresa' – Gertrudis often read St Teresa – 'said of her brother-in-law, don Juan de Ovalle, husband to doña Juana de Ahumada: "He is very childlike in certain matters".' How could she make Ramiro childlike?

XII

Al fin Gertrudis no pudo con su soledad y decidió llevar su congoja al padre Alvarez, su confesor, pero no su director espiritual. Porque esta mujer había rehuído siempre ser dirigida, y menos por un hombre. Sus normas de conducta moral, sus convicciones y creencias religiosas se las había formado ella con lo que oía a su alrededor y con lo que leía, pero las interpretaba a su modo. Su pobre tío, don Primitivo, el sacerdote ingenuo que las había criado a las dos hermanas y les enseñó el catecismo de la doctrina cristiana explicado según *el Mazo,* sintió siempre un profundo respeto por la inteligencia de su sobrina Tula, a la que admiraba. «Si te hicieses monja – solía decirle – llegarías a ser otra santa Teresa... Qué cosas se te ocurren, hija ...» Y otras veces: «Me parece que eso que dices, Tulilla, huele un poco a herejía; ¡hum! No lo sé... no lo sé.... porque no es posible que te inspire herejías el ángel de tu guarda, pero eso me suena así como a... qué sé yo ...» Y ella le contestaba riendo: «Sí, tío, son tonterías que se me ocurren, y ya que dice usted que huele a herejía no lo volveré a pensar.» Pero ¿quién pone barreras al pensamiento?

Gertrudis se sintió siempre sola. Es decir, sola para que la ayudaran, porque para ayudar ella a los otros no, no estaba sola. Era como una huérfana cargada de hijos. Ella sería el báculo de todos los que la rodearan; pero si sus piernas flaquearan, si su cabeza no le mantuviese firme en su sendero, si su corazón empezaba a bambolear y enflaquecer, ¿quién la sostendría a ella?, ¿quién sería su báculo? Porque ella, tan henchida del sentimiento, de la pasión mejor, de la maternidad, no sentía la filialidad. «¿No es esto orgullo?», se preguntaba.

No pudo al fin con esta soledad y decidió llevar a su confesor, al padre Álvarez, su congoja. Y le contó la declaración y proposición de Ramiro, y hasta lo que les había dicho a los niños de que no le llamasen a ella todavía madre, y las razones que tenía para mantener la pureza de aquel hogar y cómo no quería entregarse a hombre alguno, sino reservarse para mejor consagrarse a los hijos de Rosa.

–Pero lo de su cuñado lo encuentro muy natural – arguyó el buen padre de almas.

XII

In the end, Gertrudis's loneliness got the better of her, and she decided to share her anguish with Father Alvarez. He was her confessor, but not her spiritual director: this woman had always shied away from being led, especially by a man. She had forged her standards of moral conduct, her convictions and religious beliefs out of what she heard around her and what she read, interpreting them in her own way. Her poor uncle, don Primitivo, the innocent priest who had brought up the two sisters and had taught them Mazo's Catechism[20] of Christian doctrine, had always felt a profound respect for the intellect of his niece Tula, which he admired greatly. 'If you became a nun', he used to say to her, 'you'd make another St Teresa... The things you think of, child!' At other times, he would say 'I think what you've said might be a little heretical ... hmmm ... I don't know... I'm not sure ... it's surely not possible that your guardian angel would incite you to heresy, but that doesn't sound ... oh, I don't know!' Laughing, she would reply, 'Uncle, it's just nonsense that comes into my head, and now that you've said it may have a heretical ring, I won't think about it anymore.' But who erects barriers against thought?

Gertrudis always felt alone. That is to say, she felt alone in the sense of having no-one to help her; she on the other hand was never slow to help others, and never felt alone or lonely in that sense. She was like an orphan with many children. She supported all those around her, but if her step faltered, or if her gaze wavered from the correct path, or if her heart began to palpitate or give way, who would support her? Who would be her shoulder to lean on? Although she was so full of maternal feeling – or rather maternal *passion* – she had no feeling of filiality, of 'daughterliness'. 'Isn't that a sin of pride?', she would ask herself.

Gertrudis's loneliness overcame her, and she decided to take her anguish to Father Alvarez. She told him of Ramiro's declaration, his proposal, and even of what he had said to the children about not calling her 'mother' yet; she told him why she wanted to maintain the purity of their home, and how she did not want to give herself to any man, wanting instead to reserve herself in order better to devote herself to Rosa's children.

'But I find your brother-in-law's position entirely natural', argued the good spiritual father.

–Es que no se trata ahora de mi cuñado, padre, sino de mí; y no creo que haya acudido a usted también en busca de alianza...

–¡No, no, hija, no!

–Como dicen que en los confesonarios se confeccionan bodas y que ustedes, los padres, se dedican a casamenteros...

–Yo lo único que digo ahora, hija, es que es muy natural que su cuñado, viudo y joven y fuerte, quiera volver a casarse, y más natural, y hasta santo, que busque otra madre para sus hijos...

–¿Otra? ¡Ya la tiene!

–Sí; pero... y si esta se va...

–¿Irme? ¿Yo? Estoy tan obligada a esos niños como estaría su madre de carne y sangre si viviese...

–Y luego eso da que hablar…

–De lo que hablen, padre, ya le he dicho que nada se me da...

–¿Y si lo hiciese precisamente por eso, porque hablen? Examínese y mire si no entra en ello un deseo de afrontar las preocupaciones ajenas, de desafiar la opinión pública...

–Y si así fuese, ¿qué?

–Que eso sí que es pecaminoso. Y después de todo, la cuestión es otra...

–¿Cuál es la cuestión?

–La cuestión es si usted le quiere o no. Esta es la cuestión. ¿Le quiere usted, sí o no?

–¡Para marido..., no!

–Pero ¿le rechaza?

–¡Rechazarle... no!

–Si cuando se dirigió a su hermana, la difunta, se hubiera dirigido a usted...

–¡Padre! ¡Padre! – y su voz gemía.

–Sí, por ahí hay que verlo...

–¡Padre; que eso no es pecado...!

–Pero ahora se trata de dirección espiritual, de tomar consejo... Y sí, es pecado, es acaso pecado... Tal vez hay aquí unos viejos celos...

'But this is not about him now, Father, it's about me. And I didn't come here to ask your advice as a matchmaker...'

'No, no, of course not, my child!'

'You know what they say about the confessional: that you priests devote yourselves to making matches there...'

'The only thing I will say, my child, is that it's natural that your brother-in-law – a young, healthy widower, should want to remarry. And it's even more natural – indeed even saintly – that he should seek out another mother for his children.'

'*Another* one? He already has one!'

'Yes, but... if that one should leave...'

'Leave? Me? I'm as committed to those children as their own flesh-and-blood mother would be if she were still alive...'

'Well then that gives rise to talk...'

'I've told you before Father, I couldn't care less about what people say.'

'And what if you were doing it precisely because of that, so that people *would* talk? Examine your motives and consider whether a desire to confront other people's concerns and go against public opinion doesn't enter into this.'

'But even if that were the case, what would be wrong with that?'

'That would be sinful indeed. Anyway, the issue at hand is a different one.'

'What *is* the issue here?'

'Whether you love him or not. *That* is the question. Do you love him, yes or no?'

'As a potential husband, no!'

'So you're rejecting him?'

'Rejecting him?... No!'

'If instead of first approaching your sister, who has now passed away, he had approached you...'

'Father! Father!' she whimpered.

'Yes, that's how you have to see it.'

'Father! That is not a sin...!'

'But now it's a question of spiritual direction, of taking advice ... and yes, it is, perhaps, a sin ... perhaps there is some old jealousy at play here...'

–¡Padre!

–Hay que ahondar en ello. Acaso no le ha perdonado aún...

–Le he dicho, padre, que le quiero; pero no para marido. Le quiero como a un hermano, como a un más que hermano, como al padre de mis hijos, porque estos, sus hijos, lo son míos de lo más dentro mío, de todo mi corazón; pero para marido, no. Yo no puedo ocupar en su cama el sitio que ocupó mi hermana... Y sobre todo, yo no quiero, no debo darles madrastra a mis hijos...

–¿Madrastra?

–Sí, madrastra. Si yo me caso con él, con el padre de los hijos de mi corazón, les daré madrastra a éstos, y más si llego a tener hijos de carne y de sangre con él. Esto, ahora ya... ¡nunca!

–Ahora ya...

–Sí, ahora que ya tengo a los de mi corazón... mis hijos...

–Pero piense en él, en su cuñado, en su situación...

–¿Que piense...?

–¡Sí! ¿Y no tiene compasión de él?

–Sí que la tengo. Y por eso le ayudo y le sostengo. Es como otro hijo mío.

–Le ayuda... le sostiene...

–Sí, le ayudo y le sostengo a ser padre...

–A ser padre... a ser padre... Pero él es un hombre...

–¡Y yo una mujer!

–Es débil...

–¿Soy yo fuerte?

–Más de lo debido.

–¿Más de lo debido? ¿Y lo de la mujer fuerte?

–Es que esa fortaleza, hija mía, puede alguna vez ser dureza, ser crueldad. Y es dura con él, muy dura. ¿Que no le quiere como a marido? ¡Y qué importa! Ni hace falta eso para casarse con un hombre. Muchas veces tiene que casarse una mujer con un hombre por compasión, por no dejarle solo, por salvarle, por salvar su alma...

–Pero si no le dejo solo...

'Father!'

'We have to delve into this. Perhaps you haven't yet forgiven him...'

'I've told you, father, that I love him, but not as a potential husband. I love him as a brother, as someone who is more than a brother, as the father of my children because they, his children, come from the very core of my being too, they are the offspring of my heart. I don't love him in the way a woman would love her husband. And I can't take the place of my sister in the marital bed... Above all, I don't want to – and I must not – become a stepmother to my children.'

'Stepmother?'

'Yes, stepmother. If I marry him, the father of my beloved children, I will be giving them over to a stepmother, all the more so if I then have children of my own flesh and blood with him. And that I could never do!'

'*Never* do...?'

'No, not now that I have the children born of my own heart ... my own children...'

'But think of *him*, your brother-in-law, think about his situation.'

'You want me to think of *him*...?'

'Yes! Don't you have any sympathy for him?'

'Yes, of course I do. That's why I help and support him. He's like another child of mine.'

'You help him ... you support him...'

'Yes, I support and help him to be a good father...'

'To be a father... But he's a *man*.'

'And I'm a woman!'

'He's weak...'

'And am I so strong?'

'Too strong by half.'

'Too strong by half? What about the ideal of the strong woman?'

'That kind of strength, my child, can sometimes be harshness or cruelty. And you are being hard – very hard – on him. So you don't love him as a potential husband!... What does that matter? You don't need to feel that kind of love in order to marry a man. Often a woman has to marry a man out of compassion, so that he won't be alone or lonely ... to save him, to save his soul...'

'But I don't allow him to be lonely.'

–Sí, sí, le deja solo. Y creo que me comprende sin que se lo explique más claro...

–Sí, sí que se lo comprendo, pero no quiero comprenderlo. No está solo. ¡Quien está sola soy yo! Sola...sola...siempre sola...

–Pero ya sabe aquello de «más vale casarse que abrasarse...»

–Pero si no me abraso...

–¿No se queja de su soledad?

–No es soledad de abrasarse; no es esa soledad a que usted, padre, alude. No, no es esa. No me abraso...

–¿Y si se abrasa él?

–Que se refresque en el cuidado y amor de sus hijos.

–Bueno, pero ya me entiende...

–Demasiado.

–Y por si no, le diré más claro aún que su cuñado corre peligro, y que si cae en él, le cabrá culpa.

–¿A mí?

–¡Claro está!

–No lo veo tan claro... Como no soy hombre...

–Me dijo que uno de sus temores de casarse con su cuñado era el de tener hijos con él, ¿no es así?

–Sí, así es. Si tuviéramos hijos llegaría yo a ser, quieras o no, madrastra de los que me dejó mi hermana.

–Pero el matrimonio no se instituyó sólo para hacer hijos...

–Para casar y dar gracia a los casados y que críen hijos para el cielo.

–Dar gracia a los casados... ¿Lo entiende?

–Apenas...

–Que vivan en gracia, libres de pecado...

–Ahora lo entiendo menos.

–Bueno, pues que es un remedio contra la sensualidad.

–¿Cómo? ¿Qué es eso? ¿Qué?

–Pero ¿por qué se pone así ...? ¿Por qué se altera ...?

–¿Qué es el remedio contra la sensualidad? ¿El matrimonio o la mujer?

'But you do ... you do. And I think you understand me well enough. I don't think I need to spell things out more plainly, do I?

'No, no, I understand. But at the same time I don't want to understand. He is not alone; I'm the one who is alone! Alone, always alone...'

'But you know the saying "it is better to marry than to burn"'[22]

'But I am not burning to death with passion...'

'Weren't you complaining about being on your own?'

'It's not that kind of loneliness ... it is not the kind of loneliness you are alluding to father, no ... it's not that... I am not burning with passion.'

'But what if *he* is?'

'Well, he can extinguish the fire in the care and love of his children...'

'Yes, but you know what I mean...'

'Only too well.'

'Just in case there is any lingering doubt, let me make it clearer still: your brother-in-law is at risk, and if he falls into danger, you will bear some of the responsibility...'

'*Me?*'

'Naturally!'

'I don't see it as clearly as that. As I'm not a man...'

'You told me that one of your fears about marrying your brother-in-law was having children with him, didn't you?'

'Yes, that's right. If we had children, I would become, like it or not, stepmother to the children my sister left me.'

'But marriage wasn't instituted just to create children...'

'To marry and allow the spouses to gain grace through the sacrament of marriage so that they may bring forth children that will attain heaven ... that's what the Catechism says...'

'To allow the spouses to gain grace ... do you understand what that means?'

'Not really.'

'That they should be in a state of grace, free from sin...'

'Now I understand you even less...'

'Well ... it's a remedy against sensuality.'

'What? What do you mean?'

'Why are you becoming agitated? Why is this upsetting you?'

'*What's* the remedy against sensuality: marriage or woman?'

–Los dos... La mujer... y... y el hombre.

–¡Pues, no, padre, no, no y no! Yo no puedo ser remedio contra nada. ¿Qué es eso de considerarme remedio? ¡Y remedio... contra eso! No, me estimo en más...

–Pero si es que...

–No, ya no sirve. Yo, si él no tuviera ya hijos de mi hermana, acaso me habría casado con él para tenerlos..., para tenerlos de él... pero ¿remedio? ¿Y a eso? ¿Yo remedio? ¡No!

–Y si antes de haber solicitado a su hermana la hubiera solicitado...

–¿A mí? ¿Antes? ¿Cuando nos conoció? No hablemos ya más, padre, que no podemos entendernos, pues veo que hablamos lenguas diferentes. Ni yo sé la de usted ni usted sabe la mía.

Y dicho esto, se levantó de junto al confesonario. Le costaba andar; tan doloridas le habían quedado del arrodillamiento las rodillas. Y a la vez le dolían las articulaciones del alma y sentía su soledad más hondamente que nunca. «¡No, no me entiende – se decía –, no me entiende; hombre al fin! Pero ¿me entiendo yo misma? ¿Es que me entiendo? ¿Le quiero o no le quiero? ¿No es soberbia esto? ¿No es la triste pasión solitaria del armiño, que por no mancharse no se echa a nado en un lodazal a salvar a su compañero ...? No lo sé.... no lo sé ...»

'Both ... woman ... and man...'

'Well then no, father, no, no and *no*! I will *not* be a remedy against anything! What *is* all this? See myself as a remedy? And a remedy ... against that! No, I think more of myself than that.'

'But...'

'No, it won't do! If he had not already had children with my sister, then perhaps I would have married him to have them ... to have them with him ... but a *remedy*? And against *that*? Me, a remedy? No!'

'And if he had proposed to you before proposing to your sister?'

'To me? Before my sister? When he first knew us? Let's not discuss this further, father, because we can't see eye to eye. I can see that we are speaking different languages. I don't speak yours and you don't speak mine.'

That said, she stood up and walked away from the confessional grille. She had difficulty walking, so sore were her joints from kneeling. By the same token, the joints of her soul also hurt, and she felt more alone than ever. 'No, he just doesn't understand me,' she said to herself, 'he doesn't understand me. He *is* a man after all! But do I understand myself? Do I? And do I love him or not? Isn't this about pride? Isn't this the solitary sad passion of the mink who, so as not to sully itself, won't swim across a quagmire to save its companion? I don't know..., I just don't know.'

XIII

Y de pronto observó Gertrudis que su cuñado era otro hombre, que celaba algún secreto, que andaba caviloso y desconfiado, que salía mucho de casa. Pero aquellas más largas ausencias del hogar no le engañaron. El secreto estaba en él, en el hogar. Y a fuerza de paciente astucia logró sorprender miradas de conocimiento íntimo entre Ramiro y la criada de servicio.

Era Manuela una hospiciana de diecinueve años, enfermiza y pálida, de un brillo febril en los ojos, de maneras sumisas y mansas, de muy pocas palabras, triste casi siempre. A ella, a Gertrudis, ante quien sin saber por qué temblaba, llamábale «señora». Ramiro quiso hacer que le llamase «señorita».

–No, llámame así, señora; nada de señorita...

En general parecía como que la criada le temiera, como avergonzada o amedrentada en su presencia. Y a los niños los evitaba y apenas si les dirigía la palabra. Ellos, por su parte, sentían una indiferencia, rayana en despego, hacia la Manuela. Y hasta alguna vez se burlaban de ella, por ciertas maneras de hablar, lo que la ponía de grana. «Lo extraño es – pensaba Gertrudis– que a pesar de todo no quiera irse... Tiene algo de gata esta mozuela.» Hasta que se percató de lo que podría haber escondido.

Un día logró sorprender a la pobre muchacha cuando salía del cuarto de Ramiro, del señorito –porque a éste sí que le llamaba así– toda encendida y jadeante. Cruzáronse las miradas y la criada rindió la suya. Pero llegó otro en que el niño, Ramirín, se fue a su tía y le dijo:

–Dime, mamá Tula, ¿es Manuela también hermana nuestra?

–Ya te tengo dicho que todos los hombres y mujeres somos hermanos.

–Sí, pero como nosotros, los que vivimos juntos...

–No, porque aunque vive aquí esta no es su casa...

XIII

Suddenly Gertrudis noticed that her brother-in-law had become a different man. He seemed to be hiding some kind of secret. He was brooding about something, and suspicious. He spent a lot of time out of the house. But these unusually long absences did not fool Gertrudis: she knew that the secret lay within the home. And thanks to her patience and astuteness she managed to catch an exchange of glances between Ramiro and the maid, Manuela – glances that implied an intimate relation.

Manuela was an orphan of about nineteen years of age, pale and sickly-looking, with a feverish glaze to her eyes. She was very gentle and submissive in her ways. She was a young woman of very few words, and was almost always sad. Without knowing quite why, she trembled in the presence of Gertrudis, whom she always addressed as 'señora'. Ramiro tried to make her call Gertrudis 'señorita'.

'No, call me "señora"; I'll have none of this "señorita" business'.

On the whole it seemed as though the maid were frightened of Gertrudis, as if she were embarrassed or intimidated in her presence. And she avoided the children, speaking to them only rarely. For their part, the children felt an indifference verging on mild dislike for the young woman they pejoratively referred to as 'La Manuela'. Sometimes they even laughed at her, because of the way she would say certain things, and that would make her blush. 'The strange thing,' thought Gertrudis, 'is that in spite of everything, she doesn't seem to want to leave ... that girl's like a cat that clings to the house it knows.' Or at least that is what she thought before she realised what Manuela might be hiding.

One day Gertrudis managed to surprise the poor girl leaving Ramiro's room – or the master's room, as that was how Manuela would refer to it – all flushed and out of breath. Their eyes met, and the maid submissively lowered her gaze. But another day came when little Ramiro asked his aunt,

'Mama Tula, is Manuela one of our sisters too?'

'I've told you more than once that all men and women are brothers and sisters.'

'No, but I mean like us, the ones who live together...'

'No, because although she lives here, this isn't her home...'

–¿Y cuál es su casa?

–¿Su casa? No lo quieras saber. ¿Y por qué preguntas eso?

–Porque le he visto a papá que la estaba besando...

Aquella noche, luego que hubieron acostado a los niños, dijo Gertrudis a Ramiro:

–Tenemos que hablar.

–Pero si aún faltan ocho meses...

–¿Ocho meses?

–¿No hace cuatro que me diste un año de plazo?

–No se trata de eso, hombre, sino de algo más serio.

A Ramiro se le paró el corazón y se puso pálido.

–¿Más serio?

–Más serio, sí. Se trata de tus hijos, de su buena crianza, y se trata de esa pobre hospiciana, de la que estoy segura que estás abusando.

–Y si así fuese, ¿quién tiene la culpa de eso?

–¿Y aún lo preguntas? ¿Aún querrás también culparme de ello?

–¡Claro que sí!

–Pues bien, Ramiro; se ha acabado ya aquello del año; no hay plazo ninguno; no puede ser, no puede ser. Y ahora sí que me voy, y, diga lo que dijere la ley, me llevaré a los niños conmigo, es decir, se irán conmigo.

–Pero ¿estás loca, Gertrudis?

–Quien está loco eres tú.

–Pero qué querías...

–Nada, o yo o ella. O me voy, o echas a esa criadita de casa.

Siguióse un congojoso silencio.

–No la puedo echar, Gertrudis, no la puedo echar. ¿Adónde se va? ¿Al hospicio otra vez?

–A servir a otra casa.

–No la puedo echar, Gertrudis, no la puedo echar –y el hombre rompió a llorar.

–¡Pobre hombre! –murmuró ella poniéndole la mano sobre la suya–. Me das pena.

–Ahora, ¿eh?, ¿ahora?

–Sí; me das lástima... Estoy ya dispuesta a todo...

'Where is her home?'

'Her home? You won't want to know about that. Why do you ask?'

'Because I saw daddy kissing her...'

That night, after they had put the children to bed, Gertrudis said to Ramiro,

'There's something we must discuss.'

'But there are still eight months to go...'

'Eight months to go?'

'Wasn't it four months ago that you said you were going to take a year to think over our situation?'

'I'm not referring to that; it's something more serious.'

Ramiro's heart stopped and he went pale.

'More serious?'

'Yes, more serious. It's about your children, about the way they should be brought up. And it's also about that poor workhouse orphan, who I'm convinced you're exploiting.'

'And if that were the case, whose fault would it be?'

'How can you ask that? Are you still trying to blame me for all this?'

'Naturally!'

'Well then Ramiro, you can forget about waiting for a year. That option is no longer possible. And now I really am going to leave, and, whatever the law may say, I'll take the children with me, or rather, they'll come with me.'

'Have you gone mad, Gertrudis?'

'*You're* the one who is mad.'

'But what did you expect?'

'Never mind that: it's either me or her. Either you throw that little maid out, or I'll leave.'

There was an anguished silence.

'I can't throw her out Gertrudis. I just can't. Where will she go? Back to the workhouse?'

'She can serve in another household.'

'I can't throw her out, Gertrudis, I can't.' And the man burst into tears.

'Poor man...!', she murmured, putting her hand on his. 'I feel sorry for you.'

'Now you feel sorry for me, eh? *Now*?'

'Yes, I feel sorry for you... I'm prepared to do anything...'

–¡Gertrudis! ¡Tula!

–Pero has dicho que no la puedes echar..

–Es verdad; no la puedo echar –y volvió a abatirse.

–¿Qué, pues?, ¿que no va sola?

–No, no irá sola.

–Los ocho meses del plazo, ¿eh?

–Estoy perdido, Tula, estoy perdido.

–No, la que está perdida es ella, la huérfana, la hospiciana; la sin amparo.

–Es verdad, es verdad...

–Pero no te aflijas así, Ramiro, que la cosa tiene fácil remedio.

–¿Remedio? ¿Y fácil? –y se atrevió a mirarle a la cara.

–Sí; casarte con ella.

Un rayo que le hubiese herido no le habría dejado más deshecho que esas palabras sencillas.

–¡Que me case! ¡Que me case con la criada! ¿Que me case con una hospiciana? ¡Y me lo dices tú!...

–¡Y quién si no había de decírtelo! Yo, la verdadera madre hoy de tus hijos.

–¿Que les dé madrastra?

–¡No, eso no!, que aquí estoy yo para seguir siendo su madre. Pero que des padre al que haya de ser tu nuevo hijo, y que le des madre también. Esa hospiciana tiene derecho a ser madre, tiene ya el deber de serlo, tiene derecho a su hijo, y al padre de su hijo.

–Pero Gertrudis...

–Cásate con ella, te he dicho; y te lo dice Rosa. Sí – y su voz, serena y pastosa, resonó como una campana –. Rosa, tu mujer, te dice por mi boca que te cases con la hospiciana. ¡Manuela!

–¡Señora! – se oyó como un gemido, y la pobre muchacha, que acurrucada junto al fogón, en la cocina, había estado oyéndolo todo, no se movió de su sitio. Volvió a llamarla, y después de otro «¡Señora!», tampoco se movió.

–Ven acá, o iré a traerte.

–¡Por Dios! –suplicó Ramiro.

'Gertrudis! Tula!'

'But you've said that you can't throw her out...'

'That's right; I can't throw her out,' he said, dispirited once more.

'So ... she won't be thrown out on her own?'

'No. Not on her own.'

'What about those eight months?'

'I'm done for, Tula, I'm a hopeless case.'

'No – the one who is done for is her – the orphan, the foundling – *she's* the defenceless one.'

'That's true – you're right of course.'

'But don't be so upset Ramiro, the situation is easily mended...'

'Mended? Easily?' and he dared to meet her gaze.

'Yes: you marry her.'

Being struck by a lightning bolt could not have left Ramiro more flattened than those simple words.

'Marry her? Marry the *maid*? Marry a foundling? And this coming from *you*?'

'Well who else would it come from? I am, after all, the true mother of your children at the moment.'

'Do you want them to have a stepmother?'

'No, certainly not! I am here, and will carry on being their mother. But you must be a father to your next child, and you must make sure it has a mother too. That foundling has a right to be a mother too – in fact she has the duty to be a mother – and she has the right to her child and to the father of that child.'

'But Gertrudis...'

'Marry her – I've told you, and Rosa is telling you the same. Yes, that's right,' she continued, and her serene tones were as rich and clear as a bell, 'your wife, Rosa, is telling you through me that you should marry the foundling. Manuela!'

'Señora!' The poor girl's voice sounded like a groan. She did not move from where she was sitting, curled up by the stove in the kitchen. She'd been listening to everything they had been saying. Gertrudis called her again, and although she was answered by another 'Señora!', the girl still did not move.

'Come here now before I have to come and fetch you.'

'For goodness sake', implored Ramiro.

La muchacha apareció cubriéndose la llorosa cara con las manos.

–Descubre la cara y míranos.

–¡No, señora, no!

–Sí, míranos. Aquí tienes a tu amo, a Ramiro, que te pide perdón por lo que de ti ha hecho.

–Perdón, yo, señora, y a usted...

–No, te pide perdón y se casará contigo.

–¡Pero señora! –clamó Manuela a la vez que Ramiro clamaba: «¡Pero Gertrudis!»

–Lo he dicho, se casará contigo; así lo quiere Rosa. No es posible dejarte así. Porque tú estás ya..., ¿no es eso?

–Creo que sí, señora; pero yo...

–No llores así ni hagas juramentos; sé que no es tuya la culpa...

–Pero se podría arreglar...

–Bien sabe aquí Manuela –dijo Ramiro– que nunca he pensado en abandonarla... Yo le colocaría...

–Sí, señora, sí; yo me contento...

–No, tú no debes contentarte con eso que ibas a decir. O mejor, aquí Ramiro no puede contentarse con eso. Tú te has criado en el hospicio, ¿no es eso?

–Sí, señora.

–Pues tu hijo no se criará en él. Tiene derecho a tener padre, a su padre, y le tendrá. Y ahora vete... vete a tu cuarto, y déjanos.

Y cuando quedaron Ramiro y ella a solas:

–Me parece que no dudarás ni un momento...

–¡Pero eso que pretendes es una locura, Gertrudis!

–La locura, peor que locura, la infamia, sería lo que pensabas.

–Consúltalo siquiera con el padre Álvarez.

–No lo necesito. Lo he consultado con Rosa.

–Pero si ella te dijo que no dieses madrastra a sus hijos...

–¿A sus hijos? ¡Y tuyos!

The girl appeared, her tearful face hidden in her hands.

'Take your face out of your hands and look at us.'

'No, señora, no!'

'Yes! Look at us! Here is your master, Ramiro, who would like to apologise for what he's done to you.'

'I'm the one who should be sorry, señora, and I'd like to apologise to you too...'

'No – he should be the one to apologise. He'll marry you.'

'But señora...', cried Manuela at the same time that Ramiro cried 'But Gertrudis...!'

'I've told you: he'll marry you. It's what Rosa wants. It's impossible to leave you like this. Because you *are* ... I think you do know what I'm referring to, don't you?'

'Yes, I think so señora, but I...'

'Don't weep like that or use vulgar language; I know it's not your fault.'

'But it can be fixed...'

'Manuela well knows,' said Ramiro, 'that I would never dream of abandoning her ... I'd find her a position...'

'Yes, señora, that is enough for me...'

'No: what you were about to say is not something that you should be content with. Or rather, Ramiro shouldn't be content to settle for that. You were brought up in the orphanage weren't you?'

'Yes, señora.'

'Well, your child will not grow up there. He or she has a right to have his or her own father, and that right will be honoured. Now, please leave us ... go to your room.'

And when Gertrudis and Ramiro were alone, she said,

'I can't countenance that you'll waver even for a second...'

'But what you're proposing is madness Gertrudis!'

'What *you* were thinking of was madness; no, worse than that, it was monstrous.'

'At least consult Father Alvarez about it.'

'I don't need to. I've consulted Rosa.'

'But she asked you to make sure that her children wouldn't have a stepmother...'

'*Her* children? They're yours too!'

–Bueno, sí, a nuestros hijos...

–Y no les daré madrastra. De ellos, de los nuestros, seguiré siendo yo la madre, pero del de ésa...

–Nadie le quitará de ser madre...

–Sí, tú si no te casas con ella. Eso no será ser madre...

–Pues ella...

–¿Y qué? ¿Porque ella no ha conocido a la suya pretendes tú que no lo sea como es debido?

–Pero fíjate en que esta chica...

–Tú eres quien debió fijarse...

–Es una locura... una locura...

–La locura ha sido antes. Y ahora piénsalo, que si no haces lo que debes el escándalo le daré yo. Lo sabrá todo el mundo.

–¡Gertrudis !

–Cásate con ella, y se acabó.

'Well, *our* children then…'

'And they won't. I'll continue to be the mother of *our* children, but hers…'

'No-one will take away her right to be a mother…'

'*You* will if you don't marry her. That wouldn't be being a mother…'

'But she…'

'What, because she didn't know her own mother you think it doesn't matter if we don't deal with this properly?'

'But think carefully … this girl…'

'You're the one who should be thinking about this carefully…'

'It's madness … madness…'

'The madness happened a while ago. And consider this: if you don't do what you have to do, *I* will make a scandal of it. The whole world will get to hear about it.'

'Gertrudis!'

'Marry her, and let that be an end to it.'

XIV

Una profunda tristeza henchía aquel hogar después del matrimonio de Ramiro con la hospiciana. Y ésta parecía aún más que antes la criada, la sirvienta, y más que nunca Gertrudis el ama de la casa. Y esforzábase ésta más que nunca por mantener al nuevo matrimonio apartado de los niños, y que estos se percataran lo menos posible de aquella convivencia íntima. Mas hubo que tomar otra criada y explicar a los pequeños el caso.

Pero, ¿cómo explicarles el que la antigua criada se sentara a la mesa a comer a los de casa? Porque esto exigió Gertrudis.

–Por Dios, señora – suplicaba la Manuela –, no me avergüence así..., mire que me avergüenza... Hacerme que me siente a la mesa con los señores, y sobre todo con los niños..., y que hable de tú al señorito..., ¡eso nunca!

–Háblale como quieras, pero es menester que los niños, a los que tanto temes, sepan que eres de la familia. Y ahora, una vez arreglado esto, no podrán ya sorprender intimidades a hurtadillas. Ahora os recataréis mejor. Porque antes el querer ocultaros de ellos os delataba.

La preñez de Manuela fue, en tanto, molestísima. Su fragilísima fábrica de cuerpo la soportaba muy mal. Y Gertrudis, por su parte, le recomendaba que ocultase a los niños lo anormal de su estado.

Ramiro vivía sumido en una resignada desesperación y más entregado que nunca al albedrío de Gertrudis.

–Sí, sí, bien lo comprendo ahora – decía –, no ha habido más remedio, pero...

–¿Te pesa? – le preguntaba Gertrudis.

–De haberme casado, ¡no! De haber tenido que volverme a casar, ¡sí!

–Ahora no es ya tiempo de pensar en eso; ¡pecho a la vida!

–¡Ah, si tú hubieras querido, Tula!

–Te di un año de plazo; ¿has sabido guardarlo?

–¿Y si lo hubiese guardado como tú querías, al fin de él qué, dime? Porque no me prometiste nada.

XIV

The household was filled with a profound sadness after Ramiro's marriage to the foundling. Manuela seemed more the maid than ever, and Gertrudis seemed more the lady of the house than ever. Gertrudis also had to put even more effort than before to keep the newlyweds away from the children, so they would be as little aware as possible of the intimacy of the new living arrangements. Nevertheless, she had to take on a new maid, and explain this new situation to the children. How could she explain to them that the old maid would now be eating with them all at the same table? This was a point that Gertrudis had insisted on.

'Please, señora…', Manuela implored, 'please don't embarrass me like this … I would feel so ashamed … sitting at the same table as the master and mistress of the house … and I'd feel even more ashamed sitting at the same table as the children… As for addressing the master as if he were my equal … no, I couldn't ever do that!'

'You can call Ramiro whatever you like, but it's essential that the children, whom you fear so much, know that you're part of the family now. Once that is resolved, they won't be able to surprise you in moments of furtive intimacy. Now you'll be more cautious, because previously, it was your desire to hide your relations that gave you both away.'

Meanwhile, Manuela's pregnancy was proving to be very difficult. The delicate production plant of her body didn't tolerate pregnancy at all well. As for Gertrudis, she advised Manuela to hide her 'interesting state' from the children.

Ramiro was plunged into a resigned desperation, and seemed more under Gertrudis's thumb than ever.

'Yes, I understand now,' he said 'I see that things had to be this way, but…'

'Are you sorry?' asked Gertrudis.

'Not to have married, no, but to have had to remarry, yes!'

'This is not the time to be thinking about that. We must all make the best of things!'

'If only you'd wanted to marry me, Tula.'

'I gave you a year to prove yourself: were you able to respect that?'

'What if I *had* respected it in the way that you wanted me to? What then? You never promised me anything, after all.'

–Aunque te hubiese prometido algo habría sido igual. No, habría sido peor aún.

En nuestras circunstancias, el haberte hecho una promesa, el haberte sólo pedido una dilación para nuestro enlace, habría sido peor.

–Pero si hubiese guardado la tregua, como tú querías que la guardase, dime:¿qué habrías hecho?

–No lo sé.

–Que no lo sabes..., Tula..., que no lo sabes...

–No, no lo sé; te digo que no lo sé.

–Pero tus sentimientos...

–Piensa ahora en tu mujer, que no sé si podrá soportar el trance en que la pusiste. ¡Es tan endeble la pobrecilla! Y está tan llena de miedo... Sigue asustada de ser tu mujer y ama de su casa.

Y cuando llegó el peligroso parto repitió Gertrudis las abnegaciones que en los partos de su hermana tuviera, y recogió al niño, una criatura menguada y debilísima, y fue quien lo enmantilló y quien se lo presentó a su padre.

–Aquí le tienes, hombre, aquí le tienes.

–¡Pobre criatura! – exclamó Ramiro, sintiendo que se le derretían de lástima las entrañas a la vista de aquel mezquino rollo de carne viviente y sufriente.

–Pues es tu hijo, un hijo más... Es un hijo más que nos llega.

–¿Nos llega? ¿También a ti?

–Sí, también a mí; no he de ser madrastra para él, yo que hago que no la tengan los otros.

Y así fue que no hizo distinción entre uno y otros.

–Eres una santa, Gertrudis – le decía Ramiro –, pero una santa que ha hecho pecadores.

–No digas eso; soy una pecadora que me esfuerzo por hacer santos, santos a tus hijos y a ti y a tu mujer.

–¡Mi mujer!...

–Tu mujer, sí; la madre de tu hijo. ¿Por qué le tratas con ese cariñoso despego y como a una carga?

–¿Y qué quieres que haga, que me enamore de ella?

–Pero ¿no lo estabas cuando la sedujiste?

–¿De quién? ¿De ella?

'Even if I'd made a promise to you, nothing would have changed ... no, actually, it would have been worse. In the circumstances we found ourselves in, my having made you a promise, or my just having asked for a delay before we went on to marry, would have been worse.'

'But what if I had kept to your conditions as you had wanted, what would you have done at the end of the period?'

'I don't know.'

'You don't know, Tula? You don't *know*?

'No. I'm telling you that I just don't know.'

'But what about your feelings...?

'You should be thinking now of your wife. I don't know whether she will be able to withstand the state you have put her in. The poor thing is so weak! And she is so scared. She is still frightened at the thought of being your wife and the lady of the house.'

When the perilous moment arrived, Gertrudis once again gave herself over entirely to assisting with the birth, and she was the first to gather up the terribly weak newborn creature. It was she, too, who wrapped him in a shawl, and presented him to his father.

'Here he is, here he is!'

'Poor little thing' Ramiro exclaimed, and felt himself melt with pity at the sight of that piteous little bundle of living, suffering flesh.

'Your son ... another child..., we have another child.'

'*We*? You're including yourself?'

'Yes! I am not going to be a stepmother to him; the others don't have a stepmother, and nor will this baby.'

And so it came to pass that no distinction was made between any of the children.

'You're a saint, Gertrudis,' Ramiro would say, 'but you're a saint who has made sinners of others.'

'Don't say that; I'm actually a sinner who tries her best to make saints – of your children, of you and of your wife.'

'My wife?'

'Your wife, yes: the mother of your son. Why do you treat her so coolly, as if she were a burden to you?'

'What do you want me to do? Fall in love with her?'

'But weren't you in love when you seduced her?'

'In love with whom? With her?'

–Ya lo sé, ya sé que no; pero lo merece la pobre...

–¡Pero si es la menor cantidad de mujer posible, si no es nada!

–No, hombre, no; es más, es mucho más de lo que tú te crees. Aún no las has conocido.

–Si es una esclava...

–Puede ser, pero debes libertarla. La pobre está asustada... nació asustada... Te aprovechaste de su susto...

–No sé, no sé cómo fue aquello...

–Así sois los hombres; no sabéis lo que hacéis ni pensáis en ello. Hacéis las cosas sin pensarlas...

–Peor es muchas veces pensarlas y no hacerlas...

–¿Por qué lo dices?

–No, nada; por nada...

–¿Tú crees sin duda que yo no hago más que pensar?

–No, no he dicho que crea eso...

–Sí, tú crees que yo no soy más que pensamiento...

'I know, I know you weren't, but the poor thing deserves it.'

'She is just a slip of a thing; there's nothing to her.'

'No, no, you're wrong; she's much more substantial than you think she is. You haven't even got to know her yet.'

'But she is a slave...'

'Maybe, but you should emancipate her ... the poor thing is frightened. She was born frightened ... you took advantage of her fear.'

'I don't know... I don't really know how it happened.'

'You men are all like that; you never know what you're doing, and you never think about what you do. You do things without thinking.'

'It's worse to think about things and not do them.'

'What makes you say that?'

'Oh, no reason, no reason...'

'No doubt you believe that I do nothing *but* think?

'No, I didn't say that...'

'You think I am nothing more than thought....'

XV

De nuevo la pobre Manuela, la hospiciana, la esclava, hallábase preñada.
Y Ramiro muy malhumorado con ello.
–Como si uno no tuviese bastante con los otros... – decía.
–¡Y yo qué quieres que le haga! – exclamaba la víctima.
–Después de todo, tú lo has querido así –concluía Gertrudis.
  Y luego, aparte, volvía a reprenderle por el trato de compasivo despego
que daba a su mujer. La cual soportaba esta preñez aún peor que la otra.
–Me temo por la pobre muchacha – vaticinó don Juan, el médico, un
viudo que menudeaba sus visitas.
–¿Cree usted que corre peligro? –le preguntó Gertrudis.
–Esta pobre chica está deshecha por dentro; es una tísica consumada
y consumida. Resistirá, es lo más probable, hasta dar a luz, pues la
Naturaleza, que es muy sabia...
–¡La Naturaleza, no! La Santísima Virgen Madre, don Juan – le
interrumpió Gertrudis.
–Como usted quiera; me rindo, como siempre, a su superior parecer.
Pues, como decía, la Naturaleza o la Virgen, que para mí es lo mismo...
–No, la Virgen es la Gracia...
–Bueno, pues la Naturaleza, la Virgen, la Gracia o lo que sea, hace
que en estos casos la madre se defienda y resista hasta que dé a luz al
nuevo ser. Ese inocente pequeñuelo le sirve a la pobre madre futura como
escudo contra la muerte.
–¿Y luego?
–¿Luego? Que probablemente tendrá usted que criar sola, sirviéndose
de un ama de cría, por supuesto, un crío más. Tiene ya cuatro; cargará
con cinco.
–Con todos los que Dios me mande.
–Y que probablemente, no digo que seguramente, a no tardar mucho,
don Ramiro volverá a quedar libre – y miró fijamente con sus ojillos
grises a Gertrudis.
–Y dispuesto a casarse tercera vez – agregó ésta haciéndose la
desentendida.

XV

Once again poor Manuela, the orphan, the slave, found herself pregnant. And Ramiro was very ill-tempered about it.

'As if one didn't have enough on one's plate with the others...', he said.

'What can *I* do about it?', exclaimed the victim.

'Well, this is the way you wanted things, after all', was Tula's judgement on Ramiro.

And then, when they were alone, Tula reproached him again for the pitying coolness with which he treated his wife. And she in turn was having an even worse pregnancy than the first.

'I fear for the poor girl', was the prognosis of don Juan, the doctor, a widower who visited the house frequently.

'Do you think she is in danger?', asked Gertrudis.

'Her insides are ruined; she is completely consumed by tuberculosis. In all likelihood she'll last out until she gives birth, after all Nature, who is very wise...'

'Not nature! The Blessed Virgin Mary, don Juan', Gertrudis interrupted.

'As you wish; I bow, as ever, to your superior wisdom. As I was saying, Nature, or the Virgin Mary, which for me are one and the same thing...'

'No, the Virgin Mary is Grace...'

'Well, Nature, the Virgin Mary, Grace or whatever it may be, usually arranges things so that the mother holds out until she gives birth to the new life. That innocent little thing acts as the mother-to-be's shield against death.

'And afterwards?'

'Afterwards? You'll probably have to bring up another baby alone, with the help of a wet nurse of course. You already have four; you'll have five on your hands.'

'I'll bring up all the children that God sends me.'

'And probably, although I'm not saying it's certain, before long don Ramiro will be a free agent again,' said don Juan, his small grey eyes giving Gertrudis a meaningful look.

'Ready to marry for a third time', Gertrudis added, as if she did not capture the intention of his remark.

–¡Eso sería ya heroico!

–Y usted, puesto que permanece viudo, y viudo sin hijos, es que no tiene madera de héroe.

–¡Ah, doña Gertrudis, si yo pudiese hablar!

–¡Pues cállese usted!

–Me callo.

Le tomó la mano, reteniéndosela un rato, y dándole con la otra suya unos golpecitos, añadió con un suspiro:

–Cada hombre es un mundo, Gertrudis.

–Y cada mujer, una luna, ¿no es eso, don Juan?

–Cada mujer puede ser un cielo.

«Este hombre me dedica un cortejo platónico», se dijo Gertrudis.

Cuando en la casa temían por la pobre Manuela y todos los cuidados eran para ella, cayó de pronto en cama Ramiro, declarándosele desde luego una pulmonía. La pobre hospiciana quedóse como atontada.

–Déjame a mí, Manuela – le dijo Gertrudis–; tú cuídate y cuida a lo que llevas contigo. No te empeñes en atender a tu marido, que eso puede agravarte.

–Pero yo debo...

–Tú debes cuidar de lo tuyo.

–Y mi marido, ¿no es mío?

–No, ahora no; ahora es tuyo tu hijo que está por venir.

La enfermedad de Ramiro se agravaba.

–Temo complicaciones al corazón – sentenció don Juan –. Le tiene débil; claro, ¡los pesares y disgustos!

–Pero ¿se morirá, don Juan? – preguntó henchida de angustia Gertrudis.

–Todo pudiera ser...

–Sálvele, don Juan, sálvele, como sea...

–Qué más quisiera yo...

–¡Ah, qué desgracia! ¡Qué desgracia! – y por primera vez se le vió a aquella mujer tener que sentarse y sufrir un desvanecimiento.

–Es, en efecto, terrible –dijo el médico en cuanto Gertrudis se repuso– dejar así cuatro hijos, ¿qué digo cuatro?, cinco se puede decir, ¡y esa pobre viuda tal como está!...

–Eso es lo de menos, don Juan; para todo eso me basto y me sobro yo. ¡Qué desgracia! ¡Qué desgracia!

'That *would* be heroic.'

'And you, a widower who has not remarried, and who has no children, don't have the mettle to be a hero.'

'Ah, Doña Gertrudis, if only I could speak!'

'If you cannot, please remain silent.'

'I shall do that.'

He took her hand, holding onto it for a good while, and gently tapping it with his other hand, he added with a sigh:

'Every man is a world of his own, Gertrudis.'

'And every woman a moon, is that it, don Juan?'

'Every woman could be a heaven.'

'This man is courting me platonically', Gertrudis noted to herself.

Just when all in the house were fearing for Manuela and caring for her, Ramiro suddenly had to take to his bed, ill. He was diagnosed with pneumonia. The poor orphan Manuela seemed bewildered.

'You leave things to me, Manuela,' said Gertrudis. 'Just look after yourself and the little creature inside you. Don't insist on looking after your husband, because that could make *your* condition worse.'

'But I must...'

'You must look after your own.'

'Isn't my husband one of my own?'

'No, not at the moment. Right now your future child is what concerns you and what you should be looking after.'

Ramiro's illness worsened.

'I fear complications with his heart', pronounced don Juan. 'It's weak; hardly surprising given the grief and upset he has had to bear.'

'But will he die, don Juan?', Gertrudis asked, full of anguish.

'Anything could happen...'

'Save him don Juan, save him, any way you can...'

'There is nothing I'd like more, but...'

'Oh, what a terrible, terrible thing to happen!' And it was the first time anyone had known the woman to have to sit down and to suffer a fainting fit.

'It is indeed terrible,' said the doctor as soon as Gertrudis had recovered. 'To leave behind four children like that. But what am I saying? It will actually be five ... and the condition of the poor widow...'

'That's the least of it, don Juan, I can deal with all that. But Ramiro ... it's terrible ... just terrible.'

Y el médico se fue diciéndose: «Está visto; esta cuñadita contaba con volver a tenerle libre a su cuñado. Cada persona es un mundo y algunos varios mundos. Pero ¡qué mujer! ¡Es toda una mujer! ¡Qué fortaleza! ¡Qué sagacidad! ¡Y qué ojos! ¡Qué cuerpo! ¡Irradia fuego!»

Ramiro, una tarde en que la fiebre, remitiéndosele, habíale dejado algo más tranquilo, llamó a Gertrudis, le rogó que cerrara la puerta de la alcoba, y le dijo:

–Yo me muero, Tula, me muero sin remedio. Siento que el corazón no quiere ya marchar, a pesar de todas las inyecciones; yo me muero...

–No pienses en eso, Ramiro.

Pero ella también creía en aquella muerte.

–Me muero, y es hora, Tula, de decirte toda la verdad. Tú me casaste con Rosa.

–Como no te decidías y dabas largas...

–¿Y sabes por qué?

–Sí, lo sé, Ramiro.

–Al principio, al veros, al ver a la pareja, sólo reparé en Rosa; era a quien se le veía de lejos; pero al acercarme, al empezar a frecuentaros, sólo te vi a ti, pues eras la única a quien desde cerca se veía. De lejos te borraba ella; de cerca le borrabas tú.

–No hables así de mi hermana, de la madre de tus hijos.

–No; la madre de mis hijos eres tú, tú, tú.

–No pienses ahora sino en Rosa, Ramiro.

–A la que me juntaré pronto, ¿no es eso?

–¡Quién sabe ...! Piensa en vivir, en tus hijos...

–A mis hijos les quedas tú, su madre.

–Y en Manuela, en la pobre Manuela...

–Aquel plazo, Tula, aquel plazo fatal.

Los ojos de Gertrudis se hinchieron de lágrimas.

–¡Tula! –gimió el enfermo abriendo los brazos.

–¡Sí, Ramiro, sí! –exclamó ella cayendo en ellos abrazándole.

Juntaron las bocas y así se estuvieron sollozando.

–¿Me perdonas todo, Tula?

–No, Ramiro, no; eres tú quien tienes que perdonarme.

And the doctor left thinking to himself, 'It's all too clear: this sister-in-law was counting on her brother-in-law's being free again. Every person is a world, and some are various worlds. But what a woman! She is all woman! Such strength! Such wisdom! And those eyes! That body! She radiates fire!'

One evening in which his fever had abated and left him slightly more composed, Ramiro called for Gertrudis, asked her to shut the bedroom door and said to her,

'Tula, I am dying, and there is nothing to be done about it. I sense that my heart doesn't want to go on beating, in spite of all the injections; I am dying…'

'Don't think about that, Ramiro.'

But Gertrudis also believed that Ramiro would die.

'I'm dying, Gertrudis, and it's time that I was completely truthful with you. You married me off to Rosa.'

'Well, you were dithering….'

'But do you know why I was doing that?'

'Yes, I do.'

'At first, when I saw you both, I only had eyes for Rosa; one noticed Rosa from a long way off. But, when I got to know you both, it was only you that I had eyes for; up close one notices only you. From a distance, *she* eclipsed *you*; up close *you* eclipsed *her*.'

'Don't talk about my sister, and the mother of your children, in those terms.'

'The mother of my children is you, you, *you*.'

'Don't think about anyone except Rosa right now, Ramiro.'

'Whom I'll be reunited with soon, is that what you mean?'

'Who can know? Concentrate on life, on your children…'

'My children will always have you, their mother.'

'And think about Manuela, poor Manuela…'

'That terrible trial period, Tula, that terrible period…'

Gertrudis's eyes filled with tears.

'Tula', groaned the invalid, holding out his arms to Gertrudis.

'Yes, Ramiro, yes!', Gertrudis cried, falling into his embrace.

Their lips touched, and they remained there entwined, sobbing.

'Can you forgive me for everything Tula?'

'Ramiro, it's you who must forgive me.'

–¿Yo?

–¡Tú! Una vez hablabas de santos que hacen pecadores. Acaso he tenido una idea inhumana de la virtud. Pero cuando lo primero, cuando te dirigiste a mi hermana, yo hice lo que debí hacer. Además, te lo confieso, el hombre, todo hombre, hasta tú, Ramiro, hasta tú, me ha dado miedo siempre; no he podido ver en él sino el bruto. Los niños, sí; pero el hombre... He huido del hombre.

–Tienes razón, Tula.

–Pero ahora descansa, que estas emociones así pueden dañarte.

Le hizo guardar los brazos bajo las mantas, le arropó, le dió un beso en la frente como se le da a un niño – y un niño era entonces para ella – y se fue. Mas al encontrarse sola se dijo: «¿Y si se repone y cura? ¿Si no se muere? ¿Ahora que ha acabado de romperse el secreto entre nosotros? ¿Y la pobre Manuela? ¡Tendré que marcharme! ¿Y adónde? ¿Y si Manuela se muere y vuelve él a quedarse fiebre?» Y fue a ver a Manuela, a la que encontró postradísima.

Al siguiente día llevó a los niños al lecho del padre, ya sacramentado y moribundo; los levantó uno a uno y les hizo que le besaran. Luego fue, apoyada en ella, en Gertrudis, Manuela, y de poco se muere de la congoja que le dió sobre el enfermo. Hubo que sacarla y acostarla. Y poco después, cogido de una mano a otra de Gertrudis, y susurrando: «¡Adiós, mi Tula!», rindió el espíritu con el último huelgo Ramiro. Y ella, la tía, vació su corazón en sollozos de congoja sobre el cuerpo exánime del padre de sus hijos, de su pobre Ramiro.

'Forgive *you*?'

'Yes! You talked once about saints who created sinners. Perhaps my idea of virtue has been inhuman. But when you approached my sister first, I did what I had to do. In any case, men – all men, and even you Ramiro, even you – have always scared me. I have only ever been able to see the brute in man. Boys are fine, but men… I have always shied away from men…'

'You're right Tula.'

'But get some rest now. All this emotion might be bad for you.'

She placed his arms beneath the blankets, tucked him up, kissed him on the forehead as one would a child – that was how she now saw him – before leaving the room. When she was alone, she asked herself, 'What if he recovers from all this? What if he doesn't die now that the secret between us has been shattered? And what about poor Manuela? I would have to leave! But where would I go? And what if Manuela dies and Ramiro is free to marry once more?' Gertrudis went to see Manuela, who was in a very weak state.

The next day, she led the children to the bedside of their dying father, who had now been given the last rites. One by one, she lifted them up and made them give him a kiss. Then Manuela came, physically supported by Gertrudis, and was so upset that it seemed she would die herself. She had to be led away and put to bed. Shortly afterwards, holding Gertrudis's hand, and whispering 'Goodbye my Tula', Ramiro gave up the ghost with a final sigh. And she sobbed her heart out, her tears falling onto the lifeless body of her poor Ramiro, the father of her children.

XVI

Apenas, fuera de la soberana, hubo abatimiento en aquel hogar, pues los niños eran incapaces de darse cuenta de lo que había pasado, y Manuela, la viuda casi sin saberlo, concentraba su vida y su ánimo todos en luchar, al modo de una planta, por la otra vida que llevaba en su seno y aun repitiendo, como un gemido de res herida, que se quería morir. Gertrudis proveía a todo.

Cerró los ojos al muerto, no sin decirse: «¿Me estará mirando todavía...?» Le amortajó como lo había hecho con su tío, cubriéndole con un hábito sobre la ropa con que murió, y sin quitarle ésta, y luego, quebrantada por un largo cansancio, por fatiga de años, juntó un momento su boca a la boca fría de Ramiro, y repasó sus vidas, que era su vida. Cuando el llanto de uno de los niños, del pequeñito, del hijo de la hospiciana, le hizo desprenderse del muerto e ir a coger y acallar y mimar al que vivía.

Manuela iba hundiéndose.

–Yo, señora, me muero; no voy a poder resistir esta vez; este parto me cuesta la vida.

Y así fue. Dió a luz una niña, pero se iba en sangre. La niña misma nació envuelta en sangre. Y Gertrudis tuvo que vencer la repugnancia que la sangre, sobre todo la negra cuajada, le producía. Siempre le costó una terrible brega consigo misma el vencer este asco. Cuando una vez, poco antes de morir, su hermana Rosa tuvo un vómito, de ella Gertrudis huyó despavorida.

Y no era miedo, no; era, sobre todo, asco.

Murió Manuela, clavados en los ojos de Gertrudis sus ojos, donde vagaban figuras de niebla sobre las sombras del hospicio.

–Por tus hijos no pases cuidado – le había dicho Gertrudis –, que yo he de vivir hasta dejarlos colocados y que se puedan valer por sí en el mundo, y si no les dejaré sus hermanos. Cuidaré sobre todo de esta última, ¡pobrecilla!, la que te cuesta la vida. Yo seré su madre y su padre.

–¡Gracias! ¡Gracias! ¡Gracias ¡Dios se lo pagará! ¡Es una santa!

Y quiso besarle la mano, pero Gertrudis se inclinó a ella, la besó en

XVI

Apart from that felt by its female sovereign, the household contained little dejection: the children weren't able to take in what had happened, and Manuela, barely aware of having being widowed, concentrated all her efforts in an almost vegetable way on struggling to keep alive the being that she was carrying inside, even as she moaned, like a wounded beast of burden, that she wanted to die. Gertrudis saw to everything.

She closed Ramiro's eyes, but not without asking herself, 'Is he still watching me?' She dressed him just as she done for her uncle, placing a shroud over the clothes he had died in, and then, shattered by a long exhaustion, by a fatigue that had lasted for years, she momentarily joined her lips to his, which were now cold. She relived their lives together, which was her life. The cries of one of the children – the youngest, the orphan's child – tore her away from the dead and she went to comfort the living.

Manuela was deteriorating.

'Señora, I am dying. I won't be able to withstand this one: this birth will cost me my life.'

And so it proved. She gave birth to a little girl, but the mother bled to death. The little girl herself was born covered in blood. And Gertrudis had to overcome the disgust she felt for blood, particularly when it was dark and clotted. It was always a tremendous struggle for her to overcome this disgust. Once, just before she died, Rosa had vomited blood, and a completely overwhelmed Gertrudis had had to flee. Not through fear; what she felt above all was disgust.

Manuela died with her gaze fixed upon Gertrudis's. In her mind's eye, the poor orphan could see indistinct figures wandering around against a backdrop of the orphanage.

'Don't be anxious about the children,' Gertrudis had said to her, 'I'll live long enough to see them well placed, and in a position to fend for themselves. And if I don't, I'll make sure their brothers and sisters look after them. And I'll look out especially for this last one – poor little thing! – the one who is costing you your life. I'll be mother and father to her.'

'Thank you, thank you, thank you! God bless you! You are a saint!'

Manuela tried to kiss her mistress's hand, but Gertrudis leaned down,

la frente y le puso su mejilla a que se la besase. Y esas expresiones de gratitud repetíalas la hospiciana como quien recita una lección aprendida desde niña. Y murió como había vivido, como una res sumisa y paciente, más bien como un enser.

Y fue esta muerte, tan natural, la que más ahondó en el ánimo de Gertrudis, que había asistido a otras tres ya. En ésta creyó sentir mejor el sentido del enigma. Ni la de su tío, ni la de su hermana, ni la de Ramiro horadaron tan hondo el agujero que se iba abriendo en el centro de su alma. Era como si esta muerte confirmara las otras tres, como si las iluminara a la vez.

En sus solitarias cavilaciones se decía: «Los otros se murieron; ¡a ésta la han matado...!, ¡la ha matado...!, ¡la hemos matado! ¿No la he matado yo más que nadie? ¿No la he traído yo a este trance? ¿Pero es que la pobre ha vivido? ¿Es que pudo vivir? ¿Es que nació acaso? Si fue expósita, ¿no ha sido *exposición* su muerte? ¿No lo fue su casamiento? ¿No la hemos echado en el torno de la eternidad para que entre al hospicio de la Gloria? ¿No será allí hospiciana también?» Y lo que más le acongojaba era el pensamiento tenaz que le perseguía de lo que sentiría Rosa al recibirla al lado suyo, al lado de Ramiro, y conocerla en el otro mundo. Su tío, el buen sacerdote que les crió, cumplió su misión de este mundo, protegió con su presencia la crianza de ellas; su hermana Rosa logró su deseo y gozó y dejó los hijos que había querido tener; Ramiro... ¿Ramiro? Sí, también Ramiro hizo su travesía, aunque a remo y de espaldas a la estrella que le marcaba rumbo, y sufrió, pero con noble sufrir, y pecó y purgó su pecado; pero, ¡y esta pobre que ni sufrió siquiera, que no pecó, sino se pecó en ella y murió huérfana!... «Huérfana también murió Eva...», pensaba Gertrudis. Y luego: «¡No; tuvo a Dios padre! ¿Y madre? Eva no conoció madre... ¡Así se explica el pecado original...! ¡Eva murió huérfana de humanidad!» Y Eva le trajo el recuerdo del relato del *Génesis,* que había leído poco antes, y cómo el Señor alentó al hombre por la nariz soplo de vida, y se imaginó que se la quitase por manera análoga. Y luego se figuraba que a aquella pobre hospiciana, cuyo sentido de vida

kissed Manuela on the forehead and offered up her cheek to the kiss. The orphan went on to repeat her expressions of gratitude, like someone reciting a lesson learned very young. And she died as she had lived, like a docile, patient beast of burden, or chattel.

And it was this death, for all its naturalness, that made the biggest impression on Gertrudis, who had already been present at three deaths beforehand. It was in relation to this death that she had the keenest sense of its enigma. None of the previous deaths – not her uncle's, nor her sister's nor Ramiro's – had penetrated so deeply the hole that was gradually opening in the centre of her soul. It was as if this death confirmed the other three, and as if at the same time it also illuminated them.

In her solitary musings, she used to say to herself, 'The others died; this woman was killed! Ramiro killed her! *We* killed her! In fact aren't *I* the one with most responsibility for killing her? Wasn't it me that brought her to death's door? Did the poor thing ever really have a life? Was she able to live? Was she even really *born*? If she was abandoned at birth, hasn't her death also been a kind of abandonment? And her marriage too? Haven't we shuffled her off this mortal coil so that she can enter the orphanage of heavenly glory? Won't she be a foundling there too?' And what upset her most was a thought that obstinately pursued her: what would Rosa feel when she received her at her side, and at Ramiro's side, when she met her in the other world. Her uncle, the kindly priest who had brought them up, had fulfilled his mission in this world, protecting their upbringing with his presence; her sister Rosa fulfilled her wishes, leaving behind the children she had wanted to have and had enjoyed; Ramiro … Ramiro? yes, Ramiro had also made the crossing, though he had had to row hard, his back to the star marking out his path, and he had suffered, but had suffered nobly, having sinned and having purged his sin; but this poor thing who hardly even suffered, who had not sinned but was sinned against, and died an orphan…? 'Eve also died an orphan,' thought Gertrudis. But then she thought 'No. She had God as her father! What about her mother? Eve never knew a mother … that's the explanation for original sin…! Eve died as an orphan of humanity!' Thinking of Eve brought to mind the story told in Genesis that she had read shortly before, and how the Lord breathed life into man through his nose, and she imagined that life was taken away in an analogous manner. And then she imagined that poor foundling, whose sense of life she did

no comprendía, le quitó Dios la vida de un beso posando sus infinitos labios invisibles, los que se cierran formando el cielo azul, sobre los labios, azulados por la muerte, de la pobre muchacha, y sorbiéndole el aliento así.

Y ahora quedábase Gertrudis con sus cinco crías, y bregando, para la última, con amas.

El mayor, Ramirín, era la viva imagen de su padre, en figura y en gestos, y su tía proponíase combatir en él desde entonces, desde pequeño, aquellos rasgos a inclinaciones de aquél que, observando a éste, había visto que más le perjudicaban. «Tengo que estar alerta – se decía Gertrudis – para cuando en él se despierte el hombre, el macho más bien, y educarle a que haga su elección con reposo y tiento.» Lo malo era que su salud no fuese del todo buena y su desarrollo difícil y hasta doliente.

Y a todos había que sacarlos adelante en la vida y educarlos en el culto a sus padres perdidos.

¿Y los pobres niños de la hospiciana? «Esos también son míos – pensaba Gertrudis –; tan míos como los otros, como los de mi hermana, más míos aún. Porque estos son hijos de mi pecado. ¿Del mío? ¿No más bien el de él? ¡No, de mi pecado! ¡Son los hijos de mi pecado! ¡Sí, de mi pecado! ¡Pobre chica!» Y le preocupaba sobre todo la pequeñita.

not understand, and God taking her life with a kiss, placing his infinite, invisible lips – lips that shut to form the blue sky above us – over the blue lips of the poor girl and sucking out her life in that way.

And now Gertrudis was left with her five children, struggling with wet nurses for the youngest one.

The oldest child, Ramirín, was the spitting image of his father, both in his appearance and his actions, and his aunt was determined to combat, from his earliest years, all the paternal character traits and inclinations that had been most harmful to him. 'I have to be alert,' Gertrudis would say to herself, 'for when the man, or rather the male begins to emerge from the child, and to educate him into making his choice of wife in a measured and careful way'. Unfortunately, his health was not perfect, and his development was difficult and even painful.

She would have to give them all a good start in life, and bring them up to worship at the altar of their lost parents.

'And what about the foundling's poor children? They're mine too,' thought Gertrudis, 'they belong to me as much as the others, my sister's children. In fact they are more mine than the others because they are the fruit of my sin. *My* sin? Or, rather, *his* sin? No, definitely *my* sin. They are the fruits of my sin! Yes, *mine*. Poor girl!' She worried above all about the smallest one.

XVII

Gertrudis, molesta por las insinuaciones de don Juan, el médico, que menudeaba las visitas para los niños, y aun pretendió verla a ella como enferma, cuando no sabía que adoleciese de cosa alguna, le anunció un día hallarse dispuesta a cambiar de médico.

–¿Cómo así, Gertrudis?

–Pues muy claro: le observo a usted singularidades que me hacen temer que está entrando en la chochera de una vejez prematura, y para médico necesitamos un hombre con el seso bien despejado y despierto.

–Muy bien; pues que ha llegado el momento, usted me permitirá que le hable claro.

–Diga lo que quiera, don Juan, mas en la inteligencia de que es lo último que dirá en esta casa.

–¡Quién sabe!...

–Diga.

–Yo soy viudo y sin hijos, como usted sabe, Gertrudis. Y adoro a los niños.

–Pues vuélvase usted a casar.

–A eso voy.

–¡Ah! ¿Y busca usted consejo de mí?

–Busco más que consejo.

–¿Que le encuentre yo novia?

–Yo soy médico, le digo, y no sólo no tuve hijos de mi mujer, que era viuda, y perdimos el que ella me trajo al matrimonio, ¡aún le lloro al pobrecillo!, sino que sé, sé positivamente, sé con toda seguridad, que no he de tener nunca hijos propios, que no puedo tenerlos. Aunque no por eso, claro está, me sienta menos hombre que otro cualquiera; ¿usted me entiende, Gertrudis?

–Quisiera no entenderle a usted, don Juan.

–Para acabar, yo creo que a estos niños, a estos sobrinos de usted y a los otros dos acaso...

–Son tan sobrinos para mí como los otros, más bien hijos.

–Bueno, pues que a estos hijos de usted, ya que por tales les tiene, no les vendría mal un padre, y un padre no mal acomodado y hasta regularmente rico.

XVII

Gertrudis had been annoyed by the way that the doctor, don Juan insinuated himself into the household, making frequent visits to tend to the children, and persisted in viewing her as if *she* were ill, without knowing her to suffer from a single thing. One day, she announced to him that she was ready to change doctor.

'Why, Gertrudis?'

'It's very simple. I see peculiarities that lead me to fear that you're on the verge of an early dotage, and we need a clear-headed and alert doctor.'

'Very well. At this point, I hope you will allow me to speak my mind clearly.'

'Please feel free to speak as you wish, but bear in mind that it'll be the last thing that you say in this house.'

'Who knows?'

'Do speak your mind, please.'

'I'm a widower with no children, as you know Gertrudis. And I adore children.'

'Then you should remarry.'

'I'm getting to that.'

'Ah … and you're looking for my advice?'

'I'm actually looking for more than that.'

'You want me to find you a woman to marry?'

'I'm a doctor, as I've noted, and not only did I not have children with my wife, who was a widow; we also lost the child that she brought to the marriage. I still grieve for the poor little thing! And I know that I will never have children of my own; I cannot have children. Although I feel no less of a man for it. Do you understand me Gertrudis?'

'I wish I *didn't* understand you, don Juan'

'In short, I think that these children, your nieces and nephews, and perhaps the other two as well…'

'"The other two" are as much my niece and nephew as the others. They're all my children.'

'Well, it would be no bad thing for these children of yours – as that is how you see them – to have a father…and a father who wasn't badly off; a father, in fact, who was quite comfortably off.'

–¿Y eso es todo?

–Sí, que yo creo que hasta necesitan padre.

–Les basta, don Juan, con el Padre nuestro que está en los cielos.

–Y como madre usted, que es la representante de la Madre Santísima, ¿no es eso?

–Usted lo ha dicho; don Juan, y por última vez en esta casa.

–¿De modo que...?

–Que toda esa historia de la necesidad que siente de tener hijos y de su incapacidad para tenerlos, ¿le he entendido bien, don Juan?

–Perfectamente, y esto último, por supuesto, quede entre los dos.

–No seré yo quien le estorbe otro matrimonio. Y esa historia, digo, no me ha convencido de que usted busque hijos que adoptar, que eso le será muy fácil y casándose, sino que me busca a mí y me buscaría aunque estuviese sola y hubiésemos de vivir solos y sin hijos; ¿le he entendido, don Juan? ¿Me entiende usted?

–Cierto es, Gertrudis, que si estuviese sola lo mismo me casaría con usted, si usted lo quisiera, ¡claro!, porque yo soy muy claro, muy claro, y es usted la que me atrae; pero en ese caso nos quedaba el adoptar hijos de cualquier modo, aunque fuese sacándolos del Hospicio. Pues ya he podido ver que usted, como yo, se muere por los niños y que los necesita y los busca y los adora.

–Pero ni usted ni nadie ha visto, don Juan, que yo haya sido y sea incapaz de hacerlos; nadie puede decir que yo sea estéril, y no vuelva a poner los pies en esta casa.

–¿Por qué, Gertrudis?

–¡Por puerco!

Y así se despidieron para siempre.

Mas luego que le hubo así despachado entróle una desdeñosa lástima, un lastimero desdén de aquel hombre. «¿No le he tratado con demasiada dureza? – se decía –.El hombre me sacaba de quicio, es cierto; sus miradas me herían más que sus palabras, pero debí tratarle de otro modo. El pobrecillo parece que necesita remedio, pero no el que él busca, sino otro, un remedio heroico y radical.» Pero cuando supo que don Juan se remediaba empezó a pensar si era, en efecto, calor de hogar lo que

'Have you finished?'

'Yes. I think they might need a father.'

'Our Father in heaven is all the father they need.'

'And you, as the representative of the Holy Mother is all the mother they need – is that what you're saying?'

'You said it, don Juan. And it is the last time you'll say it in this house.'

'You mean…'

'This whole story about your need to have children and your not being able to have them … have I understood you correctly?'

'Yes, perfectly well … the last part being strictly between you and me.'

'It won't be me that stymies your chances of remarrying. And let me say, this story of yours doesn't convince me that you're looking for children to adopt – that would be very easy to achieve by remarrying. What you're actually looking to do is marry me, and you'd marry me even if I were childless and we had to live alone without children. Have I understood correctly, don Juan? And do you understand me?'

'It's true, Gertrudis, that if you had no children, I would still marry you – if you wanted me to, of course – because, to speak completely plainly, it's you I'm attracted to. But in that case we could still have adopted, by any means necessary, even if we had to resort to the orphanage. Because I've seen that you, like me, dote on children: you seek them out, you need them and you adore them.'

'But neither you nor anyone else, don Juan, knows whether I might have children or whether I'm unable to have them. No-one can say that I'm infertile. Please don't set foot in this house again.'

'Why not, Gertrudis?'

'For having been so coarse.'

And so they parted forever.

But after she had despatched him, she began to feel a scornful pity, a pitying scorn for the man. 'Have I been too hard on him?', she wondered, 'the man really got on my nerves. The way he looked at me hurt me more than anything he said to me, but I shouldn't have treated him like that. It seems that the poor thing needs a remedy, but not the remedy that he's seeking; he needs a radical, heroic remedy.' But when she then found out that he was indeed finding himself a remedy, she began to think that it

buscaba, aunque bien pronto dió en otra sospecha que le sublevó aún más el corazón. «¡Ah –se dijo–, lo que necesita es un ama de casa,[22] una que le cuide, que le ponga sobre la cama la ropa limpia, que haga que se le prepare el puchero...peor, peor que el remedio, peor aún! ¡Cuando una no es remedio es animal doméstico, y la mayor parte de las veces ambas cosas a la vez! Estos hombres... ¡O porquería o poltronería ! ¡Y aún dicen que el cristianismo redimió nuestra suerte, la de las mujeres!» Y al pensar esto, acordándose de su buen tío, se santiguó diciéndose: « ¡No, no lo volveré a pensar...!»

Pero ¿quién enfrenaba a un pensamiento que mordía en el fruto de la ciencia del mal? «¡El cristianismo, al fin, y a pesar de la Magdalena, es religión de hombres – se decía Gertrudis–; masculinos el Padre, el Hijo y el Espíritu Santo ...!» Pero ¿y la Madre? La religión de la Madre está en: «He aquí la criada del Señor; hágase en mí según tu palabra» y en pedir a su Hijo que provea de vino a unas bodas, de vino que embriaga y alegra y hace olvidar penas, y para que el Hijo le diga: «¿Qué tengo yo que ver contigo, mujer? Aún no ha venido mi hora.» ¿Qué tengo que ver contigo...?

Y llamarle mujer y no madre... Y volvió a santiguarse, esta vez con verdadero temblor. Y es que el demonio de su guarda –así creía ella– le susurró: «¡Hombre al fin!»

was, actually, the warmth of a hearth that he was seeking, although she soon had another suspicion that infuriated her to her core. 'Ah...', she said to herself, 'what he needs is a housekeeper. Someone to look after him, someone to put clean sheets on his bed, and feed him ... that's even *worse* that being a remedy for his desire! When one is not a remedy, one is a working animal, and most often one is both at the same time. Men! When it's not filth, it's laziness! And they still say that Christianity redeemed us women from our fate.' But no sooner had she thought this than her kindly uncle came into her mind, and she made the sign of the cross, saying 'No, no, I won't think that again.'

But who curbs a thought that bites from the fruit of the tree of the knowledge of evil? 'Christianity, after all, in spite of Mary Magdalene, is a male religion', Gertrudis said to herself. 'Father, Son and Holy Spirit are all male! But the Mother? The religion of the Mother consists of "Behold the handmaid of the Lord; be it unto me according to thy word."[23] It also consisted in asking her son to provide wine for a wedding, wine that would intoxicate and make happy and cause pain to be forgotten, only to receive the answer "Woman, what have I to do with thee? Mine hour is not yet come..."[24] And to call her woman, not mother....'

And Gertrudis crossed herself again, this time with a real shiver. It was her 'guardian demon' – as she would say – whispering 'He is a man after all'.

XVIII

Corrieron unos años apacibles y serenos. La orfandad daba a aquel hogar, en el que de nada de bienestar se carecía, una íntima luz espiritual de serena calma. Apenas si había que pensar en el día de mañana. Y seguían en él viviendo, con más dulce imperio que cuando respirando llenaban con sus cuerpos sus sitios, los tres que le dieron a Gertrudis masa con qué fraguarlo, Ramiro y sus dos mujeres de carne y hueso. De continuo hablaba Gertrudis de ellos a sus hijos. «¡Mira que te está mirando tu madre!» o «¡Mira que te ve tu padre!» Eran sus dos más frecuentes amonestaciones. Y los retratos de los que se fueron presidían el hogar de los tres.

Los niños, sin embargo, íbanlos olvidando. Para ellos no existían sino en las palabras de mamá Tula, que así la llamaban todos. Los recuerdos directos del mayorcito, de Ramirín, se iban perdiendo y fundiendo en los recuerdos de lo que de ellos oía contar a su tía. Sus padres eran ya para él una creación de ésta.

Lo que más preocupaba a Gertrudis era evitar que entre ellos naciese la idea de una diferencia, de que había dos madres, de que no eran sino medio hermanos. Mas no podía evitarlo. Sufrió en un principio la tentación de decirles que las dos, Rosa y Manuela, eran, como ella misma, madres de todos ellos, pero vió la imposibilidad de mantener mucho tiempo el equívoco; y, sobre todo, el amor a la verdad, un amor en ella desenfrenado, le hizo rechazar tal tentación al punto.

Porque su amor a la verdad confundíase en ella con su amor a la pureza. Repugnábanle esas historietas corrientes con que se trata de engañar la inocencia de los niños, como la de decirles que los traen a este mundo desde París, donde los compran. «¡Buena gana de gastar el dinero en tonto!», había dicho un niño que tenía varios hermanos y a quien le dijeron que a un amiguito suyo le iban a traer pronto un hermanito sus padres. «Buena gana de gastar mentiras en balde –se decía Gertrudis; añadiéndose–; toda mentira es, cuando menos, en balde.»

XVIII

A few pleasant, uneventful years went by. That home, where wellbeing and comfort abounded, was given a special spiritual light of calmness and serenity by orphanhood. The future hardly needed to be considered. With even sweeter authority than when their living bodies occupied their place, the three people that had given Gertrudis the material with which to forge such authority continued to occupy the home: Ramiro and his two flesh-and-blood wives. Gertrudis was always mentioning them to the children. 'Your mother is watching you, you know', or 'Careful, your father can see you', were her two most frequent reprimands. And the portraits of those who were no longer physically there had pride of place in what had been their home.

The children, however, gradually began to forget them. For the children, the only things that existed were the words of mama Tula, as they all called her. The direct memories of the oldest child, little Ramiro, began to fade and become confused with the things that his aunt had told him about them. For him, his parents were, by now, a creation of his aunt.

What most concerned Gertrudis was preventing the idea of any difference between the children taking hold – the thought that they had two separate mothers, and that they were only half-brothers and sisters. But she was unable to prevent it. At first, she was tempted to say that the two other women, Rosa and Manuela, were, like her, mothers of all of them, but she saw it would be impossible to perpetuate that equivocation for any length of time. Above all though, it was her love of the truth – an unbridled love in her case – that led her to dismiss the temptation out of hand.

In actual fact, she confused her love of truth with her love of purity. She loathed those commonplace stories that people use to abuse the innocence of children – like the story that they come into this world via Paris, where their parents had bought them. 'What a silly thing to waste money on!', said one child with several brothers and sisters on being told that a friend of his was going to be brought a brother or sister by his parents. 'What a silly thing to waste lies on', Gertrudis used to say to herself, adding 'all lies are, at the very least, in vain'.

–Me han dicho que soy hijo de una criada de mi padre; que mi mamá fue criada de la mamá de mis hermanos.

Así fue diciendo un día a casa el hijo de Manuela. Y la tía Tula, con su voz más seria y delante de todos, le contestó:

–Aquí todos sois hermanos, todos sois hijos de un mismo padre y de una misma madre, que soy yo.

–¿Pues no dices, mamaíta, que hemos tenido otra madre?

–La tuvisteis, pero ahora la madre soy yo; ya lo sabéis. ¡Y que no se vuelva a hablar de eso!

Mas no lograba evitar el que se transparentara que sentía preferencias. Y eran por el mayor, el primogénito, Ramirín, al que engendró su padre cuando aún tuviera reciente en el corazón el cardenal del golpe que le produjo el haber tenido que escoger entre las dos hermanas, o mejor el haber tenido que aceptar de mandato de Gertrudis a Rosa, y por la pequeñuela, por Manolita, pálido y frágil botoncito de rosa que hacía temer lo hiciese ajarse un frío o un ardor tempranos.

De Ramirín, del mayor, una voz muy queda, muy sumisa, pero de un susurro sibilante y diabólico, que Gertrudis solía oír que brotaba de un rincón de las entrañas de su espíritu – y al oírla se hacía, santiguándose, una cruz sobre la frente y otra sobre el pecho, ya que no pudiese taparse los oídos íntimos de aquélla y de éste –, de Ramirín decíale ese tentador susurro que acaso cuando le engendró su padre soñaba más en ella, en Gertrudis, que en Rosa. Y de Manolita, de la hija de la muerte de la hospiciana, se decía que sin su decisión de casar por segunda vez a Ramiro, sin aquel haberle obligado a redimir su pecado y a rescatar a la víctima de él, a la pobre Manuela, no viviría el pálido y frágil botoncito.

¡Y lo que le costó criarla! Porque el primer hijo de Ramiro y Manuela fue criado por ésta, por su madre. La cual, sumisa siempre como una res, y ayudada a la vez por su natural instinto, no intentó siquiera rehusarlo a pesar de la endeblez de su carne, pero fue con el hombre, fue con el marido, con quien tuvo que bregar Gertrudis. Porque Ramiro, viendo la flaqueza de su pobre mujer, procuró buscar nodriza a su hijo. Y fue Gertrudis la que le obligó a casarse con aquélla, quien se plantó en firme en que había de ser la madre misma quien criara al hijo. «No hay leche como

'I've been told that I am the son of one of my father's maids. And that my mother was a maid to the mother of my brothers and sisters.'

This is what Manuela's son said to her one day. Aunt Tula, in her most serious voice, and in front of everyone, answered,

'Here you are all brothers and sisters. You are all children of one and the same father, and one and the same mother – me.'

'But didn't you say, mamita, that we've also had another mother?'

'You did have, but now *I* am your mother. Now you know. And we will not speak of this again.'

But she could not prevent it becoming apparent that she had her own preferences. One of her favourites was the first-born son, little Ramiro, begotten by his father when the latter still bore fresh in his heart the wound of having to choose between the two sisters (or rather, to be more accurate, to have to accept Rosa on Gertrudis's orders). The other favourite was the tiny Manolita, the pale and fragile rosebud, whom, she feared would be snatched away by a chill or a fever while still young and delicate.

A very quiet voice, submissive – but nevertheless sibilant and diabolical – a voice which sprang up from the most intimate depths of her spirit – and when she heard it she would make the sign of the cross on her forehead and her chest given that she could not shut herself off from its intimate whisperings – would murmur temptingly that perhaps little Ramiro, the oldest, had been conceived when his father was dreaming more of her – Gertrudis – than of Rosa. And as for Manolita, the daughter whose birth had been the death of her mother – the foundling, Gertrudis used to say to herself that without her decision to marry off Ramiro a second time – if she had not forced him to redeem his sin and to rescue the victim of it – poor little Manolita, the pale and fragile little creature, would not even be alive.

And what it had cost Gertrudis to nurse her! Ramiro and Manuela's first-born, the son, had been nursed by his mother. She, as submissive always as a beast of burden, aided also by her natural instinct, did not even try to refuse him the breast, despite the weakness of her flesh, but it was with man – with Manuela's husband – that Gertrudis had had to struggle. Seeing his poor wife's frailty, Ramiro had tried to find a wet nurse for his son. Gertrudis, who had forced him to marry Manuela, was the one insisting that it must be the mother herself who suckled the child.

la de la madre», repetía y al redargüir su cuñado: «Sí, pero es tan débil
que corren peligro ella y el niño, y éste se criará enclenque», replicaba
implacable la soberana del hogar: «¡Pretextos y habladurías! Una mujer
a la que se le puede alimentar, puede siempre criar y la naturaleza ayuda,
y en cuanto al niño, te repito que la mejor leche es la de la madre, si no
está envenenada.» Y luego, bajando la voz, agregaba: «Y no creo que le
hayas envenenado la sangre a tu mujer.» Y Ramiro tenía que someterse.
Y la querella terminó un día en que a nuevas instancias del hombre, que
vió que su nueva mujer sufrió un vahído, para que le desahijaran el hijo,
la soberana del hogar, cogiéndole aparte, le dijo: «¡Pero qué empeño,
hombre! Cualquiera creería que te estorba el hijo...»

—¿Cómo que me estorba el hijo...? No lo comprendo...

—¿No lo comprendes? ¡Pues yo sí!

—Como no te expliques...

—¿Que me explique? ¿Te acuerdas de lo de aquel bárbaro de Pascualón,
el guarda de tu cortijo de Majadalaprieta?

—¿Qué? ¿Aquello que comentamos de la insensibilidad con que recibió
la muerte de su hijo...?

—Sí.

—¿Y qué tiene que ver esto con aquello? ¡Por Dios, Tula... !

—Que a mí aquello me llegó al fondo del alma, me hirió profundamente
y quise averiguar la raíz del mal...

—Tu manía de siempre...

—Sí, ya me decía el pobre tío que yo era como Eva, empeñada en
conocer la ciencia del bien y del mal.

—¿Y averiguaste...?

—Que a aquel... hombre...

—¿Ibas a decir…?

—Que a aquel hombre, digo, le estorbaba el niño para más cómodamente
disponer de su mujer. ¿Lo entiendes?

—¡Qué barbaridad!

Pero ya Ramiro tuvo que darse por vencido y dejó que su Manuela
criara al niño mientras Gertrudis lo dispusiese así.

Y ahora se encontraba ésta con que tenía que criar a la pequeñuela, a

'There's nothing like a mother's own milk', she would repeat. And when her brother-in-law argued back, saying, 'Yes, but she's so weak that both she and the baby are at risk, and the baby will grow up to be sickly', the sovereign lady of the house would unyieldingly reply, 'Old wives' tales! A woman who is herself able to take in food can always suckle, and nature gives a helping hand. As far as the child is concerned, as I've said, nothing is as good as mother's milk – as long as it has not been poisoned of course.' Then, lowering her voice, she said, 'and I don't think you've poisoned your wife's blood.'[25] And Ramiro would have to give in. The quarrel came to an end on the day when, at the husband's renewed insistence after his new wife had suffered a dizzy spell, the child was taken from his mother's breast definitively. The sovereign of the house took him aside and said 'But why are you so insistent? Anyone would think that the baby was getting in your way...'

'What do you mean, the baby getting in my way? I don't understand...'

'You don't understand? Well *I* do...'

'Look, if you won't explain yourself...'

'Do you want me to explain myself? Do you remember the barbarous Pascualón, the guard at your farmhouse at Majadalaprieta?'

'The one we said was insensitive to his son's death?'

'Yes.'

'What's that got to do with this? For goodness sake Tula...!'

'What happened there affected me deeply: it really wounded me, and I wanted to get to the root of the evil...'

'You don't change...'

'Yes, I know. My poor uncle used to say to me that I was like Eve, determined to acquire knowledge of good and evil.'

'And did you get to the bottom of things about Pascualón?'

'That man ... that...'

'What?... What are you saying?'

'That man ... the baby was preventing him from having his wife at his disposal whenever he wanted... *Now* do you understand?'

'But that's awful!'

And Ramiro had to admit defeat and let his wife nurse the child for as long as Gertrudis decreed.

Now Gertrudis found herself in the position of having to nurse this

la hija de la muerte, y que forzosamente había de dársela a una madre de alquiler, buscándole un pecho mercenario. Y esto le horrorizaba. Horrorizábale porque temía que cualquier nodriza, y más si era soltera, pudiese tener envenenada, con la sangre, la leche, y abusase de su posición. «Si es soltera – se decía –, ¡malo! Hay que vigilarla para que no vuelva al novio o acaso a otro cualquiera, y si es casada, malo también, y peor aún si dejó al hijo propio para criar al ajeno.» Porque esto era lo que sobre todo le repugnaba. Vender el jugo maternal de las propias entrañas para mantener mal, para dejarlos morir acaso de hambre, a los propios hijos, era algo que le causaba dolorosos retortijones en las entrañas maternales. Y así es cómo se vió desde un principio en conflicto con las amas de cría de la pobre criatura, y teniendo que cambiar de ellas cada cuatro días. ¡No poder criarle ella misma! Hasta que tuvo que acudir a la lactancia artificial.

Pero el artificio se hizo en ella arte, y luego poesía, y por fin más profunda naturaleza que la del instinto ciego. Fue un culto, un sacrificio, casi un sacramento. El biberón, ese artefacto industrial, llegó a ser para Gertrudis el símbolo y el instrumento de un rito religioso. Limpiaba los botellines, cocía los pisgos cada vez que los había empleado, preparaba y esterilizaba la leche con el ardor recatado y ansioso con que una sacerdotisa cumpliría un sacrificio ritual. Cuando ponía el pisgo de caucho en la boquita de la pobre criatura, sentía que le palpitaba y se le encendía la propia mama. La pobre criatura posaba alguna vez su manecita en la mano de Gertrudis, que sostenía el frasco.

Se acostaba con la niña, a la que daba calor con su cuerpo, y contra éste guardaba el frasco de la leche por si de noche se despertaba aquélla pidiendo alimento. Y se le antojaba que el calor de su carne, enfebrecida a ratos por la fiebre de la maternidad virginal, de la virginidad maternal, daba a aquella leche industrial una virtud de vida materna y hasta que pasaba a ella, por misterioso modo, algo de los ensueños que habían florecido en aquella cama solitaria. Y al darle de mamar, en aquel artilugio, por la noche, a oscuras y a solas las dos, poníale a la criatura uno de sus pechos estériles, pero henchidos de sangre, al alcance de las manecitas para que siquiera las posase sobre él mientras chupaba el jugo

tiny creature, the baby that had caused her mother's death. She would be forced to find a mother for rent, a mercenary breast. And that horrified her. It horrified her because she feared that the milk from a wet nurse – all the more so if she were single – would be poisoned through her blood, and that she would abuse her position. 'It's a very bad sign if she is single!', she said to herself. 'She'll have to be watched over to make sure that she does not go back to her sweetheart, or start a relationship with another man. And it's no good if she is married either, it's even worse leaving her own child so she can suckle someone else's.' That was what revolted her above all. To sell one's own mother's milk while neglecting or even starving one's own child to death caused her dreadful pain, pain that she felt deep inside her own womb. And this was how, from the very start, she came to be in conflict with the wet nurses of the poor little creature; she would change nurses every few days. Not to be able to suckle the baby herself was almost unbearable! In the end she had to resort to bottle-feeding her.

But she was able to turn what was artificial into an art, and then into poetry, and finally into a naturalness even deeper than that of blind instinct. It became a form of worship, a sacrifice, almost a sacrament. The baby's bottle, that industrially-produced device, became for Gertrudis the symbol and instrument of a religious rite. She washed the little bottles and boiled the teats after each use, and she sterilised the milk with all the anxious ardour and care that a priest employed to carry out a ritual sacrifice. When she used to put the rubber teat into the little one's mouth, she felt her own breast throb and burn. The poor little creature would sometimes place her little hand on Gertrudis's as she held the bottle.

She would lie down with the little girl, and warm her with her own body, keeping the bottle by her in case the baby woke during the night and wanted to feed. And she imagined that the heat of her body, sometimes inflamed by the fever of her virginal motherhood – of her maternal virginity – gave that industrially-produced milk the virtue of maternal life, and even that she was passing on to the baby, in some mysterious way, some of the dreams that had flourished in that lonely bed. And when at night, when it was dark and they were on their own, Gertrudis gave the bottle to the baby, she would also expose one of her own breasts, infertile but swollen with blood, so that it was within reach of the little girl if she wanted to rest her hand on it as she suckled on the vital fluid.

de vida. Antojábasele que así una vaga y dulce ilusión animaría a la huérfana. Y era ella, Gertrudis, la que así soñaba. ¿Qué? Ni ella misma lo sabía bien.

Alguna vez la criatura se vomitó sobre aquella cama, limpia siempre hasta entonces como una patena, y de pronto sintió Gertrudis la punzada de la mancha. Su pasión morbosa por la pureza, de que procedía su culto místico a la limpieza, sufrió entonces, y tuvo que esforzarse para dominarse. Comprendía, sí, que no cabe vivir sin mancharse y que aquella mancha era inocentísima, pero los cimientos de su espíritu se conmovían dolorosamente con ello. Y luego le apretaba a la criaturita contra sus pechos pidiéndole perdón en silencio por aquella tentación de su pureza.

She imagined that in this way a vague and gentle hope would animate the poor orphan. And it was she, Gertrudis, who dreamed in this way. Not even she was fully aware of what she was doing.

Sometimes the little creature would throw up on the bed, which was always as spotlessly clean as the paten during mass, and Gertrudis would feel the pang of the contaminating stain. Her morbid obsession with purity, the root of her mystic cult of cleanliness, would cause her suffering at such times, and she had to struggle to overcome her obsession. She did understand that one could not live without occasionally being dirty, and that this particular stain could not be more innocent; even so, the depths of her soul were pained by it. And then she would hold the little creature tightly to her, silently asking her forgiveness for that temptation against her purity.

XIX

Fuera de este cuidado maternal por la pobre criaturita de la muerte de Manuela, cuidado que celaba una expiación y un culto místicos, y sin desatender a los otros y esforzándose por no mostrar preferencias a favor de los de su sangre, Gertrudis se preocupaba muy en especial de Ramirín y seguía su educación paso a paso, vigilando todo lo que en él pudiese recordar rasgos de su padre, a quien físicamente se parecía mucho. «Así sería a su edad», pensaba la tía y hasta buscó y llegó a encontrar entre los papeles de su cuñado retratos de cuando éste era un chicuelo, y los miraba y remiraba para descubrir en ellos al hijo. Porque quería hacer de éste lo que de aquél habría hecho a haberle conocido y podido tomar bajo su amparo y crianza cuando fue un mozuelo a quien se le abrían los caminos de la vida. «Que no se equivoque como él – se decía –, que aprenda a detenerse para elegir, que no encadene la voluntad antes de haberla asentado en su raíz viva, en el amor perfecto y bien alumbrado, a la luz que le sea propia.» Porque ella creía que no era al suelo, sino al cielo, a lo que había que mirar antes de plantar un retoño; no al mantillo de la tierra, sino a las razas de lumbre que del sol le llegaran, y que crece mejor el arbolito que prende sobre una roca al solano dulce del mediodía que no el que sobre un mantillo vicioso y graso se alza a la umbría. La luz era la pureza.

Fue con Ramirín aprendiendo todo lo que él tenía que aprender, pues le tomaba a diario las lecciones. Y así satisfacía aquella ansia por saber que desde niña le había aquejado y que hizo que su tío le comparase alguna vez con Eva. Y de entre las cosas que aprendió con su sobrino y para enseñárselas, pocas le interesaron más que la geometría. ¡Nunca lo hubiese ella creído! Y es que en aquellas demostraciones de la geometría, ciencia árida y fría al sentir de los más, encontraba Gertrudis un no sabía qué de luminosidad y de pureza. Años después, ya mayor Ramirín, y cuando el polvo que fue la carne de su tía reposaba bajo tierra, sin luz de sol, recordaba el entusiasmo con que un día de radiante primavera le

XIX

Aside from her maternal care for the poor creature born of Manuela's death, a care that concealed an expiation and a mystical cult, and without neglecting the others – while also forcing herself not to show favouritism towards those of her own flesh and blood – Gertrudis worried especially about little Ramiro. She was there at every step of his upbringing, looking out for any character traits that might have come from his father, whom he took after physically so closely. 'That's what he would have looked like at this age', she would think, and she even looked amongst her brother-in-law's papers to find some portraits of when he was a boy. She would spend hours poring over them to find traits of the son in the father. She wanted to make of little Ramiro what she would have made of Ramiro if she had met him in time, and been able to take him under her care and protection when he was still young enough for life's horizons to be wide open. 'I don't want him to make the same mistakes as his father', she would say to herself, 'I want him to learn how to hold back before choosing, so that his will is not constrained before it has had a chance to settle and find its taproot in a perfect and properly enlightened love.' Gertrudis believed that it was not to the ground but to the sky that one should look when planting a new shoot; one should not be looking to the earth but to the sun's rays which would shine on it. She believed that the sapling that took root on a rock exposed to the gentle midday breeze from the east would grow better than the shoot planted in rank, greasy soil in the shade. Light was purity.

She used to go over Ramiro's lessons with him every day, and so learned everything that he had to learn. She was thus gradually able to satisfy a hunger for knowledge that had pursued her since she was young, and had once led her uncle to compare her with Eve. Amongst all the things she learned in order to be able to teach her nephew, almost nothing interested her more than geometry. She would never have believed it! And in those geometrical proofs, which others thought a cold and arid science, Gertrudis found something luminous and pure. Years later, when little Ramiro had long grown up, and when his aunt's flesh had long become dust under the ground, away from the sunlight, he would remember the enthusiasm with which, one radiant spring day, she explained to him

explicaba cómo no puede haber más que cinco y sólo cinco poliedros regulares; tres formados de triángulos: el tetraedro, de cuatro; el octaedro, de ocho, y el icosaedro, de veinte; uno de cuadrados: el cubo, de seis, y uno de pentágonos: el dodecaedro, de doce. «Pero ¿no ves qué claro?» , sólo cinco y no más me decía – contaba el sobrino –, «¿no lo ves?, ¡qué bonito! Y no puede ser de otro modo, tiene que ser así!», y al decirlo me mostraba los cinco modelos en cartulina blanca, blanquísima, que ella misma había construido, con sus santas manos, que eran prodigiosas para toda labor, y parecía como si acabase de descubrir por sí misma la ley de los cinco poliedros regulares... ¡pobre tía Tula! Y recuerdo que como a uno de aquellos modelos geométricos le cayera una mancha de grasa, hizo otro, porque decía que con la mancha no se veía bien la demostración. Para ella la geometría era luz y pureza.

En cambio huyó de enseñarle anatomía y fisiología. «Esas son porquerías – decía – y en que nada se sabe de cierto ni de claro.»

Y lo que sobre todo acechaba era el alborear de la pubertad en su sobrino. Quería guiarle en sus primeros descubrimientos sentimentales y que fuese su amor primero el último y el único. «Pero ¿es que hay un primer amor?», se preguntaba a sí misma sin acertar a responderse.

Lo que más temía eran las soledades de su sobrino. La soledad, no siendo a toda luz, la temía. Para ella no había más soledad santa que la del sol y la de la Virgen de la Soledad cuando se quedó sin su Hijo, el Sol del Espíritu. «Que no se encierre en su cuarto – pensaba –, que no esté nunca, a poder ser, solo; hay soledad que es la peor compañía; que no lea mucho, sobre todo, que no lea mucho; y que no se esté mirando grabados.» No temía tanto para su sobrino a lo vivo cuanto a lo muerto, a lo pintado. «La muerte viene por lo muerto» – pensaba.

Confesábase Gertrudis con el confesor de Ramirín, y era para, dirigiendo al director del muchacho en la dirección de éste, ser ella la que de veras le dirigiese. Y por eso en sus confesiones hablaba más que

how there could only ever be five regular polyhedrons; three made up of triangles: the tetrahedron made of four, the octahedron of eight, and the icosahedron of twenty; one of squares: the cube, made up of six sides; and one of pentagons: the dodecahedron, made of twelve sides. 'Don't you see the clarity of it all?', she said to her nephew. 'Don't you see? Five and only five – no more and no fewer. How lovely! And it cannot be any other way – it has to be like that.' 'And as she was speaking she showed me the five models, made from white card – snow-white card – models she had made herself with her saintly hands (she was always very good with her hands) and it was as if she herself had discovered the law of the five regular polyhedrons … poor Aunt Tula! And I remember how a drop of oil fell onto one of the geometrical models, and how she made another because she said that the grease spot meant that one could not see the demonstration of the proof clearly. For her, geometry was light and purity.'

In contrast, she shied away from teaching him anatomy and physiognomy. 'Filth!', she declared, 'and where nothing is clear or known for sure.'

What she watched out for most of all were the first signs of puberty in her nephew. She wanted to guide him in his first romantic discoveries, and she wanted his first love to also be his last and only love. 'But is there such a thing as first love?', she wondered, without being able to answer her own question.

What she feared most were the times that her nephew was alone. Solitude, where everything was not out in the light or out in the open, frightened her. For Gertrudis, the only holy solitude was that of the sun, and that of Our Lady of Solitude, when the Virgin Mary was left without her son, the Sun of the Holy Spirit. 'I don't want him to shut himself in his room', she would think. 'And I don't want him ever to be alone, if at all possible. Solitude can be the worst company. Above all, I don't want him to read. I hope he reads as little as possible, and that he doesn't pore over illustrations.' In relation to her nephew, she feared what was living less than what was dead, what was painted. 'Death comes from what is already dead', she used to think.

Gertrudis used to confess with little Ramiro's own confessor, and so it happened that, in addressing herself to the spiritual director of her nephew, she intended to be Ramiro's true spiritual director. It was for this

de sí misma de su hijo mayor, como le llamaba. «Pero es, señora, que usted viene aquí a confesar sus pecados y no los de otros», le tuvo que decir alguna vez el padre Álvarez, a lo que ella contestó: «Y si ese chico es mi pecado ...»

Cuando una vez creyó observar en el muchacho inclinaciones ascéticas, acaso místicas, acudió alarmada al padre Alvarez.

–¡Eso no puede ser, padre!

–Y si Dios le llamase por ese camino...

–No, no le llama por ahí; lo sé, lo sé mejor que usted y desde luego mejor que él mismo; eso es... la sensualidad que se le despierta...

–Pero, señora...

–Sí, anda triste, y la tristeza no es señal de vocación religiosa. ¡Y remordimiento no puede ser! ¿De qué ...?

–Los juicios de Dios, señora...

–Los juicios de Dios son claros. Y esto es oscuro. Quítele eso de la cabeza. ¡Él ha nacido para padre y yo para abuela!

–¡Ya salió aquello!

–¡Sí, ya salió aquello!

–¡Y cómo le pesa a usted eso! Líbrese de ese peso... Me ha dicho cien veces que había agotado ese mal pensamiento...

–¡No puedo, padre, no puedo! Que ellos, que mis hijos –porque son mis hijos, mis verdaderos hijos–, que ellos no lo sepan, que no lo sepan, padre, que no lo adivinen...

–Cálmese, señora, por Dios, cálmese... y deseche esas aprensiones.... esas tentaciones del Demonio, se lo he dicho cien veces... Sea lo que es...la tía Tula que todos conocemos y veneramos y admiramos ...; sí, admiramos...

–¡No, padre, no! ¡Usted lo sabe! Por dentro soy otra...

–Pero hay que ocultarlo...

–Sí, hay que ocultarlo, sí; pero hay días en que siento ganas de reunir a sus hijos, a mis hijos...

–¡Sí, suyos, de usted!

–¡Sí, yo madre, como usted... padre!

reason that in confession she used to speak about her oldest son (as she referred to him) more than about herself. 'But Doña Gertrudis, you are here to confess your own sins, not those of others', Father Alvarez had to tell her at one point. To which she replied 'But that child *is* my sin.'

And when at one time she thought she saw ascetic, or perhaps even mystical inclinations in the boy, she consulted Father Alvarez, alarmed.

'We can't have this, Father!'

'Well, if that is the path that God has marked out for him...'

'No, that is not where his calling lies. I know that better than you, and of course better than little Ramiro himself can know. It is ... sensuality awakening in him.'

'But Doña Gertrudis...'

'Yes, that's it. He's seemed sad recently, and sadness is not the sign of a religious vocation. And it cannot be remorse! Remorse for what?'

'Doña Gertrudis ... the judgments of God...'

'The judgments of God are very clear ... and this is obscure. Please, get this out of his head. He was born to be a father, and I to be a grandmother.'

'This again!'

'Yes, this again!'

'This is weighing on you too much. Free yourself of this burden... You've told me a thousand times before that you had overcome this immoral thought...'

'I can't Father, I can't! I hope that my children – because they *are* my children, my real children – never find out, Father, I hope they never guess...'

'Calm yourself, Doña Getrudis, calm yourself, and disregard these fears, these temptations of the devil... I've told you a thousand times... Be who you are... Aunt Tula whom we all know, revere and admire ... yes, admire...'

'No father, no ... you know that's not true. Inside I'm someone else.'

'But you must hide that...'

'Yes, it must be hidden. But there are days when I feel like gathering all his children, all my children...'

'Yes, they *are* your children!'

'Indeed. I am a mother in the way that you are father...'

'Let's leave that to one side, Doña Gertrudis...'

–Deje eso, señora, deje eso...

–Sí, reunirles y decirles que toda mi vida ha sido una mentira, una equivocación, un fracaso...

–Usted se calumnia, señora. Esa no es usted, usted es la otra..., la que todos conocemos .... la tía Tula...

–Yo le hice desgraciado, padre; yo le hice caer dos veces: una con mi hermana, otra vez con otra...

–¿Caer?

–¡Caer, sí! ¡Y fue por soberbia!

–No, fue por amor, por verdadero amor...

–Por amor propio, padre – y estalló a llorar.

'I feel like gathering them together and telling them that my whole life has been a lie, an error, a failure...'

'You are slandering yourself, Doña Gertrudis. That person isn't you ... you're the other person, the one we all know... Aunt Tula.'

'I made him unhappy Father; I made him fall into temptation twice: once with my sister; the other time with another woman...'

'You made him *fall*?'

'Yes, fall! And it was because of my own pride!'

'No, it was because of love...true love.'

'*Self*-love, Father.' And she burst into tears.

XX

Logró sacar a su sobrino de aquellas veleidades ascéticas y se puso a vigilarle, a espiar la aparición del primer amor. «Fíjate bien, hijo – le decía –, y no te precipites, que una vez que hayas comprometido a una no debes dejarla...»

–Pero, mamá, si no se trata de compromisos... Primero hay que probar...

–No, nada de pruebas; nada de esos noviazgos; nada de eso de «hablo con Fulana». Todo seriamente...

En rigor la tía Tula había ya hecho, por su parte, su elección y se proponía ir llevando dulcemente a su Ramirín a aquella que le había escogido, a Caridad.

–Parece que te fijas en Carita–le dijo un día.

–¡Pse!

–Y ella en ti, si no me equivoco.

–Y tú en los dos, a lo que parece...

–¿Yo? Eso es cosa vuestra, hijo mío, cosa vuestra...

Pero les fue llevando el uno al otro, y consiguió su propósito. Y luego se propuso casarlos cuanto antes. «Y que venga acá –decía– y viviremos todos juntos, que hay sitio para todos... ¡Una hija más!»

Y cuando hubo llevado a Carita a su casa, como mujer de su sobrino, era con ésta con la que tenía sus confidencias. Y era de quien trataba de sonsacar lo íntimo de su sobrino.

Le obligó, ya desde un principio, a que le tutease y le llamase madre. Y le recomendaba que cuidase sobre todo de la pequeñita, de la mansa, tranquila y medrosica Manolita.

–Mira, Caridad – le decía –, cuida sobre todo de esa pobrecita, que es lo más inocente y lo más quebradizo que hay y buena como el pan... Es mi obra...

–Pero si la pobrecita apenas levanta la voz..., si ni se la siente andar por la casa...Parece como que tuviera vergüenza hasta de presentarse...

–Sí, sí, es así... Harto he hecho por infundirle valor, pero en no estando arrimada a mí, cosida a mi falda, la pobrecita se encuentra como perdida. ¡Claro, como criada con biberón!

XX

She managed to draw her nephew away from his ascetic whims, and watched over him carefully, looking out for the signs of his first love. 'Be attentive, and don't rush into anything: once you have made a commitment to someone, you must not leave her.'

'But mama, it's not a question of commitment ... one has to put things to the test first...'

'No, no testing things out; there'll be none of those kinds of relationships – none of that "Oh, I'll have a word with so-and-so"... Everything must be done seriously...'

Actually, Gertrudis had already made her choice, and her plan was to lead her little Ramiro gently toward the young woman she had chosen, whose name was Caridad,

'You seem to be paying a lot of attention to young Carita', she said one day.

'Bah...'

'And *she* has noticed *you* if I'm not mistaken...'

'And *you* have noticed both of *us* it seems...'

'Me? This is between the two of *you*, my darling son...'

But little by little she brought the two closer together, and she achieved her aim. And then she planned to marry them off as soon as possible. 'She should come here to live, and we'll all live together – there is plenty of room for everyone. Another daughter!'

After she had brought Carita into her home as wife to her nephew, she made her her confidante. She tried to coax the most intimate details about her nephew from Carita. And from the start, she made Carita use the familiar form of address towards her, and insisted that she call her 'mother'. She also advised her to care most of all for the little one, the gentle, calm and timid Manolita.

'Caridad,' she said 'look after that poor little thing above all others ... she's so fragile, and she's as good as gold ... I was the one who shaped her.'

'But one can barely hear her speak ... or sense her move around the house ... it is as if she's ashamed even to appear in front of others...'

'Yes, you're absolutely right ... I've done so much to try and give her courage, but unless she's next to me, tied to my apron strings, the poor little thing seems lost! Of course, she was bottle-fed.'

–El caso es que es laboriosa, obediente, servicial, pero ¡habla tan poco...! ¡Y luego no se la oye reír nunca... !

–Sólo alguna vez, cuando está a solas conmigo, porque entonces es otra cosa, es otra Manolita..., entonces resucita... Y trato de animarla, de consolarla, y me dice: «No te canses, mamita, que yo soy así... y además, no estoy triste...»

–Pues lo parece...

–Lo parece, sí, pero he llegado a creer que no lo está. Porque yo, yo misma, ¿qué te parezco, Carita, triste o alegre?

–Usted, tía...

–¿Qué es eso de usted y de tía?

–Bueno, tú, mamá, tú... pues no sé si eres triste o alegre, pero a mí me pareces alegre...

–¿Te parezco así? ¡Pues basta!

–Por lo menos a mí me alegras...

–Y es lo que nos manda Dios a este mundo, a alegrar a los demás.

–Pero para alegrar a los demás hay que estar alegre una...

–O no...

–¿Cómo no?

–Nada alegra más que un rayo de sol, sobre todo si da sobre la verdura del follaje de un árbol, y el rayo de sol no está ni alegre ni triste, y quién sabe .... acaso su propio fuego le consume... El rayo de sol alegra porque está limpio; todo lo limpio alegra... Y esa pobre Manolita debe alegrarte, porque a limpia...

–¡Sí, eso sí! Y luego esos ojos que tiene, que parecen...

–Parecen dos estanques quietos entre verdura... Los he estado mirando muchas veces y desde cerca. Y no sé de dónde ha sacado esos ojos... No son de su madre, que tenía ojos de tísica, turbios de fiebre... ni son los de su padre, que eran...

–¿Sabes de quién parecen esos ojos?

–¿De quién? – y Gertrudis temblaba al preguntarlo.

–¡Pues son tus ojos ...!

–Puede ser... puede ser. No me los he mirado nunca de cerca ni puedo vérmelos desde dentro, pero puede ser... puede ser… Al menos le he enseñado a mirar.

'The thing is, she is industrious, obedient and obliging, but one never hears a peep out of her! And we never hear her laugh!'

'Only occasionally, when she is with me … then she laughs … she's a different person when we're alone together … she comes to life then… I try to encourage her, and console her, and she says to me "Don't tire yourself, mamita, this is just how I am … besides, I'm not sad…".'

'Well that's how it seems…'

'It may seem like that, but I've come to believe it's not the case. What about me Carita? How do I seem to you? Happy or sad?

'You, aunt?'

'What's all this formality? All this "aunt" business?'

'Well then, mamita, I don't really know if *you're* happy or sad, but you *seem* happy to me…'

'That's how I seem to you? Then that's enough!

'Well, you make *me* happy, at least…'

'And that's what God orders us to do on this earth – to make others happy.'

'But to make others happy, one has to be happy oneself…'

'Not necessarily…'

'What do you mean "not necessarily"?'

'Nothing engenders happiness more than a ray of sunlight, especially if it falls on the leaves of a tree, but the ray of sun is neither happy nor sad … and who knows? Perhaps it's being consumed by its own fire: the ray of sun makes others happy because it's clean; all that is clean makes others happy … and that poor Manolita should make you happy, because in terms of cleanliness…'

'That's true! And those eyes of hers, which seem…'

'They are like two still pools amongst the foliage… I've often looked at them, close-up too. And I don't know whom her eyes take after … they're not from her mother … who had the eyes of a consumptive, clouded by fever … and they're not from her father, whose eyes…'

'Do you know whose eyes she has?'

'Whose?' Gertrudis felt a shiver as she asked

'She has *your* eyes!'

'It's possible, it's possible… I've never really looked at my eyes close up, and I can't see them from inside, but it's possible, it's possible… At least I have taught her how to look…'

XXI

¿Qué le pasaba a la pobre Gertrudis que se sentía derretir por dentro? Sin duda había cumplido su misión en el mundo. Dejaba a su sobrino mayor, a su Ramiro, a su otro Ramiro, a cubierto de la peor tormenta, embarcado en su barca de por vida, y a los otros hijos al amparo de él; dejaba un hogar encendido y quien cuidase de su fuego. Y se sentía deshacer. Sufría frecuentes embaimientos, desmayos, y durante días enteros lo veía todo como en niebla, como si fuese bruma y humo todo. Y soñaba; soñaba como nunca había soñado. Soñaba lo que habría sido si Ramiro hubiese dejado por ella a Rosa. Y acababa diciéndose que no habrían sido de otro modo las cosas. Pero ella había pasado por el mundo fuera del mundo. El padre Alvarez creía que la pobre Gertrudis chocheaba antes de tiempo, que su robusta inteligencia flaqueaba y que flaqueaba el peso mismo de su robustez. Y tenía que defenderla de aquellas sus viejas tentaciones.

Cuando un día se le acercó Caridad y, al oído, le dijo: «¡Madre...!», al notarle el rubor que le encendía el rostro, exclamó: «¿Qué? ¿Ya?» «¡Sí, ya!», susurró la muchacha. «¿Estás segura?» «¡Segura; si no, no te lo habría dicho!»Y Gertrudis, en medio de su goce, sintió como si una espada de hielo le atravesase por medio el corazón. Ya no tenía que hacer en el mundo más que esperar al nieto, al nieto de los suyos, de su Ramiro y su Rosa, a su nieto, a ir luego a darles la buena nueva. Ya apenas se cuidaba más que de Caridad, que era quien para ella llenaba la casa. Hasta de Manolita, de su obra, se iba descuidando, y la pobre niña lo sentía; sentía que el esperado iba relegándole en la sombra.

–Ven acá – le decía Gertrudis a Caridad, cuando alguna vez se encontraban a solas, ocasión que acechaba –, ven acá, siéntate aquí, a mi lado... ¿Qué, le sientes, hija mía, le sientes?

–Algunas veces...

XXI

What was wrong with Gertrudis? She felt as if she were beginning to melt from the inside out. No doubt she had completed her mission on earth. She was leaving her oldest nephew, Ramiro – her other Ramiro – safe from even the harshest storm, the co-ordinates of his life's course set, with the other children under his protection; she was leaving a home with a well-tended hearth and someone who could continue tending the home fires. She felt as if she were dissolving inside. She became confused, and suffered frequent fainting spells. For entire days it seemed as if she were seeing everything through a fog, as if everything were made of mist and smoke. And she had many dreams; she dreamed as she had never dreamed before. She dreamed about what would have been if Ramiro had left Rosa for her. She eventually concluded that things would not have been any different. But she had passed through the world while remaining outside it. Father Alvarez thought that Gertrudis was becoming prematurely senile, and that her robust intelligence was declining; he thought, in fact, that her intelligence was declining under the very weight of her robustness. And he had once again to defend her from those old temptations of hers.

When one day Caridad approached her and breathed the word 'Mother' into her ear, Gertrudis, seeing the blush on her cheeks, exclaimed 'What? Are you...?' 'Yes, I am,' whispered the girl. 'Are you sure?' 'Absolutely sure. I wouldn't have told you if I weren't.' And in the midst of her joy, Gertrudis felt as if a sword of ice had been plunged into her heart. She had nothing left to do in this world except wait for her new grandchild, the grandchild of those who belonged to her, Ramiro and Rosa, and then go and give them the good news. From that point on, she barely noticed anyone except Caridad, who for Gertrudis loomed so large as to fill the house. She even began to neglect Manolita, whom she herself had raised and shaped, and Manolita was able to sense it: she felt overshadowed by the baby to come.

'Come over here', Gertrudis used to say to Caridad when, occasionally, she came across her when the young woman was alone – an opportunity Gertrudis actively sought out. 'Come over here and sit by my side. Can you feel the baby, my darling girl, can you feel the baby?'

'Sometimes...'

—¿No llama? ¿No tiene prisa por salir a la luz, a la luz del sol? Porque ahí dentro, a oscuras... aunque esté ello tan tibio, tan sosegado... ¿No da empujoncitos? Si tarda no me va a ver..., no le voy a ver... Es decir: ¡si tarda, no!, si me apresuro yo...

—Pero, madre, no diga esas cosas...

—¡*No digas,* hija! Pero me siento derretir..., ya no soy para nada... Veo todo como empañado .... como en sueños... Si no lo supiera no podría ahora decir si tu pelo es rubio o moreno...

Y le acariciaba lentamente la espléndida cabellera rubia. Y como si viese con los dedos, añadía: «Rubia, rubia como el sol ...»

—Si es chico, ya lo sabes, Ramiro, y si es chica ... Rosa...

—No, madre, sino Gertrudis... Tula, mamá Tula.

—¡Tula..., bueno ...! Y mejor si fuese una pareja, mellizos, pero chico y chica...

—¡Por Dios, madre!

—¿Qué? ¿Crees que no podrías con eso? ¿Te parece demasiado trabajo?

—Yo... no sé.... no sé nada de eso, madre; pero...

—Sí, eso es lo perfecto, una parejita de gemelos... un chico y una chica que han estado abrazaditos cuando no sabían nada del mundo, cuando no sabían ni que existían; que han estado abrazaditos al calorcito del vientre materno... Algo así debe de ser el cielo...

—¡Qué cosas se te ocurren, mamá Tula!

—No ves que me he pasado la vida soñando...

Y en esto, mientras soñaba así y como para guardar en su pecho este último ensueño y llevarlo como viático al seno de la madre tierra, la pobre Manolita cayó gravemente enferma. « ¡Ah, yo tengo la culpa – se dijo Gertrudis –, yo, que con esto de la parejita de mi ensueño me he descuidado de esa pobre avecilla... ! Sin duda en un momento en que necesitaba de mi arrimo ha debido de coger algún frío ...» Y sintió que le volvían las fuerzas, unas fuerzas como de milagro. Se le despejó la cabeza y se dispuso a cuidar a la enferma.

'Isn't the baby calling? Isn't he or she impatient to come into the world, into the sunlight? Because in there, in the dark..., although it is so warm and peaceful ... can't you feel the baby kick? If the baby is late, he or she won't see me... I won't see the baby ... if he or she is late I mean... If I am not long for this world...'

'Please don't say things like that, mother...!'

'Don't say things like that, *mamita* – no need to be so formal... It's just that I feel that I'm dissolving inside... I'm good for nothing now... I feel as if I am looking at the world through a mist, or as if I am dreaming ... if I didn't know already, I wouldn't be able to tell you whether you have fair hair or dark...'

And Gertrudis slowly stroked Caridad's luxuriant fair hair. And as if she could see with her fingertips, she added 'Fair, fair, and as bright as the sun...'

'If it's a boy, you know to call him Ramiro, and if it's a girl...Rosa.'

'No, mother, Gertrudis... Tula, mama Tula.'

'Tula ... all right... It would be even better if there were two of them, twins, but a boy and a girl...'

'For goodness sake, mother!'

'What? You think you wouldn't be able to cope with that? Does it seem like too much work?'

'I... I don't know... I don't know about that mother, but...'

'Yes, that would be perfect, a little pair of twins ... a boy and a girl, embracing each other before they knew anything about the world, before they even knew that they existed; in each other's arms in the warmth of their mother's womb... Heaven must be rather like that...'

'The things you think of, mama Tula!'

'Can't you see that I've spent my life dreaming?'

And at this, as Gertrudis dreamed on, as if to keep this last fantasy within her heart – clutched to her as if it were a vital provision she could take with her on her journey to the bowels of mother earth, poor Manolita fell gravely ill.

'Oh, it's my fault', Gertrudis said to herself. What with all these fantasies about little pairs of twins, I have neglected this tiny little chick ... clearly when she needed me to be there she must have caught a chill when I wasn't...' And she felt her strength returning to her ... it was like a miracle. Her mind became clear again, and she resolved to look after the invalid.

–Pero, madre – le decía Caridad –, déjeme que le cuide yo, que le cuidemos nosotras... Entre yo, Rosita y Elvira le cuidaremos.

–No; tú no puedes cuidarla como es debido, no debes cuidarla... Tú te debes al que llevas, a lo que llevas, y no es cosa de que por atender a ésta malogres lo otro... y en cuanto a Rosita y Elvira, sí, son sus hermanas, la quieren como tales, pero no entienden de eso, y además la pobre, aunque se aviene a todo, no se halla sin mí... Un simple vaso de agua que yo le sirva le hace más provecho que todo lo que los demás le podáis hacer. Yo sola sé arreglarle la almohada de modo que no le duela en ella la cabeza y que no tenga luego pesadillas...

–Sí, es verdad...

–¡Claro, yo la crié ...! Y yo debo cuidarle.

Resucitó. Volvióle todo el luminoso y fuerte aplomo de sus días más heroicos. Ya no le temblaba el pulso ni le vacilaban las piernas. Y cuando teniendo el vaso con la pócima medicinal que a las veces tenía que darle, la pobre enferma le posaba las manos febriles en sus manos firmes y finas, pasaba sobre su enlace como el resplandor de un dulce recuerdo, casi borrado para la encamada. Y luego se sentaba la tía Tula junto a la cama de la enferma y se estaba allí, y ésta no hacía sino mirarle en silencio.

–¿Me moriré, mamita? – preguntaba la niña.

–¿Morirte? ¡No, pobrecita alondra, no! Tú tienes que vivir...

–Mientras tú vivas...

–Y después... y después...

–Después... no... ¿para qué...?

–Pero las muchachas deben vivir...

–¿Para qué...?

–Pues... para vivir... para casarse... para criar familia...

–Pues tú no te casaste, mamita...

–No, yo no me casé; pero como si me hubiese casado... Y tú tienes que vivir para cuidar de tu hermano...

–Es verdad..., de mi hermano..., de mis hermanos...

'Mother,' said Caridad, 'let me look after her … between me, Rosita and Elvira, we'll take care of her…'

'No, you won't be able to look after her properly … and *you* shouldn't be caring for her … all your care should be concentrated on the baby you're carrying, to the little bundle you're carrying inside. There's no need to endanger the little one by tending to Manolita… As for Rosita and Elvira, they are indeed her sisters, and they love her as sisters should, but they don't understand these things. Besides, the poor thing will agree to anything, but she's lost without me … a simple glass of water given to her by me will do her more good than anything the rest of you could do for her. I'm the only one who can arrange the pillow to stop her head hurting so that she doesn't have nightmares later…'

'That's true'

'Of course! I should know – I was the one who raised her…and I am the one who should look after her.'

Gertrudis came back from the dead. All the bright, sturdy assurance of her most heroic days returned. Her hand was steady once more and her legs no longer trembled. And when Gertrudis was holding the glass with the medicinal drink that she sometimes had to give Manolita, the poor invalid would place her feverish hands in Gertrudis's fine, firm hands, and something like the glimmer of a sweet memory, almost forgotten by the bedridden young woman, would pass between the two. And then Aunt Tula would sit by the patient's bed and stay with her, and the young woman would simply watch her in silence.

'Am I going to die, mamita?'

'Die? No my poor little sparrow, no! You have to live…'

'For as long as you do…'

'And beyond … beyond that too…'

'No, not beyond that … what for…?'

'Girls must live…'

'What for…?'

'Well, to live … to marry … to have a family…'

'But you didn't marry, mamita…'

'No, I didn't marry, but I might as well have done … and you have to live to look after your brother…'

'That's true… I must look after my brother … my brothers and sisters.'

–Sí, de todos ellos...

–Pero si dicen, mamita, que yo no sirvo para nada...

–¿Y quién dice eso, hija mía?

–No, no lo dicen..., no lo dicen..., pero lo piensan...

–¿Y cómo sabes tú lo que piensan?

–¡Pues... porque lo sé! Y además, porque es verdad..., porque yo no sirvo para nada, y después de que tú te me mueras yo nada tengo que hacer aquí... Si tú te murieras me moriría de frío...

–Vamos, vamos, arrópate bien y no digas esas cosas... Y voy a arreglarte esa medicina...

Y fue a ocultar sus lágrimas y a echarse a los pies de su imagen de la Virgen de la Soledad y a suplicarla: «¡Mi vida por la suya, Madre, mi vida por la suya! Siente que yo me voy, que me llaman mis muertos, y quiere irse conmigo; quiere arrimarse a mí, arropada por la tierra, allí abajo, donde no llega la luz, y que yo le preste no sé qué calor... ¡Mi vida por la suya, Madre, mi vida por la suya! Que no caiga tan pronto esa cortina de tierra de las tinieblas sobre esos ojos en que la luz no se quiebra, sobre esos ojos que dicen que son los míos, sobre esos ojos sin mancha que le di yo..., sí, yo... Que no se muera..., que no se muera... Sálvala, Madre, aunque tenga yo que irme sin ver al que ha de venir...»

Y se cumplió su ruego.

La pobre niña enferma fue recobrando vida; volvieron los colores de rosa a sus mejillas; volvió a mirar la luz del sol dando en el verdor de los árboles del jardincito de la casa, pero la tía Tula cayó con una bronconeumonía cogida durante la convalecencia de Manolita. Y entonces fue ésta la que sintió que brotaba en sus entrañas un manadero de salud, pues tenía que cuidar a la que le había dado vida.

Toda la casa vió con asombro la revelación de aquella niña.

–Di a Manolita – decía Gertrudis a Caridad – que no se afane tanto, que aún estará débil... Tú tampoco, por supuesto; tú te debes a los tuyos, ya lo sabes... Con Rosita y Elvira basta... Además, como todo ha de ser inútil... Porque yo ya he cumplido...

–Pero, madre...

–Nada, lo dicho, y que esa palomita de Dios no se malgaste...

'Yes, all of them...'

'But they say I'm good for nothing, mamita.'

'Who said that, my darling girl?'

'Well, they haven't actually *said* it ... but they think it...'

'And how do you know that?'

'I just do ... and besides, it's true!... I *am* good for nothing. After you die, there is nothing more for me to do here. If you died, I would die of cold...'

'Come come, wrap up warm now, and don't say things like that. I'm going to prepare your medicine...'

And she left so that Manolita wouldn't see her cry. She knelt down at the feet of her image of Our Lady of Solitude and beseeched the Virgin, 'I'll give my life to spare hers, Blessed Mother, my life for hers. She senses that I'm going ... that my dead are calling me, and she wants to go with me...; she wants to huddle close to me, draped in the earth, down below, where the light doesn't reach, and she wants me to pass my warmth to her... My life for hers, Mother, my life for hers! Don't let the dark curtain of the earth fall so soon over those eyes whose light remains, those eyes that cry out that they're my eyes, those unblemished eyes that I gave her ... yes, *I* gave her... Don't let her die..., don't let her die. Save her, Mother, even if it means I must go before the baby arrives...'

And her request was granted.

The poor sick girl slowly came back to life; the colour came back into her cheeks; she was able once again to see the sun shining onto the leaves of the trees in the house's little garden. But Aunt Tula was struck down by a bronchial pneumonia she caught during Manolita's convalescence. And it was Manolita who then felt a wellspring of healthiness and strength surge through her, because she now had to look after the woman who gave her life.

The whole house was amazed at Manolita's revelation.

'Tell Manolita,' said Gertrudis to Caridad 'not to go to so much trouble ... she must still be weak ... and you shouldn't either; you must attend to your own, you know... Rosita and Elvira are more than enough... Besides, it is all futile... I have done my duty...'

'But, mother...'

'I don't need or want anything, and don't let that angel waste her efforts on me...'

–Pero si se ha puesto tan fuerte... Jamás hubiese creído...

–Y ella que se quería morir y creía morirse... Y yo también lo temí... ¡Porque la pobre me parecía tan débil...! Claro, no conoció a su padre, que estaba ya herido de muerte cuando la engendró... y en cuanto a su pobre madre, yo creo que siempre vivió medio muerta... ¡Pero esa chica ha resucitado!

–¡Sí, al verte en peligro ha resucitado!

–¡Claro, es mi hija!

–¿Más?

–¡Sí, más! Te lo quiero declarar ahora que estoy en el zaguán de la eternidad; sí, más. ¡Ella y tú!

–¿Ella y yo?

–¡Sí, ella y tú! Y porque no tenéis mi sangre. Ella y tú. Ella tiene la sangre de Ramiro, no la mía, pero la he hecho yo, ¡es obra mía! Y a ti yo te casé con mi hijo...

–Lo sé...

–Sí, como le casé a su padre con su madre, con mi hermana, y luego le volví a casar con la madre de Manolita...

–Lo sé.... lo sé...

–Sé que lo sabes, pero no todo...

–No, todo no...

–Ni yo tampoco... O al menos no quiero saberlo. Quiero irme de este mundo sin saber muchas cosas... Porque hay cosas que el saberlas mancha. Eso es el pecado original, y la Santísima Virgen Madre nació sin mancha de pecado original...

–Pues yo he oído decir que lo sabía todo...

–No, no lo sabía todo; no conocía la ciencia del mal... que es ciencia...

–Bueno, no hables tanto, madre, que te perjudica...

–Más me perjudica cavilar, y si me callo cavilo... cavilo...

'But she has become so strong... I would never have believed...'

'And to think that she wanted to die, and believed that she was going to die ... and I was also afraid that she would! Of course she never knew her father who was already mortally ill when she was conceived ... and as for her poor mother, I think she always lived her life as if she were half dead. But this girl has come back from the dead!'

'Yes, seeing you in peril has revived her!'

'Naturally: she's my daughter!'

'More?'

'Yes, more! I want to declare it now that I am on the threshold of eternity ... yes, more than that! She and you!'

'She and I?'

'Yes, she and you! And it's because you are not my flesh and blood. She and you. She's Ramiro's flesh and blood, but it was me that made her. She's my work! And I married you to my son.'

'I know...'

'Yes, just as I married his father to his mother, my sister, and then I married him again to Manolita's mother...'

'I know, I know...'

'I know you know, but you don't know the whole of it...'

'No, I don't know everything...'

'And nor do I ... or at least I don't want to know the whole truth. I want to leave this world in ignorance of many things... There are some things that soil one to know them ... original sin for example ... the Blessed Virgin Mary was born without the stain of original sin...'

'But I have heard that she knew everything...'

'No, she didn't know everything ... she didn't possess knowledge of evil ... which is still a body of knowledge...'

'All right now, mother, don't talk so much, it's not good for you...'

'It's worse for me to ruminate ... and when I am not talking I ruminate... I ruminate...'

XXII

La tía Tula no podía ya más con su cuerpo. El alma le revoloteaba dentro de él, como un pájaro en una jaula que se desvencija, a la que deja con el dolor de quien le desollaran, pero ansiando volar por encima de las nubes. No llegaría a ver al nieto. ¿Lo sentía? «Allá arriba, estando con ellos –soñaba –, sabré cómo es, y si es niño o niña... o los dos.... y lo sabré mejor que aquí, pues desde allí arriba se ve mejor y más limpio lo de aquí abajo.»

La última fiebre teníala postrada en cama. Apenas si distinguía a sus sobrinos más que por el paso, sobre todo a Caridad y a Manolita. El paso de aquella, de Caridad, llegábale como el de una criatura cargada de fruto y hasta le parecía oler a sazón de madurez. Y el de Manolita era tan leve como el de un pajarito que no se sabe si corre o vuela a ras de tierra. «Cuando ella entra – se decía la tía –, siento rumor de alas caídas y quietas.»

Quiso despedirse primero de ésta, a solas, y aprovechó un momento en que vino a traerle la medicina. Sacó el brazo de la cama, lo alargó como para bendecirla, y poniéndole la mano sobre la cabeza, que ella inclinó con los claros ojos empañados, le dijo:

–¿Qué, palomita sin hiel, quieres todavía morirte...? ¡La verdad!

–Si con ello consiguiera...

–Que yo no me muera, ¿eh? No, no debes querer morirte... Tienes a tu hermano, a tus hermanos... Estuviste cerca de ello, pero me parece que la prueba te curó de esas cosas... ¿No es así? Dímelo como en confesión, que voy a contárselo a los nuestros...

–Sí, ya no se me ocurren aquellas tonterías...

–¿Tonterías? No, no eran tonterías. ¡Ah!, y ahora que dices eso de tonterías, tráeme tu muñeca, porque la guardas, ¿no es así? Sí, sé que la guardas... Tráeme aquella muñeca, ¿sabes? Quiero despedirme de ella también y que se despida de mí... ¿Te acuerdas? Vamos, ¿a que no te acuerdas?

XXII

Aunt Tula's body was giving up. Her soul fluttered around inside it, like a bird in a cage that was falling apart: leaving it was as painful as the bird's being stripped of all its feathers, its longing to fly above the clouds still intact. She would not live to see the arrival of her grandchild. Was she sorry? 'Up there I'll find out whether it is a boy or a girl.., and what he or she is like, or, if it's twins, what they are like, and I'll know better than I could ever learn here, because the view from there is purer and better than from down here.'

Her final fever confined her to bed. She could hardly tell her nephews and nieces apart – only their steps allowed her to pick out Caridad and Manolita. Caridad's step was heavy, as if she were weighed down by heavy fruit: she even smelled ripe to Gertrudis; Manolita's step, in contrast, was as light as a little bird. It was hard to say whether the bird was running over the ground or flying just above it. 'When Manolita comes in,' remarked the aunt to herself, 'I hear the rustle of drooping, stilled wings.'

She wanted to say farewell to Manolita first, and she took the chance when Manolita popped in to administer her medicine. Gertrudis slipped her arm out from under the sheets, holding it out as if to bless Manolita, and then placed her hand on the young woman's head. Misty-eyed, Manolita bowed her head as Gertrudis asked her,

'So, my sweet little fledgling … do you still want to die?'

'If by dying I could prevent…'

'My death? Is that what you were going to say? No, you mustn't wish to die … you have your brother … your brothers and sisters … You were near death, but I believe that the test you were put to cured you of those things, didn't it? Talk to me as if you were before me in the confessional; I'll be telling our families up above…'

'Yes, those silly notions don't occur to me anymore.'

'Silly notions? They weren't silly. Ah! And now that you mention silly things, bring me your doll – you still have it, don't you? Yes, I know you must still have it … bring me that old doll … you know the one… I want to say goodbye to her, and I want her to be able to say goodbye to me… Do you remember? I bet you do…'

–Sí, madre, me acuerdo.

–¿De qué te acuerdas?

–De cuando se me cayó en aquel patín de la huerta y Elvira me llamaba tonta porque lloraba tanto y me decía que de nada sirve llorar...

–Eso... eso... ¿y qué más? ¿Te acuerdas de más?

–Sí, del cuento que nos contaste entonces...

–A ver, ¿qué cuento?

–De la niña que se le cayó la muñeca en un pozo seco adonde no podía bajar a sacarla, y se puso a llorar, a llorar, a llorar, y lloró tanto que se llenó el pozo con sus lágrimas y salió flotando en ellas la muñeca...

–¿Y qué dijo Elvirita a eso? ¿Qué dijo? Que no me acuerdo...

–Sí, sí te acuerdas, madre...[27]

–Bueno, ¿pues qué dijo?

–Dijo que la niña se quedaría seca y muerta de haber llorado tanto...

–¿Y yo qué dije?

–Por Dios, madre...

–Bueno, no lo digas, pero no llores así, palomita, no llores así... que por mucho que llores no se llenará con tus lágrimas el pozo en que voy cayendo y no saldré flotando.

–Si pudiera ser.

–¡Ah, sí! Si pudiera ser yo saldría a cogerte y llevarte conmigo... Pero hay que esperar la hora. Y cuida de tus hermanos. Te los entrego a ti, ¿sabes?, a ti. Haz que no se den cuenta de que me he muerto.

–Haré todo lo que pueda...

–Y yo te ayudaré desde arriba. Que no se enteren de que me he muerto...

–Te rezaré, madre...

–A la Virgen, hija, a la Virgen...

–Te rezaré, madre, todas las noches antes de acostarme...

–Bueno, no llores así...

–Pero si no lloro, ¿no ves que no lloro?

'Yes, mother, I remember.'

'What do you remember?'

'I remember when I fell over in the garden and Elvira said that I was silly to cry so much about it, and that crying never made anything better...'

'Oh yes, yes ... and what else ... do you remember anything else...?'

'Yes, I remember the story you told us then...'

'What story was that?'

'The one about the little girl whose doll fell into a dried-up well, where it couldn't be recovered, and she cried so much that eventually her tears filled the well, and the doll floated up to the surface...'

'And what did Elvira say about *that*? What did she say? I can't remember...'

'Oh you *do* remember, mother...'

'Well, tell me anyway, what did she say?'

'She said that the little girl would dry up and die from having cried so much...'

'And what did I say to her?'

'For goodness sake, mother...'

'All right, you don't have to tell, but don't cry like that, my sweet, don't cry like that ... however much you cry, the well I'm falling into won't fill up and I won't float to the surface...'

'But if only it could be like that...'

'If it could only be like that, I'd pop up and catch hold of you and take you with me... But one must await one's time. And look after your brothers and sisters. I am placing them in your care. You do realise that, don't you? I want you to look after them so well that they don't even realise that I have died.'

'I'll do all I can.'

'I'll help you from up above. I don't want them to realise that I've even died.'

'I'll pray for you, mother...'

'Pray to the Virgin Mary, my darling daughter, pray to the Virgin.'

'I'll pray for you every night, mother, just before I go to bed...'

'All right, don't cry...'

'But I am not crying. See? I'm not crying.'

–Para lavar los ojos cuando han visto cosas feas no está mal; pero tú no has visto cosas feas, no puedes verlas...

–Y si es caso, cerrando los ojos...

–No, no, así se ven cosas más feas. Y pide por tu padre, por tu madre, por mí... No olvides a tu madre...

–Si no la olvido...

–Como no la conociste...

–¡Sí, la conozco!

–Pero a la otra, digo, a la que te trajo al mundo.

–¡Sí, gracias a ti la conozco; a aquella!

–¡Pobrecilla! Ella no había conocido a la suya...

–¡Su madre fuiste tú, lo sé bien!

–Bueno, pero no llores...

–¡Si no lloro! – y se enjugaba los ojos con el dorso de la mano izquierda mientras con la otra, temblorosa, sostenía el vaso de la medicina.

–Bueno, y ahora trae a la muñeca, que quiero verla. ¡Ah! ¡Y allí, en un rincón de aquella arquita mía que tú sabes.... ahí está la llave... sí, esa, esa!... Allí donde nadie ha tocado más que yo, y tú alguna vez; allí, junto a aquellos retratos, ¿sabes?, hay otra muñeca... la mía... la que yo tenía siendo niña... mi primer cariño ... ¿el primero?... ¡bueno! Tráemela también... Pero que no se entere ninguna de esas, no digan que son tonterías nuestras, porque las tontas somos nosotras... Tráeme las dos muñecas, que me despida de ellas, y luego nos pondremos serias para despedirnos de los otros... Vete, que me viene un mal pensamiento – y se santiguó.

El mal pensamiento era que el susurro diabólico allá, en el fondo de las entrañas doloridas con el dolor de la partida, le decía: «¡Muñecos todos!»

'Crying's good to wash out one's eyes when they've seen unpleasant things, but you've seen nothing unpleasant – you're not capable of seeing such things.

'And if I did, by closing my eyes…'

'No, no, one can see even more unpleasant things by closing one's eyes. And pray for your father, your mother, and me … don't forget your mother.'

'I would never forget her!'

'Well, as you never knew her…'

'I *do* know her!'

'I mean your other mother … the one who brought you into this world.'

'Yes, thanks to you I *do* know her…'

'Poor thing! She never knew *her* mother…'

'*You* were her mother! That much I know…'

'There's no need to cry…'

'I'm *not* crying'. As she said this, she wiped her eyes with the back of her left hand whilst her trembling right hand held the glass of medicine.

'All right. Now bring me the doll – I want to see it. Oh, and in a corner of that chest of mine – you know the one – there's a key – yes, that's the one!…No-one has touched anything in there except me, and perhaps you once or twice. Together with those portraits – you know the ones – there's another doll, my one, the one I've had since I was a little girl … my first love … wait … *first* love? Anyway, bring that to me too … but don't let any of the others know … so they can't say that we are just being silly, because we're the silly ones… Bring me both dolls, so that I can say goodbye to them, and then we'll be serious and say goodbye to the others … go now, I've just had a bad thought…', and she crossed herself.

The bad thought was that diabolical whisper deep inside her, deep inside where the pain of parting from her loved ones was keenest. It whispered 'They are all dolls!'

XXIII

Luego llamó a todos, y Caridad entre ellos.

–Esto es, hijos míos, la última fiebre, el principio de fuego del Purgatorio...

–Pero qué cosas dices, mamá...

–Sí; el fuego del Purgatorio, porque en el Infierno no hay fuego... el Infierno es de hielo y nada más que de hielo. Se me está quemando la carne... Y lo que siento es irme sin ver, sin conocer, al que ha de llegar... o a la que ha de llegar... o a los que han de llegar..

–Vamos, mamá...

–Bueno, tú, Cari, cállate y no nos vengas ahora con vergüenza... Porque yo querría contarles todo a los que me llaman... Vamos, no lloréis así... Allí están... los tres...

–Pero no digas esas cosas...

–¡Ah!, ¿queréis que os diga cosas de reír? Las tonterías ya nos las hemos dicho Manolita y yo, las dos tontas de la casa, y ahora hay que hacer esto como se hace en los libros...

–Bueno, ¡no hables tanto! El médico ha dicho que no se te deje hablar mucho.

–¿Ya estás ahí tú, Ramiro? ¡El hombre! ¿El médico, dices? ¿Y qué sabe el médico?

No le hagáis caso... Y además es mejor vivir una hora hablando que dos días más en silencio. Ahora es cuando hay que hablar. Además, así me distraigo y no pienso en mis cosas...

–Pues ya sabes que el padre Álvarez te ha dicho que pienses ahora en tus cosas...

–¡Ah!, ¿ya estás ahí tú, Elvira, la juiciosa? Conque el padre Alvarez, ¿eh?... el del remedio... ¿Y qué sabe el padre Álvarez? ¡Otro médico! ¡Otro hombre! Además, yo no tengo cosas mías en qué pensar... yo no tengo mis cosas... Mis cosas son las vuestras... y las de ellos..., las de los que me llaman... Yo no estoy ni viva ni muerta... no he estado nunca ni viva ni muerta... ¿Qué? ¿Qué dices tú ahí, Enriquín? Que estoy delirando...

–No, no digo eso...

–Sí, has dicho eso, te lo he oído bien... se lo has dicho al oído a Rosita... No ves que siento hasta el roce en el aire de las alas quietas de Manolita. Pues si deliro... ¿qué?

XXIII

Gertrudis summoned everyone to her bedside, Caridad included.
'This, my children, is my last fever, and is the beginning of the fires of Purgatory...'
'The things you say, mother...'
'It is indeed the fires of Purgatory, because in hell there is no fire... Hell is ice and nothing more. My flesh is burning ... and what I regret is leaving you without being able to see, or know, the little one yet to be born, boy or girl ... or perhaps the little *ones* yet to be born...'
'Come now, mother.'
'Now then Cari, shh, and don't be embarrassed... I wanted to be able to tell all to those up there who are calling me ... come now, don't cry ... there they are, the three of them...'
'Don't say things like that...'
'Would you rather I made you laugh? You should have heard the silly things Manolita and I have been talking about this morning, just the two of us, the fools of the house ... but now we have do things by the book...'
'Don't talk so much! The doctor has said that you shouldn't be allowed to speak much.'
'Is that you there too Ramiro? The man!... The doctor, you say? And what does he know? Don't take any notice ... besides, it's better to live for an hour and speak than live two days more in silence ... now is when we need to speak. And anyway, this distracts me, and I don't brood on my own affairs.'
'Well, you know that Father Alvarez has told you that now is precisely the time to be thinking about your affairs...'
'Ah, you're there too Elvira, oh wise one? So ... Father Alvarez ... he of the "remedy" ... what does he know? He's another doctor! Another man! Besides, I have no affairs that I need to be thinking about... I don't have any affairs ... my affairs are your affairs ... and their affairs, those who are calling me from up high ... I'm neither alive nor dead... What? What's that you're saying Enriquín? That I'm delirious...?'
'No, I didn't say that...'
'Yes, you did, I heard you clearly ... you whispered it in Rosita's ear ... aren't you aware that I can hear even Manolita's still wings move through the air ... and if I am delirious, what of it?'

–Que debes descansar...

–Descansar..., descansar..., ¡tiempo me queda para descansar!

–Pero no te destapes así...

–Si es que me abraso... Y ya sabes, Caridad, Tula, Tula como yo... y él, el otro, Ramiro... Sí, son dos, él y ella, que estarán ahora abrazaditos... al calorcito.

Callaron todos un momento. Y al oír la moribunda sollozos entrecortados y contenidos, añadió:

–Bueno, ¡hay que tener ánimo! Pensad bien, bien, muy bien, lo que hayáis de hacer, pensadlo muy bien... que nunca tengáis que arrepentiros de haber hecho algo y menos de no haberlo hecho... Y si veis que el que queréis se ha caído en una laguna de fango y aunque sea en un pozo negro, en un albañal, echaos a salvarle, aun a riesgo de ahogaros, echaos a salvarle... que no se ahogue él allí... o ahogaos juntos... en el albañal... servidle de remedio... sí, de remedio... ¿que morís entre légamo y porquería?, no importa... Y no podréis ir a salvar al compañero volando sobre el ras del albañal porque no tenemos alas... no, no tenemos alas... o son alas de gallina, de no volar..., y hasta las alas se mancharían con el fango que salpica el que se ahoga en él... No, no tenemos alas... a lo más de gallina...; no somos ángeles... lo seremos en la otra vida... ¡donde no hay fango... ni sangre... Fango hay en el Purgatorio, fango ardiente, que quema y limpia... fango que limpia, sí... En el Purgatorio les queman a los que no quisieron lavarse con fango... sí, con fango... Les queman con estiércol ardiente... les lavan con porquería... Es lo último que os digo, no tengáis miedo a la podredumbre... Rogad por mí, y que la Virgen me perdone.

Le dió un desmayo. Al volver de él no coordinaba los pensamientos. Entró luego en una agonía dulce. Y se apagó como se apaga una tarde de otoño cuando las últimas razas del sol, filtradas por nubes sangrientas, se derriten en las aguas serenas de un remanso del río en que se reflejan los álamos – sanguíneo su follaje también – que velan a sus orillas.

'Well, you should rest...'

'Rest? Rest? I'll have plenty of time to rest later...'

'Don't push the bedclothes down though...'

'But I'm burning up ... and Caridad, you know to call the little one Tula, Tula, like me ... and the other one Ramiro... Yes, there are two of them ... a boy and a girl, curled up in each other's arms in the warm.'

Everyone was silent for a moment. And when the dying woman heard the choked, contained sobs around her, she added,

'Come now, you must keep your spirits up! Think, think carefully, about what it falls to you to do ... think about it very carefully ... and may you never have regrets about doing something, or, worse, regret *not* doing something ... and if you see that the one you love has fallen into a muddy pool, or even into a cesspool, or a sewer, jump in and save him, even if you risk drowning ... throw yourselves in and save him ... don't let him drown there ... or at least drown together ... there in the sewer, serve as his remedy, yes, his remedy ... so what if you'd die in and amongst slime and filth? It doesn't matter ... and you won't be able to save your companion by flying low over the sewer because we don't have wings ... no, we don't have wings, or if we do they are chicken's wings, not made to fly ... and even the wings would be stained by the mud that splashed the person drowning in it... No, we don't have wings ... or at least nothing more than chicken's wings ... we're not angels ... we may become them in the next life ... where there *is* no mud. Or blood! There's mud in Purgatory, flaming mud that cauterises and cleanses ... mud that cleanses, indeed ... in Purgatory those that didn't want to wash themselves in mud are burned, yes, those that didn't want to cleanse themselves with mud ... they are cauterised with burning manure ... they clean them with filth... This is the last thing I'll say to you: don't be afraid of putrefaction ... pray for me, and may the Virgin Mary forgive me.

She fell into a faint. When she came to, she could no longer think straight. She then gently entered the death throes. She faded as an October afternoon fades when the last rays of sun, filtered through blood-coloured clouds, melt into the calm waters of a river pool in which the poplars – their leaves also the colour of blood – keeping vigil on the banks reflected in the water.

XXIV

¿Murió la tía Tula? No, sino que empezó a vivir en la familia, e irradiando de ella, con una nueva vida más entrañada y más vivífica, con la vida eterna de la familiaridad inmortal. Ahora era ya para sus hijos, sus sobrinos, la Tía, no más que la Tía, ni *madre* ya ni *mamá,* ni aun tía Tula, sino sólo la Tía. Fue este nombre de invocación, de verdadera invocación religiosa, como el canonizamiento doméstico de una santidad de hogar. La misma Manolita, su más hija y la más heredera de su espíritu, la depositaria de su tradición, no le llamaba sino la Tía.

Mantenía la unidad y la unión de la familia, y si al morir ella afloraron a la vista de todos, haciéndose patentes, divisiones intestinas antes ocultas, alianzas defensivas y ofensivas entre los hermanos, fue porque esas divisiones brotaban de la vida misma familiar que ella creó. Su espíritu provocó tales disensiones y bajo de ellas y sobre ellas la unidad fundamental y culminante de la familia. La tía Tula era el cimiento y la techumbre de aquel hogar.

Formáronse en éste dos grupos: de un lado, Rosita, la hija mayor de Rosa, aliada con Caridad, con su cuñada, y no con su hermano, no con Ramiro; de otro, Elvira, la segunda hija de Rosa, con Enrique, su hermanastro, el hijo de la hospiciana, y quedaban fuera Ramiro y Manolita. Ramiro vivía, o más bien se dejaba vivir, atento a su hijo y al porvenir que podían depararle otros y a sus negocios civiles, y Manolita, atenta a mantener el culto de la Tía y la tradición del hogar.

Manolita se preparaba a ser el posible lazo entre cuatro probables familias venideras. Desde la muerte de la Tía habíase revelado. Guardaba todo su saber, todo su espíritu; las mismas frases recortadas y aceradas, a las veces repetición de las que oyó a la otra, la misma doctrina, el mismo estilo y hasta el mismo gesto. «¡Otra tía!» , exclamaban sus hermanos, y no siempre llevándoselo a bien. Ella guardaba el archivo y el tesoro de la otra; ella tenía la llave de los cajoncitos secretos de la que se fue

XXIV

Did Aunt Tula die? No. She began, rather, to live in the family, illuminating the eternal life of immortal familiarity with a new, more intimate and revitalised life. Already now for her children, her nephews and nieces, she was known as 'Aunt', just 'Aunt', no longer *mother*, nor *mama*, and not even 'Aunt Tula', just 'Aunt'. It was a term of invocation, true religious invocation, like the domestic canonization of a household sanctity. Even Manolita, whom Gertrudis had considered closest to a daughter, spiritual heir and the repository of her tradition, only ever referred to her as the Aunt.

She had maintained the unity and union of the family. If, on her death, previously hidden, deeply buried divisions came to the surface, making visible and obvious to all the defensive and offensive alliances between the siblings, it was because they sprang from the very family life that she had created. Her spirit provoked such disagreements, but, beneath and above them remained the fundamental and culminating unity of the family. Aunt Tula was both the foundations and the roof of that household.

Two groups formed within the home: on one side was Rosita, Rosa's oldest daughter, who formed an alliance with Caridad, her sister-in-law, and not with her brother, Ramiro; on the other side was Elvira, Rosa's second daughter, who was in alliance with Enrique, her stepbrother, the foundling's son. Ramiro and Manolita remained outside the two factions. Ramiro lived, or rather was swept along by life, attentive towards his son and the future that others might furnish him with, and to his business and social affairs; Manolita put care into maintaining the cult of her aunt and the traditions of the household.

Manolita began to prepare herself to be the possible bridge between four future families. Ever since the death of their Aunt, her behaviour had been a revelation to the others. She had preserved all her aunt's knowledge, her whole spirit. She used the same clipped, mordant phrases – some of them parroted from her aunt – and preserved the same doctrine, style and even facial expressions. 'Another Aunt!' exclaimed her brothers and sisters, not always intending it to be complimentary. She was the guardian of her aunt's archive and of her treasures; she was the keeper of the keys to the flesh-and-blood aunt's secret drawers. Alongside her

en carne y sangre; ella guardaba, con su muñeca de cuando niña, la
muñeca de la niñez de la Tía, y algunas cartas, y el devocionario y el
breviario de don Primitivo; ella era en la familia quien sabía los dichos
y hechos de los antepasados dentro de la memoria: de don Primitivo,
que nada era de su sangre; de la madre del primer Ramiro; de Rosa; de
su propia madre Manuela, la hospiciana – de ésta no dichos ni hechos,
sino silencios y pasiones –, ella era la historia doméstica; por ella se
continuaba la eternidad espiritual de la familia. Ella heredó el alma de
ésta, espiritualizada en la Tía.

¿Herencia? Se transmite por herencia en una colmena el espíritu de
las abejas, la tradición abejil, el arte de la melificación y de la fábrica del
panal, la *abejidad,* y no se transmite, sin embargo, por carne y por jugos
de ella. La carnalidad se perpetúa por zánganos y por reinas, y ni los
zánganos ni las reinas trabajaron nunca, no supieron ni fabricar panales,
ni hacer miel, ni cuidar larvas, y no sabiéndolo, no pudieron transmitir
ese saber, con su carne y sus jugos, a sus crías. La tradición del arte de las
abejas, de la fábrica del panal y el laboreo de la miel y la cera, es pues,
colateral y no de transmisión de carne, sino de espíritu, y débese a las
tías, a las abejas que ni fecundan huevecillos ni los ponen. Y todo esto lo
sabía Manolita, a quien se lo había enseñado la Tía, que desde muy joven
paró su atención en la vida de las abejas y la estudió y meditó, y hasta
soñó sobre ella. Y una de las frases de íntimo sentido, casi esotérico,
que aprendió Manolita de la Tía y que de vez en cuando aplicaba a sus
hermanos, cuando dejaban muy al desnudo su masculinidad de instintos,
era decirles: «¡Cállate, zángano!» Y zángano tenía para ella, como lo
había tenido para la Tía, un sentido de largas y profundas resonancias.
Sentido que sus hermanos adivinaban.

La alianza entre Elvira, la hija del primer Ramiro que le costó la vida
a Rosa, su primera mujer, y Enrique, el hijo del pecado de aquél y de
los hospicianos, era muy estrecha. Queríanse los hermanastros más que
cualesquiera otros de los cinco entre sí. Siempre andaban en cuchicheos y
en secretos. Y ésta a modo de conjura desasosegábale a Manolita. No que

own childhood doll, she kept the Aunt's childhood doll too, together with some letters and Don Primitivo's prayerbooks. She was the family fount of knowledge as regards the sayings and deeds of those forebears still within living memory: don Primitivo, who wasn't even her flesh and blood, Ramiro's first, flesh-and-blood mother, and her own mother, the orphan, even if, in the latter's case it was less a question of sayings and deeds than silences and passions. She was the historian of the household; it was through her that the eternal spiritual continuity of the family was ensured. She inherited the soul of the family which had been spiritualised in the Aunt.

Inheritance? The spirit of the bees is passed on through inheritance within the hive. The apian tradition – the art of making honey and constructing the honeycomb – and the apian essence are not transmitted by flesh and blood. Carnality is perpetuated by the drones and the queens, and neither the queens nor the drones ever did any work: they didn't even *know* how to make the honeycomb, or the honey, or how to look after the larvae. Having no knowledge of these things, they couldn't then transmit this knowledge through their flesh and blood to their offspring. The traditional apian art of making the honeycomb, manufacturing the honey and the beeswax, is, then, *collateral* and not a transmission through the flesh. It is, rather, a transmission via the spirit, attributable to the aunts, to the bees that neither fertilise nor lay the eggs. Manolita knew all this because she had been taught it by Aunt, who, from a very young age, had been very struck by the life of the bee, and had studied, reflected on and even dreamed about it. She had learned one particular phrase with intimate, almost esoteric meaning from Aunt, and occasionally applied it to her brothers when their instinctive masculinity became particularly apparent. She would say 'Be quiet, you drone!' The word 'drone' had a long-standing and profound resonance for her, just as it had done for her aunt. It was a resonance and meaning that her brothers were able to sense.

The alliance between Elvira – daughter of the older Ramiro, and therefore the baby that had cost his first wife, Rosa, her life – and Enrique – the son of the sinful relation between Ramiro and the maid from the orphanage – was very close. The stepsiblings loved each other more than any of the other five children. They were always whispering and sharing secrets together. And this type of conspiracy made Manolita uneasy. It

le doliera que su hermano uterino, el salido del mismo vientre de donde ella salió, tuviese más apego a la hermana nacida de otra madre, no; sentía que a ella no había de apegársele ninguno de sus hermanos y complacíase en ello. Pero aquel afecto más que fraternal le era repulsivo.

–Ya estoy deseando – les dijo una vez – que uno de vosotros se enamore; que tú, Enrique, te eches novia, o que a ésta, a ti, Elvira, te pretenda alguno...

–¿Y para qué? –preguntó esta.

–Para que dejéis de andar así, de bracete por la casa, y con cuentecitos al oído y carantoñas, arrumacos y lagoterías...

–Acaso entonces más... – dijo Enrique.

–¿Y cómo así?

–Porque ésta vendrá a contarme los secretos de su novio, ¿verdad, Elvira?, y yo le contaré, ¡claro está!, los de mi novia...

–Sí, sí... – exclamó Elvira a punto de palmotear.

–Y os reiréis uno y otro del otro novio y de la otra novia, ¿no es así?... ¡qué bonito!

–Bueno, ¿y qué diría a esto la Tía? – preguntó Elvira mirándole a Manolita a los ojos.

–Diría que no se debe jugar con las cosas santas y que sois unos chiquillos...

–Pues no repitas con la Tía – le arguyó Enrique – aquello del Evangelio de que hay que hacerse niño para entrar en el reino de los cielos...

–¡Niño, sí! ¡Chiquillo, no!

–¿Y en qué se le distingue al niño del chiquillo ...?

–¿En qué? En la manera de jugar.

–¿Cómo juega el chiquillo?

–El chiquillo juega a persona mayor. Los niños no son, como los mayores, ni hombres ni mujeres, sino que son como los ángeles. Recuerdo haberle oído decir a la Tía que había oído que hay lenguas en que el niño no es ni masculino ni femenino, sino neutro.

–Sí – añadió Enrique –, en alemán. Y la señorita es neutro...

–Pues esta señorita – dijo Manolita, intentando, sin conseguirlo, teñir de una sonrisa estas palabras – no es neutra...

wasn't that she found it hurtful that the brother born from the same womb as her felt closer to a sister born of a different mother; she did not feel that any of her brothers or sisters had perforce to feel special affection for her, and took pleasure in that. But their affection, which was more than fraternal, was repulsive to her.

'I'm counting the days,' she said to them once 'till one of you falls in love; till you, Enrique, start courting, or she – I mean you, Elvira – should find a suitor...'

'Why?', asked Elvira.

'So that you stop wandering around here arm-in-arm, with your endearments, whispering sweet nothings in each other's ear.'

'Maybe we'd do it all the more in that case...', said Enrique.

'How so?'

'Because she would come and tell me her suitor's secrets, wouldn't you Elvira? And of course I'll tell her my sweetheart's secrets too.'

'Yes, yes!', exclaimed Elvira, almost clapping.

'And you'll both laugh at the other suitor or the other sweetheart, won't you? How charming!'

'Well, what do you think Aunt would think of that?', asked Elvira, looking Manolita in the eye.

'She'd say that you shouldn't be playing with sacred things and that you're both very childish ...'

'Don't keep going on about what Aunt would say...', Enrique countered. 'Remember what the gospel says about having to be a child to enter the kingdom of heaven...'

'One has to be child*like*, yes! But not child*ish*!'

'And how can you tell the difference?'

'How? In play.'

'How? What is childish "play"?'

'The childish person plays at being an adult. Children don't have sexes, unlike adults; they're like angels. I remember Aunt saying that she'd heard of languages in which the child isn't considered a female or male noun but a neuter one...'

'Yes, that's the case in German,' added Enrique, 'and "señorita" is also neuter in German'.

'Well, *this* señorita', said Manolita, trying – and failing – to soften her words with a smile, 'is certainly not neuter...'

—¡Claro que no soy neutra; pues no faltaba más...!

—Pero ¡bueno, nada de chiquilladas!

—Chiquilladas, no; niñerías, eso, ¿no es eso?

—¡Eso es!

—Bueno, y ¿en qué las conoceremos?

—Basta, que no quiero deciros más. ¿Para qué? Porque hay cosas que al tratar de decirlas se ponen más oscuras...

—Bien, bien, tiíta —exclamó Elvira abrazándola y dándole un beso—, no te enfades así... ¿Verdad que no te enfadas, tiíta...?

—No; y menos porque me llames tiíta ...

—Si lo hacía sin intención...

—Lo sé; pero eso es lo peligroso. Porque la intención viene después...

Enrique le hizo una carantoña a su hermana completa y cogiendo a la otra, a la hermanastra, por debajo de un brazo, se la llevó consigo.

Y Manolita, viéndoles alejarse, quedó diciéndose: «¿Chiquillos? ¡En efecto, chiquillos! Pero ¿he hecho bien en decirles lo que les he dicho? ¿He hecho bien, Tía?» – e invocaba mentalmente a la Tía –. La intención viene después... ¿No soy yo la que con mis reconvenciones voy a darles una intención que les falta? Pero, ¡no, no! ¡Que no jueguen así! ¡Porque están jugando...! ¡Y ojalá les salga pronto el novio a ella y la novia a él!»

'Of course I'm not neuter! The very thought...'

'Now, now, that's enough childishness...'

'So, childishness, no; childlikeness, yes – is that it?'

'Yes, exactly so!'

'And how will we distinguish them?'

'Enough. I don't want to discuss this any further with you... What would be the point? Because there are things that when you attempt to talk about them become even more obscure...'

'All right, auntie dear...,' exclaimed Elvira, hugging Manolita and giving her a kiss, 'don't get cross ... you're not cross are you?'

'No, and not because you called me auntie either...'

'I didn't mean anything by it...'

'I know, but therein lies the danger. The intended meaning comes afterwards...'

Enrique made an affectionate gesture towards his full sister, and, putting a hand under his other, stepsister's arm, led her away...

Watching them walk away, Manolita was left to think,

'Childish? Yes, childish, indeed! But was I right to say what I did? Was I right, Aunt?' She invoked their Aunt mentally. 'The intended meaning comes afterwards... Aren't I the one who, with my reprimands, am imputing an intention to them that they don't really have? But, no! No! They shouldn't be playing around like that! Because it *is* a game that they're playing... And I hope that they both find a sweetheart soon!'

XXV

El otro grupo lo formaban en la familia, no Rosita y Ramiro, sino la mujer de éste, Caridad, y aquella su cuñada. Aunque en rigor era Rosita la que buscaba a Caridad y le llevaba sus quejas, sus aprensiones, sus suspicacias. Porque iba, por lo común, a quejarse. Creíase, o al menos aparentaba creer, que era la desdeñada y la no comprendida. Poníase triste y como preocupada en espera de que le preguntasen qué era lo que tenía, y como nadie se lo preguntaba sufría con ello. Y menos que los otros hermanos se lo preguntaba Manolita, que se decía: «¡Si tiene algo de verdad y más que gana de mimo y de que nos ocupemos especialmente en ella, ya reventará!» Y la preocupada sufría con ello.

A su cuñada, a Caridad, le iba sobre todo con quejas de su marido; complacíase en acusar a este, a Ramiro, de egoísta. Y la mujer le oía pacientemente y sin saber qué decirle.

–Yo no sé, Manuela –le decía a ésta Caridad, su cuñada–, qué hacer con Rosa...Siempre me está viniendo con quejas de Ramiro; que si es un orgulloso, que si un egoísta, que si un distraído...

–¡Llévale la hebra y dile que sí!

–Pero ¿cómo? ¿Voy a darle alas?

–No, sino a cortárselas.

–Pues no lo entiendo. Y además, eso no es verdad; ¡Ramiro no es así!...

–Lo sé, lo sé muy bien. Sé que Ramiro podrá tener, como todo hombre, sus defectos...

–Y como toda mujer.

–¡Claro, sí! Pero los de él son defectos de hombre...

–¡De zángano, vamos!

–Como quieras; los de Ramiro son defectos de hombre, o si quieres, pues que te empeñas, de zángano...

–¿Y los míos?

–¿Los tuyos, Caridad? Los tuyos... ¡de reina!

XXV

The other grouping in the family was formed not by Rosita and Ramiro, but by his wife, Caridad, and her sister-in-law. Although strictly speaking, it was Rosita who sought Caridad out, taking her complaints, fears and suspicions to her sister-in-law. Most often, it was complaints. She believed, or seemed to believe, that she was scorned and misunderstood. She would put on a sad or worried expression in the hope that someone would ask her what was wrong; as no-one ever asked the question, she used to suffer as a result. And of all the brothers and sisters, Manolita was the least solicitous towards her. Manolita would say to herself, 'If there is really something wrong with her, it will soon become more than clear. That will be more helpful than our pampering her or showing special concern for her in the meantime!' And the concerned woman was tormented by all this.

Above all, Rosita would go to Caridad, her sister-in-law, with complaints about her husband; she enjoyed accusing Ramiro of being selfish. And Caridad would listen patiently without knowing what to say.

'Manuela, I don't know what to do about Rosa', said Caridad to her sister-in-law. 'She's always coming to me with complaints about Ramiro. According to her, he's too proud … he's selfish … he doesn't pay attention to her…'

'Oh, you should go along with it and agree….'

'You mean encourage her?'

'No, that way you'll nip it in the bud….'

'I don't see that at all. Anyway, it's not true! Ramiro's not like that…'

'I know, I know. Ramiro may have his faults, like all men…'

'And women!'

'Of course! But his faults are male faults'

'Or rather, the faults of a drone!'

'If you say so. Ramiro's faults are male faults, or, if you insist, the faults that a drone has.'

'What are my faults?'

'Your faults, Caridad? The faults of a queen bee!'

—¡Muy bien! ¡Ni la Tía...!

—Pero los defectos de Ramiro no son los que Rosa dice. Ni es orgulloso, ni es egoísta, ni es distraído...

—Y entonces ¿por qué voy a llevarle la hebra, como dices?

—Porque eso será llevarle la contraria. Lo sé muy bien. La conozco.

Cierta mañana, encontrándose las tres, Caridad, Manuela y Rosa, comenzó ésta el ataque.

R.–¡Vaya unas horas de llegar anoche tu maridito!

Nunca hablando con su cuñada le llamaba a Ramiro «mi hermano», sino siempre: «tu marido» .

C.–¿Y qué mal hay en ello?

M.–Y tú, Rosa, estabas a esas horas despierta.

R.–Me despertó su llegada.

M.–¿Sí, eh?

C.–Pues a mi apenas si me despertó...

R.–¡Vaya una calma!

M.–Aquí Caridad duerme confiada y hace bien.

R.–¿Hace bien...? ¿Hace bien...? No lo comprendo.

M.–Pues yo sí. Pero tú parece que te complaces en eso, que es un juego muy peligroso y muy feo...

C.–¡Por Dios, Manuela!

R.–Déjale, déjale a la tía...

M.–Con el acento que ahora le pones, la tía aquí eres ahora tú...

R.–¿Yo? ¿Yo la tía?

M.–Sí, tú, tú, Rosa. ¿A qué viene querer provocar celos en tu hermana?

C.–Pero si Rosa no quiere hacerme celosa, Manuela.

M.–Yo sé lo que me digo, Caridad.

R.–Sí, aquí ella sabe lo que se dice...

M.–Aquí sabemos todos lo que queremos decir y yo sé, además, lo que me digo, ¿me entiendes, Rosa?

R.–El estribillo de la Tía...

M.–Sea. Y te digo que serías capaz de aceptar el peor novio que se te presente y casarte con él no más que para provocarle a que te diese celos, no a dárselos tú...

'That's a good one! Not even Aunt would have said that...!'

'But Ramiro's faults are not the ones that Rosa accuses him of. He's not too proud, selfish, or inattentive.'

'Then why should I agree with Rosa as you advise?'

'Because it is a way of challenging or contradicting her. I know what I'm saying. I know her.'

One fine morning when the three of them were together, Rosa began her customary attack.

R. 'Your husband came home very late last night!' When she was speaking to her sister-in-law, she never referred to Ramiro as 'my brother'; it was always 'your husband'.

C. 'What's wrong with that?'

M. 'And clearly *you* were awake at that time, Rosa.'

R. 'His coming back woke me up.'

C. 'Well I hardly heard him coming in...'

R. 'How wonderful to be so calm about it...'

M. 'Caridad can sleep without the slightest concern here, and she is right to do so.'

R. 'Right to do so?... I don't understand...'

M. 'Well I do ... and you seem to be taking pleasure in this ... you're playing a nasty, dangerous game.'

C. 'For goodness sake, Manuela!'

R. 'Leave her to it ... leave Aunt to it...'

M. 'The way you're speaking, *you* seem to be Aunt here at the moment...'

R. 'Me? *Me*?'

M. 'Yes, you. *You*, Rosa. Why would you want to make your sister jealous?'

C. 'It wasn't Rosa's intention to make me jealous, Manuela.'

M. 'I know what I meant...'

R. 'Yes, she knew what she meant.'

M. 'We all know what we mean here, and I know very well what I meant. Do you understand, Rosa?'

R. 'Aunt's favourite refrain!'

M. 'What of it? And do you know what, I wouldn't put it past you to accept the worst suitor that approaches you and marry him solely to provoke him into making you jealous. Not make *him* jealous, no; make *you* jealous of him.'

R.–¿Casarme yo? ¿Yo casarme? ¿Yo novio? ¡Las ganas... !

M.–Sí, ya sé que dices, aunque no sé si lo piensas, que no te has de casar, que tú no quieres novio... Ya sé que andas en si te vas o no a meter monja.

C.–¿Y cómo lo has sabido, Manuela?

M.–Ah, ¿pero vosotras creéis que no me percato de vuestros secretos? Precisamente por ser secretos...

R.–Bueno, y si pensara yo en meterme monja, ¿qué? ¿Qué mal hay en ello? ¿Qué mal hay en servir a Dios?

M.–En servir a Dios, no, no hay mal ninguno... Pero es que si tú entrases monja no sería por servir a Dios...

R.–¿No? ¿Pues por qué?

M.–Por no servir a los hombres... ni a las mujeres...

C.–Pero por Dios, Manuela, qué cosas tienes...

R.–Sí, ella tiene sus cosas y yo las mías... ¿Y quién te ha dicho, hermana, que desde el convento no se puede servir a los hombres...?

M.–Sin duda, rezando por ellos...

R.–¡Pues claro está! Pidiendo a Dios que les libre de tentaciones...

M.–Pero me parece que tú más que a rezar «no nos dejes caer en la tentación» vas a «no me dejes caer en la tentación...»

R.–Sí, que voy a que no me tienten...

M.–¿Pues no has venido acá a tentar a Caridad, tu hermana? ¿O es que crees que no era tentación eso? ¿No venías a hacerle caer en la tentación?

C.–No, Manuela, no venía a eso. Y además sabe que no soy celosa, que no lo seré, que no puedo serlo...

R.–Déjale, déjale, Caridad, déjale a la abejita, que pique..., que pique...

M.–Duele, ¿eh? Pues hija, rascarse...

R.–Hija ahora, ¿eh?

M.–Y siempre, hermana.

R.–Y dime tú, hermanita, la abejita, ¿tú no has pensado nunca en meterte en un panal así, en una colmena...?

M.–Se puede hacer miel y cera en el mundo...

R. 'Me, marry? Have a suitor? Chance would be a fine thing...'

M. 'Yes, I know you say – although I don't know if you really think it – that you won't marry, and that you don't want a sweetheart ... I know that you can't decide whether or not you are going to become a nun.'

C. 'How did you find out about that, Manuela?'

M. 'Ah, but do you think I don't know about your secrets? I know about them precisely because they *are* secrets...'

R. 'But if I *were* thinking of taking the veil, what of it? What's wrong with that? What's wrong with serving God?'

M. 'There's absolutely nothing wrong with serving God ... but if you were to enter a convent, it wouldn't be because you wanted to serve God...'

R. 'Oh? Then why would I be entering? Do tell...'

M. 'It'd be because you didn't want to serve men ... or women...'

C. 'For goodness sake, Manuela... The way your mind works...'

R. 'Her mind works a certain way, and mine in another ... and anyway, Rosa, who said that one cannot serve men within a convent...?'

M. 'You can, of course, by praying for them...'

R. 'Naturally! By asking God not to lead them into temptation...'

M. 'But it seems to me that rather than praying "lead us not into temptation" you would say "lead *me* not into temptation"...'

R. 'That's right: I don't want to be led into temptation...'

M. 'But haven't you come to Caridad to lead *her* into temptation? Or don't you think that constitutes temptation? Didn't you mean to lead her into temptation?'

C. 'No Manuela, she didn't mean to do that. Besides, she knows that I am not the jealous type, and never will be. I'm not capable of such a thing.'

R. 'Leave her, Caridad, leave the little bee to her own devices: let her sting if she wants to...'

M. 'It hurts, does it? Well then I suggest you have a good scratch my dear girl ...'

R. 'Oh, "my dear girl" now is it?'

M. 'And sister of course, always.'

R. 'Tell me, little sister, haven't you ever thought of being part of a honeycomb, of entering a beehive...?'

M. It's possible to make honey and beeswax while remaining part of the world...'

R.–Y picar...

M.–¡Y picar, exacto!

R.–Vamos, sí, que tú, como tía Tula, vas para tía...

M.–Yo no sé para lo que voy, pero si siguiera el ejemplo de la Tía no habría de ir por mal camino. ¿O es que crees que marró ella el suyo? ¿Es que has olvidado sus enseñanzas? ¿Es que trató ella nunca a encismar a los de casa? ¿Es que habría ella nunca denunciado un acto de uno de sus hermanos?

C.–Por Dios, Manuela, por la memoria de tía Tula, cállate ya... Y tú, Rosa, no llores así..., vamos, levanta esa frente..., no te tapes así la cara con las manos..., no llores así, hija, no llores así...

Manuela le puso a su hermanastra la mano sobre el hombro y con una voz que parecía venir del otro mundo, del mundo eterno de la familia inmortal, le dijo:

–¡Perdóname, hermana, me he excedido..., pero tu conducta me ha herido en lo vivo de la familia y he hecho lo que creo que habría hecho la Tía en este caso..., perdónamelo!

Y Rosa, cayendo en sus brazos y ocultando su cabeza entre los pechos de su hermana, le dijo entre sollozos:

–¡Quien tiene que perdonarme eres tú, hermana, tú!... Pero hermana... no, sino madre... ni madre... ¡Tía! ¡Tía!

–¡Es la Tía, la tía Tula, la que tiene que perdonarnos y unirnos y guiarnos a todos! – concluyó Manuela.

R. 'And to sting…'

M. 'And to sting – exactly!'

R. 'Ah, yes, and you intend to be an aunt, like Aunt Tula.'

M. 'I don't know what I intend to do, but if I *did* follow Aunt's example, it would not be a bad path to go down. Or do you think that she failed in the path that she took? Have you forgotten what she taught us? Did she ever try to create any schism within the family? Would she ever have condemned any of the acts of one of her brothers or sisters?'

C. 'For goodness sake, Manuela, out of respect for Aunt Tula's memory, don't say any more… And Rosa, don't cry like that … come on now, raise your head … don't cover your face with your hands … don't cry like that my dear, don't cry…'

Manuela put her hand on her stepsister's shoulder, and in a voice that seemed to come from the other world, from the eternal world of the immortal family, said to her, 'Forgive me sister, I've gone too far … but the way you behaved hurt me in my most sensitive spot – the family – and I did what I believe Aunt would have done in this case … forgive me!'

Falling into her sister's arms and burying her head in Manolita's bosom, Rosa sobbed, '*You're* the one who should forgive *me*, sister. No, *sister* no … mother … no, nor that … aunt! Aunt!'

'Aunt, Aunt Tula is the one who must forgive us, unite us and guide us all!', was Manuela's final word.

NOTES

1. Unamuno's 'paratexts' (the prologues, epilogues, or other material intended to be read alongside his fictional or dramatic works) often contain barbs aimed at supposedly undiscerning, inattentive or over-ingenuous readers (and writers who cater to them). In the 'Post-Prologue' to Unamuno's most famous novel *Niebla*, the 'prologuist' Victor Goti notes that in response to articles he had published in the periodical press, Unamuno would receive letters and cuttings from provincial journals which laid bare the sheer ingenuousness and simplicity of the Spanish reading public. Goti also claims that Unamuno had confessed to highlighting certain words in his articles entirely at random in order to parody those writers who insulted their readers' intelligence by patronisingly emphasising 'important' words or concepts. Elsewhere, Unamuno's approach is less mischievous: in the 'Autocrítica' ['Self-Criticism'] of his 1926 play *El otro* [The Other One], Unamuno is dismissive of those unwilling to engage with the ideas of the work: 'I did not write this play to be a mere distraction for theatre-goers [...] or to serve as a pleasant way for spectators to while the time away, munching on chocolates as they watch the action' (Miguel de Unamuno, *Obras completas*, XVI vols (Madrid: Afrodisio Aguado, 1958–1964), XII, 801–802 (802). Such comments have tended to be seen as evidence of a distinctive commitment on Unamuno's part to shaking others' complacency and encouraging them to think critically. Be that as it may, they also place him squarely within a much broader strand of early twentieth-century modernist writing which set itself against mass culture and the reading preferences and practices such culture supposedly fostered. The prologue to *Aunt Tula* is amongst Unamuno's most thematically dense and allusive paratexts. Perhaps, in part, this complexity derives from a certain defensiveness about the subject-matter of the novel. Given its female protagonist (the first in Unamuno's novelistic oeuvre), and its concentration on unconsummated love, marriage, maternity and religious faith, it is possible that Unamuno used the prologue to place a firm distance between his novel and popular romance, or popular religious writing.
2. Saint Teresa of Avila (1515–1582) is one of Spain's most prominent saints. She was a mystic, and an energetic reformer of the Carmelite order, founding several convents and male cloisters. See the further discussion of this comparison in the Introduction.
3. Bees and the social organization of the beehive are referenced at several points in the novel: what seems particularly to interest Unamuno is the altruistic industriousness of the chaste female worker bee inasmuch as it might be paralleled with the maiden aunt figure.
4. Unamuno used the term *nivola* to distinguish some of his prose fiction texts from novels. As Unamuno's 'prologuist' Víctor Goti explains, as a *nivola* is not a novel, it has no obligation to conform to the generic laws or conventions of the novel. Goti, and Unamuno, are vague about the particular distinguishing qualities of the

nivola, but Goti notes that it contains much direct speech and dialogue as opposed to long descriptions, lectures or tales. See Miguel de Unamuno, *Niebla* [Mist] trans. John Macklin [Oxford: Aris and Phillips, forthcoming], Chapter XVII). *Aunt Tula* may be safely categorised as a *nivola* on this basis.

5. Precisely because Unamuno is commenting on the lack of common terms to describe the relation between female siblings, this translation has opted for the unusual English words 'sororal' and 'sorority' rather than 'sisterly' and 'sisterhood'.

6. It is significant that Unamuno emphasises domesticity and the domestic here. Antigone is traditionally seen as illustrative of the priority that emotional family ties or loyalties have for women, a priority that disqualifies them from the more rational loyalties of civic life and duty: Hegel, for example, reads Antigone as 'one of the most sublime presentations of [the] virtue [of] family piety [...] the law of woman [...] a law opposed to public law, to the law of the public land' (*Hegel's Philosophy of Right*, trans. T. M. Knox [Oxford: Clarendon, 1952], 114–115), but Unamuno's concentration on the domestic may betray a more contemporaneous concern with women and the spaces they occupied. During and after the First World War, in most belligerent countries, campaigners for women's suffrage, female workers and students began to leave the home. Although this social change was slower to arrive in Spain, it was certainly a prominent topic for discussion and debate in the press. See the further discussion in the Introduction.

7. Unamuno did indeed return to the figure of Abishag, but not in novel form; her maidenly yet maternal selflessness is the subject of a chapter in the 1924 essay *L'agonie du christianisme* [The Agony of Christianity], published while Unamuno was in exile in France.

8. John Macklin has produced an English translation of *Abel Sánchez* (Oxford: Aris and Phillips, 2009).

9. The translation cannot capture here the word play in the Spanish: Unamuno creates a transgendered bee by changing the feminine word *abeja* to a masculine *abejo*, and makes the masculine drone feminine by changing it from its masculine form *zángano* to *zángana*.

10. Here Tula may be referring to the popular beliefs that (unsatisfied) cravings during pregnancy could give rise to a baby's being born with birthmarks, or that contact with a dog during pregnancy means that the baby will have birthmarks?

11. This may be a reference to Hegel's notorious comments about women and dependency in the *Philosophy of Right*. In an addition to §166, Hegel remarks: 'The difference between men and women is like that between animals and plants. Men correspond to animals, while women correspond to plants because their development is more placid and the principle that underlies it is a vague unity of feeling.' (*Hegel's Philosophy of Right*, trans. T. M. Knox [Oxford: Clarendon, 1952]). But if Rosa is represented as highly dependent, Tula is a notably autonomous figure (see, for example, chapter VIII, where she cites a distaste for being governed by others as one of the reasons she does not want to enter the church as a nun), even if it is a state she at times laments (see chapter XII, where her feelings of loneliness are emphasised). Unamuno's complex stance on the question of women and autonomy certainly cannot be reduced to Hegel's simple dichotomy, even if

Unamuno, too, has to resort to dichotomy, this time *between* women – the corporeal, dependent Rosa (the maid Manuela is also referred to as plant-like in chapter XVI) and the spiritual, independent Tula. See also the further discussion of this question in the Introduction.

12.   As C. A. Longhurst has pointed out, although all the initial references to the new baby in this chapter indicate that he is male, through what is presumably an authorial oversight, this third child becomes female in later chapters. As Longhurst also notes, Rosa and Ramiro's first daughter is referred to variously as 'Rosa' and 'Tulita' (also from Gertrudis) at different points in the text. (Miguel de Unamuno, *La Tía Tula*, edición de C. A. Longhurst (Madrid: Cátedra, 1988), 102, n.17; 107–8, n. 19. See chapter XXIV, which gives what appears to be the definitive list of the now adult children that Ramiro has had with Rosa and Manuela. These oversights are significant in that they are indicative of the pre-eminence of ideas (philosophical, social and political even if the latter two are presented obliquely) over finely-honed fictional craft in Unamuno's novels as a whole.

13.   See note xii above about Hegel's equation of women and plants.

14.   Tula's words about the institution of marriage echo the Roman Catholic catechism. Here, as in several other episodes in the novel, she takes on a quasi-priestly role. See the Introduction for further discussion of this role.

15.   The distinction in Spanish between '*te amo*' and '*te quiero*' has not been fully captured by the contrasted translations 'I am in love with you' and 'I love you'. The meaning of the less commonly used '*amar*' is usually confined to the contexts of romantic or sexual love; '*querer*' can also denote such types of love, but also embraces a much wider set of feelings, including those of friendship, affection and fondness.

16.   Although the patronising and dismissive set phrase '*quedar para vestir santos*' is usually most idiomatically rendered simply as 'to end up an old maid', a more literal translation has been preserved here. The phrase in Spanish reflects the belief that it would be mature unmarried women who would volunteer to help maintain the interior of their parish church, including adorning the statuary with appropriate robes. Here Tula plays with the set phrase to make the point that unmarried women might also have a contribution to make to the spiritual or religious welfare of children.

17.   Ramiro is here playing on the double meaning of '*elección*' which can denote a (political) election, but also, more broadly a 'choice'. Here he is referring to the deadline for Gertrudis's choice about whether she will marry him.

18.   Tula is here reciting part of the 'Hail Mary', the Catholic prayer for the intercession of the Blessed Virgin – a prayer that emphasises Mary's role as both spiritual and material mother. Tula is perhaps not being completely honest with herself when thinking through her reluctance to marry Ramiro; Rosa had made it clear she would be happy for Tula and Ramiro to wed. Tula's recalcitrance is clearly at least in part conditioned by a feared loss of autonomy and primacy: that Ramiro will think of Rosa when physically intimate with Tula; that she will become less than a mother to the children if she is their stepmother. In both cases, Tula thinks that it is only the

spiritual that will save her from a dangerous material sexuality, and hence perhaps her appeal to the virgin mother Mary.

19. Although Tula does not finish the sentence, it is clear that she is referring to a procurer or pimp.
20. Santiago José García Mazo's catechism (a summary of Catholic doctrine, often used in religious education) was a standard and very well-known doctrinal text in nineteenth and early twentieth century.
21. The word '*ama*' was inadvertently omitted from the first edition.
22. I Corinthians 7.9. This became orthodox Catholic teaching on marriage.
23. Luke 1. 38.
24. John 2. 4.
25. Here Tula means poisoned with venereal disease.
26. As Carlos Longhurst notes, the first edition of the text contains an inadvertent error here: the familiar second-person address '*te acuerdas*' appears, incongruously, as the more formal '*se acuerda*'.